CREATIVE

DIFFERENCES

CREATIVE
DIFFERENCES

Buffy Shutt Robinson

I want to thank Kate for being my best friend; Edite Kroll for believing in me; Juri Jurjevics for his kind, insightful editing; Ginny Fay for typing the manuscript; Kathy for showing me that a friendship begun at work can last a lifetime and my parents for showing me there could be joy in hard work.

Copyright © 1990 by Buffy Shutt Robinson.
All rights reserved under International, Berne and Pan-American
Copyright Conventions. Published in the United States by
Soho Press, Inc.
1 Union Square
New York, NY 10003

Library of Congress Cataloging-in-Publication Data
Creative differences : a novel / Buffy Shutt Robinson.
p.   cm.
ISBN 0-939149-32-X
I. Title.
PS3568.0285C7   1990
813'.54—dc20   89-77189   CIP

Manufactured in the United States
10 9 8 7 6 5 4 3 2 1

Book design & composition by
The Sarabande Press

To Peter

SECRETARY

1

—————————————————————

I'm trying to decide if I should get my hair cut today at lunch. I've made an appointment at Michael's. One of the other secretaries suggested I go there. She goes there. I'm not crazy about how her hair looks. It's so layered I don't think any two strands are the same length. But since I made the mistake of asking her advice, I guess I'll go there if I decide to go. My hair is dark brown, very thick and hangs just below the middle of my back. Hangs is the operative word here. It has no real style, which was fine at school, but somehow it seems out of place at work. In the business world. My mother always said "business world" as if business took place in a separate world from the one we live in. A different solar system.

My boss wants coffee. She doesn't look well this morning. I don't mind getting her coffee. I mind that she's always acting guilty about asking me but never stops asking me. She drinks a lot of coffee during the day. I've worked for her for about a year and a half. Each day she seems more and more unhappy about coming to work. She's been a publicist for seven years. A good one. If she knew some other way to make as much money, she'd leave in a minute. Her husband works for an insurance company and makes a good salary. She thinks he's going to ask her for a divorce. She's been drinking lately. I think she's hung over this morning. I'm not sure. She has those watery blue eyes that always look a little bloodshot.

She wants to talk. She likes to talk. She tells me everything about her life. She tells me so much I get it all confused, and I have a good memory. She comes from a big family. Nine brothers and sisters, a father who wasn't around much and an overweight mother. Poor Minnesota farmers. Growing up was parochial school, chores, cold winters and the Church. Of course, the Church was everything. She regrets she didn't become a nun.

"I can't talk. I haven't finished my summaries," I tell her.

My summaries are these daily reports that one other secretary and I do for the executives of the company. We summarize in short paragraphs what all the magazines and newspapers write about our studio each day. Frankly, I can't believe these guys don't have the time to read the papers themselves. The executives here in New York get it and the executives at the studio, on the Coast, get it over the telecopier. They used to get it in the overnight pouch, but recently they discovered they couldn't wait the one day.

"You're lucky you grew up on the East Coast. You met John at college, didn't you?" My boss is a real believer in geography as destiny. I'm listening and trying to look at my watch. If I don't have the summary upstairs by 10:45 A.M., the president's secretary always calls me and asks where it is. I hate to admit it, but she intimidates me. She's older than most of the secretaries. She's worked for him for years. Every time he moved up in the company, she acted like she was the one getting promoted. My third day on the job, she called me. She said whenever she called I should act like he was calling. I made a great impression. I said, "Who's he?" I really did it by mistake, but she got so angry it took me months to get on her good side. Now that I've been on her good side for a few months, I don't see any difference.

So this morning when she calls, which she will since I can't get out of my boss's office, I'm going to lie and say the newspapers were late being delivered.

"He locked me out of the apartment last night."

I try to keep my face still. I don't want to hurt her feelings by looking shocked. I imagine the ugly hall in my apartment building. I wonder how long she stood in the hall and if there were acoustical tiles in the ceiling to count. I really don't want to know all of this. She keeps her office door open. We might be talking about work. When other publicists walk by or stand in the doorway for a minute, she talks to them easily, like nothing happened to her last night.

When the publicity manager walks in, I get up to go. I think it's only mannerly to leave when your boss's boss walks in. Neither one of them wants me to go. The publicity manager is asking her for last night's screening report. Since I've been writing the screening reports for her lately, I guess he thought he could ask for it in front of me.

Her phone rings. I get up again, but my boss hands me her extension to answer. It's John.

"I'll be right back." Back out in the hall, sitting at the first in a row of four secretaries' desks, partitionless and public, I feel more comfortable.

"Do you think I should get my hair cut?"

John laughs. I love to talk to him on the phone. He makes me laugh about something that happened last night and for a few seconds I'm flying free, away from work. The other line rings. I slap John on hold and answer the other line, put them on hold and bounce back to John.

"I can't talk anymore. I've got to finish my summaries. She's okay. She's just driving me a little crazy. I'll tell you later." I hang up. He has not told me whether or not I should get my hair cut.

When I first started working for her I didn't mind listening to her stories. I thought it was part of working. Part of the business world. I figured this was how you made your boss happy. And even if I hadn't worked in an office before, I knew making your boss happy was important. Sort of like making your parents happy or your teachers. I did notice that the other secretaries didn't spend as much time in their boss's office as I did, but I didn't pay it much attention. Besides, my boss is a good storyteller. She tells me everything about her job. She teaches me stuff, which I like. The problem is, she tells me everything. Some of the things she tells me about her feelings, her childhood, her husband, I don't think she should tell me. I'm not her girlfriend.

Lately, she has begun to depress me. You just can't tell me that working can get you so down. It's only a job and you've all the rest of your life waiting for you after work. I don't get it. I feel sorry for my boss, but I don't want to sit on that blue chair in her office all day and listen to how easily everything can come apart. I'd rather do my summaries.

The phone rings constantly. Late R.S.V.P.s for tonight's screening. The screening room is nearly filled and fire regulations keep me from overbooking it. One wants to bring an extra guest. I say okay, since it's an editor from *Newsweek*. An editor from *Woman's Day* wants his secretary to go in his place.

"No, sorry," I tell him, "the screening's full."

"Put your boss on the phone."

"She's on the other line, but she'd tell you the same thing."

"Did you hear me?" He's screaming now. I put him on hold to answer the other line. I guess I should put my boss on, but I don't want to. I don't know why suddenly it's so important to me that I handle him. Besides, the way my boss has been feeling lately, she'd probably give in, probably tell him to bring his family. I get back on. "How about tomorrow night?" I offer. He hangs up on me.

I hear my boss typing away in her office. I wonder what she's doing. I need tea. "Want anything from the kitchen?"

She jumps a little at the question. "More coffee?"

I take her mug. I still use the white Styrofoam cups in the kitchen. Most people use mugs. At night the maid washes all the cups and leaves them in the kitchen.

I ask Joycelyn, the secretary two desks down, if she will answer my phones while I'm in the kitchen. She has a call director on her desk. She's on the phone and while I know she hears me, she ignores me. She works for the publicity manager and has seniority over the other secretaries. She likes us to remember that. She definitely has seniority over me and the one secretary who sits between us, but not really over the fourth secretary, Charlotte. She's worked for the company for forty years. Years ago she worked in Hollywood with producers and directors. She once worked for Charlie

Chaplin. She says the head of the studio wanted to put her in pictures. She's still pretty enough for us to believe this. But she says she was too smart for that. Joycelyn says what the head of the studio really wanted was for her to be his mistress. Six months after he asked her one of these two things Charlotte was transferred to the New York office to work for someone in legal. As for why she was transferred, Joycelyn has a hundred scenarios: she wouldn't have sex with him, they did have sex and it wasn't any good, he was married, she was demanding, she got pregnant, he got bored. On and on. Charlotte never married, though she was engaged once. She's a little deaf and cranky.

Four years ago, Charlotte was transferred from legal to the publicity department. No one really likes her. Years ago she extracted a promise out of the company. Now there's no one left in the company who knows why the promise was made. She'll have a job until she dies. Not because people are nice here or think thirty years should count for something. No, it's because they're superstitious. Retiring her might cause something horrible to happen.

I walk over to Joycelyn's desk and scribble "Will you watch my phones?" on her Ziggy stationery pad. She crumples up the note and holds up one finger telling me to wait. A few months ago this would have made me nuts. But I like her. I understand now how sitting in the hall at the same desk for eight years could make you a little crazy. The very fact that she hasn't melted through the floor by now and disappeared does deserve some special attention. Since she's not going to get it from her boss, she might as well get it from the other secretaries.

She hangs up the phone and screams into her boss's office that so-and-so called and she took care of it. She treats her boss like a husband she's grown tired of.

"Wanna have lunch, hon?" she asks me.

"Can't. I'm getting my hair cut today."

She cracks her gum and picks up her pink-pink nail polish. She keeps it, two other darker shades, polish remover, and two bottles of White Out in a row on the right-hand corner of her desk. Her desk looks like she orders regularly from the Miles Kimball catalogue. She keeps her monogrammed magenta pencils in a ceramic frog's mouth. She tells time from a clock that looks like a miniature computer. About once a week she buys something new for her desk. Joycelyn once worked for a record company. She liked her job. She worked there about two years. One day the head of the company was fired. The only change anyone could see that the new boss made was that all the secretaries had to clean everything off their desks at night. So Joycelyn quit.

"Good," she says. "Your hair looks terrible." The other secretary in our row puts her mother on hold to tell me she's glad I'm getting it cut, too.

Walking back from the kitchen I think maybe they think I'll look more like them and any allowances they've made for the college girl can be done away with finally.

"Any calls?" She hands me a stack of pink papers marked "From the desk of Joycelyn." I accidentally smear one of her nails when I take the messages.

"Shit. Answer your own phones till my nails are dry."

"Yeah, okay. Thanks." I look through the stack. The president's secretary has called.

I stand just inside my boss's office to say, "I'm going upstairs to distribute the summaries."

My boss sits at her desk making lists on yellow legal pads. "Here's the screening report. Can you Xerox it and give it out at the same time?"

I take the report from her. "Sure."

In the Xerox room I read her report. She's made up what the critics think. I know because she didn't stay until the movie was over; I did. Doesn't matter to me, only she makes it sound as if people really liked this movie. People didn't really like this movie. I watch the copies fly into the sorter. The room smells of toner and new paper. I don't mind Xeroxing. The room has a door so I can be alone for a few minutes. I sometimes offer to Xerox for the other secretaries when I'm going to do something for myself. They think I'm nuts. But it's private the way a tent built in the middle of the living room when you're a kid is private. I think about John in here. I think about being in love. I think about meeting him for lunch and seeing him at home at night. And I think about how loving him is something I'm good at. I stop the machine to Xerox my hand. I put back the screening report and hit the start button again. I study the Xerox of my hand. I draw a wedding ring on the fourth finger and think about the first time I met John:

The train creeps along. I think of the train as an old man and every jerk is the old man's cane stabbing the ground for balance. It's snowing like crazy. It's been snowing all day. The snow is inconvenient. It's costing me the time I need to finish my term paper. It's also beautiful and belligerent in a way that almost hypnotizes me.

The train stops. The lights go on and off and now the railroad car is lit only by the dim emergency light halfway down the aisle. I give up. I've been on this train for five hours. I'm dead. Luckily, I'm not out in the snow, because I'm sure I would find the smoothest snow drift and lie down in it.

"Looks like we'll be here a while. Train stalled ahead of us." The conductor is motioning to people behind him. "Come up here. Up ahead. This car is the warmest."

I turn and watch other passengers move into my car. The way they light up when they enter the car, you'd think they'd all been hanging on the outside of the train for the last fifty miles. They are mostly students like me going back to college after the Christmas break.

"Mind if I sit here?"

"Sure." I push my parachute bag under my legs so he has room.

He tells me I look familiar. "Do I know you?"

"No, but would you like to?" He smiles and settles his green eyes on me the same way he just settled his leather shoulder bag on the rack above us. We start to talk. He's not much on small talk. Doesn't mention the weather. Doesn't mention we're stuck on a train in a snowstorm. He tells me about a movie he just saw. I saw the same one over the holiday, too. We decide we haven't seen anything quite like it before. He's animated. He listens to me in such a way I try to say stuff worth listening to. He laughs at my jokes. I like that. I keep talking but now I'm busy trying to figure something out. I'm trying to figure out how I can be so attracted to this guy I just met. He could be a mass murderer. A drug dealer. Worse, a law student.

"Want something to drink?"

"Sure." I pull my jacket around me. It's cold in the car. It's dark outside now and the snow hangs like heavy drapes against the windows. He gets his bag down from the rack. He pulls out a sweater and hands it to me.

"Put this on." Then he pulls out a bottle of wine, two plastic glasses and finally a Swiss army knife.

"Always carry around a good bottle of red wine?"

He says something I don't hear. All I can think about is that he was on his way to see someone. And that this wine was for her. He's on his way to see his girlfriend. What did I think? That he was out looking for me?

The bottle is nearly gone when the conductor says the stalled train has been removed and we're on our way. The passengers whoop it up. Personally, I was hoping the train wouldn't be able to move until the spring thaw. Nearing the stop before mine, he starts to gather up his things.

"I thought you lived on campus."

"No, I don't."

Now I can see the woman who was expecting the wine we've been drinking. I can see her waiting for him at the station stop in a warm, idling car. I fold up the sweater and hand it to him. He grabs part of my hand when he takes the sweater. I'm sure he can feel my bones jump inside my skin.

He stands up, his bag slung over his shoulder, his eyes on me, over me. "When will you be through with your paper?"

"Thursday, I guess."

"See you Thursday, then."

The machine jams. I open up the white front that accordions back easily, revealing the innards of the machine. I don't know how to fix it and I don't want to learn. I stab at a few buttons and slam it shut. It starts up. I'm glad because I don't feel like going from floor to floor looking for a machine that works, and, if I was lucky enough to find one, having to stop each time one of the secretaries who works on the floor wants to use it. I staple the summaries together. By the time Thursday had come around I had found out that John was three years older than I, a graduate student in world literature and considered a wunderkind in certain academic circles. I waited all day Thursday for him to call me and tell me when he was coming. At nine o'clock I figured he wasn't coming. I figured the woman who had been waiting for the wine wasn't letting him out alone in the snow anymore. I was lying in bed reading when someone knocked on my door. It was about 11:30. "Come in." John walked in, a leather bag in one hand and a bunch of daisies in the other. He told me I looked pretty. He never said anything about being late.

The executive floor is unnaturally quiet. We have carpet on our floor, too, but it doesn't absorb the irregular noises of our work. I guess executives know how to work without making noise. All the secretaries up here have their own offices. I smile at the receptionist who barely looks up from her *Cosmo*. She buzzes me through the locked door. I wonder who the lock is supposed to keep out. Maybe it's just part of the mystery of senior management. I walk down the long, narrow hall toward the president's office. On both sides of the wall hang portraits of movie stars. At first glance they look glamorous in their gold frames. But all the stars look like they're living in the 1950s and all are some tone of red. For weeks I thought Martha Hyer was Kim Novak. The same strawberry-colored hair threw me off. It's a hideous gallery, but even so it thrilled me once, on my very first walk down the hall.

I lay my summaries on the secretary's desk. She nods without looking up from the leather-bound calendar she's writing in. I turn to leave and see a youngish woman. Everyone says she's the president's girlfriend. Joycelyn prefers to say mistress. I have absolutely no reason for staying, but there aren't that many chances for a close-up look. Besides, it's practically part of my job to pick up any gossip from the executive suite that I can.

She has no job as far as anyone can tell. She sits in an expensively decorated pale pink office. She has the kind of looks that seem attractive at first but are really all makeup and high cheekbones. She is wearing a pale yellow sweater and a matching pale yellow skirt. Her nipples are clearly defined. I wonder about this since she's wearing a bra. A bra with holes in it? I open the door to go. She asks me if we are screening a movie tonight. I love that. I love when women act like you're invisible until they want something.

"Yes. Want me to put your name on the list?"

The president's secretary taps her silver pen against an ashtray. What's she annoyed about? I want to tell her she can't bring her stupid little dog with the rhinestone collar and the pale yellow bow on its head to the screening. But I don't. I leave without getting an answer.

I'm in the elevator going back down to my floor. It's a quick ride, like taking a gulp of water. The reason I started thinking about getting my hair cut is because of something that happened last week. My boss asked me to take a cup of coffee into the conference room for an actor who was waiting for an interview to begin. As I put the coffee mug down beside him, he reached out and ran his fingers through my hair. He told me I had pretty hair. I wanted to pour the coffee in his lap. Instead I told him he had pretty hair, too. My boss heard me and later she said that wasn't the way to handle actors. I'm still wondering if that means I shouldn't have cared that some actor from a canceled TV series touched my hair. I don't think he would have done it if I had more businesslike hair.

I walk in, ready to tell Joycelyn about Miss Matching Outfit's bra.

"It's about you," she says.

"What is?"

"The commotion in there." She jerks her head toward her boss's office. The door is only partially shut. I hear raised voices.

"What about me?" As much as I don't care whether I get fired, figuring I can type and Xerox for anyone, I'm nervous. I wonder if what I call my sense of humor and what John calls my mouth has gotten me into trouble. All of a sudden I'm tired. I didn't get home last night until midnight.

Joycelyn is enjoying this. It's that strange thing in an office. She's not enjoying that I'm uncomfortable. It's just that she can't resist the fun of something different happening practically right in front of her. Something she can work up some enthusiasm about. The kind of thing she'll stop painting her nails to talk about.

Her phone buzzes. "Go in, they want you."

I dump the extra copies of my summaries on her file cabinet. My fingers are Xerox gray.

"Hi, you wanted me?"

All five publicists and the publicity manager are here. At first they don't seem to notice me. I hop up on the heating convector and listen. When I first came to work here I didn't know what a publicist was. I didn't know publicists seem to single-handedly keep New York's cultural world afloat. There isn't a new book, fiction or nonfiction, a play, an opera, a restaurant or a movie they haven't seen, read or heard about. I didn't know they would talk as much as they do in movie dialogue. I also didn't know that gossiping is as necessary and natural to them as breathing.

"It's about your starting that screening yesterday." My boss looks at her boss, the publicity manager.

"I just got off the phone with the producer and he wants me to fire you."

"Why?" I run my mind back to yesterday when I greeted the critic for the *New York Post*, handed her a copy of the production notes, watched her select a seat midway down the screening room, buzzed the projectionist to start the movie, waited three minutes to make sure it wasn't too loud or out of focus and left. It was a lunchtime screening. I did it because none of the publicists wanted to give up their lunch. If I don't meet John for lunch, I just have a salad at my desk.

"The producer said a publicist should have been there, not a secretary." The publicity manager gets up and tries to pace but his office isn't big enough. He seems angry, but I'm not sure yet at whom. "I told the producer you graduated from Swarthmore. That didn't cut any ice with him. He never heard of Swarthmore. In fact, it made him even angrier. The producer said, 'What's a college got to do with anything? All I know is somebody's girl started the screening and the critic didn't like my movie.'"

Now the publicists are interrupting each other to tell other stories about this producer. Their stories are funny. I'm trying to laugh. I love a good story. But I can't concentrate. The thing I remember most about the interview for this job was that my boss kept referring to me as her assistant. She never said secretary. She said there was a lot I could learn. Then she told me she had never finished college. I wasn't sure what that had to do with anything, but I smiled. She walked me out of her office and introduced me to her assistant, the one who was leaving.

This woman looked older than my boss. That threw me a little. I thought secretaries were supposed to be young. At least younger than their boss. Her desk was a mess. Scraps of paper were everywhere. You couldn't see the surface of her desk. Her bulletin board was so full of things, she couldn't possibly have known where anything was. There were stacks of magazines and old newspapers piled all around the desk. Dried White Out was splattered all over her typewriter. It was the funniest feeling, but seeing this desk almost made me refuse the job. Looking at my boss looking at the desk, it occurred to me that she had asked her secretary to leave because she could not stand looking at her desk any longer.

I always keep my desk neat. For the longest time the only identity I had in the office was in terms of my predecessor. And that was almost exclusively in terms of the neatness of my desk. Actually, I had to work hard to get people to say other things to me besides how neat my desk was.

Pretty soon after I started my boss began to let me do certain things the other secretaries don't do. I used to think it was because she thinks I'm smart. Capable even. But it's probably just because she's bored with certain parts of her job. But now I'm wondering if my days of doing things that secretaries aren't usually allowed to do are over. And if that's the case, I want out. Now. That's it, I want to quit. Suddenly, I realize what's wrong with me. My feelings are hurt. I don't want to quit, I just don't want to be a secretary any longer. I don't want to sit out in the hall and be called somebody's girl. I want to be a publicist. I look down at my arms, turn my hands over, touch my face. I expect to find a rash or something weird popping out all over my body. No, nothing. I guess this must be ambition. It feels like hidden acne and hot flashes.

CREATIVE DIFFERENCES

One of the publicists suggests I be sent tomorrow to cover an interview with this producer.

"Let's not get carried away," I say. No one hears me. Of course, having me cover the interview would be using me to send a message to the producer. In business, people are always sending messages. I guess the message this time would be "Fuck you". That they want me to be their messenger makes me feel partnered with them. That feels good. But I don't really want to go to that producer's hotel tomorrow.

The meeting spills out into the hall. One of the publicists taps me on the shoulder.

"Come on, let's have lunch."

Without turning around I can feel Joycelyn watching me. Publicists usually take secretaries out to lunch only on their birthdays.

"Can't. I'm getting my hair cut." My neck is free of Joycelyn's eyes.

2

_I_ have a lot of work to do this afternoon. I have to select some black-and-white photos of our upcoming movies for the fall forecast issue of three weekly magazines. Working in the stills department isn't exactly my favorite job. The head of the department is that attractive combination of short and fat. Every time I walk in, he gives me a slow look. I ignore it. I ignore it every time.

"Over there."

That's his idea of telling me where I can find the contact sheets. Over there is one huge wall of unmarked file cabinets.

"Great." I look over at his assistant, who clandestinely motions toward the third stack.

I think my hair looks okay. I'll never go to Michael's again. I'll find some place without uniformed maids who serve tea in better china than my mother has. The hairstylist wore a white jacket and had hair more beautiful than any woman's in the salon. We spoke different languages. I said I wanted something easy to take care of. He said, something I could just shake and spin. I said I'd like my hair cut shoulder length. He grabbed my chin like it was the Greenwich of all measurement. Sure, I'm angry with myself for being intimidated by a man with streaked hair, dressed like a butcher.

Joycelyn said if I could only get some clothes now I'd be okay. She wants to take me to a store on Broadway, a discount place. I don't want to go. I went with her once to a store on 47th Street called 660. Everything cost $6.60. Under her impatient eye, I bought a sweater for $6.60. I've never worn it. My boss is calling me. She won't come into the stills department. She gets along with him even worse than I do. That's why I go. I grab the forms I need to fill out in triplicate that won't matter three days from now when they've lost my order.

I go into my boss's office. "You wanted me?" There is a tall glass of clear liquid sitting on her desk. For some reason I know it's not water. I can't think of anything to say and I can't hear her. I can't take my eyes off the glass. I see her life floating on top; invisible, but I can see it. The office squeezes in on her. For a second I want to pull her out into the hall.

"Well?" She's asked me a question and now is waiting for me to answer her.

"Yeah, I know his secretary pretty well. Yeah, I guess she likes me. Why?" My boss has been on the phone trying to get an advance copy of *Metropolitan Magazine*.

"There's an article in it about the president of the company and he wants it right away." My boss hasn't been able to convince her contact to let her have it. Usually she's very good at this kind of thing.

"Why won't he give it to you? What's in the article?"

"Never mind. Just get it." The publicity manager is standing at her door blocking any air from getting through. He's nervous. My boss seems irritated by all the fuss. She acts like she's been interrupted. Work does seem like an interruption a lot of times. Sometimes all work seems to me a long interruption from John.

I ease out of her office and go back to my desk to call. "Can you hold on? Yes, Mother, is that you? I'll have to call you back. I'm busy." Now I'm on hold. I convince the secretary to give me an advance copy of the magazine. She says she's afraid she'll lose her job if anybody finds out she was the one who gave it to me. I promise her no one will find out.

"Come around six tonight after everyone has gone home."

"She's afraid of being fired," I tell my boss and the publicity manager. They ignore me. I guess I just said something you're not supposed to say out loud. Talking about getting fired is bad manners. My father practically whispered whenever he talked about someone losing his job. A part of him was sorry for him, but a bigger part acted as if getting fired might be contagious. They are on the phone now, each one on an extension, finding out where the president will be later so I can personally deliver the article to him. The president must be thanking them.

"It's part of the job," they say in unison. It wouldn't do to say it was a secretary who got the article. I don't care. Standing here, listening, I'm just glad I can do it.

I work. Joycelyn gets ready to go to the canteen. She goes at the same time every day with a friend of hers who works in personnel. The friend is a good contact. She works in some office that handles executive profiles. Joycelyn is always saying there are no secrets in a corporation. It's just a matter of contacts. She asks me if she can bring me something.

"Yeah, some lemonade." I hand her fifty cents. They are both made up like they're going out on dates. There's an eerie, interchangeable quality about a lot of the secretaries in this building. It's the eye makeup mostly. It's also the jewelry. Lots of it. All of it gold. None of it expensive. Much of it bought from street vendors.

My boss walks by my desk on her way to the ladies' room. "When are you going to get to the filing?" she asks me. She's out the door before I can answer. I try John.

"Away from his desk. Any message?" I hang up. I wish I had some Xeroxing to do so I could close myself off in that hot little room.

I wonder if my boss means to hurt my feelings. Or if this is just her way of reminding me that I'm still a secretary. Her secretary. And it doesn't matter that I'm the one who's going to get the advance copy of the article. I carry all the filing out of her office and stack it on the floor next to me. A couple of folders slip off the pile and they rip under the wheels of my chair.

Joycelyn is angry. She heard something about the article from someone at the canteen who works for one of the lawyers on the executive floor. She slops the lemonade on my desk. Some of it spills across the memo I've just finished typing. She waits until she is sitting at her desk to hold up my nickel change.

I tell her my boss told me not to say anything.

"So?" There is not a trace of understanding in the set of her hands around her milkshake. I tell her I'm sorry and I am. Then I go ahead and tell her everything I know. I even tell her the name of the restaurant where I'm supposed to meet the president later. For the rest of the afternoon she's on the phone. She gloats over the other secretaries who know nothing. Most don't even know what an advance copy is. She beckons for me to come over to her desk again.

"I betcha this article gets him fired."

How can she possibly know this? It hadn't even occurred to me. I feel ignorant in the ways of office drama. Joycelyn's like an old farmer who can predict storms and bad harvests. It's five o'clock and she's on her way out. She's going to a screening at another company. She doesn't bother to tell her boss goodnight.

I have enough time before I have to go to call my mother back. I ask one of the other secretaries to work with my boss at the screening tonight. You'd think I just asked her to balance the federal budget. "It's easy," I tell her. "You stand in the lobby with this list and check people off. If they're not on the list and they seem okay, let them in. Or if someone gives you a hard time, let them in."

Standing in the lobby is fairly new. The building has a new security honcho and he says it's dangerous to let just anyone come in the building. I get overtime to work in the lobby, but there's nowhere to sit. I've gotten friendly with the guys in the lobby. The ones who work the 6:00 P.M. to 6:00 A.M. shift.

The secretary takes the typed, alphabetical list. "Will anyone give me a hard time?"

"No," I lie.

My boss wants me to come in her office to talk. It's a toss-up which I want to do less. Talk to her or call my mother. I decide to call my mother because I'm afraid my boss will want to talk about me and John. She likes to talk about our relationship. She doesn't even need me to say anything. When she talks about him I start to feel numb, like I've been riding on a bus in the dark for miles and miles.

"Hi, Ma. What's up?" She asks me what are my plans for Thanksgiving. It's the middle of September and she wants to know what I'm doing at the end of November. Asking me like this could be her way of saying she's inviting John. I can't tell. I don't think my mother likes John much. But I can't really tell. She's very good at acting kind of even all the time. Particularly with people outside the family. But I think she's been a little easier lately. I think about the lunch we had the other day. She keeps on talking to me.

I went to the lunch determined to find out once and for all what she thought about John. I keep waiting to get to the age when you stop caring what your mother thinks. Why do I see myself with gray hair before this happens? We left the restaurant without my having said one word about John. So much for determination.

"I have a couple of errands to do, Ma." I lean over to kiss her goodbye.

"I'll walk with you." We go up Fifth Avenue and into Doubleday's. I buy a book. It is a book my company intends to make into a movie. We walk uptown along the park, all the way up to the Frick. My mother gives me a quick tour of the gallery without our leaving the sidewalk. She tells me all this effortlessly. She knows her stuff. Listening to her, I remember how she taught us the names of the flowers and trees around our house. She used to say not knowing a flower's name is like not knowing the names of your own family.

We walk over to Madison where I stop in another bookstore and buy the same book. My mother looks at me and then at the Doubleday bag but says nothing.

I lead her farther up Madison into another bookstore and for the third time buy the same book.

"What are you doing?"

CREATIVE DIFFERENCES

Outside the bookstore I explain that my boss has asked a bunch of us to buy this book so that it will get on the best-seller list.

"And then what?"

I look at her as if she has suddenly become incredibly dense. "If it's on the best-seller list, Mother, people will know about it and will want to see the movie when it comes out. Movie companies do this all the time."

She says, "I see." Mercifully she isn't asking me anything about the ethics of what I'm doing. We walk back over to Fifth and down to Brentano's. The last store. I buy the fourth copy. Coming out of the store she asks me if John knows about this. She makes it sound as if I'm seeing another man.

"Does John know what?" That I buy copies of the same book at stores whose sales are reported to the best-seller list? She waits for an answer. She could never work in the movie business. She doesn't get that I just answered her.

"Of course, he doesn't know, Mother. He'd hate it. He'd kill me." I put my mother into a taxi and she smiles at me. A good smile, like I'm her favorite daughter. That I am her only daughter I try to ignore.

The other phone rings. I put my mother and my reverie on hold. There's no one on the other line. I get back on with my mother.

"So will you be here on Thanksgiving?" Hard to turn down a sweet-sounding invitation like that. Maybe I was wrong about her coming around about John.

I answer by telling her I got my hair cut today. Her voice is low and full of reproach. I tell her about Michael's. She asks why I didn't go to Saks. I hang up. I feel disloyal to John.

My taxi driver thinks he's at Le Mans. But at least expecting to die at any moment in a fiery crash on Seventh Avenue makes me forget work and my mother for a while. My mother and work. Twin demons. All my powerlessness strung between the two. My mother has a way of dismissing my work. She came to a press screening once. I handed her a program and helped her find a seat. The next day she called to say she hadn't realized I was a hostess.

Now, I know I'm just a secretary, but I guess I want my mother to think at least I have good prospects.

A big white truck careens in on us, almost hitting the taxi. It's so close I can see a network of crisscrossed silver lines. Scratches from other accidents. The driver slams on the brakes, swerves. His engine cuts off. Back on the road again he seems to have lost his edge. He inches through the garment district, not even trying to run over commuters crossing against the light on their way into Penn Station. I don't think he's slowed down because of the truck. A close call is part of the job. The problem is the job. He's telling me he thinks the Church should okay birth control. He says he has six daughters and they all want to go to college. He's tired. He's been driving all day, twelve hours. He's been driving for fifteen years. He didn't go to college.

Upstairs at the magazine I wait by the water fountain until two men in dark suits get on the elevator. The magazine's offices are grimy. Narrow windows let in some of the evening light. The sills are crammed with ugly plants that have deformed themselves in search of light. I prefer the artificial sleekness of my office. More people walk by. I study the wall that separates the receptionist from the editorial offices. Here everyone tapes up cartoons from the *New Yorker*, misprinted headlines, grammatical jokes, published oddities of all sorts. I suppose you could think of it as homey.

"Here." The secretary holding the article is not much older than I am. She seems to be aging even as I watch her flatten the silver clasp on the envelope. For a minute I think of not taking it.

"I don't like my boss," she tells me.

"Really?"

She edges toward me holding out the envelope. I reach for it, but she doesn't let go.

"My boss hates movie people." Slowly I work the envelope loose from her hands. I fold it into my shoulder bag.

"Thanks. Don't worry. No one will know."

The elevator button doesn't light up so I keep pushing it over and over and she stands beside me. I know she has more to say. I wonder which will happen first. The elevator will come or she will say what's on her mind.

"I didn't know he was married," she says finally.

So that's it. That's why she's giving me the article. It would be worth getting fired if she can get back at her boss, her ex-lover. I admire her recklessness. Of course, personally, I can't imagine continuing to work for a man who has betrayed me.

"Maybe we can have lunch," I tell her. I don't think she hears me, which is probably just as well. The elevator opens. I'm inside going down. It's not the smooth ride at my building, where I feel I'm being carried on the back of a strong bird.

I have some time before I'm supposed to meet him at the restaurant. I walk uptown several blocks. I'm pulled along by other people leaving their offices. It's not an unpleasant crowding. It's more of a gentle herding. I want to keep walking until I don't feel so sorry for that woman. I see a bench, but it's covered in old newspapers. Someone's home, no doubt. I keep walking.

It occurs to me that work causes me to fall into other people's lives. Sometimes I just stumble in a little ways. Other times I lose my balance altogether and slide down deep. John helps pull me out at night.

Sixteen blocks later, I sit on a low, black marble wall in front of a Sixth Avenue skyscraper. I read the article. It's in galleys and in some ways the corrections in the margin are as interesting as the body copy. I make myself look up now and then so I don't read it too fast.

It's a funny piece with lots of anecdotes about the company I work for. I keep saying I didn't know that. Of course, there is no reason why I should. It is also mean. Vicious isn't too strong a word. Probably most of this isn't true. The journalist says the president is a snob, a braggart, a tyrant. I keep reading. Well, maybe some of this might be true. But it's so embarrassing. For him, for the company, for everyone. It has ugly little stories about Miss Matching Outfit and intimate details about his marriage and quotes from men who work with him every day. Many of whom, the article tells me, owe their careers to him. It's filled with off-the-record comments. And gossip. I wonder how his wife is going to feel when she reads this. I think Joycelyn is right. He probably will get fired.

In the margin is a note describing a graph they're planning to run showing how the company's profits have risen dramatically during this last year. So if he gets fired, it won't be about money. It won't be about his performance. It won't be about good or bad movies. It won't be about movies at all.

What surprises me most is how reckless he is. He doesn't act like a man in charge of a company, in charge of hundreds of employees. It's more like there are two companies. The one most of us work for and the one a few men work for where they wheel and deal, get rich, go broke, get rich again, get angry and get away with pretending they are businesspeople, executives, managers.

I get up to go. I have to meet him in five minutes. I'm trying to figure something out. I want to figure it out in the time it will take me to walk one avenue block. I want to figure out why work keeps some people's lives together and why it splits apart the lives of others. John says I have some funny ideas about work. It's just that people spend their whole lives working. Every day. All day. Some hold real tight to their jobs and some don't hold tight enough. When they hold too tight it makes them crazy, and when they don't hold tight enough it makes everyone else in the company crazy. I wonder which kind I am?

I'm nearly there and I think of John. I've come to hundreds of tiny resolutions just by thinking of him and of our possible eternity. Let me just drop off this article. Tomorrow I'll be summarizing it.

Waiting for the maître d' to seat the couple in front of me, I wish I were dressed differently. Walking toward the bar, the room darkens. I see myself in a mirror pock-marked with gold. I push at my hair. It looks great. I look better than I thought.

He's sitting at the bar, alone. There is a drink beside him. He's looking up but not seeing anything. He's tall, not particularly handsome, with a scar shaped like a crescent moon on his right cheek. Of course, I've never really seen him up close before. But there is something charged about him.

"Hello, there."

I see the eyes. For a second I forget how to talk. How could the article have neglected to mention the eyes?

"Want something to drink?"

Again, I'm silent. I feel a little like a doctor who knows the patient is dying.

"How about a glass of wine?"

"Thanks." I'm grateful he's acting as if he knows me. I hate having to introduce myself. He orders wine for me and another martini.

"How bad is it?" He knows I've read it. And he's glad.

"It's pretty bad. I'm sorry."

He takes up his drink. He looks at me while he sips. I wonder now if he's trying to figure out who I am. I feel the wine. I didn't have time for lunch today. I'm a little surprised how sympathetic I feel.

"I should go."

"Why?"

"I don't know." I take the envelope out of my bag and lay it between us on the bar. He touches my hand picking it up. He opens it, looks down into the envelope and a part of him falls inside. He lays it back down between us.

"Aren't you going to read it?" He stares at me oddly, as if I'm a little dense. Then I realize he probably won't ever read it.

"I'm going to resign tomorrow."

"You are?" I hate that I sound surprised. What did I think he was going to do? I can't tell if resigning is causing him any real pain. If losing his job is scary. If he thinks it's fair. I ask if he's sorry. He thinks I'm talking about his having given the interview to the magazine in the first place.

"Your boss tried to talk me out of it."

So, he does know who I am.

"But I never listen to publicity people. They're usually right. Right about the press, anyway. Some of us just think we're so charming that—" He stops.

I sip my wine waiting for him to go on. We both stare at the envelope on the bar. He *is* charming.

"I would like to go somewhere and make love to you." I pretend not to hear him.

He leans over slightly. "I want to forget all of this."

So, he *is* hurt. His eyes roam across me. Joycelyn says he has an apartment at the Waldorf.

"Everything's coming apart."

He thinks I can help him keep it from happening. For a second I wish I could.

"I want to forget all of this," he says. I think about how making love with John can make me forget. Forget everything until I start to remember something or someplace from long ago. Millennia ago.

"Thanks for the wine." I slip off the bar stool. I reach out to touch his arm or shoulder, but in the darkness I misjudge the distance and never reach him.

"Didn't your hair used to be long?"

"Yeah, I got it cut today. Like it?"

He stops me with his eyes, so blue the room disappears and for a second I can see the horizon.

"No, I liked it better long."

PUBLICIST

3

*P*eople must be crazy to badmouth Los Angeles. It's beautiful. It's warm. It's sunny. I've been here almost two hours and I think it might be paradise. I just left three inches of February slush in New York. If it weren't for the color that fluorescent light stains my face, I could pass for dead.

This is my first business trip. I'm not exactly sure why I'm here. These meetings are being held for the people who work in the field. Great expression. It sounds like they're out picking cotton. What they are really doing is talking to press people around the country. In the movie business there is New York and Los Angeles, and everything in between is The Field. I work on the other side of the floor in the New York publicity department. I am finally a publicist. A new one. About eight months. After two years as a secretary, I am a publicist. The two sides of the floor hardly ever speak. We share the same boss. Come to think of it, I guess we don't speak because he doesn't want us to.

Anyway, my boss invited me and so I'm here. This is the first time I've been away from John since we were married. I flew out with Molly. She works on the field side. She's a field publicist. She handles the Midwest. I don't know her very well. Some small talk in the ladies' room or waiting for the elevator. I was glad to sit next to her on the plane. She can talk about stuff other than work.

She says I'm here because our boss is in love with me. I told her that was ridiculous since I'm in love with John. She laughed. I pretended I was making a joke. Only I wasn't.

I feel strange. Do other people who don't really know me think the same thing? I don't know Molly well enough to ask her that. She calls me The Pet. I've been pretty lucky so far. I've done a good job. My old boss taught me a lot. And I work hard. Since I have to work, I might as well be busy. Besides, I like work. Being a publicist is better than being a secretary. Publicists talk to the press. I didn't know how obsessed everyone — executives and filmmakers — is about what the press thinks. But since we are the ones who talk to the press, they act like what we do is important because it's important to them. Typing and filing and answering the phones aren't important to them. I like that they think our work is important.

I try John. His line is busy. I lie down on the bed. My body is vibrating from the plane ride. Eight months ago when my boss left to get a divorce in Reno, she told me she wasn't coming back. I didn't believe her. Who would stay in Nevada? When she didn't come back, I wrote a memo to the publicity director asking for her job.

"They won't give it to you." Joycelyn is leaning against my desk, examining a split nail. We've been talking about the futility of my trying to get promoted for over an hour. Frankly, I think I'd give up trying to get it if it would mean Joycelyn would stop talking.

"Why won't they give it to me?"

"Because you're a secretary."

"So what?"

"You don't understand anything, do you?" She takes her eyes off her nail for a second and looks at me like a mother who's just realized her kid hasn't listened to one single word she's said.

I don't know, maybe she's right. Just as I am about to ask her who she thinks they will hire, the director of publicity asks to see me. I want to comb my hair, check my makeup, but I go straight to his office instead.

I walk into his office. His desk is incredibly neat. There are only a few pieces of paper neatly arranged in his in-box. I notice that the telephone doesn't ring in his office. It only lights up and it does that constantly. He ignores his secretary's buzz.

"I read your memo."

My back straightens. He looks down at his desk and over to the windows, back and forth like a hammock. His eyes swinging back and forth are making me nuts. I'm about to tell him that it's okay he's not giving me the job, just to get his eyes to stand still, when he says, "We've decided to promote you. Congratulations."

I giggle a thank-you. I can't remember the last time I giggled. Now I'm sure he's going to change his mind. How can he promote someone who giggles?

He tells me my new salary. More than double what I've been making as a secretary. You'd think he was my father raising my allowance. I'm not sure why executives think they have to act as if your salary is coming out of their pocket. I play along and act like he's a generous boss and I'm lucky to be getting the money. Could it be that he doesn't think I know that publicists are all members of a union and the salaries are all determined by the union contract? Doesn't matter. I love the new salary.

Joycelyn is surprised. She picks up the phone and while I'm in the middle of telling her all the details she dials the publicity director's secretary. I can tell she's angry because she's using her finger instead of her gold-plated dialing ball. She blasts the secretary for not telling her I was going to get it. Joycelyn doesn't like being the last on the block to find out about things. She dismisses me and spends the rest of the morning on the phone to her contacts in the building, telling them about my promotion.

I have nothing to wear. John laughs at me.

"I'm serious, John. I have nothing to wear." He laughs again and I slam the closet door and walk out of the room. Who would have thought a promotion would mean a new wardrobe? On the bus I think about having an office. I don't have to sit out in the hall anymore. I think about the job. Yesterday I was so sure I could do it. Now I'm not so sure.

Someone has put my name on my office door. If everything else could just be this easy. There are flowers on my desk. They are from Joycelyn and the other secretaries on the floor. This makes me feel great. They aren't mad at me for getting promoted. Joycelyn comes into my office with a manicure bag. I hope she's not going to tell me about another friend of hers I should hire as my secretary. Unscrewing the top of a bottle of iridescent pearl nail polish, she says there is going to be an opening for a publicist on the field side in the next couple of weeks.

"Are you going to pitch for it?" I ask her.

"No, why?"

"Why? Do you want to be a secretary the rest of your life?"

Joycelyn eases a Q-tip drenched in polish remover down the left side of her thumbnail. "I like being a secretary."

"I'm sorry."

"Nothing to be sorry about." I tell her again that I'm sorry.

"No need. I don't take what I do personally. It's a job. Nothing to do with me."

I sit and watch her polish nine nails, mesmerized by the precision strokes.

I come home, my first day as a publicist behind me. I am tired. I realize how much harder work is when you can't do your job with your eyes closed. I love it. On the bed is a large box wrapped in gold foil and tied with a blue bow. The card says: "I'm so proud of you. Love, John." Inside is the most beautiful blue blazer and white silk blouse I have ever seen.

The blouse is like the kind movie stars used to wear in the 1940s. There is another card. It says: "So you'll have something to wear."

I am wearing my new blazer. I decided to save the blouse for another day. A couple of people tease me that I'm already spending my new salary. Today

I'm going to lunch with Bill Riffenfeld, the director of our newest movie, and a writer from *Newsweek*.

I'm waiting at the elevators. The publicity director walks through the double doors and stands beside me. "I understand you're going to lunch with Riffenfeld."

"Yes."

He tells me Riffenfeld can be very difficult. "Don't let him drink too much. He'll make a fool of himself and of the movie. Don't let him talk about his personal life too much. Make him concentrate on selling the movie. Don't let him talk about his next picture. We're not interested in getting his next movie any free publicity."

I nod my head. I want the elevator to come. I don't know this man — my new boss of two days — very well, so I don't know if he's always this nervous. He sounds like a man who just had this conversation with someone else only he was the one nodding his head.

He keeps at me. I wonder if being a publicist means you can control what filmmakers say the way a ventriloquist controls his dummy.

"The Coast doesn't want him mouthing off about how they took the picture away from him and edited it themselves. Nothing about that. Make sure he makes this movie sound like it's got some funny scenes. If he describes it as a moving drama, we're all dead. Got that?"

The elevators must be broken. My boss pulls a piece of paper out of his pocket. He looks down at it. And as if each word were an electric shock, he's back at me, a million more things I can't let Riffenfeld talk about.

He tells me the cast hated him. Some of them even drew up a petition to have him fired, but it was too late to change directors. "Don't let him talk about his last movie. It was terrible, but he blames the Coast. The studio didn't ruin his movie. Don't let him get off on that."

I guess the elevators are broken. I'm going to spend the rest of my life standing here listening to him unless I do something. I ask him why we're letting Riffenfeld speak to the press at all if he's such a problem.

"Why don't we cancel the interview?"

The elevator opens. "Cancel the interview?" he repeats. You'd think I said nuke the whales. "The Coast wouldn't like that."

I step in and as the doors close say, "Who cares what the Coast likes?" I think I hear him laughing as the elevator lowers me to the ground silently like a hot-air balloon might.

John laughs when I tell him about the lunch and how I kept interrupting Riffenfeld whenever he started to talk about one of the forbidden topics.

"Didn't the writer get irritated with you?" John hands me a glass of wine. I think back to the lunch.

"No, she didn't."

"You must be really good at this kind of thing."

"I'm okay, but I think I can be really good." I sip my wine and don't tell John how much I like my new job. I also don't tell him how much the promotion means to me. The way I see it, if you're going to be in a race, you might as well try to win.

4

I try John again. He's on the other line. "Can you hold?" I stretch out on the bed and look around my hotel room, waiting. It's green and gray. Gray rug, vertical green lines on the walls and oversized dark furniture. I like it. It's orderly and clean. It's not at all beautiful. This is one of the best hotels in Los Angeles. Actually it's in Beverly Hills. I love the names. Beverly Hills. Bel Air. Hollywood. The freeway.

I've left my clothes in a heap on the floor. I always hang up my clothes at home. I'm wearing a T-shirt from one of our hit movies, and panties. I haven't put on the air-conditioning. I like to feel the heat. I want to get John excited over the phone. If he ever picks up. I feel the heat between my legs. I want him.

Still waiting, I read the room service menu. I'm starved. The menu is in five languages. I look at all of them. I read the hotel information booklet next. It tells me everything from fire exits to baby-sitting service to fine jewelry stores a few minutes' walk away. Why is it I can't imagine a businessman ever reading this booklet? But what if he wants to buy his wife a ten-thousand-dollar sapphire necklace on the spur of the moment? I recheck the times the pool is open. I didn't bring my swimming suit.

"You were right."

"About what?"

"I should have brought my swimming suit. It's eighty-five degrees and I have all day free."

"Go buy one."

"I can't."

"Walk up Rodeo Drive and buy one in some expensive shop. Honey, I can't really talk now. I've got to go."

"Wait!" Now I'm telling him about the heat and what I'm wearing and how I feel and what I want.

"Are you trying to drive me crazy?"

"Yes. Yes. A million times yes."

"You do that. And sometimes you shouldn't."

"Why not?"

I keep at him. I concentrate on the flowers on the heavy quilted bedspread. I roll over on my stomach. The bedspread smells of cleaning fluid. I sit up. I'm having trouble breathing. I want him.

"I love you." He hangs up. I hold the receiver longer than I should. My brain feels small. Smaller than before. My body is huge. And, I suspect, would taste good. Someone is knocking at the door. I hesitate. Will whoever this is be able to see my new proportions? An animal heat lights up my eyes. My thick, dark hair feels heavy like a mane. I've been yearning for my mate.

"Hi, Molly." She doesn't notice anything. Her eyes skip over me. The hidden dance of sex. That's one of the great things about sex. Just thinking about sex with John brings me alive. Alive in a way that lets me off the hook. I don't have to think much, I don't have to worry about anything. Work seems far away.

The air from the hall cools the room. It shrinks my body a bit. I can think better. I can't think about John now. Molly's talking about what we should do with our free day. She's been to Los Angeles before.

I unpack quickly. I don't like any of my clothes. Looking at Molly I know I've brought the wrong stuff. She's wearing lightweight beige slacks that look like they were just pressed, a silk blouse and an expensive silver belt.

CREATIVE DIFFERENCES

Last night I pulled some stuff from the suitcase that holds our summer clothes. They're too bright, too casual. I'm not on a vacation. I still feel warm. Maybe I've picked up a virus or something. Since when do I care so much about clothes? About appearance? I pull on my airplane jeans and put a blue blazer over the T-shirt. Molly says I look great. It's the jacket.

We drive around Los Angeles in a rented yellow Mustang. Molly drives. She seems to know where to go. I don't think she likes L.A. much. We haven't seen flowers in six months. She doesn't even seem to notice them. The colors are so bright they catch on the inside of my eyes and even after we've passed them the color shimmers before me.

We share a joint. I feel like I'm playing hooky from school. She's telling me about a man she knows here. Someone she hasn't seen in a long time but would like to see tomorrow after the dinner. I get the feeling this guy is the reason she doesn't like L.A. I would ask, but she's just turned up the radio so loud I can't. Besides, it's none of my business.

She nudges the car along Sunset Boulevard. I love the billboards. I like the way they stare down at us like they're gods on Olympus. Some seem to float above us, others rise up on steel haunches. I love the way some of the bodies are too big for the space and grow up over the board of their own free will. I like the day-glo colors and the moving parts and the hundreds of lights that sparkle like diamonds. Molly keeps her eyes on the traffic or the radio.

She asks me a lot of questions. A lot about John and me. Some stuff about work. But mostly about me and John.

I don't usually like to talk about John and me, but the joint and the sun make it easy. I feel as if I'm talking about someone else. Someone so lucky.

Molly doesn't seem that interested in my answers. I'm sure she can't even hear some of them. She likes the radio loud. I like her. She seems to have a lot on her mind. She finishes the joint and lights a cigarette. She holds it like it's a family heirloom; carefully, gracefully. I remember girls in my prep school who held their cigarettes the same way. She laughs at my jokes. A quick, startled laugh. It's almost as if she forgets from laugh to laugh that you can make jokes, have fun.

"Where do you want to have lunch?"

I shrug. I don't want to tell her that a hamburger served by a huge baby-faced boy at one of these fast-food places will do.

"I don't care. Anywhere is fine."

"Okay, Pet. We'll go somewhere special." She names a restaurant. I've never heard of it. I feel as if I should have a passport with me. I like this feeling of strangeness. With the sun on me all the time I almost feel as if I'm wearing a disguise.

We leave early for the studio. I say little to Molly while we wait for the car to be brought up from some hidden underground parking lot. I slept badly last night. I'm used to sleeping with John. I woke up every hour. Each time I woke up I took my watch into the bathroom to read the time by the light I had left on. I wasn't awake enough to turn on the bedside lamp. I'm not tired exactly. I just want to be quiet. It's not as hot as yesterday. I'm glad. It will be easier to go to work. It won't seem so much like a holiday. This morning John said he missed me. He seemed surprised. His voice woke me like the warm tip of a tongue. I lay naked under the sheet, listening, still a stranger with a smallish brain.

Molly lights a cigarette. As soon as she turns the car onto Wilshire she starts talking, as if she stayed up all night thinking of things to say.

There is some morning traffic. We move slowly, closer and closer to the sun. Molly puts on her sunglasses and pulls the sun visor down. A parking stub flutters into her lap. I let the sun drape itself over me like bolts of yellow cashmere. I am melting. I am turning into liquid and she is telling me that love is trouble. I want to answer her, to stand up for love, but I can't. She's telling me about other men she's known. This is just a warm-up. What she wants is to tell me about myself.

Suddenly I'm afraid of her. Of the secrets she might make up. My fingers are wobbly, but I turn up the radio. Molly's rings, smooth gold bands, beat against the steering wheel. There is a kind of evenness in the car. If there were an earthquake right now, the Mustang would be split cleanly in two along the gear shift console in the middle.

"You're very naive."

The Mustang skis down a dry slope of road away from the sun. Molly is driving much too fast on this neighborhood street. Big, beautiful houses sit back on long stretches of perfect grass.

"About what?" Christ, what's on her mind? I hold still while the cartilage re-forms in my body.

"Everything. Work. Love."

"Well, that's pretty much everything," I joke.

"You won't be an ingenue forever." I laugh and feel my insides start to clot. I'll be okay in a few minutes. We must be almost at the studio. I'd rather be gossiping about work, about the people at the studio, about movie stars we've never met. She did hear me yesterday in the car. She sort of heard me.

"What if you fell in love with somebody else?"

"I won't."

"By mistake?"

"I won't."

"By accident?"

"I won't."

She seems angry. "It could happen."

"So could an earthquake." I look at her and she flicks her cigarette out the window. For a couple of minutes we don't talk. I ask her if she's going to see that guy tonight. I know I'm being mean. I know asking her about that guy is like poking a bruise. But I can't help it. What if she's right? She's probably right. She's known lots of guys. I've really only known John. Maybe I could fall in love with someone else or maybe he could. I don't want to know what could happen. I don't want to know how many different ways things can come apart.

Molly slows the car, ready to turn right into the studio. For a second, blinded by the sun, I want to know every single way things can come apart.

Because if I know them, then I can be on the lookout, so nothing will ever come apart.

The guard at the gate wears mirrored sunglasses. He takes our names. When we say we're from the New York office he seems irritated but somehow relieved. We have some identity other than our meaningless names.

"Shouldn't we be on some kind of list?" I ask.

Molly shrugs and with one hand wheels the Mustang smartly around the low curb while the guard watches.

The studio is so clean. It looks as if someone just swept it. The buildings are low, two or three stories. They're painted white. The sidewalks are lined with flowers. Mostly begonias. The grass looks deep and is very green. Weedless. There is no wind. The sky is clear and sunny. I think they over-react to their pollution. The air smells wonderful to me. All of it makes me think of a campus. I'm visiting a college for an interview. I want to go here.

I look back at our car. Molly parked next to a hunter green sportscar. All the cars look like they've just been washed. Our rental looks out of place. I've never seen a parking lot like this. People's names are written in white block letters. It looks like a dining table set with place cards.

We walk into the administration building. The receptionist smiles beyond us. I turn around expecting to see someone behind me. There's no one there. It's how she smiles. She holds out something in response to our questions. Molly takes it. We leave. I wonder why this reception area is so unremarkable, so ordinary. What offices like palaces must lay behind that white linen partition.

Walking outside it all seems clear to me. When you work here at the studio you are in the movie business. At home, if I get off the elevator on the wrong floor, I might be in the insurance business or retail. The people here all know that. It seems an odd choice to have some of us in New York and the rest of the company in the movie business.

I think about telling Molly this, but she seems annoyed that we can't find the commissary. The receptionist gave us a map, but I'm too embarrassed to use it.

"Let's just keep walking. We'll find it." Molly stops at one of the white wrought-iron benches. She seems worn out by the beauty. She throws her purse down and lights a cigarette. We both recognize the famous movie star walking by us. He's not visiting, like he does in New York. He has an office here. He works here. He looks at us as if we're lost. He also looks at us like he'd like to help. But the moment passes and he walks on. Molly sees some other people from New York and waves at them. We walk toward them and find the commissary.

We've been asked to a meeting that the president of the company has called. He has these meetings once a month. Sometimes less. Never in New York. It should be fun. There is no reason I can think of for my having to say one word. Any questions about my area will be answered by my boss.

No one from the studio speaks to us. A few nod and smile as if we're tourists separated from our group. We go over to our colleagues from New York and kiss them and talk as if we haven't seen them in months. Most of them were on the same plane with Molly and me. Outside of the office some of them seem smaller, others more handsome, in clothes I don't remember seeing. I see my boss talking to the L.A. people. He seems to be ignoring us. I don't remember his laugh being so loud. Molly tells me to get some tea.

"Come sit by me, Pet." We sit down around a table in the second row of chairs. One of the L.A. men says that the guests from New York should sit in the front row. I don't move. They wouldn't be talking about me. I can tell the L.A. people are just crazy about being asked to sit in the back row at their own meeting. They are talking about me. I get up and move. By chance I sit next to my boss. Molly and my tea have gotten lost in the move.

The president of the company comes in, helps himself to a cup of black coffee and sits in the vacant chair at the head of the table. The table is glass and his chair some light wood and rattan. We could be sitting on someone's very nice patio. I've seen him a few times in New York. He walked around our floor once. He's been president for about a year. He has the reputation for being difficult. Exacting. I think his light gray suit is custom made. He circles something in *Daily Variety* and pushes it across the table toward my boss. It skids to a stop in front of me. Pushing it toward my boss I read what he has circled.

There is tension in the room. The chatting has stopped. The quiet is enormous. Whatever sunlight comes into the room falls across the table. Everyone's alert, a little uneasy. I like being here, being a part of this meeting. I like listening to men with big titles and big salaries talk. It's the first time I've been on the inside. It's the first time I've been around to see how decisions get made. This doesn't seem so bad, this business world. It's kind of like watching a movie — a great b&w melodrama.

I look over at Molly. She's not liking this the way I am. She seems miles away. It's not about work for her. It might be easier if it were. At least in part. But there is no emotion for her here. It's about something else. Something that goes back as far as her childhood and that runs ahead, meeting her as she comes upon the future.

Someone is shouting. They are talking about movies and money. Someone tells the plot of a script with a kind of passion I don't think we know about in New York. Which movies to make. Who should direct them. Who will pay to see them. Someone asks my opinion. I don't think I should say what I really think, so I make a joke. The president laughs. One of the L.A. people from the back row leans forward and pats me on the shoulder. Don't pat The Pet.

I watch Molly as she drives us up and around the canyons, the tip of her cigarette a miniature orange horseshoe on the wheel. The radio is off. I know she was with someone this afternoon. Mr. L.A., I guess. I want to talk to her. See how she feels. But sex is packed around her like a deep snowdrift and it's not up to me to dig her out.

John wasn't home. I called him just before I left. Not being able to talk to him makes me jittery. I wanted to tell John my stories about work. That's how I get rid of work without losing the sense of what I've been doing. It's as if I deposit my stories in a bank. And when I can't talk to John, my stories pile up inside of me and I can't think of much of anything but work. I feel like a teenager with a crush. Would I have told John that? Sounds crazy, having a crush on Los Angeles.

CREATIVE DIFFERENCES

The Mustang rolls close to the edge of the mountainside. I look down. Looking, I think, for some clue, some sign.

The attendant opens the car door for Molly. Imagine valet parking at your own home. She takes her time slipping out from behind the wheel. Her mauve skirt follows even slower. She looks great. She has pinned a small spray of bougainvillea against an unruly curl. I guess she notices the flowers after all. The young man starts to hand her the ticket, but the perforation sticks and he tears it in two. There is much talking. Their heads bend toward each other. You'd think he was parking cars at the Hollywood Bowl.

I call over to them. "Don't worry. How many yellow Mustangs are you gonna park tonight?" I start up the steps. About eight lozenge-shaped slabs of marble. It's still warm. I don't need the shawl I brought. I'm wearing a black silk dress. It's simple with a low neckline.

Molly rings the bell. I feel as if I'm standing next to a hummingbird. She's exquisitely tense.

"He might be here tonight." Before I can ask who "he" is, we are inside.

Everyone is friendly. They know our names. For a moment just now standing under a chandelier that looks like it might be more at home in a museum, I think maybe we shouldn't be here. But someone just took my shawl. Someone else waltzes us into a beautiful high-ceilinged room. There are vases of white and red flowers everywhere. Food floats by on gold trays. Champagne finds its way to my mouth. Someone takes me by the hand and leads me down a long hall. The walls here are crowded with white-framed pictures of famous people. I follow my unnamed escort into a pink and aqua bathroom. The door locks. I see Molly's here, too. We do some coke. Everyone's face appears to be as smooth as the tiled walls.

I lose Molly for a while. I'm having a good time. I'm laughing and sipping champagne and eating a million bite-sized cheeseburgers. No one is relaxed. But they are charming. They are all wonderfully dressed, tan and supple. They are serious about their fun. We are, after all, in the president's home. One of his homes. Most of the guests have come alone. It's easier. Guiltily, I realize it's easier for me, too.

I talk to a couple of production executives; young guys, film school graduates. Both are honey-colored and have eyes that snap around the room like rubber bands. I'm careful to keep my conversation about movies. I have to monitor myself pretty carefully. I have an urge to mention the weather, the incredible view of Los Angeles just below us, the nuclear accident in Pennsylvania. I remind myself that if I want to go to college here, I better not blow this part of the interview. It's so surprising to be caught wanting someone to like you. I'm so surprised and secretly embarrassed that I almost stop talking. Almost.

It's all shoptalk. The kind that comes effortlessly to the L.A. people. Talking to them I realize it's the first work I've done since I got here. It's not the kind of work I'm used to. In fact, it's the kind I usually make fun of. I think about all the times I made fun of schmoozing. I didn't know schmoozing was such hard work.

Their words make a comfortable web around me. I feel insulated against the more complicated parts of business life. Everything seems easy and the room is warm and lit with money and power. I drink some more champagne.

"The trailer played hot last night in Westwood."

"I think they should release it instead of the movie."

"Get used to him, we've optioned his next three screenplays."

"He can't write."

"I've never heard of the writer," I tell them. "But I have read the novel he's adapting. It's not a movie." They laugh. At me? I'm not sure.

I see Molly now. She's looking at a middle-aged man. He's not particularly tall, not great-looking, but something about him tugs at people. I feel it clear across the room. Molly wants to resist. I see why now. He's with a woman. A tall, dark beauty in a red sequined turtleneck and long straight skirt. It's hard to tell if she's his wife. It doesn't matter. He's with her. He says everything to her even though there is a group of people around him. I get the feeling that if he looks away from her, if he looks at Molly, things might tip over, draperies might come unhung, glasses might shatter, furniture might split apart and topple over.

I walk toward Molly. The room is crowded, giving me time to figure out what I'm going to say to her. When I reach her spot, she's gone. I turn around looking for her. I was going to tell her that Mr. L.A. doesn't matter. I was going to tell her how great the party is. I was going to make her laugh. Inside, I'm trying not to be angry with her for spoiling this night. My boss clamps his eyes on me.

I'm caught. Now I'm sorry I've had so much champagne. Maybe I can pretend not to see him. Do to him what that man just did to Molly. Not see him. Erase him. Go back to my honey-colored boys who talk to me in a strange language of step deals and turn around and development and options. Just look at him. Just look at him. That's all he wants. Just for a second.

He looks away and then back at me.

"God," he sighs, "isn't this a great party?" But he looks so alone, so unattached. Why is he making everything more complicated than it has to be? Now I remember. The item in the trade paper this morning. At the meeting. The circled item saying he was going to another studio because of a conflict with senior management. It's been a long day for him. He's trying to act like everything's okay, but when he looks at me his eyes are empty and tired. I was right. Molly was wrong. He's not in love with me. He just likes me. But I don't want to stand here beside him. I start to drift away. He grabs my arm. He tells me the president likes me. It seems important to him. I want to ask him what the president said about me. I want to know if I've been accepted here, if this is where I will be going to college. Suddenly, I'm pretty sure he was fired this afternoon. And I feel awful for thinking about myself so much.

"Isn't L.A. paradise?"

I know we're miles from the ocean. But I'm sure I can hear the waves. My lips taste salty. I feel like crying.

SENIOR PUBLICIST

5

I meet them at JFK. It's 11:45 Tuesday night. I walk up to them.
They are the first people off the plane. They look past me, thinking I'm a
fan. I walk beside them, not close, and explain I have been sent by the
studio to pick them up. Tom and W.A. finally slow down.

"Hello." Tammi's eyes don't seem able to look sideways.

I try to stash Tom and Tammi in the limo and get W.A. to help me claim
their luggage. Tom tells W.A. to stay put and he goes with me. Tom is real
helpful and for the twenty minutes we spend watching luggage go around on
the conveyor belt, we talk. There aren't many people in the airport this time
of night. A few people recognize him, but mercifully no one comes over.
They just stare, take a few steps in our direction and hunching over try to
look up into his face. He's wearing a tobacco-colored cowboy hat so people
aren't sure if it's really him.

He pulls an olive green duffel bag off the conveyor. I'm real good at
getting people to talk to me. In my job it helps to get along with people. I'm
always surprised at how many of my colleagues don't really like journalists
or movie stars. These are the people we do most of our work with. Other than
the executives. But then we don't work with them. We work for them. I don't

like my job quite as much as I used to. Lately, almost every actor, every filmmaker is certain he knows as much about the press as I do. Maybe he does.

"How long have you been doing this?" Tom asks me.

"I've been a publicist for a little over three years."

He asks so I tell him I love my job. He smiles down at me as if I've just given him permission to go wild. After all, his hand on my shoulder seems to say, You'll be here to keep me out of trouble.

He hefts the fourth and last piece of luggage off the moving ramp. None of the pieces match. He has no claim tickets. I tell him to wait and I go over to the woman who sits at the exit matching the numbers of the claim tickets to the numbers of the luggage tags. I tell her my problem. When she isn't checking numbers, she looks up only as high as my stomach and says no tickets no luggage.

"But he's Tom Reston. You know, the big movie star."

"Where?"

"Right over there." She looks up and then back at my stomach. "I don't know him." A small crowd is gathering.

"Here's how you do it." Balancing the luggage, Tom pushes past the woman. I follow. A bell goes off, but we are in the limo before we have to find out what it means.

I can't tell if Tom is angry with me. I wonder if I should have given the woman at the exit some money. This is just the kind of thing movie stars complain about. This is just the kind of thing executives hear about and then mumble they don't know what publicists are good for.

By one o'clock we are in Tom's huge two-bedroom suite and W.A. is chopping some coke. Wiley Aronson is an ex-basketball player. Tom insisted that W.A. come with them to New York. He's chopping it on what looks like a Louis Quinze desk. I fight the impulse to go and find him a mirror to use and so spare the antique.

Before I went to the airport I came by the hotel to register them and check the suite. A few years ago, when I first became a publicist, I didn't know about checking out suites. I thought that was what hotel people did. I once arrived with a producer who, upon finding his suite had a queen-sized bed instead of a king-sized one, tried to have me fired on the spot. I was amazed that he could tell it wasn't the right size bed without even going all the way into the room. This man had produced eight or ten films so I guess he'd spent a lot of time in hotels. I didn't think it was any big deal, but he did and my boss, whom he called at home while I stood in the living room watching him, did, too. I've always checked the suites since then.

I had asked if there was anything special Tom would want. His personal publicist on the Coast said Wild Turkey. The bar at this hotel doesn't stock this brand of bourbon and I don't think they liked that I even asked for it. I had to go to three liquor stores before I found it. I do that. I ask what the star likes, then I resent spending the time to get it. It's as if the right bottle of bourbon will somehow make him easier to handle. It never works out that way.

Tammi walks out of the bedroom. She has changed the royal blue skating skirt she'd worn on the plane for white satin pants and a T-shirt with Las Vegas spelled out in pink and blue rhinestones.

"Where's the piano?" Tammi is walking from one end of the living room to the other. I count her steps. This room must be a block long.

"What piano? Do you play?" I'm not sure she hears me because she's at the other end of the room. I think this is the biggest suite in the hotel. I wouldn't call this room ugly. It's just that all the furniture has the look of being secretly bolted to the walls or to the floor.

"No. I just want one so I can say our hotel room was big enough to fit a grand piano."

I wait. I don't say anything for a few minutes. Tammi keeps punishing the carpet.

"Cut the shit, Tammi." Tom isn't angry. He could be telling her to change the television channel. She sits down and starts to flip through an issue of *Vogue*. I notice she's taken it from the plane. I also notice no one is smoking the Dunhill cigarettes the Coast told me to buy: "Tom loves them. Be sure to open a few boxes and place them around the suite."

Tammi turns on her cassette player and Patsy Cline takes over. Pretty soon Tammi seems more relaxed. She even moves the wine bottle closer to where I'm sitting. They ordered four tables of food from room service, but none of it has been touched. I think about leaving them to their fun, but Tom and W.A. are real insistent that I stay. I want to get along with these guys and besides I like them. So I stay.

Tom and W.A. are rolling joints and knocking back shots of Black Jack. Seems his publicist was wrong about the bourbon. Tammi is drinking Miller Lite. I sip a spritzer. I take my turn leaning over the glass coffee table. I split one thick line of coke between my two nostrils. Tom laughs at my carefulness.

It's almost 2:30. I want to call John. I know he will be asleep, but I want to talk to him. For the last hour or so I have sat cross-legged on the floor, my back against the softly upholstered couch enjoying Tom and W.A. jiving with each other. They're funny. They're also very dirty. They're friends and I like to watch friends. I have said very little. Tammi has said nothing. I know she's still there though because she occasionally sings along with Patsy Cline.

I feel a foolish grin on my face. I know I'm tired, but the coke has migrated toward my back as though my spine were a magnet. I feel wide awake. I should be making my pitch to Tom about his giving more interviews. I started it in the limo on the way in from the airport. It didn't go well. W.A. said talking to the press was like talking to the Man. I thought this analogy a little extreme, but I didn't say anything. Tammi whispered to Tom that he shouldn't give any interviews. Her reasoning was lost in his ear. Tom took a copy of his publicity schedule, folded it without even looking at it and wedged it between the seats where he left it. He said the writer for *The New York Times* was a cunt. I said nice talk.

Instead of convincing him to do more interviews I found myself trying to convince him to do the three he had already agreed to. Convincing usually begins with compliments. Actors like to hear how great they are. They are kind of like the rest of us in this regard.

Tom didn't waste any time living up to his reputation. Sitting in the limo, trying to keep the wonder out of his eyes when he saw the Manhattan skyline, he was every inch the sullen adolescent. Of course, I've found that not just actors act like adolescents.

W.A. nudges me. I do another line knowing, as the back of my head starts to pull away, I shouldn't have. How can I work with a hole in my head? I have a lot of work to do tomorrow. This isn't the only movie I'm working on. Suddenly I feel overwhelmed. Instead of enjoying the high all I can think about is getting up and making a list. But I keep still and try to outdream the energy racing through my body.

I look down at my knees encased in wrinkled linen and think about John. He almost never gets high anymore. I guess he's a more evolved person than I am. The last time I remember his getting high was on our anniversary four years ago. We shared a bottle of Taittinger's and a spoon of coke. We were high. All day we made love and each time I slid farther and farther to the edge. He always grabbed my hand and pulled me back. I loved that weekend. I want to be making love now. Wordless love and when I come all the coke and the tiredness and the worry will be squeezed out of my body. I miss John. Sometimes even when we are together I miss him.

"Let's go out. Come on, Tom." Tammi whines. She is standing up combing her hair in the night mirror of the hotel's window. My head jerks up and my eyes take several seconds to focus. I wonder what I'm doing here in the middle of the night getting high with people I hardly know. It's business. I'm their connection to work, to the reason they have come to New York and for the moment they are mine. Knowing them has nothing to do with it. I want Tom to trust me. But even so, I know I'm not going out with them.

"No. You all go ahead. I'll call the limo and you tell him where you want to go." I'm looking through my Runner's Daily Planner for the number of the limo service. I don't run, but I like this calendar. It fits into my shoulder bag.

I find myself apologizing to Tammi for not knowing any nightclubs. I don't understand nightclubs. I don't understand why people go to them. I know people at work who go to clubs all the time. All they do is criticize the clubs and complain about the lousy time they had. Even so, when they talk about them they seem to be describing a freedom I've never known. I tell her I don't know if any are open at 3:00 A.M. I consider reminding Tom that he's taping the "Today Show" at 10:00.

"Roll one more joint, W.A. Then we'll go." Tom walks over to where I'm sitting by the phone, leans down and kisses my cheek. "Thanks for all your help. I've never been to New York and you made us feel real welcome." A little circle in my cheek burns where he kissed it. A warmth starts to melt the iron chunks floating inside me. Maybe I should go with them. I glance at the table. All the coke is gone. I take this as an omen not to go.

Tammi is screaming at Tom. "I want to go now!" She has to shout some to be heard over the music but not this loud. All of a sudden she's angry at something.

W.A. passes the joint to Tom and before he can take it, Tammi knocks it out of his hand. It falls on the carpet near his feet. Tension circles the room like a big black bird. The joint's tip is wedged into the rug. I smell it burning. Tom bends down to pick it up. Tammi slaps at his hand again. In a second he has twisted her arm behind her back. Her body now fits tight against his. Only her face seems to struggle. There is something graceful in this quick terror. The rug is smoking. I walk over, pick up the joint, hand it to W.A., who motions for me to take a hit. I do. The smell is of simpler days. I feel the tiredness seeping back in. The dam breaks. I say goodnight. No one answers me.

6

I'm just about to open the door and let the press in when Tammi walks out of the bedroom and stands dead still beside the table where room service has laid out breakfast.

"Hi ya, Honey. What're you doin' up so early?" Tom Reston leans back, balancing his chair on two legs.

My hand drops from the doorknob as if I've just received an electrical shock. I know something is coming the way you know a hurricane is on the way. You know, but there's not a thing you can do about it.

Tom chews on a toothpick and stares at Tammi. I stare at him. Even in the midst of impending disaster I have the time to look at Tom. Tom Reston has the face of a young god. I've seen his face in statues all over Europe, his face carved and chiseled and worn away and recast centuries before he was born. Tom is a big movie star. He's also got a lot of cowboy in him.

They're still staring at each other. His wife is a former waitress. He met her at an all-night diner in College Park, Maryland. He had wound up there after lost days of drinking and drugs. She had been nice to him, helping him order coffee and rye toast when he wasn't able to talk much, unable to form the sentences that connect people to one another. They were married in

---

Elkton three days later. I don't think Tammi knew who he was then. That was four years ago.

"I didn't hear you get up." Tammi has a Southern accent. But she's not really from the South. She's from Cumberland, Maryland, from the top of the Appalachians. Tammi is a smart girl. She just doesn't have any class. She's pretty, though. Almost as pretty as Tom.

Tom switches the toothpick from the left side of his mouth to the right. It seems to take all his energy. He's wearing a white shirt and white slacks, red socks and black loafers. We bought them together yesterday after he showed me the clothes he had brought with him to New York. Looking in the closet at the two pair of jeans coupled on one gold hook and at three not especially clean shirts tossed on the floor I almost laughed. But I didn't want to hurt his feelings. How can someone who gets a million dollars a movie not have any clothes?

I took him to Brooks Brothers. Tammi came, too, but refused to get out of the limo. The whole time we were driving down Fifth Avenue she kept at Tom, telling him I should take them to Soho to some really hip store. Of course, if we went to Soho I'd be running the risk of winding up with the same kind of clothes we'd left hanging in the closet at the hotel. Only cleaner.

Tom wouldn't talk to Tammi. Instead he talked to W. A. W. A. sat in front and even though the glass partition was open neither could hear what the other was saying. It didn't help that Tammi's cassette was blasting us with country music. I had to repeat everything one was saying to the other. I didn't like repeating in front of the driver all the stuff about when they were going to score more drugs. About half the limo drivers I know are either ex-cops or are still cops driving part-time. I also had to talk to Tammi. By the time we turned east on 44th Street, I was just as glad she had decided to stay in the car.

Tom is not interested in clothes or in shopping, but he has great taste when he sets his mind to it. He was fast. W. A. sat down in the first chair he found and tapped his boot on the carpet. Tom picked out two outfits, tried them on and I paid $1,358.67 in twenty minutes.

CREATIVE DIFFERENCES

I still haven't told my boss that I spent this much money yet. He won't like it. Actually, he won't understand it. Executives never understand. They sit in offices. You can't possibly understand movie actors if you sit in an office. You have to spend some time with them. Well, the $1,358.67 is on my American Express card for now.

Someone knocks on the door. It feels as if a croquet mallet just smacked me in the middle of my back. "Just a minute. Be right there," I sing out gaily through the closed door.

"You're ready, eh, Tom?"

Tammi picks up a full pitcher of fresh orange juice. The pulp sticks mouth-wateringly to the sides of the glass pitcher.

"Honey," he tells her, "I'm gonna do this press conference real fast and then we're going out shopping." Actually, he's promised to do two more interviews after the press conference, but I don't say anything.

"Okay, Sweet." All three of us stare at the orange juice. Tammi sets the pitcher down on the white linen tablecloth. She stares at it. Now and then she lets her eyes circle around Tom. Then she's back to the orange juice. Tom picks up the pitcher and pours it over his head. It drips down his face, some of the pulp catches on his thick black mustache. It runs all over his clothes.

"I'll be waiting for you." She turns, smiles at me and walks back into the bedroom. We hear the door lock.

"Jesus, Tom. Are you all right?" I walk over to the table, stopping a few steps away. I guess I think the juice might splash onto me.

"Yeah. Can you stall those suckers for a few minutes? I gotta shower and change if that bitch will let me in the room." Tom looks just as handsome covered in orange juice as he did before. And he knows it. So much for the $1,358.67 wardrobe.

He forces the bedroom door open with his shoulder. Just before he closes it, I see Tammi lying naked on the king-sized bed reading *Vogue*.

I look at my watch: 10:20. This press conference was called for 9:30. I had wanted everyone to have plenty of time to file their stories so they would break Friday on the movie's opening day. Now I'll be lucky if any of the press stays. I know I have to open the door and say something. I stall for time by calling room service to come clean up the mess. I order more juice while I'm on the phone. Tom likes it and maybe it will give me some energy.

I have been with Mr. and Mrs. Tom Reston for three nights and two days now. I have today, tomorrow, and Friday night's premiere, then I can go home to John and thank him for not being in the movie business. My boss thought it would be a good idea if I stayed overnight at the same hotel with Tom, to keep an eye on him, to make sure he did what he was supposed to do. My boss doesn't mind spending this money. It beats giving out his own home telephone number to a movie star. John thought it was peculiar, but he didn't say much about it. He just watched me throw things into my suitcase the other night. Besides, I think my boss believes the rumor that Tom destroyed a $25,000 hotel suite in Los Angeles. Looking at the broken bedroom door, I'm beginning to believe the rumor myself.

Before leaving the Coast, Tom agreed to tape the "Today Show"—his personal publicist explained that Tom could never get up early enough to do a live appearance. I mentioned something about Olivier having gotten up to appear live, but I don't think his publicist knows who Olivier is. He also agreed to an interview with *The New York Times* and one with *Vogue*. He's done two. He's wavering on *Vogue*, which is fine. The studio wants him to do *Vogue* about as much as they want a profile in *Fortune*. *Vogue*'s readers aren't exactly Tom Reston's biggest constituency. I thought it was odd. Once I met Tammi I understood.

To do these, Tom demanded a five-hundred-dollar per diem. I told my boss that was too much, but he didn't listen. I had to sit in his office while he told Tom's publicist that it sounded reasonable. I figure these three interviews are costing the studio roughly twenty thousand dollars: per diem, three first-class round-trip air fares, two hotel suites, on-call limo service, food, expenses, etc. Of course, last week my boss turned down my secretary's request for a ten-dollar-a-week raise. I understand it though. There's no chance my secretary is going to make fifty million dollars for the studio some day.

I've gotten Tom to do six other interviews. It hasn't been easy. For every one he agrees to in the morning, he tries to back out of another one in the afternoon. Tammi's not much help. I did get one publication to agree to interview them both, but Tammi only seemed crankier after that.

But more interviews are better value for the money. Better for Tom. He's really good in this movie. I bet he gets an Oscar nomination. Besides, this is what I get paid to do. This is my job. I think.

I face the press. I joke with them. I can be pretty funny. I order expensive tidbits from the hotel's elaborate hors d'oeuvre menu, offer them my room as a temporary office and place to hang out. Even as I am leading them down the hall to my room, I think that later when I go back to change I will find it used, and what I love about hotel rooms, the sterile orderliness, will be gone. I have no choice though.

Some of the journalists give me a hard time. They say Tom's no better than a rock star. A pretty cheap shot. They say they don't understand why I can't make him behave. I tell them I'm not his mother. Someone says something unkind about Tammi. I say nothing, but I'm not sure my eyes don't give me away. I tell them a couple of stories about Tom that might make good copy.

A young reporter from the *Daily News* tosses a copy of his paper at me, centerfold out. It has a picture of Tom and Tammi at the Rodeo Club, a country and western bar we had gone to last night. In the foreground I can just make out my arm on the table, my hand clamped around a glass. "Looks like you guys were out pretty late last night."

We were out late and for a few minutes I want to start the day over. I want to have the time to take a slow bath, to wash and blow-dry my hair, to put on makeup under good hotel light, to drink a whole lot of coffee from the tall, silver pot room service stylishly wheels in. I went to sleep at 4:00 A.M. and was outside Tom's door at 7:00 trying to wake him. I knocked, pounded, whistled, kicked. Went back to my room and asked the operator to call their room only to be told Mrs. Reston had left a do-not-disturb message on the phone until 10:00 A.M. I went back to my post. I knocked some more. Other guests in the hotel came out of their rooms and stared at me. One asked what the fuck was the matter with me? It occurred to me to be embarrassed, but I was only doing my job. When they didn't answer, I imagined them dead. I imagined them asleep wearing earplugs. I imagined them just inside the door laughing at me.

I must look terrible. I'm glad John can't see me. By Friday when I see him I'll look better. John has this way of telling me I look pretty when I'm least expecting it. Not when I'm dressed up about to go someplace, but weird times like in the middle of a Saturday afternoon when it's raining and we're making sandwiches or sometimes just when I'm waking up. He's always awake before me. I always seem to be trying to catch up on my sleep.

Ninety minutes later I am back in Tom's suite. All the reporters have promised to stay. Tammi comes out of the bedroom wearing the white terrycloth robe provided by the hotel. It is untied. She isn't wearing any makeup except for dark green eyeliner along each lower lid. She has combed her streaked blond hair. She looks beautiful.

"Sorry, Honey. One of those husband and wife things. You know." She looks at me as if I can't possibly understand about husband and wife things, but she's at a loss to explain it any other way. The funny thing is, she's right. I don't understand.

"Tom'll be right out. Meantime, show the press in. Tom wants me to start. He says they'll want to ask me some questions."

I smile, an elusive, meaningless smile and say nothing. I half-expected Tom to cancel the press conference, so I'm relieved. I pour myself another cup of coffee, ignoring the orange juice. For some reason room service has put the juice in a silver-plated thermos and it doesn't appeal to me. I wait for Tammi to argue with me or perhaps open the door herself. But Tammi's smart. She makes a big show of tying her robe and sitting down on the wheat-colored loveseat. She turns on her cassette player. George Strait sings and a quivering sadness fills the room. She turns up the volume.

I try to get off the phone. Marshall Wheeling, my boss, keeps talking. I look at my watch. I'm getting dressed. As I'm putting on my blouse the receiver slips. The white telephone cord tangles in my hair. My boss is telling me how glad he is that Tom is doing more interviews. My boss is greedy and I tell him so. Jokingly. His management style doesn't leave a whole lot of room for individual satisfaction. He's not a bad boss as bosses go. He has an underdeveloped sense of humor, but at least he has a sense of humor. My boss is good-looking, ambitious and lazy. I used to think laziness canceled out ambition. It doesn't. As head of publicity, Marshall seems to be just passing through on his way to bigger things within the corporation. He loves the fast lane. He won't be satisfied running beside it too much longer. Since he's always looking up ahead, he has to depend on me more than he'd like to fill him in on what's happening. I don't usually mind.

Last week in a meeting with the whole department, he told me I wouldn't be able to get Tom to do any other interviews. And that I'd be lucky if he showed up for the three he had agreed to. The publicity department's conference room has no windows and a low ceiling. Almost everyone smokes so it's hard to breathe. There is talk of turning it into a storage room. Everyone looked at me. Marshall sounded like he was challenging me. I thought someone upstairs must have challenged him. The studio hasn't had a hit in five months. We need one.

I took the challenge. This is one of the things I like about my work. I'd told him I'd get Tom to do more. I never learn. I've been a movie publicist for a little over three years and still I talk up in meetings. Meetings aren't held so that people can say they're going to do a good job. I don't know why I just didn't smile at my boss. I guess because I confuse work with business. Meetings are business. My getting Tom to do more interviews is work. My work. And my work is not necessarily or even usually my boss's work. His work is business.

I scribble a list of things to do on the small pad the hotel leaves on the desk and on the bathroom vanity. The little pencil, white, about three inches long, has almost no point. I don't know when I'm going to have time to do this work. I reread the list. Most are phone calls. Maybe once the taping starts. I've talked Tom into doing David Letterman. If I can get away from Tom, I'll make some calls. Tom was so nervous this morning that I told him I would sit right behind the reporter and he could pretend he was talking to me. It worked so well I had to sit where he could see me all day. Finally, I hang up. I'm trying to loosen my hair from the cord. Can't anyone else make these calls? I wonder if everyone in the office has been killed or something. I imagine all six of my colleagues slumped over their desks, felled by some deadly, invisible gas. I imagine my boss wearing a gas mask.

I use a pair of manicure scissors to free my hair. Shoving them back into my cosmetic bag, I drop everything onto the bathroom floor. All my stuff lying on the small white tiles, shiny under the fluorescent lights, is surprisingly pleasing to me. I'm late. I leave everything in a mess.

The television studio is cold. Tammi is wearing satin slacks and a pink and gray camisole. She looks good. This afternoon, Tom told her not to dress like a whore. She's cold. I offer her my charcoal gray linen jacket. She takes it and putting it on asks me if I have any coke. It's 5:30 in the afternoon and she's been up not quite an hour.

"Ask W.A. for me willya, Honey." Could she think my name is Honey? She hasn't called me anything else. Am I beginning to resemble a drug dealer named Honey?

Movie stars do that. Their wives do, too. They ask people they hardly know for things and expect those of us who work for movie companies to come up with the goods. It's part of being famous, asking for anything they want, demanding anything they want. It's also part of the movie business. The studio usually comes up with the goods. Who am I to try and hold the line? I might hold it if I could ever find it.

I want to sit down while the show is taping. I'm tired. I want to call John before he leaves his office. I called him this morning, early. He asked me if I was eating properly. His voice sounded deeper than I remembered it. Then he said something about what he wanted to do to my breasts. I felt weak between my legs when I hung up.

I don't sit down. Instead I look for W.A. W.A. knows right away what I want. He reaches into his jeans and cupping the vial, passes it to me. The small glass bottle is cold, as though W.A. keeps ice cubes in his pocket. I let the tip of one of my long fingernails scrape at the tiny spoon, cleaning it. The crusty coke is sand on my palm.

CREATIVE DIFFERENCES

W. A. mumbles at me. "Better come back and stand where Tom can see you."

Tammi doesn't thank me as I drop the vial into her hand. I wonder if anyone has seen me do this. She tells me she'll be waiting in the limo. "Okay, but we'll be about forty minutes." She's gone, she doesn't hear me.

Letterman is doing his monologue. Not his real monologue for the taping. This is a fast ninety seconds with the studio audience. He is complaining the set is too hot. Is he nuts? I walk over to a production assistant, a young woman dressed in pressed jeans and a sweatshirt and ask if Tom is okay. Does she think I should go backstage? She tells me he's fine. Looking up at me, she adds, maybe a little wired. She thinks I'm responsible for his being wired.

"Well, after all, Tom doesn't do television," I say. She shrugs. "Will David show the film clip?" She shrugs.

This morning Marshall changed which clip he wanted shown three times. The producer is nervous. Use the comedy clip. Another call. The director won't have his movie sold as a comedy. Use the dramatic clip. Last call. Which do you think we should use? For a second I think he's genuinely interested in my opinion. But no, I'm being used to settle the dispute between the producer and the director. I guess my boss is too busy to deal with this. I tell my boss we should use the clip we first chose. The clip that shows Tom at his best. The star clip. My boss just hung up after I said that.

I stand near one of the cameras where Tom might be able to see me. The young production assistant makes a clucking sound. But I don't move.

It's almost one o'clock. We all ate dinner together. Tammi ordered three main courses. She couldn't find anything that tasted good. Except the champagne. I ate a small mixed salad. I spent half the time in the ladies' room on the phone. It helped that most of my calls were to the Coast. I can always use an extra three hours. I have to call a couple of the honey-colored production guys, one of whom is now a vice-president. He wants to talk about long-range publicity for one of the movies he's overseeing. Personally, I think there's plenty of time to talk about publicity for a movie that doesn't even start shooting for three months, but I call him anyway. In the movie business you have to call people back right away, quicker if possible. This guy has a bigger title than I do, so I'm obliged to stand in the back of this restaurant talking about his project until someone more important or with a bigger title than he has calls him and he cuts me off.

My list is now one quarter as long. I did order a main course, broiled sole, but when I got back to the table, W.A. was just finishing it. I didn't say anything. I paid the bill, wondering if American Express has a credit limit. Tom and Tammi have been giving it quite a workout.

Tom wants to go to another Country and Western bar. He knows which one. Thank God. We pull up and there is a long line out front. I pull W.A. out of the limo.

"Let's see if we can find a side entrance so Tom doesn't have to wait." I feel, not for the first time, like a scout for a bunch of cattle drovers. Just as a scout had to know where the next watering hole was or the safest crossing of a fast river or the meaning of horse tracks or the best campsite, so a publicist has to know or find side entrances, back doors, hidden ramps, unlisted phone numbers. Am I their scout?

With a twenty-dollar bill and W.A. standing beside me, the young boy at the door reluctantly jerks his head toward the left side of the building. We nod to Tom to wait in the car and go around to the side. We bang on the fire door for ten minutes. Christ, I'm sick of banging on doors. W.A. isn't much help with the banging. A big black guy finally opens the door. As I tell him about Tom, he recognizes W.A. and pulls him through the door. W.A. disappears inside. He's not very interested in Tom, but he tells me to bring him on back.

We sit. We drink. I'm not much of a drinker, but these boys are. They tease the waitress. Tom doesn't flirt. He expects women to flirt with him. He's rarely disappointed. I see the waitress can't place Tom, though she knows he's famous. The band is good. Tammi seems happy and sings along with all the songs whether she knows the lyrics or not. People stare at us. Some dance inches from our booth. I'm the only one who seems to notice. Now and then Tammi looks around the room.

"Are there any photographers here tonight, Honey?" I shrug, not sure if she wants there to be or not. I think Tammi thought Tom's fame would mean more, make her happier somehow, but it hasn't. It just seems to give Tom an excuse to ignore her.

It's 3:10 and I'm hoping they will want to leave soon. About an hour ago I switched from wine to black coffee with shots of Tia Maria. A young giggly girl waltzes in time with the music over to our table, her hips breezy and her long, reddish hair around her face wet from dancing. Tammi's hand falls under the table. I imagine it now across Tom's thigh.

"Can I have your autograph?" Her breath smells faintly of rubbing alcohol and Dorito chips.

"Sure, Honey. For a pretty gal, I'd do almost anything." Tom winks at me. I feel like his accomplice only we haven't done anything. He did trace my backbone with his forefinger the whole way down Broadway while Tammi watched him on the "The Letterman Show" on the limo's television. He writes his name slowly like he's signing an official document. I'm just glad he gives autographs. Movie stars who don't get on my nerves.

The girl is about to leave, she's waving the signed, damp napkin at her girlfriends. Tammi reaches up and snatches it from the girl. She uses it to blot her lipstick and then she crumples it up.

"Do you want to know what a little cock he has?" Tammi asks the girl. The young girl, who I see now isn't very pretty except for her smoke-colored eyes, smiles weakly. Her body has lost the beat of the music and she's suddenly gawky. I watch her being sucked into this husband and wife thing. No longer a fan, she's involved with them. It can happen just this quickly.

W.A. says nothing. W.A. never interferes. Last night he told me how he saw his brother run over by a train when he was seven. It seems to me everything except his body stopped growing then. I think of this tiny heart floating around in his big body. Sometimes he can't take his eyes off Tammi and Tom when they fight. Like now. It's like watching a train wreck. It's loud and scary, but he can't look away.

"It's about this big." Tammi measures about three inches with her thumb and forefinger. I can't help it. I wonder if Tammi is just being mean or if it's true. Now I'm sucked in. Tammi keeps at it. Tom finishes his beer. his clear, blue eyes focused on something distant and pleasing.

The young girl backs away. Tom stands up and pulls me out of the booth onto the dance floor. W.A. stretches his legs across the seat, blocking Tammi's exit, but she makes no move to get up.

We dance. The band is playing a slow song. Tom pulls me close. Our bodies fit. Tom is over six feet. I am five-six. He isn't much of a dancer. He sways us about the floor. The singer whines down at us, trying to make me sad. I am thinking about Tammi being angry most of the time when Tom suddenly presses against me. I feel his erection large and hard. His eyes are opened to me. I look away. I suspect his erection is to prove to me that Tammi lied. I wonder if he can command an erection any time. We keep dancing. I try to think only of the music, but I can't. I press up against him. Am I trying to catch him at something? He's still big and now I am aroused.

Tom doesn't want to stay and watch his movie. He believes me when I say it's playing well. For a second I'm held by his face so huge on the screen. So handsome.

We arrive at the club the studio has taken over for tonight's premiere party. There are about fifteen paparazzi lounging against the police barricades. They don't pay us any attention when we drive up. They figure it's too early for us to be famous.

"Find a side entrance. I don't want them to take my picture."

"Come on, Tom. This is what these things are for. Pictures. Publicity." I wonder what he thinks we're here for.

Tom says Tammi's not ready. She stares at her husband. Her eyes look as if she has painstakingly separated each eyelash. Dark green foliage grows out of them. There is something desperate in the way she suddenly opens the car door.

"Hi, you all." Her Southern accent drools all over the place. She tugs at the front of her short skirt. After one flashbulb goes off, Tom is right beside her.

CREATIVE DIFFERENCES

My colleagues don't seem pleased to see us here so early. None of them speaks to me. They talk to each other while looking at me. Once inside I see why. Nothing is set up. The place is a mess.

"What the fuck's going on?" Tammi is loud, heads turn, but it's all for me. I fight panic. I look around for Molly. I study my watch but can't figure out what time the movie will break and whether they have enough time to clean up and decorate this enormous space before the five hundred guests arrive. Tom seems a little upset with me, too.

"Can we get a drink?"

"No problem." I find their reserved table. "Sit down." I take their orders. Of course Tammi wants a mixed drink. I hesitate for a second hoping Tom will tell her to cut the shit, but he says nothing. Am I a waitress?

It turns out getting them a drink is a big problem. There must be ten or twelve bars scattered around this huge room. Every young boy I approach is dressed in black pants and a tight white T-shirt. They all have short, spiky hair. None of them will fix me a drink. Not for Tom, not for anyone until 9:30. It's 8:20.

The room is dark except for tiny white pinspots that shine down from the ceiling. As I look for their boss, I feel like a tiny plane taxiing down a huge airfield. I find their boss. He's ugly and he calls me Honey, too. But he says okay.

Tom must be nervous. I've never seen him drink so much, so fast. W. A. takes him off into the shadows where the spotlights can't reach and they come back wired. I envy them a little. This is the first time in days they haven't offered me any coke. I think maybe it's because I always say no. But I know that's not the reason.

I feel tired. I'm cold again. I suppose once this place is filled with people, it will warm up. I'm wearing a black silk jumpsuit with spaghetti straps and a necklace with five diamonds that John gave me two years ago when I was made a senior publicist. I don't know if it was really expensive. I never buy jewelry. But I know the diamonds are real and I like that. Tom said I looked good when I knocked on their door this evening.

The room is filling up now. People are coming over to Tom's table and telling him how great he is in the movie. What a big hit it will be. He listens, his eyes squinting as though the sun were in them. He's eating this up. I remind him that in an hour or so Channel 4's TV crew will be here for the live remote he promised to do.

"Okay?" No answer. I place my hand on his forearm. It flexes, but he doesn't look at me. I stand up. He nods. I go look for John.

I can't wait to see John. He was in a great mood this morning when we talked. I told him to meet me at 10:15. I walk around asking my friends if they've seen John. Two say no, one says yes, two say they think so and try to get me to talk about Tom. They're starved for gossip. I stay with them long enough to get them laughing and walk on. It's so dark in here that I have to walk right up to someone before I can tell who it is. I find myself spilling into conversations with people I would rather have avoided. Everyone likes the movie. All except one of the critics from *The New York Times*. I spend nearly twenty minutes talking about the movie. The critic doesn't change his mind, except maybe a little about Tom's performance. Just as I'm leaving he tells me he won't be the one reviewing the movie. Great. Twenty minutes wasted.

I stop my search for John to get a glass of white wine. I sit at the bar. Watching the young boy in the tight T-shirt pour my drink, I see he's very cute. He doesn't look old enough to be a bartender. He's dishing the crowd to his friend who leans against the bar, exhausted and sexy. He looks as if he might have just finished making love. The boy is very funny in his dismissal of the famous. Marshall should be happy. We've turned out nearly everyone on the "A" list even if this kid doesn't think so.

I feel relaxed and wonder if this is what clubs are like. I'll be finished working soon. I'll be sitting with John soon.

I stumble up a couple of steps I don't see. A hand darts out to steady me.

"Thanks." It's Marshall. He's standing with the director and the producer, neither of whom looks especially happy. Why should they look happy? They only have a hit movie. I try to slip by, but my boss reels me in.

"Everyone I've talked to just loves the movie." None of them answer me. "I think the reviews will be good. Maybe one or two will be mixed." The director repeats the word "mixed" as if I've said he has three weeks to live. I don't think my boss likes that I've been so honest. I admit it could have waited.

The producer is standing directly under one of the spotlights. His face looks like it has no features. It's so eerie and they're so quiet. I move back a little thinking they'll forget I'm here. They move with me. The producer's face now has features. It's not a big improvement.

"Why *Newsweek?* Why not *Time?*" The spotlight shining on me makes me feel like I'm at police headquarters.

"Because *Newsweek* committed three columns and color," I explain. "*Time* had talked about one and maybe a black-and-white picture." They are trying to decide if three columns in *Newsweek* is as good as one column in *Time.* Yesterday Tammi had tried to decide the same thing. I watch them trying to decide. They can't.

"We didn't like the clip you picked for Letterman."

"Oh, why not?" My wineglass feels heavy in my hand. I wish I had taken one of those little cocktail napkins. They act as though I had shown a clip from someone else's movie.

"It made the movie look small." I try not to laugh.

Halfway through my defense of the clip, I see the producer and the director aren't listening. Oddly enough, Marshall is. I talk confidently. I know how to sell their movie to the public better than they do. They don't know who the public is. They don't know they made the movie for the kids wearing the tight T-shirts standing behind the bar making fun of them.

My boss tells them I'm the reason Tom has done so much press. More than he's ever done for any of his other movies. The producer and the director both look at me, struggling it seems, to figure out who I am. The director says this is the first good movie Tom's ever made. That isn't true, I say silently.

"Tom's a good guy." They go on. "We knew he'd be cooperative." So quickly I almost think he's playing with them, Marshall says how easy Tom has been.

"Tom did everything we asked him." I take a big swallow of wine and say the same thing. Tom's a publicist's dream.

I see John. He doesn't see me. Because of the lighting I can't tell how far away he is. Just as I am narrowing the distance, I see Channel 4's TV crew. A couple of my colleagues are chatting them up, discreetly pointing out other celebrities they might want to film. My friends look tired. I guess it's been a long week for everyone. Molly signals for me. Walking up I see the reporter they've sent is the difficult blonde. Her name escapes me, but I don't think she notices. She's too busy looking at her watch and then looking at her cameraman's watch, then scanning the darkened room like she might find another clock. She asks me what time I have.

"You'd think we were launching the space shuttle." She's annoyed at my joke and for a few minutes won't talk to me. I go over the arrangements and politely ask her to follow me.

"If you see John, tell him to wait for me here. I'll be back in ten minutes." My friend nods and for some reason I think he's going to find John. But when I look back, he's sitting at one of the bars. Whatever the young boy with the spiky hair says makes my friend smile. I guess that's what goes on in nightclubs.

When we reach his table, Tom is standing, his back to me. A large crowd weaves around his table. The security guys I placed here seem to have given themselves the night off. When the crowd sees the TV crew, most move to one side.

"It's time, Tom. Channel 4 is here for the live remote. It will only take two minutes." W. A. shakes his head. I ignore him. Tammi smiles through me. I feel a sudden change in barometric pressure. Another storm. Tammi taps her red high-heeled sandal in time with the music.

"Tom!" I tap him on the shoulder.

"For Christ's sake, can't you leave me alone, you bitch!" For a second I think he must be talking to Tammi. He wheels around. His hand knocks into my cheek, then drops heavily against my arm. My wine spills all over my jumpsuit. I lose my balance briefly. Some woman screams a little. I don't want it to be so, but his face is still beautiful.

CREATIVE DIFFERENCES

The tough blonde reporter flinches. "Forget it," she says. "I'll talk to someone else."

"Turn on your camera lights." My voice surprises me a little. I was hoping to sound calm. I sound calm. My cheek stings and my wet jumpsuit clings to me uncomfortably. The cameraman hesitates.

"But he's drunk."

"Yeah, turn on your camera. He'll be fine." The blonde nods and we exchange places. Tom calls out my name, but the lights are on and he's being introduced to a live television audience. He is charming and handsome. A movie star. And I am finished working for the night.

The white spotlight makes John look like he has a halo shimmering over his head. I am too embarrassed to tell him so. He hands me a stack of little cocktail napkins. He saw it.

"You can quit, you know." I feel sorry for myself. I put my arms around him. I want to cry, but I'm too tired. He walks me over to an empty table and goes to get me another drink. I watch him. I love him. Whatever he says to the young bartender makes him smile. I don't think I'll tell him tonight that Marshall wants to promote me.

The good news is I won't have to do this kind of work any more. The bad news is I have to do another kind of work: business.

I do tell him even before he sits down with our drinks. He laughs at me and runs his fingers through my hair. He says I look pretty.

DIRECTOR

7

I try not to let my eyes bug in disbelief. I can't look at Molly or I'm going to lose it. I'm determined to act as if the sight of one of my publicists with her hair cut so short she looks bald is normal. Maybe even fashionable.

"You're free tonight. Staff meeting here in my room at nine-thirty tomorrow morning."

She nods, showing me the pink top of her skull. She looks even thinner than usual in her black jeans and WHAM T-shirt. Etta has worked for me for almost a year. Etta's French, and this is her first job in the States. She was a fashion publicist in Paris. She's a good publicist, not great. But she is a real hard worker. Relentless. And sometimes relentless is better than great.

"Her hair wasn't like that yesterday, was it?"

Molly deliberately knocks her cigarette ash into the hotel's ashtray. "She's gonna be trouble."

I can always depend on Molly to spell out the obvious when it comes to my staff. I leave her sitting in the suite's living room and go to my room to unpack. Neither of us said anything to Etta about her hair.

I wonder if she looked in the mirror while the hairstylist was cutting her hair. Maybe it was a barber? I glance in the mirror at my own dark brown hair and try to imagine it gone. John would kill me. He wouldn't have to. I'd kill myself first. After I killed the hairdresser. Is that what Etta's doing? Killing herself?

I push the heavy closet doors to one side and remove that part of the wooden hanger that isn't bolted down. I hang up my clothes, taking care only with Friday night's outfit: black silk pants and a black-sequined top. By Friday black will be perfect. It will match my mood. I crumple up all the tissue paper and throw it away. I won't have to protect my stuff from wrinkles on the way home. I used to carry a traveling iron. It was a real drag. Reading the directions every time and getting confused over whether I was in a country that used 110 or 220 voltage, measuring the water in the tiny plastic cup, adding the salt. How many times did I go out in the hall and steal a salt shaker from a room service tray left outside someone's door? Now that I'm no longer a publicist, they pay for my valet service. I guess it's okay for a publicist to wear wrinkled clothes but not an executive.

I think about Etta. Her head is now covered with something that resembles newborn down. Blue veins run over her skull like tiny lines on a road map. Shouldn't I have known something was wrong with her? After all, I'm her boss. Isn't your boss supposed to be watching out for you, watching in case something you do affects your work?

The phone is ringing. I ignore it, preferring to free my shoes from their pink and green travel bags and line them up in the other closet. A closet just for my shoes. Unlucky for Etta this comes at a time when I'm no longer sure the office should pretend to be like a family. It's great when work can be like a family. Comfortable and quirky. Now and then something comes up and you realize just how much you'd do for one another. And that makes you feel great. But I've been thinking that work might be easier if I didn't know the people who work for me as well as I do. I fantasize about how it would feel to work with strangers. I might be able to yell at strangers. How can I yell at people I've worked with for eight years, people who seem happy that I've been their boss for the last three?

As head of publicity I manage twenty people. If each person on my staff has only one problem a month that means I have a problem every day. And that's before I even get started on the work I'm supposed to do. The phone stops ringing and I look at it until the red message dot lights up.

John wants to kill me already. I flew out to Las Vegas today. A Sunday. I could have kept Sunday for us and come out tomorrow. I sit down in front of the mirror over the double sinks. I take my time arranging the vanity. There are no special baskets of toiletries at this hotel. It's as if giving us a plastic shower cap or a miniature bottle of almond-scented shampoo would keep us from gambling. I've seen the people in the casino and believe me none of them would give up blackjack or keno for a little free shampoo.

John doesn't shout. I don't either. I think if I lived with someone else I would shout. I don't think John ever would. I have a good memory, especially when it comes to remembering being hurt. Scientists say the body has no memory of pain. My body doesn't believe that. Anyway, I can remember our conversation last night.

"Go Monday," he begins, his voice quiet, his beautiful eyes looking lazy and green. "You're giving them too much. Do you really think a man in your position would go out a day early?"

"Thanks. I love to be reminded of my overly conscientious nature." In school being conscientious was good, but in business it's bad. It means getting taken advantage of. I speak up. Wearily. "I'm doing it for myself. I have a lot to do. I can use the extra day. Molly's going with me." As soon as I say this, I realize I've weakened my case. Another woman, someone who works for me.

His eyes enter the conversation. They sparkle now the way they do when he has a fever. I don't answer his questions about being happy at work. I prefer to slam some dishes around setting the table. Besides, I'm not sure happy enters into it. He has more questions. The dinner is long and tasteless. I manage not to cry. I feel sorry for myself. The funny thing is John feels sorry for me, too, and that's what bothers me the most. We go to bed early. In the middle of the night, he rolls over and pushes against me. I take him inside. I am greedy for him and silent. I don't think John likes my job very much anymore. I know he doesn't like the late hours or the phone calls at home at night. He wants me to be happy and he gets mad at me when I'm not. Sometimes I hate my job. Who doesn't? But most of the time I like it. I'm good at my job and I'm not bored. I put a lot of stock in not being bored.

Besides, I don't want to drive myself crazy thinking about work. The way I figure it, any job in a corporation will drive you crazy eventually. John doesn't understand that one way of staying sane is to complain a little. I complain to John and then I'm cheerful to my staff and to my boss and to the filmmakers and to the press. Besides, I can usually make John laugh about my work. I didn't last night, though.

All his questions are attached to me like tin cans on a car's bumper. They make a racket. I'd call him and say I'm sorry only I don't know what I'm sorry for. For doing my job? Besides, he would probably start talking about the quality of life and I would probably talk about saving our money for when we can buy a better quality of life. I could call though and ask him what color his eyes are because right now I can't remember if they really are that green.

Molly comes into my room saying she's hungry. I motion toward the room service menu. "The club sandwiches aren't bad."

"No. Real food in a real restaurant." Molly doesn't let herself be taken advantage of. Well, not in business anyway. She's exchanged her jeans for a flowered skirt and a dark green sweater. I leave my jeans on. The best thing about Las Vegas is you can dress any way you want. You've got to really work at looking out of place. I think Etta worked at it.

Two steps from the hotel's nicest restaurant, we run into Len, the vice-president of sales. He is not my boss, but since this event is for the sales guys, he will act like my boss for the five days we're here. My boss wouldn't be caught dead in Las Vegas for five days. Marshall never arrives until just before the cocktail party the night of our studio's dinner. Sometimes he comes on the specially chartered plane we hire for our filmmakers, sometimes he comes on the president's private plane. The words "flying commercially" make him shudder in something that can only be described as pain.

"Got a minute, Babe?" I nod and incline my head. Molly wanders off to a nearby slot machine. I watch her first unsuccessful pull.

"Could you get me four tickets to Steve and Eydie's show?"

I think he's kidding. "What's the matter, Charo all sold out?" He stacks his chips in the palm of his hand. It's a good-sized column of money.

"Can you?"

"Who are they for?"

"One of our customers. Very important." He makes his eyes big to show me how important. "Can you take care of this for me? Don't worry about the price."

I don't answer. Instead I take an index card out of my purse and start running down a list of things: the entertainment, the menu, seating for the dais, times we can run-through the product reel.

"Whoa, Babe. Can't this wait? Handle it any way you think best and tell me about it tomorrow. Okay?"

I shrug. I have this great way of showing disdain. My face remains placid, sometimes even friendly, but my shoulders say asshole.

"Work on those tickets, willya?" I guess he missed the disdain.

He turns away from me, his fingers getting all jumpy around the chips, his eyes scanning the casino. Just my luck. He remembers something else and turns back.

"By the way, I saw Etta." I stare unblinking into his paste-colored face, more at the eyebrows than the eyes. "She looks like a freak. She better not be any trouble."

I look at him more carefully. Never in danger of being named to the best-dressed list, he's outdone himself tonight. He is wearing a white polyester suit. His shirt is open and I can see several gold chains lying flat against his hairless chest. He is dressed like Elvis at the end of the king's career. He's even wearing white shoes. Did he buy this outfit just for this trip? Who's calling who a freak?

"There won't be any trouble. Etta's fine," I assure him. I assure myself. I watch him walk away. Len has an artificial leg. You'd have to know, otherwise you'd think he just walked real slow.

"Steve and Eydie. Is he kidding?" Molly and I are sharing a bottle of pouilly-fuissé. Of course I have already called two people in the hotel to see if they can get me tickets. Our waiter says he's sorry but the kitchen is very busy. I don't care how long it takes for them to bring our dinner. We're having fun. We are telling each other work stories. Stories we've told each other before, but stories that always make us laugh.

I tell her about the time, years ago, when I was standing in the hall at work talking to another secretary about a big movie star who was in a meeting on our floor. This movie star was old, in some sort of state of preservation. We were making fun of him and what appeared to be the corset under his sweater. Just as I started making fun of his facelift, he walked out of the office and caught the two of us staring at him and laughing.

He walked over to us and asked what we were talking about. When he was close to us, I forgot how old he was. All I could think of was all the great movies he'd been in, even if they were made twenty years ago. I said I couldn't believe how great he looked and that we thought he was the handsomest guy who had ever been up to the office. In a funny way I was only half lying. He smiled and asked our names. The next day I received a box by messenger. I opened the card first. It was from the movie star. He wrote: "You look pretty great, too." Inside the Bergdorf box was a white lace bed jacket.

Molly laughs until tiny tears run out of the corners of her eyes. Twenty minutes or so go by and we keep telling stories. I don't know about Molly, but I feel a little like Scheherazade, worried about what will happen to me if ever I finish my stories.

Our waiter comes over and says there is no more lobster. Molly had ordered the lobster. He's very sorry; he's also very hassled. I expect Molly to order the crab. She likes the idea of ordering fish in the desert. Personally, I stick to pasta. Suddenly, she is very angry and asks to see the maître d'. I don't understand what's wrong.

"Who cares if the lobster is gone?" She looks at my wineglass. She's so mad, she can't even look at me. While she's arguing with the maître d', I wonder if it has anything to do with Mr. Los Angeles. There was some talk of him meeting her here so they could spend some time together. As far as I know, he's still coming. I think he's a jerk. Of course, I don't tell Molly that. I don't have to. She thinks he's a jerk, too. But that doesn't stop the heart from beating fast. I always call Molly's men friends by the city they live in. I'm sure one of these days, I'll call one of them by name. I hope so. Molly's pretty worked up. Maybe it was all that talk about work that's upset her. We agree we don't like work as much as we used to when we were both publicists, before we found out what being management was really like. But we can't stop talking about it. We can't stop the way some people can't stop looking at a traffic accident.

"She can have my lobster."

I turn to look at the man sitting by himself who has just spoken to us. He's so handsome I forget for a moment what the fuss is all about.

"Oh, no, Mr. Darling." The waiter is clearly upset.

"No, I insist." He has the voice of money and patience.

The maître d' immediately leaves our table and goes over to Handsome's table. They confer in low tones. Molly is once again herself and tells the waiter to bring her a Caesar salad.

A few minutes later the biggest lobster I have ever seen is placed before Molly. She laughs. I turn and ask Mr. Darling if he would like to join us and share Molly's lobster. He smiles at me. He has a slight gap between his two front teeth. He has a very sexy smile.

"I'd love to." He tells the waiter to bring a bottle of champagne.

We all share each other's food. Molly and I are high from the wine and the champagne and the time change, but when he orders after dinner drinks we don't say no.

Darling and I do most of the talking. Talking to a stranger like an old friend is one of the things I do best. Besides, it's fun. Molly acts like a snob. Every time he lights her cigarette she says thank you in a way that makes it sound like she's saying, But we haven't been properly introduced. I know she's only being shy. By the time the cappuccino arrives, I feel like I've known Rick Darling for years. And when Molly says she's going up to the room, I tell her goodnight and hardly take my eyes off him. He knocks me out.

He's married and I'm married so I feel safe and keep talking. The moment Molly is gone, we settle into a quiet conversation. It's all very personal and now there seems to be an invisible string connecting us.

Rick Darling lives in Monaco. "My wife doesn't like to fly so she spends most of her time there with our two daughters. Jenny is eight and Alexandra is three." I can tell he is no longer in love with his wife. He's a gambler. I tell him I've never met a gambler.

"Oh, sure you have," he says. "They've just called themselves by other names."

He walks me through the casino to the elevator bank. His workday is just beginning. Everyone in the hotel knows him.

"I'll call you tomorrow," he says. I smile.

I am inside the gold elevator before I realize how late it is. Two men stand on the other side of the elevator.

"This isn't gold." He pats the wall like he might a woman's fanny. "If you want real gold, you've got to stay at Caesar's." The other man nods. The doors open and I get off on my floor.

"He wants a private plane."

"Fuck him."

"I've had worse. He wants the plane."

"What's wrong with the charter? All the others are taking it. Does he know who's coming? Stars, Oscar-winning directors, talented screenwriters. They're all going on the charter."

Molly puts her hand over the receiver. "Do I have to remind you who Mark Ludlow is? Do I have to remind you that without Mark Ludlow you have no one to honor with your Male Star of the Year award?"

I start to tell Molly that I do know who Mark Ludlow is. He's the guy who when he got his first job in a movie used to come up to the office and hang out with us, picking our brains about how to be a star. That was only five years ago.

"Well?" Molly waits.

"Tell him I'll call him back. Don't promise anything." I have to remind Molly to say no; she'd much rather say yes. It saves wear and tear. She believes in giving in to actors' demands, no matter how crazy. She's always telling me life's too short to argue with filmmakers. And besides, if we don't say yes, some guy higher up will. That's usually true.

Molly lights a cigarette and says to no one in particular: "It's just money." In some ways she's right about it being just money, but even so I can't do it. There's more to it than that. I'm making it sound like I face a moral dilemma every time I make a business decision. It's not quite that bad since there are no morals in the movie business.

"Are you ready to meet with Bruce?"

"Who's Bruce?" I question our temporary secretary. She's looking at me as if I've just started speaking Chinese. I tell her to ask Molly if I'm ready.

Our temporary secretary, Lynette, is supposedly Manpower's best. She's an older woman who I imagine has just started working again full time. She was fine on Monday when the most she had to do was arrange for a typewriter to be sent to our suite and put a hold on twenty-five limos for Thursday and Friday. Well, she did have to find a company with twenty-five limos. The company we used last year said they didn't want our business. They said it wasn't worth the aggravation. Last year we spent $35,000 with them in two days.

Anyway, each day Lynette has gotten more and more tense. At first I thought it was our language. I swear I see her flinch every time we use the F word. I guess I expect people who live in Las Vegas to be more blasé about cursing. But that's stupid. Living in a town where there's gambling doesn't necessarily mean you don't have standards. Today, I think something else is worrying Lynette. And I think she's going to tell me what it is.

I get another cup of coffee and sit down with my legal pad, which is covered with notes and telephone numbers and things I have to do. This is the third year I have put on this event. Each year I swear I'm never coming back. I've promised myself not to say that this year and instead really not come back next year. Our event is tomorrow night. Tomorrow night we host a sit-down dinner for fifteen hundred people — theater owners and their wives — in the Grand Ballroom of this hotel. We come to Las Vegas once a year to show these men clips from our upcoming movies. We give them lots to drink, mediocre hotel food to eat and a Vegas show to watch. We do this so they will like our movies. We also do this so they will like us. Us, the studio.

We spend a lot of money. Every year we spend more. Before I leave New York I always show Marshall and Len the budget. They glance over it. They never question it. They're just so glad that they don't have to do the work. Any price seems cheap to them. Of course, two months from now I will be asked to attend a meeting with Marshall and Len and the head of finance to explain the budget, which by then will seem excessive to everyone, including me. My boss will say it was Len's show and leave to take a more important meeting about this or that ad campaign. Len will swivel in his chair first toward me and then back to Mr. Finance and say, "She's got all the answers." The head of finance will then begin the interrogation. And I will have fallen behind enemy lines once again.

I've brought five publicists plus Molly to Las Vegas to put on this extravaganza. They don't like coming here much either, but the overtime is good. I watch them eating breakfast, smoking, talking, waiting for me to give them their assignments and get their day started. They all look nervous and tired and today is the day we really have to pump. They've been staying up too late. They've been spending too much time in the casino. Last year one of the publicists gambled away his return ticket to New York.

I get myself another cup of black coffee and piece of cinnamon toast. I love cinnamon toast. It reminds me of my childhood. I never make it at home. It's too much trouble. Molly hands me a list of things to do. By each task I put a pair of initials. Handing the list back to her, I notice my initials appear way too often.

It's 10:45. I finally start the staff meeting I had called for 9:30. I give them their assignments, trying not to let myself sound tired or depressed.

CREATIVE DIFFERENCES

There is some discussion about tomorrow's dinner. Why did I think they would take their assignments and leave silently? One of the publicists says rain is expected in Los Angeles and maybe the chartered plane won't be able to take off. Someone else says there is a power shortage in the ballroom and maybe we won't be able to project the product reel. They're all making me crazy. If I yell at them, they will become sullen and I'd much rather deal with hysteria than sullenness.

Etta stands against the sliding glass doors that overlook the Strip. She doesn't make any dire predictions about tomorrow night. I'm not sure she's even been listening to any of this. The sunlight through the sheer curtains skips across her head, making it appear as if she still has her hair. She asks to speak with me.

I nod. "Sure, but first I have to call Len."

Len answers. I explain about the plane and why I don't think we should give it to Ludlow. I think I may have woken him up. His voice goes in and out of the receiver, like he's groping around for something—a robe, a watch, a person?

"No fucking way! No! Tell him no private plane." I let him go on longer than necessary. I'm enjoying the outrage in his voice.

I hang up and ask Lynette to get me Mark Ludlow. Molly says it would be easier to call back his agent. I ignore her. A part of me doesn't think it was Mark who asked for the plane in the first place. Mark has a big ego, but he has some sense of proportion. Besides, Mark has made all five of his movies for our company. All five have been hits. He'll be saner than his agent.

I hang up from Mark Ludlow. Molly is kind enough not to ask what he said. He was not saner than his agent.

"Molly, ask Len to stop by if he has a minute, willya?" Molly lights a cigarette and nods. She's irritated with me.

I pick up the phone. It's Rick Darling. "Can we have dinner?" I hesitate. I hadn't expected his voice to catch me quite this way. For a few seconds there is nothing else—just his voice and my breathing.

"Yes."

"Lynette, see if Bruce and his friends would like any coffee. I'll be with them in a minute." Bruce and his friends have been up for three days. They've probably got something stronger than coffee and for a second, looking at them, I wish they'd give me some. They're awake, but floating about two feet off the ground.

Lynette seems irritated. She wants to talk to me, not serve coffee to three guys who look like casualties from a drug war. I look at her. She told me the other day her husband sells juvenile furniture at Sears.

Len comes in. His face is chapped from too hasty a shave.

"Coffee?" He nods but makes no move to pour himself a cup from the urn that stands not three feet from him. I pour him some coffee and look around unsuccessfully for some Sweet 'N Low. I have another cup, black.

"What did Ludlow say?" He slurps his coffee. I never noticed that before. He drinks a lot of coffee in meetings and I have never noticed that revolting noise. I tell him Ludlow said he wasn't coming.

"Oh, my God. What else did he say?"

"Let's see. He said he was going to call you and whoever else in the goddamned company he had to. He also called me a cunt just before he slammed the phone down."

"Did he say he was going to call Jake?"

"Yeah." Jake is the head of the studio and not a calm kind of guy.

Len pushes his coffee cup from side to side on the glass-topped table, making ugly little brown streams of spilled coffee. He looks around the room.

"Give him the plane."

I sit back in the club chair, cradling my coffee the way I might if my hands were cold, and stare at him. Out of the corner of my eye I see Etta moving toward me. Just when I think my stare is making Len uncomfortable, I have to give it up to look at Etta. Her eyes are big. I know instantly that she feels like a kid who's happened upon her parents quarreling. She wants to leave, but she's got to know what I'm going to do. Am I going to stand up to him? I'd like to know the answer myself.

Len holds out his cup to Lynette who has been watching him ever since he came into the suite. This is the first time in four days another executive has come into our work suite. Now a man is here, and he is someone who clearly outranks me. Her world seems ordered once again. She takes his cup but pours his coffee into a clean one. She also hands him a saucer to go with it and two packets of Sweet 'N Low. Four or five years ago this little act of domesticity would have made me nuts. Now it just deflates me a little.

"You want me to give him the plane?" I repeat his order, hoping he might change his mind. I'm angry. I'm the one who told Mark Ludlow no. I was convincing in my delivery, convinced the company was behind me. I did not let the fact that Ludlow has made tens of millions of dollars for the company sway me. Besides, it isn't about money. It's about our treating Ludlow the same way we are treating all the other filmmakers. I had said no. I had listened to him call me a cunt. Now Len is going to cave. He's going to give in.

I listen to him slurp his coffee. My anger is beginning to give way to something else. I am stunned by Len's ignorance. He is truly surprised that Ludlow threatened not to come. He's asked me three times if he really said it. It had never occurred to him. I see now that Len knows nothing about handling actors or filmmakers. Why am I surprised? I guess I expect an executive, a vice-president, to have some feel for the kind of people we work with. Some vague sense, at least. He might as well be working for a company that makes widgets. Even as I think this, I wonder why I'm so outraged. Obviously, no one else in the company cares what he knows or doesn't know about handling people. Why should I? Probably because his ignorance is about to make my job harder.

He's talking about Ludlow and how we should handle him. I have to stop myself from telling him I would be glad to introduce him to Mark some time. He is gathering confidence from his very ignorance. The odd thing is Len never asked me one question about how giving the plane to Ludlow or not giving it to him would affect the other filmmakers. He must have reasoned that any messiness could be handled by me. It is a reckless way of doing business. But maybe that's what it takes to be successful in business. Len would give his opinion on open heart surgery if someone asked him.

One thing's for sure. He isn't going to make any enemies. And he sure as hell isn't going to let some movie star go over his head. There's something else. I can hear in his voice that some mystery has just been unlocked for him. The mystery of marketing-advertising and publicity. It isn't so hard. He could do it. He even thinks he was right all along when he says the people in marketing aren't any more creative than his sales force. There was always a sneer in his voice when he said the word "creative." Well, in a way I can understand that. Certain people in advertising are called the creatives. It is akin to calling them dauphins. I am not called a creative. I like to think that this doesn't necessarily mean I'm not creative.

"Yes, give Ludlow the plane. How much will it cost?"

"Isn't it a little late to ask?" The room has no air. None of the windows is open. It's one hundred degrees outside. It's the desert. Even so I wish a window were open and a hot breeze was coming in. Len's mouth has shrunk into a thin line. He's grim and he's trying to hold his temper. That makes two of us. I decide to answer his question without the benefit of oxygen.

"About twenty thousand with insurance, down-time, overtime, everything." I try and ease up. "Maybe less. I'll work something out." Etta sits down, relaxes a little. I think she expected more of me, but even so she seems relieved there will be no fight.

Len gets up to leave. The way he pulls his sports jacket around his chest tells me he thinks he's handled this pretty well. Unfortunately, this is the crack in the dam. He will now want to be more involved. Just what I need.

He's almost out the door when he asks me sotto voce who Bruce is. I look over at Bruce. He is thirtyish, black, dressed in blue jeans and a work shirt and has a small, gold stud in his ear. It consoles me to see someone dressed like this. It confirms that the sixties did happen.

"Oh, Bruce? He's the road manager for tomorrow night's entertainment. He's also the man who got you the tickets to Steve and Eydie's show." An opportunity to say thank-you lies before him. He walks around it. At the door, he turns once more to tell me to call him later.

"Where?"

"Have me paged."

I turn back around. Great. What that really means is I should check with him before doing anything. Let me amend that. Doing anything that might make him look bad. Better not to think about this now. I've got a lot to do. Etta stands up.

"Can I talk to you now?"

"Sure." My lack of enthusiasm is embarrassing even to me. "First, let me grovel to Mark Ludlow."

I ask Molly to talk to Bruce. "It's something about a special grand piano and a certified check." You'd think we were Fly-by-Night Studios the way he wants the check handed to him before his man goes out on stage.

Molly whispers in my ear. "Do you want a Valium?"

"No, thanks. I'm fine. I'm just feeling a little tired." A little depressed. A little angry. A little stupid. She whispers some more. She tells me about the health club in this hotel where we can have oxygen pep-ups.

"Pep-ups?"

"Yeah, two minutes of pure oxygen and in about thirty minutes you feel great." I can't wait.

"Oh, Molly. I'm going to have dinner with Darling tonight." She nods but no smile. "Is Mr. L. A. coming?"

She shakes her head. "Don't know yet."

"Etta, let's go into my room for a minute. It won't be so noisy." I sit down on the couch and Etta sits cross-legged on the floor and starts talking.

"My parents are very rich. They haven't lived together since I was a kid. My mother lives in Paris, where I grew up. But they won't get divorced."

I want to say "too costly," but I don't. Instead I listen. Even with the jeans, the white T-shirt and the funny haircut, you can tell Etta grew up rich. It's this way she has of being detached, of missing a beat. I've known other rich people who act the same way. There is always this lag time between when someone says something to Etta and her response. It's like she's trying to decide whether or not to let life in. She usually decides to keep it at a distance so a lot of times I feel as if I'm talking to someone who has water in her ears.

"My boyfriend threw me out of our apartment. Just a couple of days before we came here. I almost asked you if I could stay in New York, but since I don't have anywhere to say . . ." Her voice trails off on this exaggeration. I wonder if this is the reason she cut her hair. As if she heard me, she runs the palm of her hand over her head. The way a boy might.

She tells me how much she still loves her boyfriend. Her ex-boyfriend. It breaks my heart to listen. What is sadder than to love someone who no longer loves you? I want to tell her to forget him, to stop loving him. But she keeps on talking and there is no way I can say it now.

I feel as if I'm on a barge, floating with Etta on a blue river. It's so dark I can't see the shore. I'm pulled along. There seems to be time here, all the time in the world.

Somewhere I hear John's voice telling me to stop. To stop being so damned sympathetic to everyone's problems: "These people work for you; you're only making things harder for them." Sympathy like mine, like most sympathy, I guess, only reminds me of my own impotence. I'm just listening. I can't help her. I get up and walk over to the windows. Maybe a dose of Las Vegas in the daylight will remind me John's right.

Molly calls to me through the half-closed door. Just my name, but I can hear in her voice there's a problem.

"I've got to go, Etta. You okay?"

As usual a beat. It's as if I'm on a mountain and she's down in the valley waiting for the echo.

"Sure." In that one word is so much anger and rebellion and fear that I am tempted to restart the conversation. Tempted to ask her who the fuck she thinks she's talking to. But I walk back into the living room. Molly and Bruce are still at it.

Lynette hands me some phone messages. John. Mark Ludlow's agent—urgent. Len's wife—can I recommend a hairdresser? I can't, maybe Etta can.

8

*A*fter dinner I sit and watch Rick Darling play baccarat. We're in a smallish casino set off from the larger one by four red-carpeted steps and security guys dressed in tuxedos. There are couches for the women who are waiting for their men. There is not one woman gambling. Everyone is dressed in evening clothes.

Darling looks great. He was born to wear a tuxedo. He drinks Scotch on the rocks. He wears a plain wedding band and an expensive watch. I think he has his nails manicured. He's winning.

I just sit and watch him. It's a funny feeling. I feel like his appendage. Nothing is expected of me. I am with Darling. Perversely, I'm enjoying this. I have no responsibility. I am not in charge. I'm tired, but for the first time today I feel okay. Maybe the oxygen pep-up is starting to kick in, eight hours later. Darling wants nothing from me. All day people have wanted something from me. That's what my kind of work is all about. I wonder if that's what all work is about. Looking at Darling I don't think so.

It's nearly 2:30 in the morning. "I have to leave soon," I whisper to Darling. He gives me his full attention; for a moment I am the most important thing in the world to him. I don't want to leave. I don't want to leave him. John would think this odd. He would say I should have called him. He would be hurt. I don't know how to tell him I'm embarrassed to call him when I feel like this. It seems funny after all these years to think I'd be embarrassed to tell John anything. But because I know he thinks I should do something about getting another job or make peace with the one I have, I can't tell him how unhappy I am right now. I'd rather tell a stranger. Darling doesn't know me, but he knows something about me. Something I want him to tell me.

I run between the smallish room where we've corralled the filmmakers at a cocktail party and the ballroom where scores of union waiters are throwing dishes and silverware onto hundreds of tables for ten.

Several filmmakers ask me where they're sitting on the dais. By the way they ask, you'd think their entire self-worth is tied up in whether they are on the first tier or the second tier.

"I don't remember." I lie and use a girlish laugh. "Somewhere great." They spare us both any further embarrassment by going over to the bar. A couple of filmmakers push past me on their way to the casino. This is exactly what I don't want. This is why I have brought them in through the back entrance. Long, vacant, white-washed concrete halls form a secret labyrinth within the hotel. They think I used the back way because they're so famous. Generally, famous doesn't stack up to gambling.

"Oh, please stay. You can gamble later." I sound a little too much like a Girl Scout leader. They look at me. In their eyes I see I am exactly, specifically, what they think is wrong with studio executives. I move aside.

Molly comes into the room. She finds me. Her eyes skate around the party taking everyone in. There's a certain desperation in her face. She's trying to hide it, but she can't. She's too tired.

"I can't find Ludlow. His plane landed twenty minutes ago, but he's not here yet." Molly's red dress is very stylish. I haven't seen it before.

"Etta went to pick him up. I'm sure they'll be here soon."

She looks at me. "You sent Etta?"

CREATIVE DIFFERENCES

Three people are all talking to me at once. Maybe I should run this like a bakery and make people take a number. Just tell them what to do and they'll go away. If I keep talking to myself, I'll get through it. I hate to admit it and wouldn't out loud, but I so want this evening, this ridiculously expensive extravaganza, to be successful. In business, it's best not to reveal how much something means to you. It gives you away. You can even scare yourself. Jake Tyler, the head of the studio, walks up to me. Everyone else, including Molly, melts away.

"So, I hear you have sound problems. The product reel is gonna sound like shit. You know how important this is?"

For a few seconds I'm sure he's right. It will sound like shit. Everything will be a disaster. He keeps at me. Why should there be sound problems? We're in a room the size of two football fields with no permanent sound system, using a projector that was not designed to project from here to Reno. I don't say this.

"The sound levels will be fine," I tell him. I say it matter-of-factly.

He's unconvinced. "Can you promise the sound will be good?"

"Can I promise?" I repeat dully.

He starts up again. I let a small ice cube from the Coke I'm drinking slide into my mouth. It tastes sweet and it cools the insides of my cheeks. I concentrate on its melting. Listening to him, it occurs to me that movie people have forgotten that there is sometimes more power in saying less than more. I think it's from talking on the phone too much.

Again he tells me how important it is; how he won't be able to face the filmmakers if their movies sound terrible. I almost laugh. He goes on.

If it were so goddamned important, where were you at 4:00 this morning when we finally got into the ballroom for the run-through? Where was Len? I want to say this, but I don't. I want to scream at him, but I don't. In business most of us never get to say what we want, instead we are reduced to fantasies, or sarcasm, or silence. Of course, the thing about the movie business is most people do, in fact, say what they want. Then those of us who are not in positions of power or who do not have someone in a position of power looking out for us or who actually like our work and want to keep doing it, act as though these crazy people are normal and have not said anything outrageous, mean or stupid.

The ice cube, now a splinter of cold, slips down my throat and temporarily lodges in my chest. I decide to act like he hasn't been yelling at me in a hoarse whisper, criticizing every decision I've made, trying to—I don't know what—scare me? I take his arm.

"What are you drinking?" I steer him over to the bar and order for him like he's my date. I start to flirt with him. He's not bad-looking. Jake is a smart man and that goes a long way with me. Most of the movies he commits the studio to make are good—that is, the idea is good, but they aren't always good in the end. The rumor about him is that he consults a numerologist every day. I'd like to get my hands on his chart. He can be very funny. That also goes a long way with me. And I know from meetings I've been to with him that he likes to look at me.

It bothers John when I flirt. It takes him by surprise. It seems so unlike me. He thinks I'm better than that. I'm not.

Jake finishes his drink in two gulps and runs his hand over the small of my back much too slowly and says he knows everything will be great. He makes me laugh.

The shard of ice shifts and continues to fall downward, chilling my insides. I ease out of the cocktail party and check on the ballroom. Molly says our entertainer, Bruce's man, will not perform without two spotlights. Bruce stands respectfully beside Molly.

"Sounds reasonable to me. What's the problem?"

"Only one union operator." Molly holds her cigarette so smoke doesn't get in her eyes. She has this great way of always looking like she's a guest.

"Shit." It occurs to me that at a time like this I could use a man to help me. I know I shouldn't let myself think like this, but Christ, the head of the electrician's local would take it a lot better if a guy went over to ask him for another spotlight operator. This is the same guy who last night threatened to pull all his electricians out of the hotel if I didn't stop asking them to change the lighting. The head of hotel operations got wind of the union's threat and was all over me. I kept at them. I even used Mark Ludlow as the reason I needed special lights. The union guy acted like he didn't know who Mark Ludlow was. He called me Doll, and it wasn't an endearment.

I reach into my purse for some money. I push several hundred dollars into Molly's hand. "Doll, go buy us a spotlight operator."

I go back into the cocktail party. Thirty minutes until the dinner starts. At least half of the dais is in the casino. Marshall comes up to me. I'm glad to see him. I figure now I have some support. He lulls me with an endearment.

"Honey?"

I'm all his. I'm waiting for the compliments, for the sympathy. I know how hard you've been working kind of thing.

"I want my room changed. It's too close to the elevators."

"What?" I ask feebly. I must have heard him wrong.

"My room." He hands me his room key. "Have someone change it."

I want to strangle him. I want to be led away in handcuffs. There are no vacant rooms in this hotel. He leans in to me.

"Everything looks great. Len's been looking for you. Something about Ludlow." Then his back is to me; he's working the room. I love that. I love the way Marshall divests himself of a problem so effortlessly.

I see Len. Mercifully he is wearing a regular tuxedo. I don't think I could bear it if he were dressed in his lounge lizard finery.

I order another Coke and wait for Len to find me. One of my publicists hands me a note. The paper is damp. I wonder if it's wet with nervous perspiration. The note is from Darling. The publicist tells me he's trying to round up the filmmakers for the head table and leaves. I feel sorry for him. He's going to have to stand beside them at the tables and wait while they ignore him for ten minutes or so. Then he will have to ask them to stop gambling and come with him to sit on a dais for three hours so fifteen hundred people can gawk at them. Yeah, they're gonna be real nice to him when he snaps their winning streak.

Len is next to me. "Ludlow's upstairs. He won't come down. I want Etta fired."

I maneuver another piece of ice into my mouth. My mother always hated us sucking on ice, so I do it surreptitiously, as if she were watching me.

"I must have missed something, Len." I'm surprised at the iciness in my voice. I realize I don't like Len and I'm having trouble hiding it.

Len tells me Ludlow called him a few minutes ago. I can't help but smirk over the instant friendship the private plane has given birth to. He says Ludlow was insulted by Etta and refuses to come to the dinner.

Another sip of Coke. Buy time. All too often a manager of people experiences this feeling of dread, this feeling of everything out of control. I have to trust my staff, they're all I have. Short hair or bald. I decide to use one of my favorite tacks.

"Fine. I'll just go remove his place card and fix the dais a bit."

"Are you nuts? Didn't you hear me? Ludlow's not coming!"

"Oh, Len, relax. He'll come. And if he doesn't, he doesn't. It's just a dinner. We're not depending on him to perform brain surgery."

Len looks beyond me and says, "If Ludlow doesn't come down, I will see to it personally that Etta is fired."

This last piece of ice has coated my insides with a thin but sturdy sheet of ice. Inside, I am now a frozen lake and Len's anger skids across me clumsily. The dinner is supposed to start in five minutes. I see the publicist arrive with the missing-in-action filmmakers.

"Len, you better get in line. We'll be seating the dais soon. Oh, and Len." I pretend to pick a piece of lint off his lapel. "If you want to fire someone, you can start with me right now. Would you like me to stop and let you handle the rest?"

Len shakes his head. He knows I've won. But he doesn't know yet how much he's going to hate me for it later on. Much later on. But I know and I don't look forward to it. It makes me hope Marshall holds onto his job. I'd hate to work for Len.

Just as I'm leading the members of the dais down the hall to the ballroom, feeling like a put-upon tourist guide, Etta delivers Ludlow. Instantly the filmmakers move into line. Movie stars can actually alter the physical world this easily.

CREATIVE DIFFERENCES

Ludlow makes a big show of being happy to see me. He is a handsome, almost beautiful man. He kisses me full on the mouth. I let him. He pulls back suddenly. I wonder if all the ice I've swallowed has somehow turned into vapors and just then fled up through by body into his mouth, chilling him.

The dinner starts and Etta finds me in the dark. She tells me Ludlow got fresh with her in the limo and she called him a pig.

"Fresh," I repeat not understanding. Fresh is a word our mothers would use. Maybe it's her English.

She whispers into my ear. "Ludlow said he always wanted to fuck a boy and my hair made him think he could pretend I was a boy."

"How'd you get him to come down?"

"You kidding me? He wasn't going to miss this."

We both look at the dais. Ludlow is accepting the Star of the Year award. Fifteen hundred people are standing and clapping wildly. Flash cameras explode.

Etta runs her hand over her head. "I also let him fuck me."

"The dinner was a success, I guess. Yeah, it was."

Darling smiles at me, the gap between his teeth making me hot. We are drinking white wine in the bar that overlooks the casino. Darling plays with a stack of chips that could probably buy John and me a three-bedroom co-op in Manhattan. Several people come by to say how great the evening turned out. None of them is Marshall, Jake or Len. Molly comes by to tell me she and the gang are going upstairs to order room service.

"We'll be waiting for you."

I don't want anyone to be waiting for me. I just want to slip away, assume a new identity, move to another city, get a new job, meet new people.

"Are you okay?" Darling's voice comes to me out of the bar's hum.

"I feel like I'm on a runaway train." He waits for me to go on, to explain what I mean. I want him magically to know what I mean. I want him to tell me why I don't feel like I thought I was going to feel if the dinner was a big success. I thought I would feel great. Why don't I feel great? I sip the wine and look down at my body trying to see it with his eyes. I wonder if he is attracted to me. I look at him. If he asks me to go to bed with him right now, I'm afraid I'll say yes.

"Rick, I don't think I can do this anymore. I think I want to quit my job."

He reaches over and takes my hand. His fingers are long and the color of some polished wood I remember from my childhood.

"You don't want to quit your job. You're just tired. You let people hurt your feelings. You keep thinking work is like life and it's not. It's not ever going to be. Work is always going to hurt. You're never going to feel at work like you feel when you're with John."

He tells me he's going to take me upstairs to Molly. He tells me John is lucky to have me. He tells me in another world he would have asked to make love to me tonight. I relax. I am flooded with warmth. The lake inside of me begins to thaw.

EXECUTIVE DIRECTOR

9

"*L*ook." My secretary, Lisa, thrusts a piece of paper in front of me. She pulls it away before I can read it.

"Look!" She repeats, only louder. She slams the door to my office.

Instinct tells me I don't want to look. Lisa has a flair for the dramatic. It's one of the things I like best about her. It's also one of the things I like least. I sit still, hands in my lap.

Lisa sits down in front of my desk in one of two leather chairs. The chairs sound nicer than they are. They are old, ripped and repaired. But my office isn't about furniture or design, it's about the view.

Lisa explores the deep pockets of her green suede skirt. Out comes a wine-colored case of soft leather. She lights a cigarette and studies the piece of paper laying flat on her lap.

I can tell this has something to do with me. She is reading it for the third time. Is she memorizing it? I lean back in my chair. It's broken and I almost tip over. I right myself just in time. I've grown used to the thrill of almost falling and now am annoyed.

"Lisa, could you call maintenance today? This chair's going to kill me."

I've been asking her to call for months. On her desk is a yellow Post-it note reminding her to call. She never calls. She won't call today.

"Wait till you see this." She looks up at me. I look down at my desk. In my absence Lisa has arranged all my mail in colored folders. One folder is a dark, almost bitter shade of blue, one is bright yellow, one is white-white and two are red. You can't requisition colored folders from the eighteenth floor. I wonder if there is a petty cash voucher waiting for my signature inside one of these. There's a lot of mail. I've been away for ten days. John and I went to Antigua right after this year's Las Vegas extravaganza. Actually, I like the folders. They dress up my morning.

"I'm going to make you a copy. Be right back." Lisa sweeps out of the room, leaving the door open.

"Welcome back." Molly stands at the door. Looking at her I can feel the heat of my suntan across my forehead. She looks pale.

"Hi, come in. Anything interesting happening?" Before she can answer me, her secretary is at the door telling her she is wanted on the phone.

"Mr. Malibu?" I sound casual. I'm dying to know what's been going on between them while I was gone. Molly nods and walks slowly out of my office. I watch her, thinking she might be going out onto a veranda to take the call so casually does she move. I think I smell some of her perfume in the air. I don't know her Mr. Malibu very well. We've been at some industry functions together. He works at another studio. It's not that Molly isn't herself around him. It's just that she seems less herself. The trick is, of course, to find someone who lets you be exactly yourself.

Twenty-four hours ago I was on a beach. A gentle curve of white sand along an aquamarine bay. John doesn't love the beach the way I do. I love it from my childhood. I'm drawn to it. He indulges me. By the fifth or sixth day he knows why I love it so much. But he will forget over the spring and the summer and next winter I will have to convince him all over again. But I never forget. It's like some part of the beach, a grain of sand perhaps, maybe some of the salt, has worked its way into my bloodstream.

I dial John. I can't start to work right away. I have to ease back into it. I feel as if I'm on stilts, heady from relaxation.

CREATIVE DIFFERENCES

John's secretary says, "Who's calling?" I laugh. She does this all the time. Maybe she's in love with John and thinks if she's mean to me, I'll stop calling or go away. Or maybe she just hates answering his phone. One of these days I'm going to ask John about her. But not today. Today I am determined to keep the wonder of our vacation alive.

"He's in a meeting. I'll have him call you back," she promises.

Lisa returns. I tell her I want to have a staff meeting at 10:30. This week shouldn't be so bad. The whole company waits for the Academy Award nominations to be announced tomorrow. No one expects us to get many. But even so, everyone goes around talking like we might, talking, in fact, about little else. They act like the ballots being counted in Los Angeles had their names on them. Still it's kind of nice. It's one of the few times the whole company draws one breath at the same time.

Lisa lays the Xerox on my desk and leaves to tell the staff about the meeting.

I take a sip of coffee. One of my vacation resolutions is to drink less coffee. I pick up the Xerox. It's a press release. Actually, it's a draft of one announcing the promotion of my boss, Marshall Wheeling, to senior vice-president. The language of the release is not our style, the publicity department's style, that is. I wonder why we weren't asked to write it. I read it again and this time I notice something. The last paragraph recapping everyone who reports to Marshall has two blanks. My name and Cassie's, the woman who runs the field department on the other side of the floor, are not typed in. They are handwritten in the margin.

My stilts go out from under me and I topple over. Suddenly I feel as if I haven't had a vacation in three years. Dialing my boss, I think how lucky I am to have Lisa. A lot of people are good at office espionage. But Lisa has a special talent for it. She's not as good as my old friend Joycelyn, but she's pretty close. She doesn't mind putting in the hours necessary to keep on top of things. This work can be exhausting. Lisa might follow a lead—a remark from a senior executive overheard in an elevator—for days, only to find it leads nowhere. But she is undaunted by such setbacks. Today's information fell into her lap, but it still counts. After all, she is the one who has made it a point to check the Xerox machine first thing every morning. Two years ago, Lisa found payroll's copy of executive salaries in the Xerox machine.

"Hi, 'Del." Marshall's secretary likes me. She likes that I sometimes dial my own calls. When you become an executive you usually forget how to dial.

"Welcome back." A few minutes of swapping Caribbean stories.

"Any chance I can see Marshall for a few minutes sometime today?" I don't think I could sound any more casual. I sound like I'm asking if my dry cleaning is ready.

"Sure. Any time. How about twelve-thirty. He has a one o'clock lunch."

"Great." I hang up pretty sure Adele didn't type the release. I'm relieved. It's not on the secretarial grapevine. Yet. I'm surprised at feeling relieved. But there it is.

Lisa comes back in with the telephone message book and still more mail. Adeptly she slides the new pieces into the proper folders. For an instant I wonder what Lisa's linen closet looks like. I realize it will be difficult to have a meeting with my boss if I don't read the mail. The memos. The reports. The reviews. The trades. The daily summaries. Not that I want the meeting to be about work.

"Well?"

"Lisa, I need more coffee." When I say it like this, there is no room for her to refuse. Ten solid days of rest and what I'd really like is some speed. "Ask Molly to come in." Before she leaves I see something in the set of her hands on the message book that tells me she doesn't want me to tell Molly. Knowing a secret, for no matter how short a time, is one of the few really satisfying experiences in business.

"Molly's gone out." She places the coffee mug on the square piece of tile I use as a coaster. When I was a secretary I used to drink coffee out of Styrofoam cups. Then I used to drink out of an old cracked mug my first boss left behind when she quit her job. Now I use one of four mugs all the same shade of midnight blue. I notice Lisa's brought me a clean mug. I appreciate it, but don't say anything. Instead, I say, "Out? Out where?"

CREATIVE DIFFERENCES

"Just out. Her secretary says she'll be back in an hour or so. Probably something about that guy she's been seeing." I wait for something more, some detail that I've missed that might explain Molly's attraction to Mr. Malibu, but Lisa doesn't say anything else.

I tell Lisa to start telling me what's been going on. I begin to sort through the folders. I look at my watch. Not yet ten. Plenty of time. I know she wants me to say something about the release, but I don't. A real nice welcome back.

"Half the staff isn't in yet. I left word for them about the meeting." Lisa doesn't approve of lateness. I look up. Lisa is a tiny, beautiful black woman with a strict code of office procedure.

Lisa talks. She tells me about the phone calls she's handled or referred to Molly or to my boss. She tells me about the staff: who worked while I was gone, who gave Molly a hard time, who took off a few afternoons. I'm half listening. She sounds like a hall monitor. I'm irritated that everyone is late. Almost a half hour late. Does this say something about my ability to manage? I look out the window at the bank with the time and temperature display: 9:58. 17 degrees. God, only seventeen degrees. I decide the cold is making the staff late. Lisa finishes and lights a cigarette. I wish I had the nerve to post a no-smoking sign in my office. But I don't. I wish I still smoked.

"What do you think?" I gesture toward the release. "Pretty clumsy leaving it in the machine."

"Clumsy?" She looks at me like I am impossibly thick. It's a look all secretaries give their bosses now and then. I recognize it. I've given it. "Right after everybody got back from Las Vegas there was a lot of talk that Marshall would finally get a new title. I figured if he got a new title, then something might happen for you. I almost called you in Antigua."

Gee, think how great that would have been. To be able to lie in the sun and think about work. I wonder what would have burned me quicker—sitting under the close, Caribbean sun or thinking about work that I just spent two thousand dollars to forget. She tells me Marshall deserves to have a title at least equal to Len's. I love that. I love her perverse sense of loyalty to my boss even as he seems to have none for her boss. I wait for her to get back to me.

She goes on. "Marshall wanted someone to find this release. Don't you get it?" Even though I more than get it, I shake my head so she'll go on.

"He's trying to decide who he should promote. You or Cassie? Which one of you should run both departments. He's hoping that by leaking this, you two will fight it out and he won't have to make a decision."

I fight an image of mud wrestlers.

"'Del says he's leaning toward Cassie." Lisa smokes her cigarette in such a way I feel the cigarette is leaning toward Cassie as well. I replay my phone call earlier with 'Del. I guess she must know, after all. I'm having a little trouble breathing, but my face shows nothing. Over the years I've taught myself to absorb this kind of casual violence without changing my expression. It's important in business to keep your face unreadable. The problem is, of course, that sometimes I forget and keep my face unreadable in my private life. John hates it. But sometimes business dribbles into real life.

"You should tell Marshall you expect to be promoted," Lisa tells me. She says expect in such a way she might as well have dragged her long, lacquered nails across a blackboard.

Now she's going on about how great I am. I think there may be some transitivity going on here. You know, if I'm great and she works for me, then she's great. I love compliments, but somehow having a tan in the middle of February is enough for me today. I don't want to upset the gods. I wish Lisa would leave me alone for a few minutes. For some odd reason I am thinking of my parents now. They told me to use my mind, which they assured me was first rate, and to mind my manners. They told me life is a meritocracy. Maybe my parents were wrong.

"Where's Etta?" I look around the room and settle my annoyance on Lisa. She shrugs. Someone says she has the flu. Someone else says something mean but wickedly funny. I laugh in spite of myself. Then I say something in her defense. I leaf through the bitter blue folder. Hers is the only status report missing. I thought Etta had been doing better lately. She let her hair grow back to a more normal length. But now she's so thin. And she's out a lot.

"Call her. Find out where she is." Lisa abdicates a leather chair reluctantly. One of the publicists slides into it and asks if we would like to hear his ten-best list of movies.

Molly comes in. She is no longer pale. The cold air has given her face a strawberry flush. Or, I wonder, was it Mr. Malibu? She asks to hear his list.

Everyone reads his or her own list except me. I don't make lists like that. One person names only eight films, declaring it a terrible year for cinema. Several name foreign films. Some I've never heard of. An argument breaks out over one publicist having put a documentary on her list. I enjoy their passion. It provides a kind of focus that gets us from one hour to the next and eventually through the day.

We talk about our chances for Academy Award nominations. We haven't had such a good year financially. But we released some good movies.

Someone asks how the movie did yesterday. We opened Lowell Reese's movie in two theaters. One in Manhattan, one in Westwood. It's what we call a special movie. A small movie. In other words it probably won't gross my annual salary.

I pick up the phone and call Len to find out. His secretary says she can give me the figures, but I tell her I'd prefer to speak with Len. If I didn't have such a nice voice, I could sound like a real bitch. She slams me onto hold. I guess I don't have such a nice voice after all.

"Hi, Len. How are you?"

"Cold enough for you, Babe?" I marvel at how effortlessly Len uses clichés. "Good news about Marshall."

"Hmmm," I say. He's fishing and we both know it. When this is official, Marshall will have the same title as Len. I can just imagine how thrilled he is about this.

Len gives me the figures. "They're soft."

"Have you told the director?" I ask sweetly.

He repeats the numbers. Numbers are what a lot of Len's work is about.

Then he says the director has his telephone number if he wants to know how much his movie grossed yesterday.

Nice, Len. That's being real supportive of our filmmaker. I don't say this. Before he hangs up he says he's sure everything will work out for me. I don't say anything. Len knows about Marshall's indecision. The guidance counselor in my prep school used to post which colleges accepted or rejected each senior. It felt terrible to have everyone in the school know who wanted you and who didn't. Right now I feel a little bit like I used to watching a classmate studying that list.

I give the staff the numbers. There is an informed sigh of disappointment. I turn into a cheerleader. "One day's gross doesn't mean anything." A couple nod sagely. I go on until I am interrupted by Lisa.

"No answer at Etta's. Lowell Reese is on the phone."

I pick up the extension. "Hi, Lowell. How are you?"

"How am I? You want to know how am I?" The connection sounds scratchy. I'm sorry I asked.

"Where are Marshall and Len? I've been trying to get them on the phone all morning?"

I'm about to lie for the two cowards, but I don't have to. Lowell keeps talking.

"The wrong people are going into my movie. They are too old. They're carrying shopping bags. They won't be able to hear the dialogue if they have shopping bags."

I laugh. He can't be serious.

"What have shopping bags to do with people's hearing?" The phone goes dead. Replacing the receiver, I think he was serious.

I start going over the staff's reports. I tell them I'm not happy with the schedule of interviews they've put together for the star of our next movie.

"What do you expect for a two-day stay in New York?" one of the publicists says.

"Two days?" I look at Molly. "I thought we had him for a week?"

Molly nods slowly, like someone being awakened from hypnosis. "Yes, a week. That sounds right."

CREATIVE DIFFERENCES

One of the publicists says Cassie wanted him in Chicago and San Francisco longer and Marshall said okay.

My face remains the same. Lisa says it's Lowell on the phone again.

"Lowell? What happened?"

"I'm calling from a pay phone across the street from the theater."

This makes me sad. The director shouldn't be standing in seventeen-degree weather watching who goes into his movie for the first show. It's hard to be a filmmaker on opening day. So much of his life up on that screen.

"I just want you to know it's your fault if we didn't do any business yesterday." It's also hard being an executive on opening day. I think about interrupting him to give him the figures and say the movie did fine yesterday when the operator comes on.

"Please deposit twenty-five cents for five minutes."

"Shit. I don't have any more change." The phone goes dead.

"Are you going to talk to Cassie?" Molly asks me, all innocence. She hasn't seen the release yet.

"Yeah, I'm going to talk to Cassie."

Adele is on the phone when I arrive at Marshall's office at 12:25. I like to be early. People in the movie business are always late. Lateness gives the impression that they've been caught up in something terribly important and couldn't get away. By the way Adele jerks her head toward the chair beside her desk, I know Marshall is caught up in something terribly important. I sit down, a dandelion yellow folder on my lap.

Before coming up to the executive floor, I went around to speak to Cassie. I asked to see the list of San Francisco and Chicago press interviews. She pulled them out of a standard cream-colored folder. I looked them over quickly, not bothering to remove the paper clips which would have made reading them easier. I saw that her staff had booked every major newspaper and TV talk show. They were strong schedules. Dammit. I said thanks and left before she could say anything. On the elevator I thought if she had asked to see the New York schedule, I would have said it was being retyped and as soon as I had a copy I'd send it over to her. Then I'd never send it. She was being pretty easy. Or was she being pretty deadly? We're not friends. We're not even very good colleagues. I don't think she ever got over my getting Molly promoted into my department a couple years back.

About a month after Molly started working for me, I was in one of the stalls in the bathroom when I heard Cassie and her secretary walk in. Cassie was saying, "She won't get very far. She makes too many jokes." I imagine Cassie straining over the sink to get as close to the mirror as she can so she can work on her eyelashes. Cassie uses a straight pin to separate each eyelash. She spends a lot of time on her eye makeup and the result is striking. I wonder who they are talking about and decide to keep still and listen.

Cassie is saying, "She works hard, but then makes a joke about it and everyone thinks what she does isn't very hard to do after all."

Her secretary says, "But she is funny and everyone likes her.

Cassie drops the pin on the tile floor. A moment later she says, "Not everyone likes The Pet."

Adele smiles at me once. I stare at the narrow piece of metal that runs along the edge of her desk. At just the right angle, which I have plenty of time to find, it becomes a mirror. My dark brown hair is a little lighter from the sun. All during our vacation I wore my hair up off my neck so I could feel the Antiguan breeze. It was hot, but the air was never still for long.

Every night John would take the pins out of my hair and brush the sand from my scalp. Then he would wash my hair. I would sit on a wicker chair and lean my head over the bathroom sink. He would rinse my hair with a large blue-and-white pitcher that the other guests used for drinking water. I would watch in the mirror as he washed and rinsed my hair and think how much I loved him, how I would do anything he asked me and how glad I was that he wasn't the kind of man to ask. The door to Marshall's office opens and some air gushes out. For a second it feels like one of the breezes off that tame, blue ocean.

I want to walk into Marshall's office like I've just won the lottery. I walk in, my black high heels kicking up static on his carpet.

CREATIVE DIFFERENCES

"You look great." My boss's eyes skip over me. Neither of us feels anything. My dress is red wool and moves gracefully on its own. John bought it for me. He likes the round neckline and the way the sleeves hold my wrists.

Marshall leans over to kiss me. I don't kiss him back. Years ago I went to kiss him and he moved funny and my lips landed on his shirt collar. And all day I had to look at him, knowing I was responsible for the lipstick on his expensive white shirt. I still wonder if he knew it was there that day.

Marshall sits down at his glass-topped desk. The glass makes everything in the office look fragile, temporary.

"Finance sent this to me." He holds out a memo like it's a piece of melting ice and it's getting him wet. I glance at it and slip it inside my folder. It's about the money we spent in Las Vegas. Three weeks ago everyone was happy with the convention. Ecstatic even. Now they want their money back.

"Shall I ask Len—"

My boss interrupts me. "Ask him whatever you want. Only handle it."

I smile. Handle it—such a great all-purpose phrase. One of Marshall's favorites.

He's asking me about Antigua, asking me if I stayed at such-and-such hotel. I shake my head and he names two others. I shake my head again. I've never heard of these hotels. He switches to restaurants. Again, I say no. He goes on. Listening to him I get the feeling we didn't see the right Antigua. I can tell he's baffled that we had a good time considering where we stayed. On the last of a rather long list of restaurants, cafes and clubs, I hear something familiar.

"Oh, yeah. We had lunch there."

"Lunch?" He is appalled. "It's a restaurant for dinner."

For a second I think he's thinking how can he promote someone who doesn't even know the right restaurant or hotel to go to.

"Etta came to see me when you were away."

I look at a stack of material swatches piled on a pine chest behind his desk. "And?"

"She's not happy."

"Who is?" Talking about Etta's state of mind isn't exactly what I want to do. Marshall likes Etta. He likes the reckless way she goes about doing her job. He thinks that if he had been born rich he would act the same way. He also likes that she comes to him for advice. I think he wishes I'd come to him for advice. If I want advice, I go to John. My problem is I don't much like advice. "I'm thinking of firing her."

Marshall looks up. He's surprised. Marshall has hardly ever fired anyone. He's not that kind of manager. He prefers to make people's lives so miserable that they leave on their own. Actually this is the more common form of management.

"Give her some time. You know who likes her?"

I can't wait to hear. That's the trouble with the movie business. It's too much about personality. Personally, I don't think it should matter who likes whom. Just do a good job.

"Lowell. Crazy Lowell Reese who doesn't like anybody."

I say nothing. Now it's my turn to be surprised. Two weeks ago Lowell couldn't stand Etta. I tell Marshall about my conversation with Lowell earlier this morning. Again, he says, "Lowell's crazy."

I don't think Lowell's crazy, despite the shopping bags. Lowell's just too smart, too intellectual smart for the movie business. I remember at one meeting with Len and Marshall a few months ago. Lowell, desperate to explain why he didn't want his dramatic movie sold as a comedy-drama, quoted Kierkegaard. Len nodded and then said something totally unrelated about the German director, Fassbinder. After he said it there were a few moments of quiet while people appeared to be mulling it over. Or possibly they were trying to recall Kierkegaard's film credits. In another context Len would have probably known who Kierkegaard was. Well, maybe not Len, but Marshall would have. But movies are talked about only in terms of other movies, other successful movies. It just never occurs to anyone to talk about them in any other way.

Marshall is talking about a photograph that appeared in this week's *Time*. It's a two-shot of the male and female leads in a comedy we have in production. I say leads because these actors aren't big stars. They aren't even little stars. They should be happy to have their unknown faces in a newsweekly. But no. The actor's agent has been on the phone to Marshall. This rings a bell.

"Yes, I remember his name on my call sheet."

Marshall says the agent claimed his client had killed that photo. I walk over to the low table that sits in front of Marshall's leather couch. Looking for the "People" section, I notice a two-page spread on one of our competitor's films. I wonder how their publicist managed this. It's such a small film for so much coverage. Obviously Marshall hasn't read this magazine or he would be all over me about this. Thank goodness for the summaries. I get to the offending picture.

"Looks all right to me. I'm pretty sure it was approved."

"Pretty sure?" Marshall doesn't like to upset The Talent. I pick up the telephone and call the head of the stills department.

"They are sure this is an approved shot since the ones the actor didn't like he stuck a pushpin through so they couldn't be used." I don't tell Marshall what else he just told me. He told me that Etta chose this shot even though it had a pushpin hole in the lower-right corner. She said it was a perfectly good shot. She's right. But that's not the point.

"A pushpin." Marshall's amused. "Okay. Handle it. I don't want to talk to that man again." Marshall picks up on Adele's buzz. He takes a call. I can't tell who it is. He talks to everyone in the same genuine way.

I look around his office. His is one of the few offices with shades at the windows. The shades block out the magnificent view. The shadows around the room are almost tropical. For a second I am back in Antigua.

Marshall is good at what he does. He's good because he doesn't fight it. This kind of work fits him. Snug. He's part artist, part con artist. Marshall is a great salesman. He can sell anything. He acts like he's never seen a bad movie. He can always find something in a movie for people to buy. It's as if he has a divining rod. Of course, he can sell himself best of all. Studying Marshall over the years, I've come to think selling is what our business is all about finally. Marshall wouldn't be as good in any other business. He needs to be in the movie business. He thrives on its glamor. It's a kind of glamor that I shy away from, figuring it doesn't belong to executives, only to filmmakers. To me it's like working in a candy store and eating all the candy. It could make you sick. I guess I'm afraid of getting sick. But not Marshall. He revels in it. And I think he's lucky. Not that many people revel in their work. In fact, most people can't bear getting up in the morning to go to the office.

Being with Marshall I am reminded of my own ambition. Or lack of it. No, I am ambitious. I just haven't had to show it. Every time I've been promoted, someone came to me and said we want to promote you and I said fine, great. I didn't have to do too much to get from secretary to publicist and then to senior publicist. I just did a good job. Since the publicists are members of a union, I didn't even have to talk about a raise. It was all laid out. Then, when Marshall fired the director of publicity and offered me the job, that was pretty easy, too. But now I see the time of sitting on a stool at Schwab's and waiting to be promoted is over. I am no longer The Pet. It just seems so humiliating, so unladylike, to have to say, Hey, I'm wonderful, I'm the best, give me the job. Hasn't my work demonstrated I'm good? My work doesn't have anything to do with this. This is business. The business of politics.

He's off the phone. He slides a copy of the New York publicity schedule across the desk. It skates onto the carpet. I bend to pick it up.

"Looks thin to me. You only wanted him for two days?"

I know this is just Marshall's way of getting things started between Cassie and me. It would be so easy to badmouth Cassie. Too easy. Marshall would probably join in. He enjoys dishing like most people enjoy breathing. I say nothing.

He swivels around on his chair to pick up the stack of material swatches. These must be for his new office. You can't have a new title without a new office to go with it. Marshall understands these things. He never lets his work get in the way of the business of ambition. Besides, the movie business is strictly judge a book by its cover. Marshall's cover is still a little too New York, but tasteful and very expensive.

He hands me three swatches. He likes the pale peach.

CREATIVE DIFFERENCES

"Nice, isn't it?" he prompts me. I stall for time by picking up the swatches and carrying them over to the window to inspect them. In the sunlight, I like them even less. These colors would look fine on someone's patio furniture. I think of John. I know all I have to do to make Marshall happy is to say I love the peach. But I don't. John once said my idea of being honest was like a reformed alcoholic's idea of taking one drink. I guess that means if I say one or two dishonest things then in no time I'll be saying whatever anyone wants to hear. John is wrong. I can say what people want to hear. I do it all day, every day. It just doesn't come easy.

I turn toward Marshall. "Which color does Cassie like?" I'm hoping he's going to say he hasn't asked her opinion.

Marshall picks up his desk lighter. It's a beautiful antique piece of leather and gold. "She loves the peach."

I pick up my folder and walk over to the door. I can't put this off any longer. With one hand resting casually on the doorknob I say, "Who are you going to promote, Marshall?"

"I haven't decided yet." He's enjoying this. A little too much.

"The reason I ask is that I think we should go ahead and announce your new title." I've got his attention now. Few of us can resist the pleasure of talking about ourselves. I go on. "Otherwise, if we wait too long, the news will leak out and the trades won't give you the space you deserve."

It's hard for people who aren't in the movie business to understand just how important titles are to us. A new title instantly makes you a more important person, a better person. Instantly, people have to give you more thought, the same people who two titles ago didn't even bother to have your number on their Rolodex. Instantly, a new set of perks is available to you. It might be a new office, first-class airfare, or a more generous expense account. Later on up the ladder, it might be a low-interest loan. Some of us would even forego a raise to get a better title. I haven't had to make that choice yet. Next in importance to getting a new title is making sure everyone knows you got a new title. So it is crucial you receive good space in the trades. This is where the publicity people come in. This is one of the reasons publicity people enjoy a special little place in the movie kingdom.

If your announcement is brief and appears on page four or five of *Variety* and *Hollywood Reporter* instead of on the front page (hopefully with a picture), you might just as well not even have gotten it. Marshall is someone who understands all this.

I open the door and walk out without waiting for Marshall's answer.

10

*M*olly and I wait for the waitress to bring our wine. Neither of us can face the prospect of a strategy meeting with Marshall on our Oscar-nominated films without a little wine. We got two nominations. It hardly calls for a strategy. Actually this is our second glass. Molly will undercut hers with a double espresso at the end of lunch. I think I'll stay a little sleepy, a little generous.

I turn to put my coat over the chair next to me and see Cassie and Marshall having lunch on the other side of the restaurant.

"It's been almost a week and Marshall hasn't said one word."

"What will you do if he chooses Cassie?" Molly gets to the bottom line. Sometimes she surprises me with her practicality. She's never that practical about herself. She looks pretty today. Her reddish hair has been blown off her face by the wind. She's wearing a hand-knit pink sweater and a thin silver necklace. She lights a cigarette and blows the smoke away from me and then she notices Cassie and Marshall. I can tell she hopes I haven't.

"I don't know what I'll do. Quit maybe."

She says everything will be okay either way. That's the difference between Molly and me. For her either way would be okay. She lives at such a distance from work. I live too close to it. If I don't get this job I will feel as if I've let John down. And Molly. And the staff. Molly doesn't think too much about promotions. I don't know what she thinks we're working for every day if it's not to get ahead. I mean what's the point if you don't move forward. Staying in the same job would be like repeating the same grade in school over and over. Getting this promotion will somehow make up for all the late hours, for all the work, for all the complaining John's had to listen to, for all the times I didn't get to say what I wanted to say. For all the times I pretended. It will have been worth it. And it will prove that the system works. Good work is rewarded. Even as I think this, there is a part of me saying I've got it all wrong. Getting this promotion is like being asked to join a cool club in high school. And I have this feeling that if I get lucky and become a member, I'm going to find out the club isn't so cool after all.

Molly says she was married once. This takes me out of myself with a jolt.

"Really," I say stupidly.

"Yes, really." Her tone says I had a life before we became friends, but her eyes are all fun. I'm really Molly's first best friend.

"When?"

"Almost eleven years ago. We had a child. It died when it was six weeks old. Crib death."

"I didn't know that." Suddenly I want to call everyone I love and make sure they are where they are supposed to be. Everything at the office seems distant and stupid. I seem stupid. Why don't I know what to say? "What happened to your husband?"

"We divorced. We didn't know each other very well."

The waitress sets down two oval platters. Crabmeat in an avocado and shrimp hung over a bowl of cracked ice. "More wine, girls?"

"Yes." Molly answers for us. She's talking about Mr. Malibu and whether or not he's going to be able to go skiing with her this weekend in New Hampshire.

"He doesn't want to be away from Los Angeles right now," Molly explains. "There's a chance there'll be some management changes where he works. He thinks he might get a better job if he's around. He really wants this job."

I know how Molly's friend feels. Right now I'm wondering whether this would be happening if I hadn't gone away on vacation. I can't remember when Marshall last took a vacation. He goes to Europe all the time. But it's business. Marshall takes promotions instead of vacations.

Molly says if he gets this new job, it will be good for them. Even as she says this I know she doesn't believe it. People don't generally calm down after getting a new job. They don't have just the one job in mind. As we get up to leave, Molly says maybe she'll meet him in Aspen instead. Aspen, in February, on a weekend, is even better than Los Angeles. Everyone in the movie business is there. No one is in New Hampshire.

We walk back to the office. The sun is bright and the sidewalk sparkles.

"Why did you tell me today?" It's an odd question but I don't know what else to say.

"Oh, because today she would have been ten years old."

I have ten minutes before the meeting. I brush my hair sitting at my desk. Etta walks in. I can't tell if she's gained weight or if it's just her big sweater and corduroy pants. She's dressed like she's on vacation.

"I'd like to take two weeks vacation starting Monday. If it's okay with you."

I keep brushing my hair. "Sit down, Etta." I check my hand mirror. Still don't need any makeup. The tan is holding. "You can take the two weeks."

Etta sighs, louder than she means to. "Thanks." Her French accent is always more pronounced when she's nervous.

I pick up my orange Academy folder. "When you get back you'll have two weeks before you're going to resign."

I wait a moment to see if she's going to fight me. When I see her eyes fill with tears I leave my office and shut the door behind me.

Waiting for the elevator I realize that Etta is the first person I have ever fired. I suppose I could have kept her, but I'm tired of doing her job for her when she won't, tired of watching over her, of babying her. I think she's tired of our talks, tired of the excuses I dream up for her. Besides, if I really want this new job, I can't afford for someone on my staff not to pull his weight.

On the elevator I keep staring at the floor numbers displayed in lights above me. At every floor I say, I had to fire her. I had to. I had to. I had to.

I'm in a little early. John and I made love this morning. He woke me up with café au lait. And then he woke me up again. Afterward I told him about Molly. For a second I thought he was angry with me for telling him about it when we were both feeling so good. Then after a while he asked me when we were going to have children. Kids is what he said.

"When are we going to have kids?" I wanted to say how about never. I mean, who in their right mind would open himself up to that kind of pain? Instead I gave him a kiss. "Someday." Actually someday would be just fine.

My chair is fixed. Lisa had someone fix my chair. I'm glad it's fixed, but I know this is just part of her campaign. Her campaign to get Etta's job.

There's so much campaigning going on around here, I feel as if our floor has been given primary state status. Cassie has spent the last two weeks taking every member of my staff out to lunch one by one. Secretaries and publicists. Someone told me she pays cash for the lunches. So she gets points for not abusing her expense account. She sends memos around soliciting my staff's ideas on her projects. She even offers them a cash award if their idea is chosen. Must make her very popular with her own staff. My mother always said you don't get paid for being part of the family. If I opened my door right now, I half expect to find Lisa and Cassie handing out leaflets, thrusting their hand into mine, saying please vote for me. I need your vote.

I think about my own campaign. Was firing Etta my campaign? It seems to have made a big impression on my staff. And no impression on Marshall. He's never mentioned it. Makes sense that my staff would sit up and take notice. They look at me a little differently in meetings now. They know I have power over their lives. No one likes to admit that someone has power over them. But they admit it in the way they act, the way they do their work, the way they look at me.

My campaign? This whole thing is making me crazy. The other day, waiting at the doctor's office, I found myself reading an article in *Cosmo* entitled, "How to Get That Promotion." I sat there taking this little eighty-question quiz, frantically checking my answers against their answers in the back of the magazine. I was real annoyed when the nurse interrupted the quiz to tell me the doctor was ready. Now this is the kind of story you hope to go to your grave keeping secret.

"What are you doing here?" Lisa walks in still wearing her coat, a black slicker. It's twenty degrees outside and she's wearing a spring raincoat.

"I work here." Her boots are red with an inlay of feathers and snakeskin along one side.

"You're supposed to be in a meeting. In Marshall's office."

"I am? When did it start?"

"Thirty minutes ago. Didn't Cassie tell you?"

The silk blouse I'm wearing suddenly feels very cold against my body. "No, she didn't."

"She called last night after you left to tell you about the meeting."

"Adele forget my extension?"

"Cassie offered to call you at home. I said okay. I really thought she was going to call you." Lisa is suddenly out of breath. I know she feels terrible. She sees the election slipping away from her. The fact is I never had any intention of promoting Lisa. I want someone with experience in that job. I should tell her. I wonder if she'll quit.

"It's not your fault, Lisa. What's the meeting about?"

Lisa doesn't know.

I find myself on the elevator, a rainbow of folders in my arms. I look down at my pleated winter white skirt and blue blazer. Am I dressed for the campaign trail?

Adele sends me right in, offering to bring me coffee. I say thanks. Cassie is talking when I sit down. She's saying how much she likes the producer's other movies. She names them. I notice the producer does not correct her when she names a film he did not produce.

Marshall says "great" every now and then. The three advertising guys lounge, talking only to one another. I start to say something, but Cassie starts talking again. I feel a little like a game show contestant who can't press the buzzer fast enough. Cassie goes on. I guess she'll get to the point eventually. The producer is eating this up.

The producer's name is Jack Wolcott. He's wearing an Armani jacket, pressed jeans and tennis shoes. I think he may have had his eyes done. He's very slim. Personally, I think it's creepy for a fifty-year-old man to have the hips of a seventeen-year-old boy. But that's California.

Cassie takes a breath and Jack Wolcott starts his pitch. He starts to tell stories. He's a very good storyteller. I guess he knows his movie isn't very good so he won't bother trying to sell that. He'll try to get by on charm. And gossip about famous people.

I'm laughing and having a good time. This isn't like work at all. Marshall's loving it, too. The advertising guys stop talking to each other. Only Cassie seems to be fighting it.

The problem with a meeting like this is that it isn't good for business. This is the atmosphere in which the producer is promised everything because he seems to be asking for nothing.

Marshall is looking at me like it's my turn to perform. I don't have any funny stories to tell. I guess I'll have to talk about his movie. I can't shake the feeling that this is the swimsuit competition between Cassie and myself. And Marshall is the only judge.

I begin. Cassie keeps interrupting me. She raises her hand like she's in class. I stop talking and look at her and she ducks her head like someone is shooting at her. I know I, for one, would like to have a gun right now. I listen to her suggestions about how I might do my job. Then I go on as if she hasn't said anything. Wolcott perks up, hoping for a gunfight.

"I think that's a very unusual idea, Cassie." Marshall acts like she's just reinvented the wheel. I go on. Now the advertising guys are offering their ideas on publicity. Is this happening to me? Maybe next Marshall will ask the lobby guys to come up and give me their ideas.

I look at Jack Wolcott. He's sitting on Marshall's leather couch with his tennis shoes propped up on the table in front of him. The heel of his shoe is wrinkling the copy of *Variety* on Marshall's table. Last week Marshall's announcement was printed on the front page. With a photo. Jack crosses his arms. He's whistling. He knows this has nothing to do with his movie. And he doesn't like it. He whistles louder. I keep talking while trying to place the tune.

The meeting's about over. Jack Wolcott stands in the middle of the room whispering to Marshall about something. I watch them. It occurs to me that Jack has spent his adult life having bouts of intimacy with strangers such as we. For months an executive and a filmmaker work with each other trying to fashion a way of presenting a movie to the public that the studio can afford and the filmmaker can live with. You are in endless meetings, you talk on the phone constantly. You exchange home phone numbers. The filmmaker even gives the executive his car phone number. Each lets the other into his life—the filmmaker because he's afraid the executive won't work on his movie if he turns his back, and the executive because it's the only way he knows how to work. A week after the movie is released the filmmaker may not recognize the executive on the street.

Jack Wolcott leaves. A sort of energy goes out of the room with him. I get up to leave. Cassie stays on the couch.

Marshall looks at me and says, "Call Wolcott in a couple of days. Tell him we're not doing the screenings we just promised him." Cynicism like a fine dust settles about the office. I had really thought we were going to do the screenings.

Marshall goes on. "How stupid does he think I am? And when you're talking to him, tell him we're not touring him, or his has-been actor, in Chicago or Dallas."

"Don't you think Cassie should tell him that?"

"No, I think you should."

The elevator is crowded. I get on but then get off on the next floor. I wait here, where I'm not known, for another elevator. The longer Marshall wavers the less I like him. The less I like myself. I think this is what's called making a living.

"Lisa, try Jack Wolcott." I can't put this off any longer. Still, I time the call so it's lunchtime on the Coast.

Molly comes into the office and shuts the door.

"Look!" She thrusts a piece of paper in front of me.

"What is it?"

She takes it back. "I just happened to be on the other side of the floor and when I got to Cassie's secretary's desk I lingered. I saw a stack of new stationery. So I picked up a sheet. Here."

I read it. I read it again. It is stationery with Cassie's name and a new title. It's the title of the job that Marshall is still trying to decide which one of us should have.

I'm angry and I'm hurt, but I start to laugh. "What nerve!" She has a real flair for playing politics. I admire it in spite of myself. But suddenly nothing feels the same. I feel like a stranger in the building I grew up in. Business is filled with Cassies. I've just been lucky so far. Lucky? Or stupid? Rick Darling said work wasn't like life. Why the fuck isn't it? I've been going along all these years thinking life and work are the same thing; if not the same thing then in the same ballpark. I thought the same rules that run my private life would also run my work life.

Maybe Darling and my mother are saying the same thing. She calls work the business world. Only the way she says business world it sounds great and mysterious. And she sounds jealous of it, of those in it. When I was little, I couldn't wait to be a part of it. The way Darling talks about the business world it sounds like there aren't any rules. No real notions of loyalty or ethics or right and wrong. But as long as you understand this, business can be an adventure. The adventure hasn't started for me yet. I'm still stuck back on the part about there being no rules. Since Darling is a gambler, I don't think his philosophy about work is reliable. And since my mother is my mother, I don't pay any attention to her either.

Lisa comes in. "Why aren't you answering my buzz? Marshall's on the phone." I don't move. "Didn't you hear me? Marshall wants to talk to you."

I pick up the phone, uncurl the cord and stand looking out over Manhattan to talk to him. "Hello."

"Congratulations."

"For what?"

"Come on. Ms. Executive Director." He strings out the word Ms. in such a way I feel a little sick to my stomach.

"So you've decided."

"Yes. You'll be great."

"What's my new salary?" Marshall puts me on hold. When we were on vacation I would lie in the sun trying to turn myself into nothingness, trying to think of nothing, and I would wind up thinking of everything. And everything would then turn into something. And I would think about John and about work and worry over the bigger picture and wonder if this is the bigger picture.

Marshall's back on. "We'll talk about the money." I know I should keep on him about it, but I let it go. I make a conscious tactical error. He'll get me cheaper than is fair.

"Does Cassie know yet?" I think of the stationery.

"No. Not yet. I thought you might want to tell her."

"Why would you think that?" I watch some kids playing ball in the park. It's so cold none of them can catch it.

"I'll be glad to tell her if you want me to, but she works for you now."

"Thanks, Marshall." I soften my tone. I've won. He'll tell her. But to be sure, I say, "She doesn't work for me until you tell her."

"All right. I'll tell her." He bumps me onto hold again. I wonder why Marshall is giving the job to me instead of to Cassie. The other day Molly said Cassie was a lot like Marshall. Only not as smart. Cassie would have stayed at the right hotel in Antigua. He gave the job to me and I really didn't have to do anything. Except maybe be miserable for a few weeks. I reach for the stationery Cassie had printed prematurely. I scribble a memo to her across it. What I write isn't very nice. I'm learning. He comes back on.

"Are you happy?"

"Sure, Marshall. I'm happy."

He hangs up. Already a part of him is regretting his choice. From time to time I will be trouble and the last thing an ambitious man wants is trouble from a female underling.

Waiting for John to pick up my call I think about our waiter at the hotel in Antigua. He was always humming or singing the same song under his breath while he served us. I thought he was happy until John told me the reggae tune was a song of hunger and revolution. You never know. People do their work, but you never really know what they're thinking.

$\mathcal{V}$ICE-PRESIDENT

11

*L*isa informed me first thing this morning that she wants to be known as Arden from now on. I've already screwed up four times since 10:00 A.M. I think the name Arden is pretentious and on the few occasions I remember it, my tongue falters and it comes out sounding like Larden.

I have a lot of work to do today. I have a lot of work every day, but they pay me a lot of money. I have a great view of Manhattan from my big office. But I'm getting bored. I need a change. There's something about being able to do your job easily that makes you think it's not worth coming in for.

Lisa/Arden just asked to see me later to discuss something personal. I know what's coming and it's more than pronouncing Arden correctly. "If we get the report done by two-thirty, we'll talk then, before my three o'clock meeting. Otherwise afterward."

She nods. "As long as I can talk to you sometime today."

"Yes, yes." I hope it's 2:30, because when I drag down from the thirty-fifth floor around 7:00 tonight, all I'll want to do is go home. But she'll be there waiting for me, encamped in the leather armchair in my office, cigarettes at the ready, one expensive purple snakeskin shoe off, foot tucked up under her.

It's 11:30 and I'm starved. I met with my staff for forty-five minutes. We gossiped about our business, about the people who work on other floors, about each other. We are all very verbal. In fact, sometimes we are so clever we become momentarily enchanted with ourselves. I told them about the report. They complained, I sympathized. Then I cracked the whip. It occurs to me that my method of managing hinges primarily on my being the most stubborn.

About twenty minutes later they start drifting back, one at a time. Lisa/Arden lets those people she likes wander unmolested into my office. The others are made to stand beside her desk while she comes into my office, pushes the door halfway shut and tells me not to see them. I see them anyway.

They each come to establish a connection to something beyond their obvious daily work. Reaffirming one's place in a company is very nearly a full-time job. For many of us who work in offices, it approaches an almost mythological quest. This search has been known to get in the way of getting the work done. My staff uses me as a conduit of sorts. I am happy to be used. It is, after all, part of my job to convince them that their work is appreciated by others higher up in the corporation.

The six of them are now compiling their parts of the bigger report that Lisa will cut and paste together for me.

I finish the fifth cup of coffee—a little powdered creamer, no sugar. I try not to let too much come between me and my caffeine. I didn't get home last night until almost midnight. John was sort of awake, watching television with my night table lamp on. He said he made a sandwich for me and that it was in the refrigerator. I was so tired my knees ached. I decided to forget about food. All I wanted was a bath. By the time I got out—one *People* magazine skim later—John was asleep. After putting the earphones into the TV, I got into bed. He mumbled something about not really being asleep and if I wanted to make love I should just wake him up, he was ready. I leaned over and kissed him. He's so sweet. He's always ready. We've been married eight years and he still wakes me up in the middle of the night to have sex. Every morning he rolls his hard erection against me.

CREATIVE DIFFERENCES

More often than I care to admit I say, "Later, I just got to get some sleep, Honey."

But I can't ask Lisa/Arden to order me food. She'd be insulted. I learned too late that it would have been better to hire a high school graduate with steno and typing than a college graduate with poise and ambition. You see, Lisa mistook this secretarial job for a management trainee program. Maybe that's partly my fault. I used to think smart and educated was important. And it is, just not necessarily in business. I'm not saying a high school graduate would like ordering me lunch, but it wouldn't necessarily be a life crisis.

At noon, Lisa buzzes me to say she's going to the cafeteria for a salad. "Do you want anything?"

"Yes, thanks, Arden." I ask for plain yogurt and trail mix. John says I eat like an old Greek. I'd like to eat real food, but it slows me down in the middle of the day. After a big meal I can feel my hands and feet growing pads like the underside of a lion's paw. My eyelids droop. It would make a canny pose at today's meeting. I could pretend to be half asleep, but by my size, my heavy mane, my sharp teeth, it would be obvious I was dangerous. Better to stay a human. There'll be so few of us in the conference room today.

I can actually see the Statue of Liberty from my window. Not well, but if it's clear, I can make out the arm holding the torch and from there reconstruct the rest of her from memory. I like to tell the people I talk to on the phone about her. Most of the people I talk to are in California. On the Coast. I talk on the phone almost nonstop. Every time I leave my office to go to the bathroom or to walk down the hall to one of my staff's offices, Lisa puts a freshly typed list of all my calls — color coded differently each day — on my desk. Today the calls I've completed she colors in yellow, those we've left word for are blue and those I have done absolutely nothing about are red. She knows red is my favorite color, so I think today's particular color code is a slight attack, a forewarning of our little talk this afternoon.

John calls. He makes me laugh. Only I ruin part of my fun by realizing I haven't laughed once all day. I set a lot of store by how often I laugh. I particularly like to laugh about what I'm doing. Now that's a satisfying laugh. Maybe I did laugh a little when Lisa told me about her name change. We're supposed to have dinner with John's sister and her husband tonight. John wants to know if I'm going to cancel. I take down the restaurant's address and promise to meet him there at 8:30. I act like I don't remember that I didn't show up for the last two dinners with his sister because something came up at the office.

Lisa/Arden comes in with the report. "How many Xeroxes do you need?"

I read over the cover sheet. "Looks okay to me. Eight copies." She tells me Harry will answer my phones while she makes the copies. I don't like when Harry answers my phones. He mispronounces my last name and tells everyone I'm right there and when I refuse to take the call, he makes up the wildest excuses. He should be writing a new edition of Tall Tales for kids. But he has this incredibly cute face, more energy than most of us have seen in years — it's probably cocaine, but who's asking — and no one, not even me, ever criticizes him.

At 2:45 I take out my makeup. There won't be time for the talk with Lisa before the meeting. I slather cover-up under my eyes, but my skin sucks it up like a dried sponge, leaving me looking just as tired. The plum-colored lipstick lightens my face, but it is worn off quickly by the coffee mug. I comb my hair. It looks great. Thank God.

Lisa/Arden puts the reports on my desk. My copy is in a canary yellow see-through plastic folder, one of those European folders that look so great in stationery catalogues, but once in hand are actually not very practical. She stands with her hands on her astonishingly slim waist. I'm thin, but my waist is nowhere near as narrow as hers. It seems impossible that I could ever exercise my body into that shape. I don't have time to exercise.

"Cassie wants to know if she should come to the meeting," Lisa asks.

I consider this. I could say yes and have her there to take some of the heat. Or I could say no and disappoint her. Two years ago when Marshall promoted me over Cassie, I thought she'd leave. And when she didn't leave, I thought she would make my life miserable. Cassie surprised me. She does a good job and acts like she's happy to do it. She doesn't seem interested in getting a bigger job anymore. But the odd thing is, I still don't like her. I tell Lisa to tell Cassie no.

I slip onto a crowded elevator, nodding and smiling to those who make contact with me. I've worked here so long it's almost impossible to ride an elevator unnoticed. People in other parts of the company are interested in what the division I work in does. I have always tried to downplay any of its misleadingly glamorous aspects, carrying on as if it were just like accounting or office services. I do it for two reasons. First, it's really not that different, and second, acting friendly and regular in a corporation gets the machinery moved a whole lot easier. Lisa still doesn't get this, which is why I always have to make the calls about a broken air-conditioner vent, a warehouse transferral, a cash advance. It drives me crazy to have to do it, but I've learned not to ask people who work for me to do something they're not good at. They'll screw it up. Sometimes intentionally; sometimes not. It will drive you crazy.

The conference room is almost filled. The two people for whom this dog-and-pony show has been called will not come in until everyone else is assembled. Some of my colleagues are resentful of this and while they will come up to the thirty-fifth floor, they won't sit down at the table. They'll get coffee or kibitz, trying to look like they've just arrived. I save my performance for the performance.

3:10. I pass copies of the report forward to be spread out in front of the empty places. I ask someone at the other end of the table to turn the air conditioner down. A few heads look in my direction but nothing is said. After all, I am one of only two women who attend these kinds of meetings and maybe women are more sensitive to the cold.

I look around. The other woman who usually comes to these meetings also works for Marshall. She runs the international publicity department. She's not here. She's pregnant. She's out a lot. I wonder if her absence has anything to do with the way movie people look at her. Movie people look at pregnant women like they have three legs. Maybe all businesses treat pregnant women like this. Like they have incredibly bad taste for letting themselves get pregnant.

We wait. I read an advance copy of an article that will be on the newsstands Friday. It will upset most of the people in this room and most of the people on the Coast. I consider whether or not I should tell them about it today. I'm quite enjoying the piece, as journalistic entertainment only. I am, of course, professionally outraged. This article is the inside story on how this movie got made. The view from the inside isn't very pretty. But it's riveting. I decide Thursday is soon enough. I just hope no one else has a friend at this magazine and that it doesn't come up this afternoon.

The filmmakers walk in with Marshall. The filmmakers are tan. They wear expensive suits, the kind male models wear in *GQ*. Back home in Los Angeles, on the Coast, they dress more casually in slacks and polo shirts. They look happy enough. Both smoke. Both are nice-looking. One is very tall, with cool blue eyes that will make a nice refuge if the meeting heats up.

Marshall begins the meeting. He's talking about the movie. He's saying how great it is. I don't have to listen. My turn will come. It's taken a while, but I have come to appreciate the pacing of meetings. I look around. I like this conference room. It's just been redone. Almost everyone hates it because it's too pastel, too mirrored, too sleek and way too modern. For instance, the lighting panel intimidates most people. Sometimes, if a secretary hasn't adjusted the lights before a meeting, we will all sit in half-darkness for hours. Of course I know the lights are activated by body temperature and one need only run a hand lightly over the panel, but it wouldn't do for me to show I know this. Executives do not possess such unseemly, pedestrian knowledge.

It amuses me that people don't like this room. It's just perfect for the movie business. The executive who designed it, who approved the design, that is, is rarely in New York. He works on the Coast. I think he believes that by turning the room into something that looks like a perfume company's boardroom, he was helping those of us in the New York office to remember we are in the movie business. Frankly, I don't need any help remembering.

Marshall is almost finished. He's just going over the numbers — how little the movie grossed this weekend. This is usually Len's part. But Len isn't here today. Lucky Len. Marshall has this uncanny way of talking about movies that don't open well as though they belong to some other studio. Even though he has called almost every shot—the ads, the publicity program, the media buys—he acts on these occasions of company failure as if he were a friend of the producer.

Last Thursday, five days ago—it seems to the director like a lifetime— we sat in this same room going over the checklist, asking each other if we had done everything we could to ensure this movie would open, would make money. Right now we are sitting here talking about ways to turn the movie around. We are wasting our time.

"I did tell you," I say to the director, trying to effect the proper balance between sympathy and honesty, "that I didn't expect the movie to get good reviews." Since he's looking at me as if I've yet to speak I keep talking. The room is very quiet. Everyone at the table freezes, like so many deer caught in headlights. They hope they won't be noticed. They hope, not at all maliciously, that I will be the only prey this afternoon. I have known this kind of hope.

The director reminds all of us that at last Thursday's meeting he said this movie would have to get good reviews if it was going to make it.

He looks at me again.

"Why did no one disagree with me then?" Can he really be begging me to state the obvious? I decide to wait him out a little. There are ten people at this table, one of them will want to take a crack at this. Surprisingly it is Don Self, the head of advertising. He is usually more cagey than this. He says how stupid critics are today; how they see so many films they can't possibly know a good one when they see one. He goes on.

"Besides, your films have never been particularly well received by the critics, especially the New York critics." Don Self has made a fairly decent play and, as if on cue, half the people at the table are now acting like small-appliance salesmen from America's heartland complaining about how provincial and ignorant New York critics are, and while they're at it, New Yorkers in general.

Silently I curse my luck. This director has made eight films over the last fifteen years. All of them made money. He is second-generation Hollywood and by Hollywood standards his lineage is as old as the Hapsburgs. When he talks I hear something in his voice. I call it divine privilege. I think this is how monarchs must talk. Now he comes to our studio and he's about to break his good luck string and lose a lot of money. Actually, the studio is about to lose a lot of money. He just won't make any, which is, to his way of thinking, equally bad.

Why me? Couldn't someone have liked his picture—just enough to get a quote to slap over the ad for this Friday.

5:26. Suddenly I am overwhelmed with tiredness. The lack of real food seems to have caught up with me. I feel a great emptiness inside. The yogurt has made a marshland of my insides and now each of my organs is threatening to slide, irretrievably, into the swamp. My brain begins the trek downward.

The producer stares at me, the tall one with the great eyes. Only now the blue reminds me of deep, treacherous water. He whispers something to the director. The director looks at me as if I just blew the cure for cancer. The stupid part is I feel like maybe it was me who dropped that test tube in the lab. Maybe I *am* responsible for no one liking his movie. Just as I'm reminding myself that the movie really isn't very good and that it probably doesn't deserve to be seen or liked by anyone, the director shouts.

"You don't like the movie!"

I smile at him. His tan seems to be melting off his face. We've been going at this for almost two hours and now he's going to bring the meeting down to a personal level; a level everyone in business really wants to deal on. The movie is no longer the issue. This is about personalities. So you think my baby's ugly?

Maybe I should tell him my brain and my heart have fallen into some kind of quagmire that was, until a few minutes ago, my stomach. I'm not really equipped to finish the meeting. I decide not to say anything. I just keep smiling. I show teeth. Maybe this will scare him off: This she-animal has teeth, beware. But no.

For most of this meeting Marshall has been like a loud, idling machine. His presence is undeniable. He has talked, but I can't remember one thing he's said. Now, in an effort to reassert himself, he's offering everyone something to drink. Coffee, soda. A regular waitress. No one wants anything. Personally, I'm dying for a Classic Coke. I'm so thirsty. Must be all the anger I've been swallowing.

"If you had liked the movie more, things would be different." The director turns to Blue Eyes who first makes a feeble gesture of agreement to his partner and then looks at me as if he would like to fuck me. I look away, not in the least flattered. I don't want a sex partner. I want a white knight. I haven't seen Blue Eyes in years, not since I was a secretary. He doesn't recognize me. He used to be president of our company. He wanted to fuck me then, too. That seems like a long time ago. I figure it up. Nine years ago. He looks the same. I probably don't. I feel the same. And yet I feel different. I feel as if I've been on one of those moving sidewalks they have at some airports. You step on and begin to glide forward. You stare ahead or at the things moving slowly beside you. You hardly notice you're moving and then suddenly you've stepped off and when you look back you've come a long way. You feel tricked, somehow. Like you missed the trip.

"Whether or not I like the movie—which by the way I happen to—has nothing to do with what the critics think." I plan on saying this as soon as the director stops ranting. I know he just had triple bypass surgery. I find that amazing since I didn't think he had a heart.

Now he's getting himself so worked up he's about to explode. He presses the heel of his hand against his forehead like he's trying to keep his head from blowing off. Will I also be responsible if he has a heart attack or a stroke right here?

6:30. "When were you going to tell us about this article?"

I haven't been paying attention to his every word. I've been dragging the swamp trying to locate my heart. Or my brain. Besides, I find it so much easier to take public humiliation when I don't concentrate on each word. I get the gist of it. So I'm not sure he has asked about the article until I see Marshall toss his expensive cigarette lighter onto the peach-colored marble and inlaid wood table. Because the newly designed room has a faux ceiling, the room has a strange echo. The lighter sounds like a small caliber gunshot. Frankly, I think Marshall's better than this gesture. But once again, he is enviably distanced from this newest problem.

"I was going to tell you about it at the end of this meeting." I lie convincingly. It comes with this line of work. Now there is much whispering at the table among those—everyone but the director, Blue Eyes and me—who do not know what the magazine is going to print. They are certain it must be pretty awful.

The director's anger knows no bounds. He personifies excess, exaggeration, overstatement, hysteria. In short, the movie business.

When all else fails, I pull out one of my standard but very effective lines. I try it now. "Well, if I did the wrong thing, I apologize."

He stands up. This is going to be good. He can't even say it sitting down. I have enough time while he's building up to the climax to wonder how this would be different if I were stoned or a little edgy from coke, or if I were a blonde instead of a brunette, or if my brain hadn't sunk into the yogurt swamp, or if I had let Blue Eyes have me years ago.

"When I'm finished with you, you'll be selling toasters."

He is so angry that I know if I laugh he will probably not rest until he gets me fired. So I make a small joke just to show everyone—Blue Eyes, the director, Marshall—I'm not hurt, I'm ready to continue the meeting. I feel tears close behind my eyes, but I can control them. After all, this isn't my first day at the conference table. Besides, I'm not sure you can cry if your heart is in a swamp. Marshall is saying something about setting up interviews for the director. I say yes to everything Marshall suggests. Marshall is winding up the meeting. I could kiss his feet.

7:45. I am back on my floor in the sanctuary of my office. I feel terrible, abused, angry, hurt, useless. Lisa/Arden is waiting for me. So is a newly typed card with my telephone calls and a few messages of encouragement left by my staff. Is it possible that his anger penetrated four floors like some sort of acid that can eat through concrete?

"Want to talk now or in the morning?"

"Now." She lights a cigarette.

"Okay, let me just call John." His secretary tells me he left quite a while ago. No answer at home. Then I remember the dinner. I sit down, look out the windows. It's about to storm.

Lisa begins to talk before I have finished straightening the papers on my desk. She doesn't have my full attention because I'm busy tallying up how hard everyone on my staff worked against how bad the movie really is. I can't reconcile the ledger. No one cares how hard anyone worked.

"I figured if I changed my name it would give me a new outlook." Lisa is looking at me so intently I push the rest of the folders aside.

"Yes, I see." I hear myself talking. I sound normal enough. I study her eye makeup. Her eyelids are intricately colored in four, no five, shades. For some reason I think these are the colors I would find in Santa Fe. It's nearly 8:00. Why hasn't her makeup worn off?

A flash of lightning splits midtown in two. Lisa is now telling me she is thirty-three years old. She doesn't have a boyfriend. Even though she goes out all the time. She tells me she is tired of going to bars and restaurants and outdoor concerts and taking shares in the Hamptons trying to meet some- one. The Right Someone. She is tired of having to fold up her Murphy bed as soon as she gets up, otherwise she can't open her closet or walk around her tiny studio. She can't wait until she makes a decent salary and can move into a larger apartment.

I knew this morning that this is what she wanted to talk about. Lisa has always picked the busiest days to come in my office and demand my attention for her personal crises. I have never, in four years, told her how much I hate this, how much better it would be if she waited until we weren't so goddamned busy. I hate to hurt people's feelings.

She is going to ask me if she can stop being my secretary. If I can promote her. If I can help her move part of her life forward. I can't promote her, I have nowhere to promote her to. I could have promoted her two years ago when Etta left. But I didn't. I had to think of myself. My department. I am frantic to find a way to tell her there will be no promotion that will not make her feel as if she has just crashed into a concrete wall. I can't seem to come up with anything. I feel sorry for Lisa. So much of Lisa is tied up in what she does. A big chunk of me is tied up in what I do, but somehow I don't think it's the same chunk. Lisa thinks a better job will make her a happier person, make her more attractive to men. She thinks if she doesn't have to be a secretary any longer, everything will be fine. I wish I could tell her it doesn't work that way. Lisa gives everything she has to work. You have to give a lot, but you don't have to give everything.

I begin. "Lisa . . . Arden. This isn't about what you're called."

She interrupts me. "I can't stand my mother calling me every Sunday from Georgia. 'What's new?' Nothing's new."

I think about my mother's calls. For what is probably the first time, I wonder how I sound to her. Do I sound the way she dreamed her daughter might sound?

I think Lisa's going to cry. I'm not one who thinks tears are bad, they just seem so out of place under fluorescent lights, close to filing cabinets. The rain is falling in windy sheets. It slaps at the windows like storm waves against a docked boat. She is telling me that I am so lucky, how I have everything. A good job, people's respect, a good salary, John. On John's name she seems to rise inches out of the chair.

We are standing outside under the narrow overhang of our building. We flatten ourselves against the lobby glass to avoid the direct hit of the rain.

"Goodnight, Arden. We'll talk more tomorrow." She puts on an absurdly stylish hat and walks directly into the storm.

Finally I'm in a taxi trying to pat myself dry with an old tissue. It's useless. I'm drenched. The driver stopped even though his off-duty light was on. I must not be taking him too far out of his way. But now, having done me this favor, he has not stopped talking. All the windows are fogged up. I can't see anything. I feel disoriented, like I'm orbiting in an airless space capsule.

He's telling me about a movie he saw Saturday night. "We don't go out much. Too expensive. They don't make movies like they used to."

I wonder why everyone always says this. I start to listen. He's talking about my movie, the director's movie, the company's bomb. Can this be happening to me?

I hear the rain as a tinny drizzle now. I rub the window with my fist and make a clearing about the size of a quarter to look out of. The storm is over.

The inside of his taxi smells like dill pickles and pine-scented room freshener. I'm back on earth. I roll down the window hoping the air will keep me from getting sick.

"My wife and I loved the movie. You should see it. It's a real good movie."

The taxi idles at a red light. He stops talking to write furiously on a clipboard. I look out. The rain has left the city looking clean and new. What usually looks so ugly, tonight looks beautiful. It's also oddly quiet. A few drops of rain slip off the roof of the taxi and fall on my arm. I lick them off. I feel my insides where they ought to be. The marsh is gone. Suddenly I remember I'm supposed to meet John at the restaurant. I give the driver the address. It's out of his way. I soften his irritation by telling him I work for the company that made the movie he liked. He likes this. He'll have something to tell the wife.

The taxi makes a left. I look up at the marquee of a theater at 48th and Broadway. They are playing *The Young and the Hung*. I suppose I could be working on that movie. Or I could be selling toasters. I laugh. I can't wait to see John. I'm ready.

A gentle snow fell last night and this morning the park looks like a steam room. It is so beautiful I want to skip work. But I won't. Being at work is now a little easier than being away from it. Away from it I would just spend all day wondering what was going on. I was trying to figure out the other day when I stopped thinking about work as a job and started thinking about it as a career. When does a woman stop thinking about a guy as a boyfriend and start thinking about him as a husband? It's actually what you want to happen, but when it does, you feel caught. It is in this sudden change-over that you lose some part of yourself. A part you expect to recover each day.

Lisa/Arden is waiting for me at the elevators. She draws me to one side. Her sweater is brown, a collage of leather and rhinestones. We are standing under a framed poster from one of our hit movies. I like that. I like that the walls are decorated with our hit movies.

She tells me Timothy Rice is in my office. "Marshall sent him."

"Doesn't sound so bad to me." I start to walk away, but she grabs my arm. In the second it takes her to figure out what she's going to say that will make her grabbing my arm the right thing to do, I wonder why she thought she had to tell me out here in the reception area. Did she think I would make a scene? You go along thinking of yourself as a pretty easygoing person, then someone grabs your arm like you're a crazy person and you've got to ask yourself how you've been acting lately. I might be acting a little harassed, a little overworked, but I wouldn't call it crazy.

"Timothy is going to share your office. For a couple of days. No one can find him an empty office." She's acting as if she just told me there is a leper waiting for me in my office.

"I see. There are fifty floors of offices in this building and not one of them is free." I push open the glass double doors and walk down the hall toward my office. I say hello to a couple of my staff. I see seven or eight boxes stacked up against one wall. They're press kits. They look terrible. Doesn't it bother the secretaries who sit out here in the hallway that they have to look at these boxes all day?

Timothy Rice is the director of our next release. He's British. I don't know him very well. Marshall has been his main contact. Marshall does this every now and then. He'll pick a filmmaker to be his very own. I'm a little surprised that my office has been offered up. In business we sometimes make the mistake of thinking that our office is our own little haven, our home away from home. But then one morning, a stranger has moved in. I guess Rice's honeymoon with Marshall is over. I wonder about my own honeymoon with Marshall. Marshall has been promising me things for almost a month now. Things, until he promised them, I didn't know I wanted.

Rice is on the phone when I reach my office. He is sitting on the couch surrounded by a leather shoulder bag and two leather appointment books. Yellow Post-its reminding him how to use the WATS line, the country and city codes for London, and the three digit tie-line to the studio, are everywhere. He's got two days' growth of beard, dark blond hair and eyes the color of unpolished bronze. He starts to get up when he sees me. He's won me over with this small show of manners. He can stay in my office forever. I motion for him to sit still and he smiles. A relieved smile. Did he think I was going to kick him out? Make a scene?

Marshall buzzes me on this special line he had installed in my office last week when I was out to lunch. "Hi."

He's telling me about Rice: "He's in some kind of jam. He may ask you to help him out. Everyone at the studio is real high on him."

I say uh-huh a few more times and hang up. I love when Marshall says The Studio, like it's the UN Security Council.

Lisa buzzes me to say Danny Castle is on the phone. Danny Castle owns one of the most successful PR firms in the business. I've worked with Danny hundreds of times. He handles everyone. Well, he'd say he handles everyone.

"Hello, Danny." He wants to know if I can have dinner with him Thursday night. I take my appointment book out of the slender middle drawer in my desk. "I can't Thursday. What's up?" He tells me it's very important that we get together. I imagine this is how he talks to those few important columnists who are always trying to let the public in on his clients' secrets. I also imagine that this is how Danny always spoke. Even as a kid. The hint of promise in his voice hits me like a blast of inexpensive perfume. I can't wait to hear his stories, for him to make good on his promise. I look down at my book. Dinner with Molly. She'll understand. I reach for a pen. "Okay, Danny, where?" "The Tea Room. And bring John." He's off the phone.

I hang up. Timothy Rice is staring at me. I wonder how I am going to get any work done today. I wonder this as I am telling him how much I like his movie. I like this part of my job, spending time with new people, talking to them. I do it well. The trick is to make the entire conversation about them. I like movie people. They enjoy their work even when they're not enjoying it. I think this is where Molly and I are the most different. She only wants to talk to filmmakers when she has to about what she has to. Conversation with them is, finally, just too much traffic in and out of her life each day.

Lisa buzzes. Phone call for Timothy. I tell Lisa to start the calls. John first. Waiting for John to pick up, I hear Timothy telling someone he won't leave his wife. My ears perk up. Is he going to sit here and let me in on his personal life? The day will move ahead and having Timothy in my office will be like having the television on in the corner.

Marshall buzzes. "I want you to be at the photo shoot this afternoon."

"Why?"

"I just think it would help."

This afternoon, Mr. Advertising, Don Self, is overseeing an ad shoot for a movie starring four young kids. He's going to love it when I come in.

"Marshall, I'm pretty busy this afternoon, I'll try to get down there if I have time."

"Find the time." He hangs up. Lisa comes in with a package. Timothy looks up like it might be for him. Silver paper, blue ribbon, very nice. I open it and laugh. It is a silver-plated toaster from Marshall.

12

*J*imothy has been leaving for an hour. I get the idea he wants to talk to me about something, but I pretend I don't know this. Every call Timothy made today lasted about twenty-five minutes. He needs a lot of attention. From what I've pieced together, his next project will be for us. It will be based on a very popular children's story. But first he has to convince the great granddaughter that he is the right person to entrust her great grand-father's story to. He's got one last deal-clinching meeting with her sometime this week. I'm sure there is a snag here, but I must have missed it when I was out to lunch. Or down at the photo session. Don was really very gracious about my being there. In fact, he let me deal with the four young stars all by myself. He talked on the phone and I got to act like a shrew. Young, inexperienced actors are so malleable.

"You've been great. I really appreciate your letting me hang out here today." Timothy smiles more thanks.

"No problem. You're welcome to hang out here tomorrow if you want." He says he will and starts to gather up his stuff. He bends over to pick up some of his notes that have slipped all day to the floor. He's clumsy in an endearing sort of way. Watching him, I think there is something funny about him. Just as he is out the door, I realize what it is; he has no ass. No ass at all.

I'm ready to go home. It's 7:00. Not bad. I fit the trades and some magazines into my bag. John will be happy to see me. Lisa comes in. "Marshall wants to see you."

"Did you say I was still here?"

"Aren't you still here?" Lisa lifts her coat off the hook on the back of my door. "Goodnight." I envy her for a moment as she walks out of the office. I envy that she can go home and I can't. Of course, the funny thing is, she probably envies me for being on my way up to Marshall's office. It's times like this that I think being a secretary was a breeze. If it only paid more, who would be anything else?

Marshall's office is dark except for the brass lamp lighted on his desk. He has had the overhead fluorescent lights turned off. Marshall goes out of his way to make his office look as if it isn't in this office building, as if it isn't in any office building. There's something about his office that makes me think this is what the private chambers of a cardinal might look like. About a year and a half ago, Marshall was all set to have his office decorated in clean, California pastels. But at the last moment he canceled all the specially ordered fabric and redesigned his office in dark, rich wine tones.

Marshall looks up at me and for a second I think he doesn't know why I'm here. As I settle myself into a wine-red chair near his desk, I wish I were on my way home. This is the part of my job I like the least. The part I understand the least. It's like work is this mansion I have been living in and I think I have seen all the rooms, but then I come upstairs to see Marshall and he leads me through a secret passage into rooms I've never seen. Big, beautiful, mysterious rooms. I like these rooms. If he had never shown them to me I would never have known they were here. I'd have been just as happy if I had never seen them.

"Goodnight."

We both wait to hear the doors click behind Adele. Marshall lights a cigarette. The smoke falls backward against his hand as if it cannot bear to be separated from the cigarette.

CREATIVE DIFFERENCES

"I hear the photo session went well. Don thinks he got the shot for the ad."
I ignore this and start to tell him about Timothy Rice. Marshall loves gossip.
He demands it. It is one of the things we have in common. I tell him Timothy
had an affair with the co-star of his movie and now his wife has found out.
Marshall seems to know this.

"If we both know this, how come his wife didn't find out until today?"
Marshall doesn't answer me. Instead, he makes a couple of quick calls. I
settle back into my role as audience. I'm fairly certain Marshall doesn't
really like me. I'm just who he has. I'm not sure how this makes me feel.
Generally, I like people to like me.

Marshall tells me how he would like the department to be reorganized.
He has a plan. He has lots of plans. But this one I am particularly interested
in. This one is about how he plans to get rid of Don Self. Marshall wants to
make me head of both publicity and advertising. Of course, he doesn't want
to do this for me. He wants to do this for himself.

Marshall says Don's not a player. "He's too interested in protecting his
turf. He doesn't see the bigger picture. He's not a player."

For an instant I feel like I'm up here to be fitted for clothes that will make
me into a player. I know this is just the muslin pattern, but if I play my cards
right, I could be back for the final fitting.

The phone interrupts us. I jump a little. Marshall smiles at my nerves. At
my lack of nerve. It is Don asking if Marshall still wants him to wait.

Marshall says yes and apologizes for keeping him so late. "I know you're
trying to get out of here so you can get to your daughter's piano recital, but
Jake is supposed to call any second. And I think you ought to be here to
defend your ad." He hangs up after he tells him to sit tight. He looked at me
when he said sit tight.

Suddenly there is an enhanced quiet. The heat in the building has been
turned off. Maybe that's why I'm having trouble breathing all of a sudden. I
can see my reflection in the window. Surprisingly, I don't look any different.

"You'd do a great job with advertising. You'd know how to handle Len.
Don is always acting like the sales guys have a right to comment on the ads.
But you'd handle them. And you'd handle the bigger salary, too."

"The money would be great." I say this twice. Marshall only wants me to be head of advertising because he thinks he can control me. He thinks I'll be happy to be a figurehead. Why does he think a fancy new office, a fancy new title, and a fancy new salary will make me happy to be a figurehead?

Marshall is over by his antique pine breakfront getting us drinks. I think of Marshall as a kind of nomad, a corporate nomad. He is forever wandering in search of more. More power. More people to report to him. More money in his budget. More money in his bank account. I think he's a little mad. I think maybe working in a corporation makes you a little mad. I am afraid of that madness. Marshall sees his opportunity in my fear. I take the glass of wine he holds out to me. It's a beautiful glass with soft etching at the base of the stem. Marshall has exquisite taste. I hold the glass as if it's a goblet of blood.

The phone rings. It's Jake. I get up and walk over and put my untouched glass down on the breakfront. I think about the new job. When there is nothing new left to discover about your job, you begin to hanker for something else. It's natural to want to keep doing new things. It keeps you from getting bored. Bored people can be dangerous.

Of course, I think there are miles between hankering and lusting. It's about as many miles as there are between Marshall and me right now. Marshall is shouting at Jake about the ad. I wonder why he doesn't call Don to come up. I whisper goodnight. He doesn't even look at me. I'm kind of glad he doesn't.

"Let me go down with you. I'll give you a ride to wherever you're going." Timothy Rice is standing beside me. We are both staring at the round disks above the elevator, waiting for one of them to light up in red or white.

"After lunch, Timothy. I don't really have time right now."

"Marshall said you would help me." His accent is slipping. His voice is miles from London now. I tear my eyes away from the elevator lights certain that the elevator will no longer feel my magnetic pull of impatience and will never come. I look at him. He thinks using my boss's name has gotten my attention.

"Have you given up shaving?" What looked charming a couple of days ago now looks reprobate. "What can I do for you?" I sound like a salesperson at Cartier's. He might look like a streetperson, he might cheat on his wife, but what the hell, he might have a lot of money to spend.

The elevator opens, offering me escape. I grab Timothy's black sports jacket and we step onto the empty elevator à deux.

Timothy tells me he's meeting with the storyteller's great granddaughter day after tomorrow.

I nod. I know this.

He names a powerful gossip columnist. "She called me this morning to ask if I had an affair with Dresser."

I nod again. Dresser is the starlet.

"Dresser told her I gave her herpes and she's going to sue me."

I don't nod.

"If this appears in the paper before I see the granddaughter, I'm dead. She'll never let me make the picture."

And with good reason, I say to myself.

"Can you keep this out of the paper? Marshall said you could."

The elevator snaps to the ground and opens. "I'll see what I can do. Timothy, is it true what the reporter wants to print?"

"Yeah, it's true, love." And he's through the revolving doors and into his on-call limo. Thanks for offering to drop me at the restaurant.

The maître d' smiles at me. I eat here three or four times a week. I once brought a big movie star here for a lunch interview with a journalist. Ever since then they always act pleased to see me and never keep me waiting. I like that. I do think, though, sometimes they are disappointed when I don't show up with someone famous. I check my coat. I wonder if it will ever be spring again. The maître d' leads me to a corner table by the window, whispering that my mother has been waiting for twenty minutes. There is a small crystal vase filled with yellow daffodils in the center of the table. For a second I wonder where the greenhouse is and how one goes about forcing bulbs to bloom in winter. I also wonder if this is a job I might like.

"Are you all right?" My mother assumes I must be ill or just missed being run over by a truck, otherwise I wouldn't have kept her waiting. I guess some people might call a director with a sexually transmissible disease a truck.

"I'm fine. I'm sorry I'm late." I flag the waiter. I wish I could ask him to join us. That way he could do the talking for me. I ask him for a carafe of white wine. My mother starts to talk. She looks pretty. Winter is her best season. She wears a navy suit with a red blouse visible only at the neckline and the cuffs. She has not checked her red fox coat.

I look around the restaurant as though I expect to find topics I can discuss with my mother written on the walls or on the diners' foreheads. I could tell her about John's tenure. I could tell her about the co-op we're bidding on that we can't afford. I guess we could afford it if I get the job Marshall is promising me. I know she doesn't want to talk about my work.

I appreciate restaurants. I like the timely interruptions of our conversation. I like the white, rosebud china. I like the manners everyone uses. The waiter is beside us. I order a Caesar salad. My mother interrogates him about the specials. I think about how I should deal with the Rice thing. I'm also thinking what will happen if I can't get this columnist to kill the item and it runs. The Coast will be disappointed if Rice isn't able to make his fairytale. They're all set to spend twenty-five million on it. The Coast will be disappointed in me. I decide to ask Danny Castle to help me out.

My mother is a good conversationalist. She brought us up to believe that being able to make conversation is as important a skill as reading and writing. She can also be very funny. I'm just having trouble concentrating on what she is saying.

I see Don Self walking across the restaurant. He is coming toward me. "Hello, Don." I introduce him to my mother. She doesn't try to engage him in conversation.

"How can you be a party to this? How dare you tell Marshall I can't handle my area? I have a wife. I have three kids. Who are you?" His voice is very loud.

"Don, I think some of the guys in the kitchen missed that last part about your family." I try for the laugh. "I don't know what you're talking about." I try for the truth.

"Three kids. Of course, you wouldn't know about kids. Or a family. Would you?" Don gives my mother a quick searching look that says surely you must have adopted her, and storms off.

Two waiters are beside our table, forming a phalanx to protect the other diners from our unfortunate lapse in manners.

"Coffee." My mother doesn't skip a beat. She acts as if no one just came over and insulted her daughter at a decibel level way above the Environmental Protection Agency's standard of acceptability. I love that about her. There is a certain kind of unpleasantness in life she refuses to acknowledge.

I order a double espresso. Maybe the caffeine will help me figure out what Don was talking about. What did Marshall tell him? My mother looks at me, waiting, I suspect, to see if I'm going to explain what that was all about. I'd like to. There are times when we want to tell our mothers about all the bad things that are happening to us. We want to tell them because they think of us as good. But we can't tell them because we don't want them to know we're involved in things devoid of goodness. My mother is only a couple of feet from me. Maybe as close as when she used to sit on the edge of my bed at night when I was a kid. Some part of me slams into reverse and wants to be back in that bed listening to her voice, a voice that filled every corner of my room with certainty and answers and love.

I stare at the thin lemon peel beside my coffee. It is almost the same shade of yellow as the daffodils.

"Well, that's the business world, isn't it? Your father works for a company for thirty-seven years and then one day they walk into his office and tell him to retire. And all he knows is work. He's forgotten how to live. They're sending him home to me. Thirty-seven years late. And I'm supposed to know what to do with him. Well, I don't know what to do with him. And I don't want to find out."

The business world. She takes a plump strawberry and gives it a deep ride in the cream. My mother always talked about the business world as if it were another woman. It was as if my father were having an affair instead of earning a living. Now his mistress is telling him he's too old and she doesn't want him anymore. And his wife is telling him she doesn't want him either.

All I want is to get out of here. All I want is the check, a smart ballpoint pen and that little, square American Express bill with the carbons I'll tear up and leave in the unused ashtray. Then I want to retrieve my coat from behind the Dutch door with the discreet gold slot and I'm out of here.

My mother is waiting for me to say something. I look down into my espresso cup. No clues there. I used to be so good at making her feel better. I understand about my father. I understand how it happens. You start a job and you just let the job's momentum carry you from day to day. You don't really have to do very much. It's as if you're on an assembly line. Then you start to feel engaged in your work. You're good at it. You like it. In fact, you're determined to like it. Then a few years slip by. Then five. Then ten. Then thirty-seven. And maybe somewhere along the way you start to like it a little less, but you've made a commitment. A commitment to doing your job and you tell yourself you're not just filling your days, you're filling them up.

"What should he have done differently?" I'm asking as much for myself as for him. She looks up. She loves this. She loves to give her opinion about work. About the business world.

"He should not have thought he could find his purpose in life in the business world. You're not going to find the purpose for your life in business."

I think a slap would have hurt less. I make a quick pact with God that I'm not doing this. I'm dying to ask her where one would find the purpose of life, but I don't think I can.

I try one more tack. "Work made him feel special."

She settles a Hermes scarf about her neck as if she's putting in earplugs. She gathers up her coat. I pay the bill. The maître d' himself brings me my receipt. He looks at me as if I've disappointed him by allowing that man to scream at me. He still likes me, but he wants me to work on my manners.

Outside I stare at the townhouse across the street. I love the way the sun goes through its eight small, leaded windows. I long to be in that person's house, sitting on that person's couch, fumbling with that person's problems.

I ask my mother if she remembers how, when we were kids, every spring she would pick out a tree, sometimes a cherry tree, or maybe a young magnolia, and say that that tree reminded her of us. She is nodding and smiling. A part of me unhinges. My childhood self rushes up and kisses her. At this moment there is no one more precious to me than my mother.

"Don't worry," I say.

She looks at me like I've missed the whole point of what she said at lunch. Walking back to the office I think she's wrong. I got the point and I'm filled with resolve.

The item ran in this morning's paper. As a blind item. The columnist disguised Timothy Rice as that blond, good-looking British director. The columnist was sympathetic. She made it sound like the actress got herpes just to spite him. I'd say Danny Castle went a bit overboard.

I'm sitting at my desk reading it over the phone to Timothy, who's just called from a pay phone around the corner from the great granddaughter's Beekman Place apartment.

"Think the other papers will pick up on this and run something using my name?"

I must have missed his thank-you. I tell him no.

"How can you be sure? This is a pretty hot item."

"It's white hot, Timothy, but it's over for now. Maybe we can get some space when Dresser actually files suit." He seems to be mulling this over. He's loving all the attention. "I've got to jump off, Timothy, but you should give Danny Castle a call. He did you a real favor."

"I'd say he did you one, Love." And the phone goes dead. So much for the public school manners that won me over four short days ago. He won't call Danny. And my promise about Danny having a client for life is worthless.

We had dinner last night, Danny, John and me. Of course, I got to the restaurant forty-five minutes late. They were talking as if they didn't expect me to join them. Trying to get into the conversation was like trying to jump onto a moving train. I had a couple of glasses of wine and relaxed into the evening. It wasn't about me. I thought it would be, but when it turned out it was going to be about Danny, I was just as glad. He asked me to join his company. He asked me once and he asked John what he thought and then he went on talking about other things.

Danny has taken the old-time Hollywood job of praise agent to new heights. To more sophisticated, literate, dizzying heights. Danny's a smart kid from the Bronx via Oberlin, Oxford and Armani. It didn't take Danny ten minutes to figure out what filmmakers, actors, anyone famous wants. They want attention. They want to be taken seriously. Danny doesn't laugh at them when they call him ten times to ask if their limo should or shouldn't have tinted windows. He takes them seriously. I take their movies seriously. I don't know if I could take them as seriously.

Danny doesn't make extended eye contact. He's always looking around the room. He makes no apologies for it. A surgeon wouldn't apologize for being beeped by the hospital. Danny's on call twenty-four hours a day.

I asked him to help me out with the Timothy Rice problem. He understood right away why a studio person couldn't call. He loved the story. He jumped to call the columnist before I had even finished the part about the great granddaughter. When he was away from the table, John said I was using Danny.

"Here, he's offered you a job and you ask him for a favor." John was wrong. Danny loves to handle these kinds of things the way some people like to go on cruises.

I buzz Lisa and tell her to send Danny champagne. Molly stands at the door, her newspaper folded to the gossip page. "Nice work." She looks pretty today. Her strawberry blond hair is pinned off her face by two tortoiseshell combs.

"You going to take the job with Danny?"

"Would you come with me?" I sound casual but halfway through asking her my body felt like someone just spilled ice water over it. Work slices friendship thinly.

"I don't know. Maybe I'd stay here if they gave me your job." Molly lights a cigarette and tosses the match into the ashtray on my desk. It's still burning. We both watch it burn.

"There's a lot of talk. I thought you would want to know."

I don't take my eyes off the burnt match. "Talk?"

Molly has a way of leaning against a wall that seems to say she's much too bored to discuss this. Or too much of a lady.

It's odd the way you're dying to know what people are saying about you, but you don't want to hear it. You just want to know it, magically.

"People say you're leaving if you don't get Don's job."

Gee, that wasn't so bad. It kind of clears things up in a way. "I think I will take Danny's job, if Marshall doesn't come through on his promise. I mean, wouldn't it be sort of humiliating to stay? It would be like not being invited to a party but showing up anyway."

Molly shakes her head as if she doesn't get what I just said.

We're about to go up to Marshall's office when Molly says, "You don't want to work for Danny. You don't want to do that kind of work."

I'd almost rather put my hand in that burning match than talk about this. I'm the struggling fish and Molly's voice the jagged hook.

"You won't give up what you've got here. You like the money too much. You like the security of a big company. You wouldn't be very good in a small shop."

As much as I know she wants me to say no, I can't. Not because she's right, but because she's upset about something. Something I've done that I don't know I've done.

I dial John and ask him to come and get me at the office at 6:30. He laughs. "You haven't left the office at 6:30 in ten years." He says he'll be there. I follow Molly out the door.

Adele offers everyone croissants and pain au chocolat. Café au lait stands in sturdy, white mugs on Marshall's black-lacquered butler table. I wish this were a Paris cafe. I ask for black coffee.

I study the croissant as though buried in its flaky layers is some information vital to my well-being. Some information about John. I seem to be paying attention to the meeting. But, as when I was a kid in school, I just separated my selves. It's kind of like splitting the atom. It lets you sort things out.

My head snaps up. Don is saying something about the item in the morning paper. He and Marshall are real chummy. They're acting like they had a pajama party last night. Don's asking me how I got the columnist to agree to run it as a blind item.

I fucked her, Don. Didn't you know? I don't say this. I don't say anything.

"Don't you just love Don's ad for Timothy Rice's new movie?" Marshall grabs the board and holds it aloft, like he might be auctioning it. I tell Don it's good. And it is. Marshall smiles at me. He acknowledges my manners the way some people acknowledge panhandlers. They hope their misfortune isn't contagious. He thinks my manners will do me in some day.

Turns out Marshall doesn't like the ad as much as he wants all of us to. He's beginning to suggest changes. Don doesn't get it. I can see it from here, that look Marshall is giving him. The look that says the only way I am letting you stay head of advertising—and he *is* letting him stay—is if you let me call all the shots. Don doesn't completely understand what he promised Marshall last night at the pj party. One of these days though it's going to hit him. He's going to understand. He will see that he was willing to give up his stake in his work to keep his job.

Now I'm not saying this is bad, I'm just saying this is the way it is. Without a stake in your work, you begin to float, you begin to get into trouble. That's what happens to Molly every now and then. She gets angry and if you ask her what's wrong, she doesn't know what to say.

Marshall has changed his mind about me. I'm not sure why.

Looking at Don, I think maybe I just lucked out. Still, I want to know why. Business is like the formal dances we used to have at my prep school. The girls get all dressed up and sit on metal folding chairs in a gym decorated to look like a luau or a 1954 cocktail lounge and wait for one of the boys to ask them to dance. Some girls don't get asked. Some girls don't get asked very often. Some girls get asked but never by the boys they want to ask them. It isn't because the girls aren't pretty or because they can't dance. It's because that's just the way things are. I'm all dressed up, but Marshall isn't going to ask me to dance.

I look at Marshall and for some reason start to think about the time, six years ago, when I was in his office. It was late. It was Halloween. Marshall asked me to sit down and wait for a minute while he dictated an important memo to his secretary. This was his secretary before Adele. I sat down on the chair next to his secretary. He began to dictate a memo about someone's job performance. This person was in a lot of trouble. Marshall made this person sound like a cross between Simple Simon and Simon Legree. I looked out the window, desperate to get some distance from this. It was raining hard, the night was turning creepy. He seemed to be at the end when his secretary suddenly stopped writing. Her body got very still and then she shuddered the way you do when you catch a chill or when a ghost crosses your path. The termination memo was about her. Marshall was dictating her termination notice. Kind of like reading your own obit. I bet he expected her to type it up before she gathered up her belongings for the last time.

The meeting's over. Marshall asks me to stay behind. Molly gives me a look like a mother might give her child who's not much of a swimmer but who has just been asked by his swimming coach to jump off the high diving board. So, she does love me.

I walk over to his desk and lean my fingers on the edge. I look down at my blue suit, red high heels. My suit's jacket is cut like a blazer and I'm not wearing a blouse underneath it. I guess this is when he explains why he didn't ask me to dance but wonders if I'm available for a little heavy petting.

"Don's going to be okay. I think we can work things out."

I look up. "Gee, that's great, Marshall. I'm glad."

Marshall starts to talk about the item. How much he appreciates my handling it. "Jake is real happy, too."

I interrupt. "Marshall, I've been offered a job. Actually, an equity position in Danny Castle's firm. I'd like to take it." I think if Marshall could figure out a way to get rid of my body, he would kill me right now.

"Why didn't you tell me?"

"I'm telling you now."

Marshall selects a cigarette from his heavy silver case. You'd think he was at the Yale Club choosing a cigar. I sit down. I'm not sure how I expected Marshall to act. I guess I thought he might say he was happy for me or that he would miss me. Or that I couldn't leave because I was indispensable. Yeah, I was hoping for indispensable.

"I'll talk to Jake about it. It would mean letting you out of your contract. But I don't see a problem." He buzzes Adele to start the calls.

I get up. "Great. I didn't think there would be a problem. Could you talk to Jake today? I promised Danny I would let him know as soon as possible." The way he just looked at me when I said promised, you'd think I threw up on his desk.

John stands at the door. "You about ready?"

Sometimes I forget how handsome John is. Sometimes, when I'm waiting for him somewhere, I panic, thinking I have forgotten what he looks like, thinking he will walk past me and I won't recognize him.

"I'm almost ready." John sits down on the leather couch. His dark green cableknit sweater begs me to come closer. I resist. He picks up *Variety* and I see he isn't going to rush me. I don't ask John to come to the office very often. I remember one time about five years ago, when I was a publicist, I asked him to meet me at a screening. I had just gotten back from taking a movie star on a ten-day press tour. I went straight from the airport to the theater on Broadway. The theater was overbooked. Throngs of people stood in an unruly line outside the theater in the freezing cold. Everyone was yelling at me. A friend of the movie's star—the friend was almost as big a star himself—was banging on the emergency fire exit door. By the time I figured out who was banging and had made my way across the choked lobby with an usher who had a key, the star's friend was walking away. I opened the door and ran after him. I ran after him for almost a block before he would stop. I apologized for the mix-up and waved my hand toward the mob in front of the theater. I apologized several times, standing coatless in December on the corner of 44th Street while he listened with his hands stuffed deep into the pockets of his sheepskin jacket. Then he said he wasn't going back to the theater since no one was treating him right. He'd just have to tell his friend the studio didn't want him at the screening. I ran back into the theater, frozen and furious. Then I saw John standing in the lobby and I burst into tears. I wouldn't have cried if I hadn't seen him.

Molly comes in. She goes over to John and kisses him. She sits beside him. Yesterday Molly told me she was angry that her life was so entwined with mine. I wanted to comfort her, but she was right. You can get used to your life being all tangled up with someone you love. But you never really get used to it with someone at work.

Molly tells me to call her later when I find out what's happening to her life. She laughs and is gone. I look at my watch. All day I've been daydreaming about how I'll leave. One dream is with dozens of boxes and lots of people, a parade of well wishers. Another dream is solitary and quiet. I steal out of the office like a kid sneaking out of the house at night.

The direct line to Marshall's office buzzes. I look over at John who seems not to have heard it. I pick up. "Hello?"

"Jake won't let you out of your contract."

"Why not?"

"Because you have a contract with this company that runs another eighteen months." Marshall's voice drops an octave. "In eighteen months, we'll talk."

I love when Marshall assumes the role of the company's guardian. I slog around in my empty brain for something to say. "This can't be right. Can I talk to Jake?"

"If you like. It won't do you any good. He's pretty worked up that you want to leave."

This is great. They won't let me go. And they think I'm some sort of ungrateful wretch for wanting to leave. I don't care if Jake is all worked up. I don't say this. I don't say anything. "I'll talk to you tomorrow." I hang up the receiver feeling like I was just denied parole.

I get up and slam the door.

"What's wrong?"

I look at John but say nothing. I sit back down behind my desk and stare out the window. The way the buildings look from my window you can hardly tell where one begins and the other one ends. They looked like a kid has snapped them together. It occurs to me that there are hundreds of people sitting in offices like mine across the avenue, sitting in their squares of this elaborate erector set. I wonder if they know of a way to deal with all this.

"Marshall's not going to promote me. And he's not letting me out of my contract either. So I can't join Danny's firm."

"Come on, Honey. It's okay."

"It's not okay, John. Saying it's okay doesn't make it okay." I feel my eyes start to burn. My throat feels raw. For some reason I see my father. He's all dressed up for work. He's smiling at us, but he doesn't hear us. He's got an absentmindedness about him. It was as if he went into a trance before going to work.

"Come over here. Come sit by me. You didn't want to go to work for Danny. Not really. Everything will be fine here. Eighteen months isn't forever."

I glance over at John. I wonder if an artist came into the office right now and saw us, John and me, what would he see? Would he see some inner world, some inner world of joy and love that is invisible to everyone else? Invisible right now to me?

"John, I love you. I want you." I get up and walk over to the couch. Even as I am standing over him I know it's wrong. It's wrong to make love here in my office. But I am going to make a mistake. I want nothing more than to make this mistake.

I pull my skirt over my hips and settle down across him. He is surprised and confused even as he is responding to me.

"What are you doing? Don't. Let's go home. Come on."

John is upset with me, but even so I see him look over at the locked door. I kiss him again. "What are you doing?"

I'm trying to stop thinking about work.

13

My boss is late. Again. We wait in the conference room for the meeting to begin. Some of my staff look at me like it's my fault. When Marshall is late, my staff takes it as a personal affront. They think he doesn't think their time is as valuable as his time. I don't take it as a personal affront. Our time isn't as valuable as his time. Once we waited for over two hours and then Marshall canceled the meeting.

I look over at Rae. I'm going to fire her soon. Not because she does a bad job. But because the company hasn't had a hit in nearly twelve months and someone has to go. Studio executives are a little like professional athletes. We're paid more money than we're probably worth, but our life span is short. Athletes are struck down by injuries. Studio executives are struck down by bad movies.

I'm sure Rae has no idea I'm going to fire her. She has a certain innocence about business that I find almost amusing. Almost as amusing as the prospect of nuclear winter. She believes her boss will protect her. Firing her is my way of protecting her.

I have to leave in forty-five minutes. We are flying to Tucson for a sneak preview of the movie we're supposed to be meeting about now.

"Coffee?"

"Yes, thanks." My staff has dug in. They've gone for supplies. John left so early this morning he didn't make coffee. I had trouble getting up. I have trouble getting up without him.

I scan my index cards. These cards were specially designed for me. They come in two colors, dark blue and sky blue. They drive my secretary, Emma, crazy. Every time I have a new thought or something changes, I make her retype the card. I hate to see my handwriting on the cards. I like the permanence of her typing. I like the way she'll choose to capitalize something she thinks deserves emphasis. It may be a small way to display her personality, but she always seems pleased when she hands me a new set of cards. Emma seems to have caught my fierce sense of organization. Emma is feverish in her devotion to being organized. Emma's a good secretary, but now and then I miss Lisa. I miss Lisa's sense of humor and her daily struggle with life. She used to drive me crazy, but I always liked that she thought about her life. When she left two years ago to move to Washington, D.C., to work for the Environmental Protection Agency, I told her she was nuts. "They won't appreciate your clothes. You'll be bored. You'll miss the movie business."

One year later, almost to the day, I was sitting in my office eating yogurt and trail mix when Emma said Lisa Worthington was on the phone. I told her I didn't know a Lisa Worthington, but then snatched up the phone before Emma could. It was Lisa Johnson. Lisa/Arden. She was calling to tell me how great D.C. was. She was calling to say she had married a lawyer who worked for a senator. Lisa said she loved her job at E.P.A. and was doing volunteer work for the same senator.

"Are you happy, Lisa?"

"I'm so busy I don't know if I am or not."

I look over at Rae. She has to go. I've known it for months. I think Marshall knows it now, too. But I'm not sure. It sometimes surprises me how slow he is to divine a personnel problem. For a while I thought by the sheer force of my will I could turn the situation around and save her. It's not ego that makes me think this. I just want everyone to be happy and the work to be good. I've seen the release schedule for the next few months. Not much to be happy about there. But I can't do anything about Rae now. I have to get through the summer movies first. Rae tells me she has another idea for the ad.

"Just show the ads we went over last night." We worked so late last night, John was asleep when I got home. He almost always waits up for me. If he falls asleep, he usually leaves a note that says, "I'm falling asleep—wake me when you get in." Last night there was no note. My side of the bed was not completely turned down. I drank a glass of milk, took a shower and a Valium and lay down beside him. I wanted to wake him up. I didn't.

"But think of this." Rae is telling me about an idea she had early this morning. I get the feeling she didn't sleep last night either. Her blond hair is frizzy and long and seems to vibrate about her face. It's her eyes mainly that give her trouble. So blue they are almost painful to look at. Especially when you're telling her, no, we don't like your ad.

"If you use that ad, you'll need the National Guard to get people into the theater." She doesn't hear me. She's always telling me that criticism doesn't hurt her feelings. This isn't true. Criticism hurts everyone's feelings. Rae is vice-president of creative advertising. She might as well be vice-president of hurt feelings. And some of these guys can be really mean. By the end of some meetings there is a faint line, like a smudge of coal, under each of her eyes. I used to think she had accidentally rubbed her heavily mascaraed eyelashes with the back of her hand. But now I know the lashes are smudged with tears. Only her tears never fall down her cheeks. They are stopped by the thick, dark lashes.

I turn to talk to someone else. I should have left her in the design studio. Personally, I sometimes can't stand the blue eyes either. They take my time. Besides, I run out of ways to explain the behavior of senior management.

It occurs to me that most problems in business are caused by one of three things: hurt feelings, lack of time or fatigue.

"He'd like to have the meeting in his office." Marshall's secretary's secretary inclines her head. She hesitates as though she expects me to have trouble understanding her statement. I let my eyes skate upwards, which I believe demonstrates annoyance, not stupidity.

On my way into Marshall's office, I stop to call Emma. I watch my staff walk on ahead. They seem happier. The wait has been worth it. It is worth it because they will be in their boss's boss's office. There will be no intermediary. Many of us in offices believe that if it weren't for the intermediary, our boss, we would soar within the corporation.

Waiting for my secretary to pick up, I notice that no one notices Rae struggling with her ad boards. Emma answers the fifth ring. Very impressive. She knows the meeting is now in Marshall's office. Marshall's secretary's secretary tells her everything. I hang up, some messages scrawled on the back of one of my cards.

John. I can't think of John right now. It's all I've been thinking about. Last night, I lay awake for hours listening to him breathe. Like a movie whose sound and picture tracks slip, mismatching the dialogue and the action, I feel out of synch with John. I lay rigid trying to match my breath to his. I was jealous of his dreams.

Marshall's office is very grand. It should be. He is a divisional president. I see Len immediately. I am surprised to see he is still seated. That's odd. He intends to stay.

"Len's going to Tucson with you. I can't go." Marshall must be talking to me, but he's looking at Len.

"Oh. Great." I look right at Marshall. This is his way of telling me Len is my new boss. Neither one of them has the nerve to tell me directly. Neither has the nerve because this hasn't anything to do with me. This is about Len and Marshall. I'm just here.

Len and Marshall have been racing each other up the corporate ladder for years now. Sometimes Len would nose ahead, sometimes Marshall. Jake has played them both very well. Neither man has gone to another studio. Each believes he is the president's favorite. Marshall's been ahead of Len for a couple of years now. Len works for him. Lately, Len has been antsy. Discontented. Nervous. Angry. A real pleasure to have as a colleague. Len and I have roughly the same title. Only Len's a guy, so his title is a little grander than mine. Now, in order for Len to continue to report to Marshall, I will have to start reporting to Len. This way two of the key players in the company will be satisfied. Temporarily. Makes sense. Makes sense if you're not me.

Makes sense for Rae. Marshall hasn't been thinking about her after all. She's got some more time.

I nod at Rae to begin her presentation. She walks over to the mirror and adjusts the antique pin that holds her silk blouse together. All eyes watch. Rae is arrogant. Of course, in business I think arrogance is next to godliness. But not today. Today I just want to get on with it.

I gently kick over one of the ad boards. It seems the nicest way to get the meeting started. Rae begins her presentation. No one is listening. Except Len. He's right. He'd better listen.

My staff, four vice-presidents, is busy trying to figure out why Len is in our meeting. Each of my vice-presidents has their own staff. The way I used to have just the publicity staff. Only not as easy. Having a staff of vice-presidents is complicated. People who have titles think they deserve something. Of course, exactly what it is they think they deserve is hard to say. It's the trying to help them figure out what they want and then telling them the company is not prepared to give it to them that is so exhausting. I think I do it well, maybe even gracefully sometimes.

After this meeting, each of these vice-presidents will say something to someone on their staff and the announcement that Marshall cannot bring himself to make—the announcement that Len is my new boss—will be handled quietly, violently, by gossip.

Marshall walks around his office looking at the fifteen boards. He asks Rae about some copy lines. She tries to rewrite them on the spot. You can't get much more cooperative than that. Few of us will actually do our job in front of people. We prefer the comfort of a memo or a closed door. Creative work leaves you so exposed. It is what filmmakers and advertising executives have in common, only neither seems to know it.

Rae gives him another line. He doesn't like it. She tries again. Rae lets people in on her mistakes. In business, you can't let people in on anything, especially your mistakes.

"Have the filmmakers seen these yet?" Marshall's voice is even. You have to be careful of Marshall. He's nicest to those he likes least.

Rae shrugs and turns to me. Marshall doesn't allow us to show filmmakers the ads until he has seen them. Of course, last week he was much too busy with something or other and didn't have time to look at the ads for the studio's biggest summer picture. I didn't know how to explain this to the filmmakers, so I showed them the ads.

"In a rougher stage, yes."

Marshall does not like my answer. I think I see a look pass between him and Len. Is this also about tightening ship? "Has Jake seen these yet?"

"Not in living color. Just stats. I'm taking them to Tucson with me to show him tonight."

Marshall looks back at the boards. It isn't lost on him that he has an advantage over Jake. For companies split on two coasts such as ours, being a successful executive often hinges on such small advantages.

Now Marshall is going around the room asking everyone which ad they like. He pretends to care about their opinions. I hate that. I hate when someone asks for an opinion, but doesn't really want it.

My staff is evasive. I fight the feeling of a nervous parent hoping her children won't embarrass her. They don't embarrass me. They disappoint me. Not one of them backs up Rae and her choice.

"Let's go with this one." Marshall walks back to his desk and picks up his call sheet. The meeting is over. I stare at his polished nails and wonder if someone comes to the office to do them. Someone to do his hair. Someone to fit his suits. Someone to exercise him. What does he think he's in, the movie business?

I know everyone is waiting for me to say something. I can't seem to keep my mind on the meeting. I think I might be having an out-of-body experience.

"Which ad?" I ask, trying to keep bewilderment out of my voice.

CREATIVE DIFFERENCES

"That one. That one!" He points to the ad I hate. To the ad the filmmakers hate.

"Great. Fine. Thanks." My staff is out the door. Len holds the door for me.

"By the way, would John like to go to Tucson with us this afternoon?" I imagine this is Len's code that his lovely wife will be joining us on the company plane.

"Gee, Len, would John like to fly five hours in a plane he can't stand up straight in, spend three hours in Tucson seeing a movie and then get back on the same plane for another five hours? He'll be heartbroken that he can't go."

"Oh, okay. See you at Teterboro, Babe." Len wouldn't understand that he was being called an asshole if you held up a sign.

The executive vice-president of finance is on hold when I get back to my office. He has never spoken ten words to me. He usually has his vice-president or his senior vice-president deal with me.

Emma hands me an index card with my itinerary typed on it. A lot of phone numbers for a turn-around trip. The limo service here and in Tucson; the tail number of the plane; the tail number of Jake's plane from Los Angeles; the theater, both the box office and the manager's direct dial; a hotel if we decide to stay; numbers for two restaurants if we decide to have dinner; Marshall's car phone and home number. Emma is thorough.

"Try John for me, willya?" I go into my office and pick up the phone.

"Your department is fucked up." These are Mr. Finance's first five words to me. I can't wait to hear the second five: "You're spending too much money."

"Can we talk about this on Monday? I have to catch a plane to Tucson."

"I want to talk about this now."

I can't imagine who upstairs has been on his case so badly he's willing to scream at me over the phone and deny himself the pleasure of screaming at me in person.

"Okay, shoot." I lay down the receiver and start to pack up my stuff. He goes on talking. Rae comes in with a large portfolio that has the ads inside.

"I should be going to Tucson with you. I should do the presenting. It's my work."

Rae's commitment to her work is partly her undoing. She thinks the work belongs to her. It's a common mistake. You see, on the one hand, it's my job to encourage my staff to think their work belongs to them. This way they work harder. They are loyal to me. On the other hand, it's also my job to make my staff understand their work belongs to the corporation and it is of more value if it seems to have been done anonymously. This way the men who run the company don't have to worry about individual personalities or prejudices or passions. Or hurt feelings.

I point to the phone laying on my desk and whisper that she can't come this time. She goes on about why she should come when Molly walks in.

Molly looks relaxed, happy. It's Friday. She leans against the far wall, lights a cigarette and looks out over Central Park. She seems untouched by work. In the meeting, when Len didn't leave, she looked over at me and smiled. Her smile said, What do you expect from these guys and this business? She stopped expecting things from work a while ago. And because I still expect things, sometimes I feel foolish around her. I think she's acquired some secret wisdom. And I'm afraid if I ever acquire this same wisdom, I won't be able to get out of bed in the morning. And the last ten years will seem stupid. Wasted.

I pick up the receiver and listen. He's still going at it. I make an inarticulate noise into the phone so he'll know I'm still with him. This man is all worked up. He's using words like extravagant, whim, drawing the line, appetites. Is he kidding? Does he know what business we're in? A part of me shares his outrage, but over the years that part has grown smaller. Acting like the company's money is your own money doesn't save money. It just makes enemies. For every time I say no, there are a dozen guys standing in line to say yes. You could say extravagance is essential to the movie business. It is what people have come to expect from us. It is what we have come to expect from ourselves. What Mr. Finance doesn't understand is that you can't trade in dreams without a little extravagance. I'd explain this to him if I had the time.

I start to put on some eyeshadow. A gold shade. Emma comes to the door to say John is holding on 09. I try to interrupt Mr. Finance so I can take John's call, but he won't stop talking. I have five minutes before I have to be downstairs to catch the limo to the airport. For Christ's sakes why doesn't he shut up?

"I know. I know. We should really have a meeting about this." I sound so concerned, he stumbles. Line nine keeps blinking. I know John is on 09, but I can't get to him.

Mr. Finance is apologizing. Sort of. As a rule finance people don't apologize. It might signal a weakness. He's saying something about corporate guidelines.

I look at the phone: 09 has stopped blinking. John has hung up. I think my heart stopped beating just for a second.

"Have you talked to Marshall about this? As I'm sure you know, he signs off on all my budgets. On every fucking penny I spend. So I'm not having any meeting with you or any of your accountants unless Marshall is there." Fuckhead. I hang up. I'm angry. I wish I had called him a fuckhead.

"Emma, please try John again." I turn to Rae. Mercifully, she's leaving, having given up the fight for Tucson.

"Oh, I've been meaning to ask you something."

I look up. "Yes?"

"Does John work down in Soho?"

My face is unreadable, but my insides start to unhinge. "Why?"

"I saw him Wednesday night at this restaurant I go to all the time. He was with this woman. She was real pretty. I figured it was business."

Molly swings away from the window. All I can see is the tip of her cigarette. She's waving it like a torch at Rae. She says something to Rae I can't hear. Rae's head snaps back. She leaves.

Molly comes over to my desk. I tell her I like her dress. It's not really an office dress. It's a lavender sundress. It's the kind of dress you wear when you know your boss will be gone by noon.

"Emma, any luck with John?"

"No."

"Keep trying and get me Marshall."

Molly moves away. She settles on the couch. She wants to say something to me, but she makes some notes on one of my cards instead.

I look out the window. Central Park is green and leafy. The lunchtime blankets look like small, square pieces of gauze to me. I need to talk to John. Otherwise I am going to be lost. That's how I feel. I feel as if I'm coming apart and being washed away. I'm looking for something to grab on to. Maybe I'll grab on to work. Maybe if I concentrate on work hard enough I won't be able to think about John. And if I don't think about John, maybe I won't get washed away.

Emma buzzes me. I pick up on Marshall. "Marshall, about that ad. I don't think it's all that strong. Besides, the director and the producer hate it."

"Why didn't you say so in the meeting?"

"Was that a meeting?"

Marshall laughs. His voice is friendly. It spreads over me like a smoky drug. He goes on. "I've talked to Jake. He agrees with me about the ad. He just wants to see it tonight. Just sell the ad. I'll take care of any problems. Don't give in."

"Marshall, I don't believe in the ad."

"You don't have to believe in it." His edginess clamps itself onto my ear. I can almost hear him saying to himself that Len would never worry about whether or not he believed in something. He'd just go out and do his job.

"What about Len?"

"What about him?"

"Is he up to speed on this ad?" I amaze myself. I don't sound the least bit angry or resentful. I pride myself on my manners. I start to think what it might be like to look for another job. I don't even have a résumé.

"Don't worry. Len doesn't know anything about advertising. He won't be any trouble." I love that. I love that Marshall thinks Len wants to be a figurehead. I mean people just don't pass up the chance to be creative. Two years ago when Marshall didn't renew Don Self's contract, he promoted me and finally gave me advertising. He promoted me just five months after he said he wouldn't promote me and he wouldn't let me out of my contract to go work for Danny Castle. It didn't take Marshall long to find out I wasn't going to pass up a chance to be creative. And neither will Len. Suddenly 09 starts to blink.

"Gotta run, Marshall. Shall I call you tonight and let you know how the movie plays?"

"Don't bother. I asked Len to call me."

"Hello, John?" It isn't John. I've gotten John's secretary.

"John had to leave. He wanted me to tell you he'd see you tomorrow morning when you get back from Tucson."

The producer asks to see the ads. Beside me is a twelve-foot-square black case. I could say it's my purse.

The pilot leans out of the cockpit. "Traffic. We'll be on the ground for a while." I contemplate escape. "But please sit tight." Can he read my mind? "They might clear us at any time." The pilots for the company plane are always smallish with blond crewcuts.

The stewardess asks what everyone would like to drink. There is not a drink imaginable that you can't get on this plane. The stewardess smiles hello at me. She calls me by name. Clearly I've been traveling too much. At least that's what John has been telling me. I haven't figured out how you tell your boss you can't travel anymore, your husband doesn't like it. Of course, John doesn't say he doesn't like it. But he doesn't like it.

A spritzer would be nice. Something stronger would be nicer. "A Classic Coke with a slice of lemon," I answer with her same smile.

I get some satisfaction out of seeing that no one recognizes Len. My manners get the better of me and I introduce him to the producer, Paul Levine; the director, Woods Wellman; the agent for both, Milt Kasen; and to the star, Billy Farrow. Billy Farrow lowers the *New York Times* and almost nods. He goes back to his reading. What a companionable guy. I haven't seen Billy Farrow in over seven years. He looks great. He's gotten even better-looking. For a second I wonder if I look better now than I did seven years ago.

I also introduce Len to the reporter, Blair Longcourt. The reporter has been following Paul Levine around for months. He's writing a piece for *Esquire:* "What Is a Hollywood Producer?" I, for one, am anxious to find out.

I wait for Len to introduce his wife. He doesn't. He's too busy talking to the reporter. He keeps saying he didn't know a reporter would be going with us. Len is going to be heartbroken when he finds out the reporter isn't interested in talking to him. As Blair Longcourt said to me a few months ago when he first talked to me about the *Esquire* piece, I know all there is to know about studio executives. Certainty oozed from every perfect Yalie pore. I'm not really sure I know what he meant. Sometimes the specifics of an insult escape me. Usually the essence does not.

Len's wife looks around. I think her name is Wanda. But I'm not sure. I don't make it clear to the filmmakers that Len is my new boss. They don't really care. They're grumbling that Marshall isn't here.

The stewardess offers us hors d'oeuvres. Shrimp, crabmeat, gravlax salmon. Does Mr. Finance know about this menu?

I unzip the portfolio. Like crows, they converge. I set up the fifteen boards around the small plane. This plane seats nine. Barely. So now there is no room for anyone's legs. I look at the men looking at the ads.

I know I'm not supposed to be showing these before I show them to Jake, but what would we talk about for five hours? We could talk about how these men have spent thirty million dollars of the studio's money and no one has seen the movie yet. Well, Jake has seen some of it. On the phone yesterday he asked me if I could guarantee him a full house at tonight's sneak preview. I asked him how the movie was. He said he hoped we don't get our ass kicked. From anyone else, I'd say that means it's a bomb. Coming from Jake, it probably means it's a pretty good film.

Given the way the reporter is looking at the ads, I'd say Paul Levine has had him sitting in front of a Kem machine. So I'm at a disadvantage. I haven't seen any of the movie, but I'm here to tell them how to sell it. You'd think it would make more sense to show us the movie before we spend thousands of dollars creating ads. Maybe other businesses let you see the product before you try and sell it. But not the movie business.

There are probably a million reasons why this is so. I can think of two. First, there never seems to be enough time for us to see the movie. I know that sounds nuts, but it's true. A lot of movies are barely finished in time for release. Of course, there is time for us to see the movie unfinished. See a rough cut. But this doesn't happen very often, which brings me to the second reason. It seems as though filmmakers hate showing their movies to the advertising people. This used to make me crazy. I'd complain to Marshall. I'd complain to Jake. I'd get Marshall to complain to Jake. But nothing ever changed. Then one day Jake explained it to me. He said it would be different if you lived in Los Angeles. It would? How? You'd be in Los Angeles. Hard to argue with that.

The reporter places his tape recorder on the coffee table. He flips it on. From behind his paper, I feel Billy Farrow flinch.

The plane takes off. Like a pebble released by a sling, we are shot into the sky. I feel the tug of gravity. For a second, I panic. Such a small plane, so many hours. I feel like I'm leaving something behind. Something precious. Claustrophobia sets in. But it will pass.

Paul Levine stands up. The top of his balding head brushes the ceiling of the plane. He is the only one of us short enough to stand up in here. His gray suit looks as if it cost two of my mortgage payments. It doesn't matter though. He's still an ugly guy pushing sixty who has spent the last thirty years turning out schlocky movies. "Which do you like, Woods?" he asks.

Woods Wellman points to the board next to me. His is the finger of authority. I purposefully set this board next to me. This way they will be forced to look at me from time to time when it's my turn to talk. You'd be surprised how many times I've given a presentation and the filmmakers won't even look at me. It's not rudeness so much as fear. They're afraid I might change their minds. A lot of my job is trying to get people to change their minds. I'm pretty good at it. But it takes a lot of energy. I don't know if I have enough energy anymore.

Len's eyes are riveted to the ad Woods is pointing to. He must be remembering how Marshall said something like over his dead body when he saw this one.

"Milt?" Levine goes on. Milt doesn't bother to look at any of the boards. He's studying his Filofax appointment book. A brown leather case crammed with the private numbers of the most famous people in the movie business. In spite of myself I wonder if my number is in there.

"I don't like any of them." Milt's voice is toneless. I imagine him asking for three million dollars for one of his clients in this same toneless way. He repeats, "I don't like any of them." I smile. Milt isn't going to waste any of his passion over something stupid like an ad. He did his work eighteen months ago when he made the deals. He's already on to other movies, other deals.

"Blair, what do you think of this ad?" Levine continues his survey. Seems to me asking the reporter is a bit out of line, but Levine has set the rules. Act like the reporter isn't really a reporter. Okay by me. I know Blair isn't out to do a hatchet job on Levine. This reporter wants to give up journalism for the movie biz. This reporter has a script. Blair Longcourt doesn't care what we say to each other up here. I gather his editor doesn't care much either. He probably just wants to get rid of Blair Longcourt. I feel the same way. A reporter who doesn't drool over the potential for great gossip at twenty thousand feet doesn't deserve to be called a reporter.

"Billy?"

Again, the *New York Times* goes to half-mast. He points to the one that has the biggest picture of him. "I guess that one." He hauls the paper back up. The way he's hiding himself you'd think we were flying commercially on a 747 crammed with his fans. I guess stars can't ever stop taking care of their celebrity.

Finally, Levine asks me. I start to sell Marshall's ad. Slowly. I talk about the other fourteen boards and why they won't work. Paul Levine says the ad I want them to use reminds him of another movie.

CREATIVE DIFFERENCES

"Which one?"

He can't remember. The reporter names a wildly successful movie of two summers ago. Paul smiles at him and nods.

"We should live so long," I say. Milt laughs, his Tiffany pen working the weeks ahead.

"The fact of the matter is," says Paul, "I don't think this ad will bring anyone into the theater." Paul makes his case to everyone on the plane. I feel my hearing give way. Paul Levine is gesturing. I reach for my Coke. It's empty. I want another Coke desperately, but I can't interrupt him now. There is a certain etiquette to these meetings.

I've heard this speech a million times before. All producers use it. Some do it so well that on occasion I have found myself apologizing for the studio's total lack of sensitivity and my own Philistinism. We're not getting anywhere.

"Well, Paul, you're probably right," I say.

"Wait!" The reporter leaps up, hands in the air and bangs his head on the ceiling. Two boards fall over. One knocks into Len. He gives it a friendly pat. The other falls on Woods. Woods is about to lose it. All six feet four inches of him. The reporter flips over the tape and restarts the machine.

"All set now?" I flirt a little with the reporter. He colors. I go on. "Maybe we better go with something safer, more obvious."

Paul Levine slumps into his seat, knocking over three boards. He's almost mine. I don't like games, but I can play if I have to. Acting like you don't care is practically an aphrodisiac to movie people.

"I don't care, Paul. I just want what's best for the movie." This is working. Woods seems to be buying it. Billy is doing the crossword puzzle with the paper folded over so he can watch us. Milt looks up. Yes, going, going . . . no. Paul Levine isn't buying, after all. He's muttering something about his contractual rights for consultation. Len straightens up like someone just pressed the muzzle of a gun into his back.

"Isn't that what I'm doing, Paul? Consulting with you?" My voice is even, you could almost say sweet.

Paul and Woods start to argue. This seems to be part of an ongoing argument. I can tell Woods thinks Paul knows nothing about moviemaking. The only thing Woods thinks Paul knows is how to fight with studio executives. Well, to be a really good producer, you've got to know how to fight. Only most producers fight the wrong thing. You don't fight the people who are trying to do their jobs. You fight cynicism. You fight being pushed through the system. You fight to make your movie special. Special to the people who work at the studio.

The reporter is staring at Woods like a puppy. A stupid puppy. I can read his mind from here. Why didn't Woods agree to the *Esquire* piece? Then Blair might have had a shot at selling his script to someone who really knows about movies. But Woods didn't want any part of the article. Of course, no one knows Paul Levine was Blair Longcourt's second choice. It's just our little secret, and Blair is hoping that neither Woods nor I will let it slip out and mess up his chances for a development deal at Levine Productions.

I take out my book. I can't read, but holding the book helps me to pretend I'm not listening to them fight. I look at Len. He's drumming his fingers on the coffee table. This gesture gives the impression that he wants to say something but will wait until everyone is quiet. He doesn't want to say anything. He hasn't said one goddamned word. I don't know what I expected from him. Support maybe.

I put my book down and start selling again. The whole time I'm talking I'm trying to figure out if what I'm doing is ethical. I mean, I don't like the ad. I don't think it's right for the movie, but my boss wants me to convince the filmmakers it's right. I'm doing what my boss wants, figuring ethics are something you keep quiet about and hope one day they don't pop out and embarrass you. Keep selling, I tell myself. Don't overthink this. You think Len is sitting over there thinking about moral choices?

"This isn't the best time to try and decide about an ad. Everyone's nervous about tonight. Why don't I put the boards away," I say finally.

Milt asks if he can use the phone.

"Sure," I say. I think it's great that he's going to call someone on the phone right in front of us. He's not at all bothered that Paul and Woods are acting like the ad I'm suggesting will kill both their careers.

CREATIVE DIFFERENCES

I start to pack up the boards when Paul Levine says, "Why don't we get an objective opinion. Why don't we research them?"

"We can," I say amiably. Research used to be something the studio did behind the filmmakers' backs. Now the filmmakers demand it. Of course, neither the studio nor the filmmakers believe in research. They don't let people who shop in malls, eat in fast-food joints and go to the movies every Friday night tell them how to run their business.

"Hey, Honey, what's your name?" Paul points to Len's wife. "Rhonda?"

"No, it's Wanda." She smiles at Paul, showing large but even white teeth. For God's sakes, you'd think he just asked her to the junior prom.

"Which ad do you like?" Wanda hands her purse to Len and gets up to inspect the ads. I love when producers do this. I love when producers ask anyone they can find what they think of an ad. It's usually a secretary, but I know one producer who always asks the shoeshine guy. His shoeshine guy is about seventy years old, almost blind and hasn't been to a movie in maybe forty years. But the producer trusts his opinion. He doesn't trust the opinion of people who do this for a living.

Wanda keeps studying the ads. Something like this makes me stop and wonder if people in other businesses are as distrustful of one another as movie people are. Maybe drug dealers.

Wanda goes over and puts her hands around the top of one ad. The way she rests her hands, it's like the board has shoulders. She smiles down at it. It's the ad Paul and Woods like.

Len looks at his wife like she's a trained dog who's just rolled over. Len doesn't get it. His wife isn't a trained dog. She's one smart woman.

"See?" Paul looks at me, triumphant.

"Gosh, Paul, I guess that's pretty definitive research." I turn to Len. "Your wife has a real knack for this business." He laughs. He thinks I'm kidding. I wish he were half as bright as his wife. I get up and inch my way past the boards. Let them pack them up if they want more room. I'm at the bathroom door. I turn back to Len. "I think you can put the purse down now."

I slide the gold bolt across the door. Maybe they'll all be gone when I get back. Maybe the plane will lose pressure and none of the oxygen masks will work except for the one in here.

I look at my watch. We've been talking about these ads for almost three hours. I sit down on a narrow, cushioned bench. I'm tired. The bathroom is mirrored, walls and ceiling, and it makes me dizzy. I stare at the little basket on the marble vanity. It's filled with miniature soaps wrapped in silver foil with the studio's logo embossed on each one.

I start to brush my hair. I look at myself in the mirror trying to see it. Trying to see what's wrong with me. Am I less pretty? Am I not home enough? Am I terrible in bed? I brush my hair. It looks great. I have to go back in there. We're only over Kansas. I can't stay in here until we hit Arizona. If I cry they'll think I'm crying because of them and their stupid ads. I'm crying because I think John is having an affair.

14

*I*t's 105 degrees. Of course the air is dry so it only feels like 95 degrees. Inside the lobby it's almost too cool. I think this is what refrigerated air must feel like. It's almost 11:00 P.M. New York time.

Jake comes over immediately. He shoves some popcorn at me. I take some. He leans into me. I think he's going to kiss me.

"Get rid of him."

"Who?" He jerks his head at the reporter.

"He belongs to Paul," I explain.

"I don't give a fuck who he belongs to. Get rid of him." Then he shakes hands with Paul Levine and Woods Wellman. He shoulders Milt Kasen over to the water fountain. I imagine they're talking about another movie, another deal. All in Milt's toneless, expensive way.

I go over to the reporter. "Blair, would you mind waiting for us inside the theater?"

He stares at me. A little tension builds around his mouth. Some of the old reporter instincts find a level. Five years ago Blair Longcourt wrote one of the nastiest pieces ever written about an actor. It made his reputation. Some say the actor never entirely got over it. Blair left the magazine that had given him his shot. He freelanced. Despite his reputation, people talked to him. Off the record and on. Each of his victims thought they could win him over. He didn't want to be won over. He wanted to be noticed. And he was.

I have lunch with him every couple of months. He makes me laugh. He has great stories and he has great manners. But Blair is a cynic. Like a lot of journalists who cover the movie business, at first Blair loved it. It was fun. He was just out of college. He was invited to screenings and premieres, parties and intimate breakfasts. People at the studios wanted to know his opinion of their movies. He hung out at Elaine's with movie stars. He stayed at the Chateau Marmont when he was in L.A. Gradually, he began to hate it. To hate the people, the excess, the waiting, the little dramas, the bad movies, even the good movies. I think that's why he wrote the infamous article. He had something to prove to himself.

But now he's back to loving the thing he hates. He loves it with a vengeance. He wants to be a part of it. He feels entitled. I think this is how a victim must feel when he starts to identify with his kidnappers. I have never let any of our filmmakers talk to him. That is, until he went after Paul Levine.

"I'll just talk to Paul," he says.

I step aside. "Blair, really, it would be better." He shrugs and then walks through the double doors into the theater. I envy his shrug. "Sit in the last row," I call after him. "It's reserved for us."

I look around for Jake. I see Billy Farrow standing by himself. Conspicuous and uneasy, he doesn't look quite so handsome now. I take him to the manager's office. He's walking so slowly, I slip my hand into his to pull him up the stairs. His hand is damp. I wish I could take mine back. You forget how nervous actors get when their movie is shown for the first time. It might be the studio's money, the producer's vision, the director's genius, but it's the actor up on the screen. It's just him up there. I look down at the turquoise carpet and up at the turquoise-tiled walls. The two-story lobby looks like a bathroom. Coming to suburban Tucson makes you realize that colors you haven't seen in years are still very much in demand.

"Okay, Billy, as soon as the movie starts, I'll send someone up to get you so you can watch with us."

I'm halfway down the spiral when I hear him say, "Not someone . . ." The noise from the video games catches me right behind the ears. Personally, I think video games should be outlawed in movie theaters.

"You. I want you to come back for me."

"Sure, Billy."

I find Jake hunched over the candy counter. The sleeve of his black sweater slides across the counter, raising static. It's so hot outside that I wonder why he's wearing a sweater, even if it is the sheerest cashmere I've ever seen.

A few people are staring at us. You'd have to be blind or stupid not to recognize movie people. We look so out of place. Sometimes at sneaks the audience sees us as they come in and silently, as a group, decide to protect us. They decide to like our film. Sometimes they decide to humiliate us. This is just my own private theory.

"Better be a full house," he says. I pat Jake's arm. This theater is a triplex. We are in the biggest house. Twelve hundred seats. He keeps at me.

"It's a disaster. No one's coming. What are you going to do?"

It's easy for me to see by looking at the line outside that there will be turn-aways. I don't tell Jake this, though. He won't want to believe me. He'd rather worry.

He points to a box of Good 'n' Plenty. "Haven't had those since I was a kid," he says. He buys two boxes and gives one to me. He hands the young girl behind the counter a fifty-dollar bill. She hollers across the lobby for change. At every sneak preview Jake does the same thing. He acts like he's been living on Mars where there's no candy or popcorn. Well, I guess Los Angeles is a little like Mars.

"Jake, I've got to talk to you about the ad." He's looking around the lobby and inhaling his cigarette like it's a joint.

"I know all about it." He's talking and holding his breath at the same time. His tan face is turning red. For a second I think he's choking on a Good 'n' Plenty. He exhales. I won't have to call 911.

"You're nervous," I say.

"Goddamn right I'm nervous." Jake is so nervous, in fact, that suddenly I feel calm. More than calm, I feel protective. I feel I have to protect Jake from his nervousness or he will explode. Even while I'm trying to think of a way to calm him down, I know I've fallen for his act. I fall for it every time. He starts to act crazy and I start to comfort him. I've done this all my life. When I was a kid and one of my parents acted crazy, I'd knock myself out trying to calm them down. John says I should stop doing this. He says everyone knows it's my weakness. I hate scenes. He says people take advantage of me. I'm just beginning to realize John's right. I'm also just beginning to realize John takes advantage of my weakness, too.

I can't really tell about Jake's nervousness. I can't tell if he's nervous because he cares so much about the movies he makes, cares about his work, his job. Or if he's nervous because he cares so much about what people will say about him if the movie is terrible. I think it might be both. I think he tries like crazy to make good movies. And I think he cares what people say about him. He can't bear the idea of people in Los Angeles sitting around badmouthing him. Did you see that shitty movie that asshole Jake Tyler put thirty million dollars into? In a funny way, if we all cared as much as Jake does about what other people think, this business wouldn't be half bad.

I press on about the ad. I don't have much time. "Jake, there's a problem. I almost got them all to agree to the ad you and Marshall want, but Paul Levine isn't going for it. You've got to tell them how much you like Marshall's ad." I'm whispering, trying to get this set up before Levine and Wellman walk over. Right now they're giving the research guy the third degree. It occurs to me that I left the ads in the plane and Jake hasn't seen the ad I'm talking about. But I can't let that stop me. "Okay, Jake?"

"Do you like the ad?"

I've been waiting for him to ask me that, hoping he would ask me so I could say, no, I don't like the ad, and so redeem myself a little. But now that he's asking, I don't know what to say. I hesitate and he doesn't wait for an answer.

Jake says, "I don't like the ad."

CREATIVE DIFFERENCES

I look at him. I look away. He couldn't have said that. Marshall told me Jake was on line about this. I see a phone booth. I want to call John. I think fleetingly of walking away from Jake to call him.

Len is beside us now with Levine, Wellman and Kasen. One of Jake's production executives stands opposite us hitting the concession counter with a nickel. It sounds a little like a firing squad.

Jake puts his hand on the small of my back and presses gently into my spine. Why don't I just tell Jake I don't care which ad they use? Why don't I?

"Is this the theater we're going to open in?" Paul Levine wheels around on the heel of his Italian loafer. Whenever anyone uses this tone, I know they haven't been in a theater except maybe in Westwood or on Third Avenue in years. Probably since their last sneak preview. It's a sobering experience being with the common people.

We file into the theater. We sit in the last row. It is roped off. The theater is sold out. The only seats left are in the first row. Some paying customers try to get into our row, but the ushers keep them at bay. They stand and stare at us for a moment. I wish I could be a little famous so they'd feel better about our taking the last good seats. I know what they're thinking. Who wants to sit in the front row so some jerks from a movie company can watch their own movie that they've probably seen a million times already?

I sit between Jake and Woods Wellman. The movie starts and I remember Billy Farrow. I whisper I'll be right back and go back into the lobby. I once left a screening without saying anything to go to the bathroom and the next day my boss told me I couldn't work on the movie. The producer said I was disrespectful. My boss said I was just stupid. It took me a while to realize how easily filmmakers' feelings get hurt. I guess that makes them like the rest of us.

The lobby is almost empty. Someone is still playing a video game. I walk upstairs to get Billy. I find him in the projection room. It's a very clean room. One guy is running all three screens. Billy is watching the movie through a little glass window. There is no sound.

"Billy?" He doesn't take his eyes off the screen.

"Yeah?"

"Wanna go downstairs?" He shakes his head. I go back down by myself. I decide to stand in the back. The audience is liking the movie. I don't like it much. But then I'm not paying attention. Except maybe to see that Marshall might be right about the ad. It's so cold in here my knees ache. How could I have been so stupid as to talk to Jake about the ad just now? Timing. What's happening to my timing?

Jake is not the kind of guy to push his feelings aside for anyone. I know that. I should have waited. As long as I've known Jake, he's never really liked any ad campaign. Usually, he's pretty affable about his dislikes. But sometimes he can be deadly. We're almost at deadly tonight.

While we wait for the research guys to count the audience cards, I talk to the manager. He confides that he doesn't like the picture much. He agrees it played well. But he says he's seen lots of movies have good sneak previews and then drop dead at the box office.

Len walks over. He clamps an arm around the manager's shoulder. The manager says, "Big Movie." Len says, "Big Movie." The manager has known Len for years. He just met me. He looks at me like he's sorry he told me the truth. I say, "Big Movie."

When he walks away, Len says, "They don't like your ad. None of them."

"Really?" I wonder when it stopped being Marshall's ad and got to be mine. "Yeah, I kind of got that impression."

"I wouldn't keep pushing it if I were you." So this is the kind of boss Len's going to be.

"Okay."

Len smiles. He didn't think I'd be this easy. "Just go over and tell them they can have their ad. Okay, Babe?"

I lean against a turquoise wall. I see one of the ushers noticing me. He's about half my age, but I get a quick thrill out of his once-over. "Len, why don't you tell them?"

He nods thoughtfully and goes over to them, his walk, as always, slow and deliberate. He thinks this is the end of it. I know Marshall. This isn't the end of it. But I don't get paid to tell Len this.

CREATIVE DIFFERENCES

Everyone is asleep except for Billy Farrow and me. The reporter decided to fly to Los Angeles with Jake. They got real chummy as soon as the research guys told Jake he had a Big Movie.

When we got back to the plane there were two magnums of champagne on the coffee table. They were from Jake. Generous of him, considering they'll probably end up on my budget. A few weeks from now my new admirer in finance will be asking me why I ordered champagne. They do that in the movie business. They spend lots of time tracking down relatively insignificant expenditures. It's the big money that no one wants to look at. I don't blame them. Who wants to stand in front of a freight train going two hundred miles an hour?

Everyone was happy and friendly. It was like a party. Len was especially happy. His first day in a new job and the company has a hit. I'm not sure there's a correlation here. But then I'm not sure there isn't either.

The movie played great. Everyone thinks it's going to be a big hit. I don't think so. It's true the audience liked it, loved it even. But I have a feeling it won't be a hit. Of course, I'll take this feeling to the grave. If I were to say it out loud and it turned out to be true, everyone would blame me. They'd act like I was somehow responsible because I didn't like it enough. Filmmakers talk. Soon they'd be saying I was bad luck. It's tough enough being a woman in this job without being a jinx, too.

Finally, everyone is asleep. Billy Farrow and I sit side by side in separate leather armchairs. He's hunched over looking at the cassettes to see if there is a movie he might want to watch on the VCR.

I don't really care that Len is my boss. It's true I feel as if I've been hit by a truck. And it's true Len doesn't have much of a sense of humor, doesn't know much about advertising or publicity. But he's dressing better. The polyester suits are gone. Besides, I've got bigger fish to fry. I've got to figure out what I'm going to do if I get home and John isn't there.

This business of fantasy is taking me over. I admit I'm letting myself be taken over. I'm trying to find out what it might be like to be out of control. Fantasizing seems as good a place to start as any. I pretend. I pretend what I'll say to John if he tells me he's having an affair. How I'll act. How I'll cry.

How I won't cry. The fantasies are brutal. I can't stop. It's not unlike imagining my own funeral.

"Nothing worth watching." Billy stretches and turns toward me. "Wanna do a couple of lines?"

"Sure." I surprise myself. I haven't done coke in years. We don't even bother to go into the bathroom. He pulls out his tray table and lays out four thick lines. I tell him to go first. He is, after all, the movie star. He hands me his silver straw.

"Good, huh?"

I nod. There are stars in my eyes and a tangy, hospital scent in my throat. I feel ready.

Billy Farrow lays out four more lines. This time I go first. I'm going almost as fast as the plane now. I like the speed, it sands away at my fears.

Coke is funny. It makes me feel like I can see through the darkness. See through any darkness. I look out the window and see my reflection. I try to see it again. Try to see what's happened. Try to see. I speed along, thinking easily.

Molly used to say that infidelity doesn't have anything to do with the person being cheated on. I used to think that was her way of excusing her philandering men friends. I guess I thought it was a weakness on her part. Molly's loving has a kind of looseness about it, an elasticity. She doesn't tug when a man pulls away from her. She feeds him slack the way a kid lets out a kite string. Now I am there, poised to tug as hard as I can. And I want desperately to stop seeing it as a weakness to excuse someone. Maybe it's like with Marshall and Len this morning. Maybe this doesn't have anything to do with me. Only my feelings are hurt.

I'm going so fast now I can't think straight. Things start to collide inside my brain. The coke is settling down inside of me, inflating me like an innertube. My head is as big as a beach ball. I just need a few minutes. A little time to sort things out.

I know I can't let this matter too much. I have to let it be. We let our days slide by. All of us. We don't try very hard to stop them from sliding along. From turning over endlessly the same. Sometimes that's how we get through them; not look at them too closely. Sometimes we have to go out looking for them. Go out looking for adventure. Go out looking for our days. I think that maybe that's where John's gone. I think of our days together as freshwater pearls. There is that sudden jolt of surprise at finding each pearl and then there is the wondrous labor of stringing them into a necklace.

Now the coke feels like a magnet running up and down my body, drawing my insides back together. Snapping them into place. I can't figure all this out. I'm not sure I want to figure this out. But I know something. I know John. Loving John is like looking directly into the sun. It's blinding.

I love him. I love him. I am hurtling across the sky. Small in space, not truly a person. A spark. But my love for John is speeding along beside me. Brushing up against me. Bumping into me making me feel alive.

"Do you remember me?" In a second I find my body, my static place. I look at Billy like he's a moron. Or he thinks I'm one.

"Oh, you mean from before. Yeah, I remember you, Billy."

Seven years ago, *Metropolitan Magazine* wanted to do a cover story on Billy Farrow. Billy had made two movies. For the first he won an Oscar. The second became the fifth largest grossing movie of all time. Billy didn't really want to do it. He said he didn't have anything to say. I talked him into the interview. I thought it would be good for his next movie. It couldn't hurt him.

He drove me crazy. Saying yes and then an hour later, a day later, three days later changing his mind. He sent me a handwritten list of questions he'd let the magazine ask him. I threw it in the trash. He'd call me at home, late. John would look right at me and say into the phone, she's not home. Billy had a million reasons not to do the interview. I told my boss I thought he would do it. My boss told the head of the studio. It would have been difficult to explain if Billy didn't do it. So I kept at him.

One day he called me with a new demand. He said he'd do the interview if I flew his girlfriend with him to New York. This was the first I heard of any girlfriend and I knew just about all there was to know about Billy. And he was right. He didn't have anything much to say. He said it was real important to him. He said he couldn't do the interview without her.

Seven years ago I was a publicist. Agreeing to fly his girlfriend in from Los Angeles was a little out of my league. Back then the studio didn't automatically pay to fly girlfriends, spouses, agents. Things have loosened up since then.

Anyway, I said yes. "Okay, Billy. I'll get her a ticket. What's her last name?"

"Wait a minute," he said. Then he hollered out, "Hey, Honey, what's your last name?"

Maybe that's the kind of girlfriend John has. Someone who doesn't mean much to him. Someone who would wear her sunglasses while looking into the sun.

SENIOR
VICE-PRESIDENT

15

I am dreaming. The phone rings.

"Did I call too early?" John's voice pulls me up from the watery deep. It's 6:30 A.M. I tell him it's not too early. We both know I'm lying. I wait for him to talk. He tells me he loves me and I don't hear much else. His voice is inside of me, roaming. I wake up.

"I love you, too. I'll call you later." I hang up and stare at the phone like a part of him is inside of it. We share a secret today.

In the shower I try to remember my dream. It seems important. I get out and turn on the infrared sunlamp in the ceiling. It ticks away the minutes until seven. At seven the phone rings. It's Emma, my secretary. I talk to her wrapped in the hotel's white terry robe. I talk while I dress. Brushing my hair I almost strangle myself with the phone's long white cord. My hair looks great. I sit down at the vanity, steadying the receiver with my shoulder. I twist off the crystal lids of four white porcelain jars. The glass is so thin it looks blue. John bought me these. It's crazy to take them on trips. They're breakable and expensive. John says it doesn't matter. He'll buy me others. I smear some cream on my cheeks. The dream is still on my face.

"Hold on, Emma." I open the door for room service. I watch breakfast being wheeled in. Cinnamon toast, strawberries, coffee. "Okay, Emma, shoot." She reads from a long list. Some answers I give her right away. She tells me the producer of an action movie wants to know if we have a shot at a *Time* cover.

"Maybe. Tell him maybe."

"Maybe?"

"Yeah, if the star of his movie finds the cure for cancer, maybe we have a shot at the cover."

Emma never laughs at my jokes. It's one of the things I like least about her. She goes on with the list. I don't mind. Just some of it seems stupid. Whenever I'm in Los Angeles, I realize how stupid it is to have half the company back in New York. The people in New York go to bed thinking one thing and wake up to find it's been changed during one of L.A.'s late meetings. Do you know how annoying it is to have a memo waiting for you in the Fax machine first thing in the morning? Before coffee? So while Los Angeles slumbers, New York works to put everything back the way it was. It's not because New York is stubborn. It's just the way it is.

Emma apologizes for all the questions. I tell her it's okay. But she keeps apologizing. It makes me think I must be a real witch some days. I think she's glad I'm in Los Angeles this week. It gives her the run of the office.

"Okay, I'll check it out and call you." I hang up. The crumbs from the toast fall down my cleavage. I dial John. His secretary answers and asks if we didn't just speak. I lie and say no.

John comes on quickly. I start to tell him about the crumbs. He's too fast for me. I feel my face growing hot. I hold my breath. His words are like fingertips.

"Don't." He laughs. I laugh and fall onto the bed. I want him. The bedsheets smell like the beach.

"Save it, I'll be home tomorrow." We hang up. I let the receiver dangle from my outstretched hand. After a lot of years, John can still make me laugh. And come. Sometimes both at once. John never told me whether he had an affair. And I never asked. It's not that I've forgotten about it. You don't forget about things like that. You walk around them. Like you would walk around a land mine.

The parking attendant opens the door to my rental car. I hand him two dollars and slide onto the leather seat. Last couple of years I've made an effort to live up to the corporate guidelines for travel and entertainment expenses. If you don't take advantage of what your title gives you, people get suspicious. By being too good, you upset the bureaucracy. Upset the people who do nothing but make up rules. These people could work in any business. But they work in the movie business and seem none too happy about it. The mistake a lot of people in the movie business make is thinking the studio doesn't care about its own bureaucracy. The studio does, though. It is the only way, finally, of having any say over the movies, over the filmmakers and over us, of course.

So this week I'm driving a red Ferrari. I turn the radio on. The day opens to me, spreading itself like a bird's great white wings. It is a beautiful morning. The air is clear and warm. The sun is in front of me leading me down Sunset. Leading me through paradise. It is the kind of day California has in the thousands. It is the kind of day that makes you feel happy to be alive. The jacaranda trees are blooming. I feel I could drive around the world.

The man in the dark blue Mercedes next to me smiles. I smile back even though it's the Ferrari he's smiling at. The kind of car you drive in Los Angeles matters. I press the accelerator hard to the floor and dash away from the light. I run over the day ahead of me.

I pass La Cienega and slow down. The billboard for our next movie rises in front of me. It's spectacular. It was my idea. It was an expensive idea. Len didn't want to spend the money. He said the movie didn't need it. He's right. The movie doesn't need it. It will be a hit. The studio needs it. For studios to stay in business they have to be talked about. All the time. Like beautiful, loose women. Jake agreed with me. The billboard went up two weeks ago. Everyone is talking about it. Monday, the *Times* ran a little piece on it. It made me feel good.

The last three years I've been coming out to Los Angeles all the time. I feel almost at home. I don't carry a map in my shoulder bag anymore. I keep it in the glove compartment with all the gloves. I miss the way I used to feel when I would come out once every three or four months. I used to feel sort of strange, like I was stoned. Like I had never seen flowers so pretty or women so thin or men so handsome. I love the way things look here. A bank of purple bougainvillea can make my whole day. I don't ask Los Angeles to do anything else. Just look good.

My job brings me out here every five or six weeks. I stay a week and work like crazy. From the other side of the country, it seems that people in Los Angeles don't work as hard as we do. It's not true. The way I look at it, if you're in the movie business in Los Angeles, your whole life is work. Every meal, every evening out, every tennis game, every everything. In New York, we tend to make a distinction between our work and our life outside the office. It is for this distinction that people in Los Angeles hate us.

The radio is loud. The speakers are in the back. The sound comes through the seat straight to my heart. It gets threaded there. Then it floats ahead of me sort of like a kite.

I drive. I keep time with the music. I think of John. A couple of weeks ago we were sitting around listening to music and drinking wine. I got a little sad. I think I was just sleepy, but I didn't have the sense to go to bed. I told John I was afraid something might happen to him. He always laughs when I talk like this. I was expecting the laugh. It made me worry less. I wasn't expecting what he said next. He said if something ever did happen to him, I wasn't to keep him alive with machines. I just sat there. I didn't know what to say. He leaned over and held onto my chin and I swam into his eyes and said okay. But I didn't really mean it. I don't think you should give up on life so easy. Who knows, maybe those machines could buy some important time. Not giving up. I guess that's part of what makes me crazy. I don't seem to know when to give up the fight and get on with life. Driving right now I think I know when to give up. But, somehow, once inside an office, I forget.

I know my fighting makes Len crazy. Sometimes in meetings he looks at me like I'm a Martian. He just doesn't get why it should matter so much to me. At first it made Len nervous that I spent so much time at the studio.

CREATIVE DIFFERENCES

Every time I came, he came with me. It was like having a chaperone. But he stopped about a year or so ago. He comes out, but I can tell he'd rather stay in New York. He'd rather stay where he's in charge. Out here, Jake's in charge and he never lets any of us forget it.

Len and I have reached a truce of sorts. I don't want his job. That takes a lot of pressure off him. It shouldn't. It should tell him something about his job. But he trusts me and I try not to think too much about him. We're almost on a par now. Our titles are similar, but he earns more money than I do. That doesn't bother me. I make a lot of money. The principle of equal pay doesn't seem to matter as much when you're making a lot of money.

I still report to Len. On paper. When Marshall was asked to move to Los Angeles, I thought it might be different. God knows why I thought this. Jake explained it: We can only have one person in New York in charge and it can't be you. In other words, it can't be a woman. Being a woman can help your career for a while until you get to where you want to be in charge. Then the guys get nervous. They know when the chips are down and a filmmaker is screaming and the studio's got twenty-five million dollars riding on one movie, they want to hear a man's voice on the other end of the phone.

My feelings were hurt at first. But I made a quick recovery. My staff thought I should have sulked. They sulked. They walked around for days acting like a company can't do what it wants. They walked around like something awful had happened to them. They had trouble getting their work done. When I got angry with them, they said they understood I was angry at the company and not at them. I was angry at them. I love that. I love when something happens to me and everyone goes around acting as if it's happening to them. Only Molly acted as if it were happening to me.

The reason I didn't sulk was that just before this happened I promised John I wouldn't complain about work anymore. Or not so much. About once every couple of months I'd get him to the point where he'd say if you hate it that much, quit. I don't hate it enough to quit. Besides, I don't hate the money. What I hate is being screamed at. What I hate is being told I have no taste. What I hate is trying to keep the people who work for me happy when the company says if they don't like it, let them work somewhere else.

When I told John all this, he looked at me so hard I thought he was going to cry. So I told him I was only kidding. I don't know if John was upset because of what I said or whether he was sorry to meet this part of me this late in our love.

But when I saw what they were doing to Marshall, I figured things could be worse. What's a little high blood pressure compared to uprooting your life to move three thousand miles to sit in an office and do nothing all day.

I see two people jogging along the sidewalk. I'm in Beverly Hills. Their outfits are shell pink with a gray trim. They look perfect. Not like the runners I see in the park in New York, sloppy, sweaty and exhausted.

Life flies by. But sometimes, like today, the flight is heady and effortless and up ahead is something wonderful, maybe even joy. I turn the Ferrari into the studio gate. The guard waves me through.

I pull into a spot marked Visitor. I use this same spot on each trip. I use the same guest office with the same secretary. I use the same reserved table at the commissary. There is something soothing about all this sameness. I lock the car and step onto the chalk white sidewalk. It is lined with hundreds of small-petaled flowers. Impatiens, I think.

I see Molly up ahead about to go into the screening room. I call to her. She smiles and waves to me. I'm happy to see her. She's dressed all in white and looks as if she's on her way to a lawn party.

"What are we doing here?" Molly asks me this all the time. Usually just before we go into a meeting. It makes me laugh. She tells me she wants to talk to me later.

I think she wants to tell me she's quitting. Up close I see there are silver threads stitched into her white summer sweater. I show her my schedule. "We can talk anytime you want."

"I think I'll go talk to the president of the United States. He's not as busy." Her sarcasm covers me like mosquito netting. She pushes me through the screening room door and her hand on my back says she was trying to make me laugh.

"Oh! Excuse me." It's so dark in here I can't see who it is I just tripped over. The legs and feet I just bumped go rigid. I take a moment to regain my balance. I move along the aisle and like a blind person feel my way into a cool leather armchair. I push my sunglasses on top of my head and free my hair from under my linen jacket. The morning's coffee pumps inside my stomach. It feels like I have two heartbeats. I promise this will be the last coffee. I'll switch to tea or decaf. I catch myself. Making promises to yourself can be dangerous. It usually means things aren't great and you've got to make some changes. But today it's okay. I'm pregnant and these promises are for someone tiny.

A sound travels over the darkness. I try to identify it. My ears feel big; my eyes, little, unseeing dots. The baby was John's idea. Mostly. But I can get used to it. The curtains hum and part. The screening begins.

The footage is roughly edited. Some parts are in black and white. There is temp music. It is the score from a big hit movie of a couple of years ago. One reel is out of synch. After ninety-five minutes, the screen goes black. Slowly, like someone is hand cranking them, the lights come up.

Now I see there are seven of us in the room. Except for Molly and me, no one in this room slept last night. I can tell. What I can't tell is what's keeping them awake. I'm hoping it's adrenaline. But whoever heard of adrenaline working for days and nights on end?

"Do you know what you just saw?" The body I tripped over comes alive.

I take a wild guess. "Your movie?" I turn toward the director. I see the beginnings of a smile, but it flattens out and disappears. He's too tired.

He nods. His profile is worthy of a Roman coin. "Yes, my movie. No one has seen it. You are the first."

My heart sinks. I slap my brain around. Being the first to see a new movie is not the compliment it may seem.

"You have to promise not to tell anyone that you've seen it." He waits. Is he expecting me to cross my heart, draw a little blood? "So what do you think?"

I'm thinking about the time years ago when I was in a screening like this with about fifteen other people. When the movie was over, the director asked the production executive in charge what he thought of the movie. This production executive was not young. Nowadays production executives are all young. He had been to maybe a million rough-cut screenings like this. He was a member of the Editor's Guild. He told the director what he thought. The director, a young guy, maybe twenty-five, on his second movie, listened and then without saying a word got up and left the room. He walked straight to the head of the studio's office where he demanded the production executive be fired or he would not finish the film. Those of us left in the screening room didn't even wonder why the director had left so abruptly. We were busy telling the production executive how right he was about the changes the movie needed when in walked the president of the studio and the director. They looked like they had just finished eighteen holes of golf. The president walked down the aisle and stood behind the production executive. He placed his hand on the executive's shoulder and said, "Don't you have something to say?" I couldn't imagine what he was talking about and by the way the production executive looked, I was pretty sure he didn't know what he was talking about either. But after a couple of minutes, he stood up, held out his hand to the young director and said, "I'm sorry." The president swept us all with his eyes and left. Then the production executive took back everything he had said about the movie. Then we all got up and left without saying a word. Later, someone explained to me that it's always best to say a movie's great. It keeps The Talent happy and when The Talent is happy, the studio is happy.

"So, what do you think?"

I buy a little time. "Of what?"

"My movie."

"I haven't seen it."

This time a real smile. He digs deep into his chinos and comes out with a pack of Chesterfields. A real man's smoke. He pats the pocket in his shirt. He might be searching for his heart. He fishes out a lighter with two fingers.

"Don't worry about these guys." He tilts his head, dismissing the producer, the editor, the writer and the director of photography who sit behind him. "Just don't tell anyone." This last is delivered like a line from a B movie. But even so, I believe the implied threat in Mr. Walsh's voice.

Ted Walsh's way of doing business is to threaten. It's effective. Sometimes I think he'd be happier as a low-level thug. Not part of any organization. Just a freelance badass. Walsh's biggest problem is being embarrassed about his television roots. He acts like he made kiddie porn instead of sitcoms. Now, ten years and tens of millions of dollars later, he wants to be a feature director. When he says the word "feature," he sounds as if he's talking about a woman, a woman way too classy for him.

"So you won't tell anyone?"

By anyone he means Jake. I hate this. Jake is supposed to see a movie first. That's the way it's supposed to work. I imagine he and Jake are fighting about something. I try to stay in the demilitarized zone in situations like this. I don't like to deceive Jake. It's not good for business. I decide to tell Walsh this.

"I don't like to lie to my colleagues." My words hang about the room like laundry caught in a downpour. I hear a cigarette being lit. I imagine it's Molly's. I consider my options. Quickly. I can make a joke out of what I just said. I can beg his forgiveness. I can appeal to his vanity.

I begin. "Teddy." I can see the diminutive of his name catches him. He rights himself in his chair. I wonder for an instant which of his four ex-wives called him Teddy. He thinks I've picked the begging option. I haven't.

"Teddy, put yourself in my place. Today I'll be in a meeting with my production colleagues. We'll be talking about movies. About your movie. Don't ask me not to tell them how great your movie is."

Walsh stands up. He sits down. I can sense his tiredness circulating around the room. I felt the president's hand on my shoulder and I said the movie was great. (That president is now head of another studio. He's probably still got that special touch.)

Walsh doesn't know whether to believe me or not. The guys behind me are busy fantasizing what they'll say when someone comes up to them in the commissary later today and tells them they hear the movie is great. Word of mouth. It's as cheap as air. But I can't think of many things more powerful.

Walsh looks at me. His eyes are dark and so steady there might be weights on them. Walsh looks like a miner who has been working the graveyard shift so long, he's forgotten what daylight is like. Now, by saying the movie is great, it's as if I switched on a giant floodlight. We sit, all of us, quiet while his eyes get used to the light. There are two kinds of directors. Those who resist the selling of their movies and those who like selling their movies better than they liked making them. Usually, I like those in the first group better. Walsh will do anything to make his movie a success. As he puts it, anything to put asses in seats. And he will complain the whole time he's doing it.

"What do you think? Really?" He has dismissed my use of the word "great." He has also for the moment tabled his request that I lie to Jake.

I cross my feet at the ankles and stretch my hands up behind my neck. This is one of the hardest parts of my job. He wants me to tell him in two minutes what I think of a movie it took him two years to make. In business, if you say let me think about this for a while, right away people think you're stupid and that you don't know how to do your job. You have to be careful in this business, because everyone is sure they know how to do your job better than you do. I start to tell him what I think. He interrupts me to tell me what he thinks.

I don't mind. Gives me some time to think. Only I'm not thinking about his movie. I'm thinking about how in business you've got to teach yourself to appreciate what other people do well. An odd thing to be thinking about. I'd never admit it to anyone, but I think I used to be envious of filmmakers. Envious of what they can make. Envious of how what they make can turn a studio upside down. You can't imagine the power movies have over the lives of those of us who work at a studio.

"So what do you think?"

I tell him exactly what he just said, only I put it into my own words. It's so easy to please people, I wonder why people don't do it more often. Besides, Walsh knows exactly what his movie is. And is not. He leans over and kisses me on the cheek. A light, Chesterfield kiss. I get up, knock into his long, inflexible legs once again and lean over to shake the hands and kiss the cheeks of the men behind me. Silently I thank the movie god. The movie's not great. But it's good. I can sell it. And, after all, isn't that what I'm here for?

CREATIVE DIFFERENCES

The young woman who greets me is beautiful. She looks like a model. Slender, carefully dressed, blond hair loose and long and icy blue eyes kept at the freezing mark by frosted eyeshadow. She is Harry Cajun's personal assistant. She is, by all accounts, also his girl friend. Harry Cajun is a big movie star, married with a new baby and just about to direct his first feature. He is, by all accounts, a son of a bitch. Most say he's good-looking. A little too Cro-Magnon for my taste.

Harry Cajun sits at a long table in a darkened room. None of the sunlight that has painted the afternoon gold is allowed in here. He is eating an apple. He strips the skin off each piece using a penknife with an ivory handle.

"Hello, Harry." I take a seat opposite him even though neither she nor Harry offered it. I take my red leather notebook out of my shoulder bag and flip to a clean page of blue graph paper. I ask him how he sees his movie. I've read the script and frankly I'm not expecting much. I tell him the script's great. It's a caper movie. Pure and simple. He's probably going to tell me it's a relationship movie. And I'm probably going to agree. Preliminaries over with, I lean back.

Harry turns to his pretty assistant and mumbles something. I ignore his rudeness. I look around his office as if it's the reason I've come. It's been a while since I've seen anything quite so ugly. Offices in Los Angeles are usually cool, easy on the eye. Hip. On the walls are pictures of hunting scenes that look like framed place mats.

"Harry isn't happy with this office. It isn't," the assistant struggles for the right word, "it isn't nice enough." Well, that's a relief. He thinks it's ugly, too.

She goes on. After a couple of tries settles on, "It isn't big enough." I look around again. It's just a shade smaller than a mausoleum. I shrug my shoulders. I try to convey sympathy even though I feel none. She stares at me. Does she think I'm in charge of office assignments? Is it possible they've got their vice-presidents mixed up and she thinks I'm building administration? For a second, I think how awful that job must be. I try to catch Harry's eye. He knows me. From years ago.

I start again. More about his script. I tell myself to talk to him like he's a director. I don't have much time. I have to be at my next meeting up on Mulholland in an hour.

Again, he turns and mumbles to the pretty assistant. Up close Harry Cajun doesn't seem as big as I remember him. He looks like he's dieted for so long that he's shrunk down to mortal size. I'm getting impatient. The assistant fondles an apple from a large wooden bowl that is kept from being the one possibly tasteful thing in the room by some crude carvings that spell out Harry's name and the name of his last movie. She offers the apple to Harry. Suddenly, he looks at her as if she might be Eve. His finger plays the blade of the knife like a harpstring. In the set of his narrow shoulders I can see he doesn't like women. Not even his mistress. We are all some form of Other.

The phone rings, interrupting this silent drama between them. The assistant answers and gives it to Harry, nodding, coaxing, treating him like a child. He mumbles into the receiver. I toy with the idea of befriending the assistant. But I don't think there's time. He sounds like he's hanging up.

I close my notebook, stand up and walk the carpeted floor. I catch him looking at my legs. My flowered silk skirt shows off my legs. John is always telling me I've got great legs. Over the years I've come to believe him. This is great. I couldn't get him to look at me to talk about his movie, but I can get him to look at my legs. I now notice the assistant is wearing slacks. Maybe her legs aren't so great.

"Harry wonders if anyone else is coming to the meeting?" The assistant speaks English as if she's just woken up from a coma and is unsure if words still mean what they did before she went to sleep. Don't worry, Sleeping Beauty, that still means, Is a man coming to the meeting? I sit down, suddenly a little tired.

I try again. This is my third or fourth try, but who's counting? "Who are you expecting, Harry?" He still doesn't look at me. This is almost funny.

She answers for him. "We're not sure. We just don't want to start and have to say everything over again if someone comes in later." I love when assistants start talking like nurses. If I ever heard Emma talk like this, I'd fire her. Or commit her.

The assistant gasps. She sounds like someone just stuck her with a straight pin. "I'm so sorry. I didn't ask you if you wanted anything. Anything to eat or drink," she clarifies her offer.

"A Perrier would be great." I smile at her. My fight's not with her. While we wait for her to bring my drink I remind Harry of the last time we worked together. I name the picture. A grunt greets this information. I just named a movie he's probably taken out of his official biography. I love when stars rewrite their histories. Make themselves younger or gentile. Delete all their bad movies. There's a few things I'd like to delete from my autobiography.

Talking about this movie has erected an invisible net between us. Better than the dead space that separated us before. We sit quietly. I imagine he's remembering an easier time. When he was a star. Not a mega-star. Not a director. Not even wanting to be a director. He was single. He was adored for his womanizing. The movie was bad. He's probably right to take it out of his bio. But it made money. I'm remembering his odd request for three theater tickets for two different Broadway shows on the same night. He and his two bodyguards watched the first act of the first show and then, during the intermission, got into his limo where, by all accounts, he drank domestic champagne and smoked sensimilla. Then he got out of the limo and went into the other theater and watched the second act of the second show. I thought it was a pretty dumb request, but I let him do it. I treated him like a kid who wants two desserts. A lonely kid.

The assistant sets the glass of Perrier in front of me. The lemon slice looks like a miniature ferris wheel. I take a sip. The cool liquid douses the fire that is beginning to catch inside of me. I look at my watch. I'll give him five minutes, then I'm out of here.

"Harry, Len will be here in ten minutes. He got held up."

So, she can open a Perrier with one hand and make a call with the other. We are waiting for a man to come and give this meeting legitimacy. You expect this kind of thing to go away, but it doesn't.

"Well, I don't have ten minutes. So if you want to talk to me about your movie, start talking." This last sounds like a line out of a B movie, but Harry's the sort of guy who eats up this kind of dialogue.

"Okay."

The assistant's pretty face goes white. I smile at her, downplaying my victory. Her blue eyes look like they've been fired in a kiln for about ten hours. She doesn't like women much more than her boss does. "I'm sure Len will be here any second." She's caught his mumble.

"Don't worry, Hon. We'll start the meeting now," Harry says, locking his smoky gray eyes on me. For the first time I realize he wears contacts on screen to make his eyes blue. "Len doesn't know anything about advertising anyway."

Well, that would make you a fine pair. One doesn't know anything about directing, the other doesn't know anything about advertising. I don't say this. Instead, I take a long swallow of the Perrier and try to snuff the anger that is back, sitting in my chest like a hot coal. I can't defend Len to Harry. I can't take away Harry's reason for taking the meeting with me. I should, but I can't. This is my chance to get something going with Harry Cajun and save myself a lot of trouble later on. These last twenty-five minutes have been like a hazing and now he's asking me to join the fraternity. I can't say no. Hopefully, later on, when I'm back in New York and he's out roaming the studio sidewalks, he won't be complaining about some broad who's trying to ruin his picture.

I open my red notebook and this time I take out my silver pen. The assistant won't be so easy to win over. The pretty ones can be dangerous in business. They feel entitled to be treated as if they know something. I'll pretend a lot of things, but pretending the director's girlfriend is smart isn't one of them.

I yell my name into the square box. Static responds. I say my name again. I feel like I'm ordering a Quarter Pounder and a chocolate shake at McDonald's.

A couple of clicks like large magnets unhinging and the gate swings open. I push the Ferrari into gear and let it wind its way up the long driveway the way sports cars are supposed to. I stop near the front door, a massive oak affair with a brass lion's head for a knocker. Getting out of the car, I am struck by the quiet. I hear the muted sounds of a gardener clipping away at some distant hedge. I know Los Angeles lies just below me, but it might as well be light years away, so removed do I feel on this five-acre estate. Hey, this isn't work. This is like visiting a rich friend.

The big door is opened by a small man in a white jacket. I didn't even have to knock. Was he watching me through some hidden panel? He leads me through a towering hall, under a crystal chandelier and past what might properly be called a sitting room. Yellow and apricot couches sit primly on Oriental rugs that probably spent their youth in a French chateau. My guide leaves me in an unfurnished solarium. A young girl dressed in gray sweatpants, an olive green T-shirt and sunglasses with hot pink frames comes toward me.

"Thank God you're here!" I feel pretty great that she's so happy to see me. I have no idea who she is. She turns and starts walking away from me into other rooms. Unasked, I follow. I follow her into the noise, into a nervous rushing around. No one planned to make this house an office. It just happened.

About three months ago the director refused to leave his house to go to the cutting room on the lot. So the cutting room came here. And everything else needed to finish a film. We pass a young girl wearing a Warren Zevon T-shirt who is slamming her hand against the top of a jammed Xerox machine. It occurs to me, walking through the seventh or eighth room, I'll need a map to get back to the Ferrari, to my little piece of heaven.

"He won't see them," she says.

"Won't see who?"

The young girl takes off the pink glasses in such a way you might think they were earplugs. "Who? The guys from *Life*."

I wonder if my one little question is going to cause her to treat me like a moron.

She goes on, "They've been waiting since nine this morning. They won't leave. I don't know what to do." The young girl looks close to tears. She's talking to me like I'm the only thing standing between her and a breakdown.

I ask her a few questions. Easy ones. Name, rank, serial number. She calms down. She sits down on the floor in the room they've turned into the production's main office, crosses her legs, drops her head forward. She begins to do head rolls. In between the slow yogic circles, she tells me she's been working for three straight days because he said they could finish the first cut if everyone would just suck it up and work harder. She tells me she's so tired she feels sick. I know that kind of tiredness, but I don't say anything. She's my only link to what's been going on here and too much sympathy could make her crumble. Then she'd be useless to me.

She says her boyfriend is so angry with her he won't answer the phone. Just leaves the machine on. She's been talking to a goddamned machine for three days. She's back on the photographer and reporter from *Life*. "Some idiot promised he'd see them."

I don't tell her I'm the idiot. I ask her what our journalist friends have been up to. She shrugs. She doesn't know and she doesn't care. I can hear Jake on the phone to me telling me *Life*'s not a good idea. I ignored him. I always ignore him. If I listened to Jake, our movies would never get any publicity.

"He's angry 'cause some assistant editor didn't show up last night," she says. "We've got enough editors around here to cut ten films."

I figure this assistant editor must be his drug connection. But I don't do my figuring out loud.

She says he went to bed at about six this morning and is still in bed. She flops forward, resting her head on the floor. It occurs to me that everyone in Los Angeles is supple. She says the accountant is quitting. She says she can't get anyone at the studio on the phone. "The only person who will take my calls is some guy in business affairs."

I stop her there. I look around for some way to staunch the flow of complaints. If this were a B movie I would slap her across the face and she'd thank me for it.

I find the reporter and the photographer by the pool. They sit sideways on a pale blue chaise. Getting comfortable might excuse his lateness somehow. I fight a desire to jump into the blue-and-white-tiled pool. The water in the sun looks silver. I look away. I decide to gossip with them a little. No sense in attacking the problem head on.

I tell them I saw Ted Walsh's new picture. "It's great." They nod good-naturedly. They like Walsh's work. They like me. They know this isn't my fault. For a quick second it feels as if time has stopped. I am a publicist again making excuses for a filmmaker. It wouldn't be so bad to go back to that.

They agree to wait. I flag down another young girl. They roam around here like a fleet of taxis. I ask her to get them some lunch and a phone they can use. They had been offered lunch at 10:30 this morning. Anything to buy a little time. Now they're hungry. It's almost 2:30. Fasting isn't going to get him out of the bedroom any quicker.

I tell them I'll go myself and see what's happening. Before I go, the reporter leads me into a cabana. It's about the size of a Manhattan studio. The walls are covered in fabric that looks and feels like bamboo. The ceiling and floor are lacquered white. The photographer stands just outside. He holds his cameras in such a way they look like guns.

The reporter talks low. "It's really nuts around here. This movie's in big trouble. We don't want to do a hatchet piece. It would be better if we didn't do any piece. Believe me."

I don't believe him. How bad can it be? Movies go over budget all the time. Movies are late. Movies get into trouble. Big deal. That's part of the business. This director has made four hit movies in a row. The last one for our studio. He has made millions of dollars for us. Tens of millions. I'm not worried.

"Thanks for telling me. But it will be all right. I'm just sorry you guys had to wait so long."

The photographer drops his artillery to his side. The reporter smiles. His smile says I'm just another studio executive walking around in a body he once knew.

"We'll be here." They walk back into the main part of the house.

Sometimes when people from New York get mad, they act like they're mad at the weather. They act like if the day wasn't so beautiful, none of this would be happening.

I knock on his door. It's just an ordinary door painted a restful shade of green. I knock louder. I wait. I don't know Quinn Lilley. During the release of his last picture, he worked only with Marshall. I knock again. I hate having to introduce myself. I hate having to introduce myself to a big-time director while he's still in bed.

A buzz and the door opens. "Who the fuck are you?"

I slip inside and shut the door behind me. I lean against it for support. Again, "Who the fuck are you?"

It's hard to see him. The room is large and he's lying on his stomach. Pink pinstripe sheets cover most of his body. He looks naked underneath. From what I can see of his body, it looks fine. Fit and tan.

I tell him who I am. I remind him of our appointment. I remind him of the two journalists cooling their heels in another part of the mansion for over five hours. I remind him of the time.

"Thanks for the update. Now be a good girl and get the fuck out of here." All this said into a pink pinstriped pillow.

A part of me wants to be a good girl and leave. Wants to get back into my cute little Ferrari and drive back down the mountain, maybe making a detour to that store on Melrose to get John a present. And then back to the studio for the afternoon meeting with Jake. But that other part of me stands against the door, ready to laugh. Ready to stay. Ready to win him over.

"Well then, Slim, stay. I don't give a shit." His face turns toward me. It looks older than it should, the eyes are bloodshot, the beard about three days' growth, but God, what a beautiful face. For a second I want to jump in bed with him. He turns on his back, tugging at the sheets.

I walk over and pick up the phone sitting on his bedside table. A young voice answers. I ask for a pot of coffee, orange juice with some vodka in it and rye toast. I cover the phone. "Anything else you want?"

"Cocaine." He looks at me as if I left my clothes at the door.

CREATIVE DIFFERENCES

I hang up and sit down in an armchair next to the bed. The chair is surprisingly feminine. His black hair is thick. The specks of gray look like slivers of ice I could melt with my tongue.

"Got a cigarette, Slim?" I shake my head. I like his voice. He starts to get up without a sheet.

"Okay, where are they?" He points to his bureau. I go over and pick up a pack of Dunhills and toss them onto the bed. Just out of reach.

He bends a match with one hand, strikes it and lights his cigarette. I knew a girl in prep school who always lit her cigarettes that way. I thought it was so cool. I still do.

He begins to talk. I guess I expected him to be incoherent or something. He's not. Except when he talks about the movie he's trying to finish. Then he sounds a little crazy. A little like an outlaw running from a posse.

I slip off my shoes and put my feet up on the side of the bed. He makes easy room for me like I've been putting my feet here for thirty years. I tell him about a poem I was reading on the plane trip out here. I recite four lines. He asks me to say them again. I do. He repeats them. My eyes are drawn into a waltz with his.

Over the years I've worked with a lot of filmmakers. I have had a chance to watch them. To watch how they handle their talent. Some fight against it. Some are overwhelmed. Some carry it around like a cross. Quinn tries to outfox his. He thinks he could live another kind of life. He thinks he could live in a small village in Ireland, run a pub, mine coal, have children, eat dinner at dusk, mend fences. Just live. But he couldn't. There is no other life for him. This is the only life for him.

We talk. He tells me about his first job on a movie. How he got into a fight with the director and was fired. I tell him about my first job in the movie business. We spin tales and trust and stay clear of the present. He tells me stories about Ireland. I tell him stories about my childhood. He stops me now and then to ask a question, to be sure he has understood me. My watch says I've been in here two hours.

I work my stocking feet under the sheet. Quinn straightens his legs and now his calves are resting over my feet. I feel the warmth of his legs.

"Hey, Slim, why don't you get in here with me?" He holds up the sheet. It is an easy, uncomplicated invitation. His words erase the world for me. His words have erased every notion of obligation and for a second I am in a new world and here there is no past, no one measures time, there are no memories. I'd like to make love to him; incredibly, I feel like I have already made love to him. I could tell him how it feels, how we fit. A memory of him drives me forward.

"I can't."

"Why?"

"Because I'm pregnant." I surprise myself. Only John and I know this. It's a secret I am pleased Quinn has found out.

He sits up cross-legged and pelts me with a million questions. "God, that's great! When are you due? What are you going to name her? Will you nurse? Have you felt her move inside of you yet?"

I am out of breath. I feel great. Quinn makes me feel as if no one has ever been pregnant before me. I grope for answers.

"How do you know it's going to be a girl," I ask.

"I have five younger sisters, Slim. I saw my mother give birth to five sisters. I know how a woman looks when she's pregnant with a girl."

I fight an impulse to run over to the mirror and look at myself. But now Quinn is telling me how children are the pieces to the puzzle we are all struggling to put together. His voice is almost a lullaby.

"Do you have kids, Quinn?"

"Yes, two." Now, it's my turn to ask the questions.

He cuts me off. "I don't see them, Slim. Not for years."

"Why not?"

"Their mother didn't want me to love them if I wasn't going to love her."

I see bits of him draining away. "You tell me when you want me to go." I hold my breath, suddenly afraid he will tell me to go now. He doesn't answer. The effort to remain whole is too much for him. He wants some drugs. This isn't the time to be Florence Nightingale. I ask him if I can get someone to get him something.

"I think there may be something in the bureau. Top drawer. In a black box. Could you see, Slim?" He touches my hand and a shiver propels me out of the armchair.

Walking over to the bureau, I ask him if I should send the reporters away. If I should send all the young girls home for a while.

"Get some rest, Quinn. Jake will understand." Even as I say this, I don't believe it. The movie business isn't about one person working for another person anymore. I'm not sure it ever was. But now it's about banks and partnerships and interest payments and product thrown on and off the shelves in a hurry.

"Jake won't understand for a fucking second. All Jake understands is that I owe him a movie."

That's funny. Quinn isn't as cynical as I am. He thinks he's working for just one guy who had the nerve to gamble on him.

"He'll get his goddamned movie."

I'm not listening to him anymore. I find the black box, but now I am staring at the small gun sitting next to it. It startles me. In a strange way, I think it's attractive. Small, silver, curved. I wonder if it has bullets. I wonder what it's doing here. I pick up the coke box and close the drawer gently, not wanting to disturb anything.

Quinn offers me some. A heroic gesture on his part. I shake my head.

"Give me ten minutes to get dressed, then I'll meet your reporter. Okay, Slim?"

"Sure," I say.

"You know something about me, don't you?"

I'm not sure what he means. But suddenly I think I do know something. But it's not about him, it's about us. I shiver, trying to loosen myself from eeriness. Why do I feel like I've known Quinn all my life?

I ask him about the movie, trying to get back to where I was before I lost track of myself. I ask him how he wants me to sell it.

"What should I tell Jake?"

He reaches over to the bedside table and hands me a flat, brown package. "Take this. It'll tell you."

I reach for the package. He moves it out of my reach and says, "I want to kiss you." I lean down obligingly. The phone rings. He picks it up and talks, loud and certain. The coke or the coffee or something has revived him. He waves me out the door.

"I'm glad you decided to join us." Jake's sarcasm hits me in the stomach. I fight nausea. I sit down at the other end of the conference table. Next to Molly. I am forty-five minutes late.

"We hear you've seen Ted Walsh's movie." Jake's hands are painted to the sides of his chair. I get the feeling he's trying hard not to leap across the table and strangle me. I still don't answer. Len tries to catch my eye. I look straight ahead into nothingness. If I had a mantra I would be chanting it now.

One of the production executives, a young girl, not very pretty, with hair as straight as string, starts to talk. She must have been talking just now when I walked in. Reluctantly, Jake tears his eyes away from me and looks at the girl. Her poise deserts her. Jake chews his bottom lip. The young girl is telling the plot of a movie we have in development. She reads off the elements attached: the director, the writer, the producers.

"What's a movie without at least four producers?" This is the first thing I've said since I came in. It is greeted with laughter. The young girl swivels her whole body to look at me. She's even younger than I thought. I feel a little sorry for her. It's the first time I can remember feeling sorry for someone young. I'm accustomed to thinking of myself as young. She doesn't get my joke. She will once filming starts.

Another production executive talks. Molly leans in to me and whispers that they haven't gone over our area. "Jake wanted to wait for you." Molly puts her hand, as cool as a shadow, on my forearm. I think she wonders if I'm the same person she saw a few hours ago.

Driving back to the studio I thought I would ask Len and Jake if we could have a drink somewhere and then I would tell them about Quinn and the mess the movie's in. Looking at Len and Jake, I don't think this is in the cards. Over the years I've noticed that men often prefer to hear bad news with a lot of people around them.

212

CREATIVE DIFFERENCES

Another production executive begins a story. He tells it beautifully. For a second I forget about Quinn. It's hard to say if the movie could ever be as good as his telling of it. This production executive has a talent. No one, except Jake and me, seems to be paying much attention to the pitch.

"I'd go see that movie."

Jake nods at what I say. We begin to make it up through the work. Even so he keeps punishing his lower lip.

I get up and walk over to the buffet. I dish some raspberries into a glass bowl. I like how the red fruit looks in the bowl, like scattered rubies at the bottom of a clear pond. I'm not hungry. I'm weak. I feel as if I left some part of me with Quinn.

I sit back down and look at the note Molly has put in front of me. It says she's taking the red-eye back tonight. Molly's been living with Joe for almost a year now. He's good for her. He doesn't work in the movie business. She wants out. She wants a job she won't have to care about so much.

I pull a piece of graph paper out of my notebook and scribble I'm sorry we didn't get to talk today. I underline sorry. I hand it to her. Suddenly I feel I might cry. I push my hair off my forehead like I think whatever's making me sad is sitting there.

I do my dog-and-pony show. I do it well. You do these things so many times, you can almost do them with your eyes closed. I save Quinn Lilley for last. I remember the package and open it. Inside is a video cassette. In pencil is written: How to Sell My Movie. Instinct tells me to put this cassette right back into its brown wrapping. I don't. Instead I hand it to Len. Let him decide what to do with it. I smile. Handing over things to someone else doesn't come easily to me.

Len drops the cassette into the belly of a large black video system. Len never seems to think anything over. I wonder if maybe his brain looks different from mine on the inside.

On comes Quinn Lilley. Clean-shaven, clear-eyed, gorgeous. The camera holds his face close, he might almost be in the room with us. He starts to tell what his movie is about. He says it's about working people. And love. And maybe heroism. Without warning, in the middle of a sentence, the tape goes black. Soon we are all staring at the white fuzz of unrecorded tape.

"What the fuck is that all about?" Jake growls at me.

I shake my head. "I don't know, Jake. I don't know what that is."

Len says, "It's a video of Quinn Lilley talking about his movie."

Can he really be this stupid? The production executives look at each other. I laugh, trying to save Len some embarrassment. Make up for earlier when Harry Cajun was so vile about him and I didn't do anything about it.

Molly gets up. I think she's going to leave. She doesn't. She walks over and turns off the video machine. I love her self-possession. I wonder if she was always so smooth. I think so. I wonder then why so many men have roughed her up over the years. It occurs to me that if she leaves work, we have a better chance of staying friends.

Jake is ranting. He's yelling at me. Asking me if I'm deaf or something. "I want to know what's going on with Quinn and I want to know now."

I tell him. I tell him about how Quinn sleeps all day and tries to work at night. How his concentration is shot. How he hollers at all the young girls who try to help him but know nothing about editing a movie. How he's spending money like crazy and has nothing to show for it. How the guys from *Life* spent three hours hanging out at the house — "just hanging out, Jake — and they know he can't finish the movie. He wants to finish it, but he can't." I tell him everything. I leave out the part about us. Then I stand up. I don't know why exactly. It just seems right. I don't raise my voice. I just say, "I'm sure Quinn's the same as he was when you last saw him."

I'm greeted with silence. It's the kind of silence that falls over a group when they realize as one that something bad is about to happen. Everyone at the table longs to be invisible.

I sit down. A strange relaxation runs up and down my body like so many taut rubber bands cut in two. I wait for Jake. It occurs to me that I am waiting for him to say something kind, something healing. I want him to say he will take care of Quinn. That the movie will be fine. We will all be fine. We will all work together and something great will come of it. Jake isn't going to say anything like this.

"I want to know how you're going to sell Quinn Lilley's movie," Jake says.

Now it's my turn to wonder if he's deaf. He hasn't heard one word I said. In business, people don't like to hear about chaos. They can't really take it in. If they could, they probably wouldn't be working in offices. That's the promise the bureaucracy makes. You won't have to deal with chaos.

Len looks at me. He knows I'm telling the truth. He knows there's a problem. I can tell he doesn't understand why Jake is acting as if he doesn't know or doesn't care. Len speaks up. I'm surprised.

"Who is the production executive on this picture?"

The storyteller says he is.

Len questions him, "When did you see Quinn last?"

"I'm on the picture. But I'm not on it. It's really Jake's picture."

Len persists. "When did you see Quinn last?"

The storyteller lights a cigarette. His hands are fair. I wonder how they have escaped the California sun. "I haven't been out to see him in two months."

"Two months!" Len is almost shouting.

"That's great. Just great." I'm talking to Jake, but he's looking at the production executive. Jake is surprised at how quickly the storyteller just squirmed away from any responsibility. What did Jake think he'd do?

"Two months. Two weeks. Who cares?" Jake bangs the table dismissing this information. I imagine he has just dismissed this talented production executive's career with the same bang.

"Just tell me how you're planning to sell the movie and we can all go home."

This must be how professional torturers keep their victims conscious. Vague promises of relief.

"It doesn't matter how I'm going to sell the movie because there isn't going to be a movie."

"There'll be a movie. Don't worry." Jake sounds so sure, so reasonable that suddenly everyone is looking at me like I'm a small child with a high fever.

"Don't you get it, Jake? Quinn Lilley is—" I stop.

"Is what?"

"Is —" I can't locate the words. I know there's a freight train coming at us but no one believes me. Len wants to believe me. But he isn't sure. Jake and Quinn are old friends. Len drags on his cigarette. Business is all about taking sides. Len throws in with Jake.

"Is what?"

"Quinn Lilley is tired."

They don't know whether I'm making a joke or not. I look around the table. We might as well all be mercenaries. Whatever is good about being a company, having a structure, is lost on us. We are all going about our work alone. When we agree about something, it is only by chance. Quinn Lilley needs us, but we can't get out of our own way.

"Tired?" Jake laughs. An authentic laugh of relief. "We're all tired." Jake relaxes. He can go from zero to sixty and back down to zero quicker than my rented red Ferrari.

16

*F*or the last three days I have come up to Quinn's house after I finish my work at the studio. I was supposed to have gone home four days ago. But I changed my plans to work with Quinn. Quinn called Jake and told him I should get a big raise, because I was the reason he had gone back to work. Jake doesn't give much credence to this. He doesn't think people do things for other people. Maybe they open doors or pass the salt for other people, but they don't do anything really important. Important things they do for themselves. I never argue with Jake about this. He's probably right.

I get there about 8:00 P.M. The feel of the house, the way people look, what they are eating, it could be 11:00 in the morning. I change my clothes in Quinn's bedroom. Tonight, I notice he has pushed his clothes to one side. There are three empty hangers for me. For some reason I think that if I could only put all my belongings on three hangers everything would be fine.

"Yes?" A young girl with plaid bows decorating the ends of her red braids stands at the door.

"Quinn wants you. He wants to know when you want to eat dinner."

I don't answer. Instead I follow the young production assistant down the hall. She cuts through the dining room on her way to the guest bedroom suite that has been turned into the editing room. I notice someone has set dazzling silver at two places. Lace place mats seem to hover inches above the antique tiger oak table. They are held down by gold and red china. Fat crystal goblets are stuffed with matching lace napkins. Quinn has beautiful things. He likes to show off for me. A couple of nights ago I mentioned how much I hated eating in restaurants, but how much I enjoyed a nice meal.

"Hello." Quinn doesn't answer me. Without taking his eyes off the editing machine, he reaches back and touches me. I feel like his good-luck charm. Quinn tells me everything he has done on the film since I saw him yesterday. Without trying, I memorize everything he says.

It occurs to me that I have been standing on my feet for almost two hours. There is a chair against the wall that I could sit in. But I don't. I'd rather stand near Quinn. Quinn sits in front of me next to his editor. His editor is about twenty-five years old. He wears his long blond hair in a ponytail. He is very pale. I know he has been working on Quinn's movie for weeks now, but even so his paleness seems to date back to when he was a kid. When he was a kid I bet a computer was his best friend. Quinn can be very difficult to work for, very loud, very demanding. With his young editor, he is gentle and patient. I imagine this is the way Quinn might be with his own son if he ever got to spend time with him.

The editor's fingers are long and slender and they work the controls on the editing machine with incredible deftness. I am almost hypnotized by his hands. Watching him, I decide Quinn's movie will be okay after all.

"Telephone call for you." I shake my head no at the young man who stands with his hand over the receiver. "It's your husband."

I take the phone. Pulling at the tangled cord, I try to walk out of the room, but it won't reach.

"I was asleep. But a dream woke me up. The hotel gave me this number. Where are you?" I stare at the back of Quinn's head. It is steady.

"I'm working." Quinn pushes his chair back from the editing machine and it brushes against me. He walks out of the room. My hand nearly crushes the phone.

"Oh, Honey. You must be dead." John's voice rights me. I find my balance long enough to tell him I'm fine, to tell him I miss him. For about five seconds I think about telling him how I feel. But I don't. I guess I don't really know how I feel. How I feel about Quinn. We hang up. I try to untangle the cord again.

"Want some dinner?" Quinn's smile is tender. I am drawn to him. I follow him into the dining room. He pulls out my chair and as I sit down, I hear a hitch in his breathing. I pull my napkin free of the goblet. I want to talk about us. About Quinn and me. Last night we sat and watched the sun come up. Quinn talked about Ireland. I said very little. I was pretty happy to just sit with my hands over my stomach.

Quinn spills a little red wine into my glass. "Pregnant women shouldn't drink." For a second I hate him for trying to take care of me. He lifts his glass and offers a silent toast. He smiles and for a moment I wonder what it would be like to live with him. What it would be like to ruin my life with John for him. I raise my glass and in that quick moment I know I won't ever find out.

"Got to go back to work." He's gone. I sit fiddling with the lacy corner of the place mat. It's not easy coming upon new parts in yourself. It's not easy finding out your heart is still looking even when it has no reason to look.

I am dreaming. In my dream I am looking for something. Desperately looking.

The phone rings. I jerk awake. "Hello?" My heart slaps at my chest. It's Jake. His voice is low.

"Jake? What's wrong?" I sit up against the wood and wicker headboard. I feel the bones in my spine. My heart is twice its natural size. "What is it, Jake?"

"It's Quinn."

I hold my breath when I'm afraid. "What about him?"

"He's dead. He killed himself."

I suck wildly for air. I get out of bed and drag the phone behind me. I push open one of the windows. Some burnt air floats up into my nostrils, making me nauseous.

"I need your help." The way he asks I know he knows he's got it. "We'll have to tell the press something."

"What time is it, Jake?" He tells me it's almost five o'clock. I start to make a list in my head of the people I can call in New York. I reach for the handle of the window and pull it closed. I try not to remember the day my brother was hit by a car and everyone waited for him to die. It took him three days to die. My parents waited. Mostly sitting on the porch. Not fighting for him. I was sadder about how my parents were giving up on him than I was about him dying. I remember thinking they would probably give up on me just as easily.

I tell Jake who I am going to call and ask him what I should tell them. "Don't call them. Wait."

"Wait for what?" These are my mother's words from a long time ago. But they seem right for now. "Jake, it will be better if I call. Let me take some of the sensationalism out of this."

"Can I pick you up in an hour?" I tell him I'll be waiting downstairs for him. I hang up. I take my red notebook and get back into bed. I feel a cramp. I look into the bathroom like I expect the aspirin to come walking out on its own.

I call eight people at their homes. I apologize for calling so early and tell them about Quinn Lilley. "It's too early to know for sure whether it was a suicide, but it looks that way."

Five to six. Almost nine in New York. I call John. No answer. I put on a pair of jeans and a Chinese red blouse John bought me years ago. I brush my hair. I find a small antique pin in my quilted jewelry pouch and fasten it to my jacket. I'm in the hall walking toward the elevator when I turn around and go back to my room.

I unlock the door and go into the bathroom. I feel another cramp. I look at the aspirin. I put some cover stick under my eyes and put my lipstick in the hip pocket of my jeans.

I'm downstairs before Jake drives up. He picks me up in a long black limo. For a second I think the funeral has started. I wave at the driver to stay put. I get into the car. Jake reaches over and gently puts his hand on the back of my head, working his fingers under my hair until he is at my skull. He's been crying.

"Where are we going?" I take the glass of orange juice he offers me from the bar.

"To the morgue."

"To the morgue?" I repeat dumbly. Easy breathing deserts me. "Why?"

He looks out at Los Angeles. A silvery dawn is heaving itself up over the smoggy night. "Someone has to identify the body."

"Isn't there someone else who can do it?" I say this as much for him as myself.

He shakes his head. "I was Quinn's best friend. And you don't think I was much of one, do you?"

I settle back into the bigness of the limo and look out the window. To tell the truth, I don't know what I think. We ride in silence. Jake smokes. "Isn't there anyone else?"

Jake doesn't answer.

"Isn't there somebody?" I wonder if there isn't a brother or sister or a mother? Someone who can say, "That's Quinn. He belongs to me."

"No." Somewhere between my asking and Jake's answering I turn cold. The idea of being that alone takes up residence inside me.

"I tried to be a good friend. I just couldn't watch him squander his talent. It was bad enough I was paying for him to do it." Jake's confession is fast. We are out of the car, walking up some stone steps.

We stand close in the elevator. "Jake, I think I'm going to be sick."

"No, you're not." He takes my hand. There is something infinitely kind in the way he holds it. I want to tell him about Quinn and me. But I don't know what to say. It's pretty quiet in here. Everyone talks low, like we're in church. I guess we are in a kind of church. You feel a sense of awe being this close to death. I don't let go of Jake, but I don't look either.

"It's him. Still a handsome son of a bitch," he says to no one in particular. It is just what I wanted to hear. I don't think it's true. Gunshots aren't usually pretty. Suicide makes you so curious. What exactly was it that made him want to exchange this world for some other? And when? Did he know he'd had enough when I was with him last night? I don't understand it. He was working again. And we were having fun together. I can't help but think he shouldn't have given up so easily. I can't visualize Quinn killing himself. But I can hear the gun going off. I hear it and each time my spine stiffens as though I am hit, too. John is always telling me there are worse things than death. Right now I'm having trouble thinking of any.

The walk back out to the limo seems long. Pushing through the heavy glass doors I remember my dream. I am looking for something. I am looking for my baby. I have lost my baby. It's hard to find. My baby is no bigger than a grain of rice and it is lost in a rug. I'm losing the baby. I don't cry, but I can't seem to catch my breath. My heart is broken in two new places. I think of John.

The world outside seems the same. I guess I half expected it to look different. I guess you always expect the world to notice when something important happens to you. Good or bad. If it does notice, you'd never know it.

The sun is beautiful. It is the kind of day California has in the thousands.

17

"*I* understand that the article in *Metropolitan* will be out Monday."

Molly nods. About a month ago I gave an interview to this magazine for a piece about movie executives. It is the only interview I've ever given and now I'm sorry I did it.

I look at Molly. Her dress is a bright floral print. Her shoes are a pale lavender. Three days ago, Molly's friend, Joe, decided they shouldn't see each other anymore. I'm not sure why. Neither is Molly. After a few tortured days, though, Molly will see she's better off without him. I think about telling her this, but when your heart is breaking you don't want to be told how much better off you're going to be when it's finally and completely broken.

The amazing thing is that she's in the office at all. I thought she would have stayed home and, in the privacy of her home, monitor her sadness, the way a nurse keeps track of a high fever. I wonder what she's thinking. Molly and I used to talk about love all the time. We used to examine love. We didn't talk too much about John's and my love. It always seemed the same. Nothing to say. Besides, I think talking about our love would be like breathing on a snowflake. We talked about Molly's loves. About generic love. But one day she stopped talking about love. It was almost as if she was suddenly superstitious that talking about love might keep it away. Not talking about love created a small desert in our friendship.

"I want an advance copy. Can you get me one?" Molly makes a note on a yellow legal pad. The silver Tiffany pen was a gift from me.

"I'll try, Pet." This is not the answer I'm looking for. It would be easier to get things done if we weren't friends. About a year ago Molly wanted to leave. She said it would be easier for me. I didn't believe her. I talked her out of leaving. Turns out, she was right.

It occurs to me that I want the person who is my second to be ready to walk through fire for me. To do whatever it takes to get the job done. Stay up all night, frighten whoever needs frightening, call in every favor, promise the moon, but get the job done. Molly's not like that. She doesn't want to walk through fire for herself, let alone for a job that drives her crazy.

"I saw Marshall in the elevator." Molly tells me he wants to have a meeting tomorrow morning. A pre-meeting before the one with Jake in the afternoon.

"I can't do it. I have an appointment." I pick up the phone and buzz Len. He comes on.

"Hi, Babe." I tell him about Marshall wanting the meeting and how I can't do it.

"No problem. I'll call Marshall." I hang up. Having Len for a boss turned out okay. I finally have someone who takes my side. I like it even if I know he is only taking my side because it's often the opposite of Marshall. About six months ago Len talked Jake into moving Marshall back out to Los Angeles permanently. I don't know how he did it. Len agreed to keep reporting to Marshall, if only he wouldn't have to deal with him every day. When Marshall got to L.A., Jake sent him to Europe. And then to Japan. And then to Australia. And then back to Europe. Marshall racked up a lot of bonus miles. Now Marshall is back in New York trying to regain his power. He's wasting his time.

Molly comes closer to my desk. Her strawberry blond hair looks exactly the way it did when I used to see her in the ladies' room or by the elevator before I knew her. She tells me I should be more respectful of Marshall. I want to laugh. "Are you kidding?"

"He's still your boss," she says.

"No, he used to be my boss. He's Len's boss. And Len is my boss. Let Len and Marshall work it out." I ignore Emma's buzz. You think over time your feelings repair themselves. I'm always surprised to find mine are as ragged as ever.

"You know what Len is trying to do to Marshall," she says.

A coldness pulls my shoulder blades together. I know what Len is trying to do. It occurs to me that one of the reasons Molly and I first became friends is because we believed in the structure. We believed in adhering to the rules. Even if we thought the rules were stupid. Even if we thought the men who made up the rules were stupid. We believed in the system. Lately, I'm beginning to see that there are no rules, no absolute rules. I used to think that the same code I used growing up, the code of what's right, what's wrong, what's acceptable, a code everyone uses as they use the same language would see me through business. It hasn't worked out that way. Eventually, you have to learn a new code. Usually your boss teaches it to you. It's a primitive code, as if some savages put it together.

"Molly, whatever Len's doing to Marshall is really none of my business."

She looks at me hard. I lean back in my chair almost afraid she's going to slap me. She doesn't understand that I just want to get through each day in one piece so there's something left over for John. Besides, my being nice to Marshall isn't going to make one bit of difference. Except maybe make Len hate me for being disloyal.

"Molly, I want the article."

She says okay, but her eyes are like hard balls smacked in a pitcher's glove about a thousand times. She's almost out the door when I try to call her back. I want to make her laugh. Tell her one of our stories. But I don't.

Emma buzzes again. "Jake on oh-eight."

Jake's voice pulls me away from myself. That's one of the things I like about work. Work comes right on in and whips you around. It doesn't care if you're ready. You either jump on or get dragged along, but you go.

We do some business. But Jake hasn't called about business. It was a year ago today that Quinn Lilley killed himself. He wants to talk about Quinn. So do I. I buzz Emma to come and close my door. We talk. I'm trying to build Quinn. Jake's trying to rebuild him. When we hang up, I feel disloyal to John. And I decide, like I do after every Jake call, to tell John about my secret love for a dead man.

I am sitting in the lobby of a quiet, tasteful hotel on Madison. I am waiting for the head of another studio to come down from his suite. I have talked on the phone to this man several times about my coming to work for him.

When I called him on the house phone just now he said he would be half an hour. Something has come up and could I possibly wait. I could wait, yes.

I ask the concierge if someone can get me a cup of coffee. The concierge looks at me like I have "ax murderer" engraved on my forehead. I give her a look that says while I know all of this is obviously much too menial for her to handle, it is, after all, her job. She notes the look in her mental ledger and goes for the coffee.

I sit with my coffee. There was one other time I was interested in getting a different job. I'm interested now because a movie mogul is pursuing me, wooing me. He tells me how great I am, he tells me how much he needs me. Now, who can resist that? I'm appreciated where I work now the way a man appreciates the wife he's been married to for twenty years. He appreciates that she has kept her figure, makes great meals, takes care of the kids and fixes anything that breaks in the house without bothering him about it. But Mr. Movie Mogul appreciates me in a different way. He thinks I'm sexy. He doesn't care if I fix him hot dogs every night. He wants a mistress, not a wife. He wants to keep the romance alive. He calls all the time to tell me how great I am. I like to hear this even if it's coming from a man who has been known to look at eleven different suites in one hotel before agreeing to sleep in one of them, a man who has been heard to say if the screenplay needs a writer like F. Scott Fitzgerald, then let's get this Scott Fitzgerald's agent on the phone right now. I can't let a little ignorance or a little neurosis get in the way of this movie mogul romancing me.

There was one other time when I was interested in getting a different job. That time was right after I thought John was having an affair. I had convinced myself it was all my fault. All my job's fault. It was odd, though. I didn't want to get another job. There had been plenty of times when I should have raced out of that building, but that wasn't one of them. Suddenly the company was making money. It seemed that kids were constantly lined up at the movies. As long as that line stayed long, I thought everything was right with the world. I liked Jake a lot and Len turned out to be an okay boss. He was really happy about the hit movies. And besides, after a while I could tell Len was more interested in finding a way to get rid of Marshall than he was in bossing me around.

But even so, eight months after I thought John had had an affair, I decided I should do something to prove I loved him no matter what. Now why does a woman, who thinks her husband has cheated on her, feel she has to prove something. It's beyond me. But there it is. There I am. I decided to go and see a headhunter. Someone who hunted heads for businesses other than the movies.

Waiting in his office, I look around. Four other people wait. All are dressed in conservative business suits. I'm wearing a cashmere skirt and sweater that John bought me. I'm not dressed properly. Doesn't matter my outfit is by a well-known designer and probably cost more than one of these applicant's biweekly salary, I am dressed wrong. The movie business makes you do a lot of things, but it doesn't make you wear a uniform. I'm worried if this will keep me from getting a new job. Suddenly, not wearing a suit means I won't be able to fix our love. I won't be able to atone for our mistakes.

The headhunter is reading my résumé. The one I wrote up last night while John sat in his chair making jokes, acting like I had lost my mind. On the walls are several African masks. I guess you could call his interior designer humorous. He asks me questions about job expectation, job satisfaction.

He says, "Before changing careers, one should always make a list of the pros and cons of the career you have." He hesitates a bit on the word "career." I don't think he thinks the movie business is a career.

He begins to quiz me. He asks me a million questions. I try to answer fast, thinking this is like a Rorschach test. He holds up the yellow legal pad he's been taking notes on. There is nothing under con. I stare at the pad. It says I can go back to doing what I like to do even if I don't like to do it. It says my job is not responsible for John's affair. Without saying a word, I get up and leave his office.

Looking back, I see it's possible that John didn't have an affair. He was probably tempted. Temptation comes along all the time. When we avoid it, we feel pretty pleased with ourselves. Sometimes we feel we're better than the person we just avoided temptation for. But whether or not he was tempted or actually made love to someone else doesn't really matter because I know something scared him. Something like finding out it's possible to fall in love with someone when you're already in love with someone else. It can happen in a moment, and like a small caliber bullet, it blew a hole inside his confidence about us.

Everybody has a different way of figuring out how to put things back the way they were. I think John's way was for us to have a baby. My way hadn't worked out, maybe his would.

I scan the lobby for a phone booth. Maybe I should call the office and tell Emma I'm going to be late. That way I could see if John has called.

This morning I got up early and made tea for John and me. We've promised to cut down on our caffeine. This is a promise John will live up to. He takes promises seriously. I don't take this one seriously. We were sitting in bed, drinking mint tea, watching TV. John asked me about trying to get pregnant again. I looked at him like he was speaking Chinese. Then I looked around the room like I was trying to locate our translator.

"Don't you think we ought to try again, Honey?" His voice is wise. It opens up rooms inside of me.

"No." My voice is loud and I imagine he must think it ugly.

"Want to tell me why?" The doors to the rooms slam shut, one after another. It's a fair question. He wants me to tell him why I'm not ready. If I tell him, maybe it'll make the two of us stronger. Tell him even if it diminishes me. Even if I will be less. Less lovable.

"I'm just not ready. I wasn't ready then. I don't want to have a baby. I don't think I ever did. I was doing it for you. I was doing it because you go along in life and you do these kinds of things. Things that mark you were here. I'm glad I had a miscarriage. I'm glad." I stop. I didn't know I was glad. Relieved, maybe. But glad? I feel sick to my stomach. There are tears on my face and somehow my cup of tea is on its side and my nightgown is wet. My thigh is burning.

John gets out of bed slowly. His great green eyes peel away from my face and I feel as if some wondrous green paint that has been on my face for years has just been stripped away. He takes the tray and goes into the kitchen. I want to scream or run a million miles away or put my hand in fire. What is the matter with me? I hear the tea dishes being thrown into the sink. All I can think about is my favorite mug being broken. And to wonder if there's any epoxy in one of the bins under the sink.

Somehow we get dressed. I pull back my thick hair into a sedate, low ponytail. I think about the interview I am having in an hour and I think about how John has no idea how much I love him. Or how sorry I am that I didn't know my secrets were so violent, so brutal.

At the door, John puts his hand around the back of my neck. "I'll see you tonight." I let him go first. I pretend to have forgotten something.

The concierge sets another cup of coffee in front of me. She tells me Mr. Mogul needs more time. I nod. I've been waiting an hour. I feel rooted to this couch. I'm content to wait. Content to sit and figure out how I might make it up to John. This morning, the hole in his confidence got bigger.

It could have been me. The days I spent with Quinn Lilley I was falling in love. I didn't really know it then. I didn't know it until I started to talk to Jake about Quinn. I figure the reason I found Quinn so attractive was because he treated me in a way only John had before. Quinn was interested in me. He was interested in me the way he might have been interested in music or mysticism or astronomy. He paid attention to me. He made me pay attention to myself. Quinn introduced me to myself. Sounds odd, I guess. But it's true. You go along in life knowing who you are the way you know the days of the week, by rote. Then you fall in love with someone and he shows you who you really are. And then that love gets to be a habit until someone else comes along. I didn't know any of this then. But when Quinn treated my feelings as if they were original and precious, I knew some part of me had been asleep. Not a bad sleep. But asleep all the same. Quinn woke me up with a start.

I guess deep down I think I lost the baby because of how I felt about Quinn. It seems one way of explaining things. After Jake and I identified Quinn's body, I went back to the hotel to deal with something unidentifiable. Something that was deserting my body at a crushingly slow pace. Life eking out.

I meet the doctor in the Emergency Room. He's dressed in white. Not white like a lab coat, white like tennis clothes. Even so, I like him and he's soft-spoken. Lying on the table while he examines me, it occurs to me that perhaps something is also wrong with my breathing. I feel like I've been holding my breath for hours.

He explains about the D&C and I nod my head as though I understand perfectly, as though we are talking about an ad campaign. He says he can do it with either a general or local anesthesia. Almost cheerily, I say I want to be awake. This is the part of me that turns everything into a business meeting. He chats about what movies he's seen lately and then he says a miscarriage is not uncommon. He wouldn't believe me if I told him a crazy Irish director killed himself last night and somehow took my baby with him. He takes my hand as he's about to leave. He's saying that the pregnancy had only just begun. The way he says "just begun" makes me think he's glad because it's been easier on him. For some stupid reason, I thank him and he's gone.

John flew out to L. A. to fly back with me to New York. We went to Quinn's funeral and then Jake drove us to the airport. When we got back to New York, I didn't talk to John much about losing the baby. I was too confused. And later when I wasn't as confused, so much time had passed it seemed stupid to bring it up.

CREATIVE DIFFERENCES

So I lost Quinn and the baby within forty-eight hours. I knew them both about equally well. That is, hardly at all. Yet they are still with me. How can I explain this to John? How can I explain that I can't get pregnant until this tiny ghost sitting weightless on my heart goes away?

A young woman looks around the lobby. She's dressed in a conservative suit but wears high heels and brushes her hair against its part so it stands up full like a model's. She sees me and walks straight toward me. She is carrying a folder. She is not carrying a purse. I wonder how she paid for the taxi. Does she keep her money rolled up in her fist?

"Molly said you wanted to see this." Suddenly I realize this is the article.

"Did you read it?" The young woman hesitates, but she is not nervous. She's trying to figure out what answer will do her the most good. Make the best impression on me. I am, after all, the boss. I don't give her a clue which answer I am hoping for.

"Yes, I did."

"And?" I'm not sure why I don't like this young woman very much. She doesn't seem sufficiently tortured by the politics of business. She's too smooth. I get the queasy feeling she's a business school graduate. You know, the kind who has sat in class and been taught about politics, about office espionage. It's all the rage now. She's cool. Cool, but not like hip; cool like not hot. Cold.

"It's a good article. You come off real strong."

"Great. Anything else?" My voice, if bottled properly, could be used to cool drinks, cool rooms, cool continents. She steps away from the icy blast. In a few years this woman will walk through fire for her boss.

"Molly told me to remind you that you're meeting with Reggie Nouri at five." I met Reggie Nouri a few years ago when he managed rock bands, one of which had written a score for one of our movies. I didn't have a real big job then, but I was the one who decided about videos . . . whether to make them, how much to spend, who should direct them. I had every intention of making a video with Reggie's band, only he didn't believe me. He wanted to show me how tough he was. He was wasting his time. I already thought he was tough. Reggie looked as if he had drugs in one pocket and a gun in the other. We invited some press to the set. We gave them a cocktail party. Just a few journalists and the filmmakers. At this party Reggie started talking to me. I wasn't very interested. Then he said something that got my attention. He pointed to his pregnant wife who was walking toward him. "I sure hope she has a boy so I don't have to fuck her again." I made two videos for Reggie, the tough guy. Until recently he was one of Hollywood's most successful producers. Only now he wants to star in one of his movies. Okay by me. But Jake is sending him to me so I can tell him I can't sell a movie with him in it. So I can tell Reggie, the tough guy, to forget about acting. Sure.

"Yes, I know. Tell Molly I'll be there. And thank her for the advance copy." I raise the folder in a kind of dwarfed salute to the absent Molly.

The young woman leaves. I take out the article. It's still in galley form. In the margin is a note about a b&w photo of me they will be running. I hope Emma sent them the right one. I read it. The girl said it was a good article. The piece begins with a rundown on corporate titles and how silly and meaningless these titles really are. Reading along, I am almost agreeing with her. Then I come to the part where she uses me as an example. She notes that no fewer than four other people in our corporation have the same title. She wonders how this can be. Then she goes on to reveal the smallness of corporate movie life. And I have a starring role in this small life.

The elevator opens; happy for any interruption from reading this piece, I look up and see Marshall stepping out of it. He doesn't see me. He walks to the revolving exit door. There might be invisible pillows under his feet, so lightly is he walking. I didn't realize Mr. "You're-the-Greatest-Kid" Movie Mogul is running a contest. And this is probably just the Parade of States for me. I think Marshall has already gotten to the Isolation Booth.

I uproot myself from the couch and walk over to the concierge. I tell her to tell Mr. Movie Mogul I couldn't wait. Her eyes grow a little taller up by the brows. "You can't wait?" For the first time this morning, I smile at this woman.

"No, I can't." Silently, she changes the sign on my forehead from "ax murderer" to "gutsy dame". Walking away, I wish I were a gutsy dame in a 1940s movie.

I stop at a pay phone on Madison Avenue and dial my office. Emma tells me the calls. Reggie Nouri has canceled his meeting. I listen and then ask her to transfer me to Len's line. When Len comes on I tell him his problem with Marshall has been solved. For a second he sounds disappointed that there won't be a chance for bloodshed. But his spirits pick right up and he says, "That's great, Babe. Just great for both of us." Len thinks I'm more than just the messenger. He thinks I had a hand in this. Len has no idea I wanted the job Marshall has probably just been offered. Len thinks I like working for him. I guess he can think what he likes.

I hang up and start walking uptown, crosstown. It's a beautiful fall day. I start to think up ways I can keep John from ever reading this article. The one way I don't really spend much time on is just to ask him not to read it.

I think about the president with the magnetic blue eyes and the crescent-shaped scar and the article that did him in. I am amazed at how the public never grows tired of reading about the movie business. They act, in fact, like it's their right to have the movie business written about, criticized, dissected and finally revealed as the bad business they're so sure it is. Funny, how outraged I was back then. Sixteen years ago. I really thought everything was black or white, right or wrong. I sat on that cool, black-marble ledge, leaning my face over now and then to catch a glimpse of my new haircut in the marble's reflection, and believed every word I read. The article said he was a tyrant. A braggart and a bad manager. I wonder. That article came out on a Monday and by Friday he had been smacked off the corporate track. This article won't hurt my career. Oddly, it might even help it. But even so I am embarrassed by it. I'm better than this article. My work is worth something. Somewhere along the way I picked up a message, like a ham radio operator might, that work has value and you want those who love you to understand its value.

18

I stop harvesting the tiny bay leaves from my meager windowsill garden. I turn and look at John. "What?"

"I've been offered the fellowship. I'll be gone six months." John is telling me that he's going to Mexico City to finish his book on Mexican poets. I rush over and kiss him. He holds me, one of his hands around the back of my neck. In my memory of John, I always feel his hand around the back of my neck.

"Oh, Honey, that's so great. I'm so proud of you." John has saved us. He has found a way to repair our confidence. A way to forget about this morning and what I said. I can see myself in a loose-fitting gauzy skirt and blouse waiting for it to be five o'clock when he'll be through writing. I can see the flowers I'll tend in terra-cotta pots during the day. I'm planning picnics in Chapultepec Park. John is our savior. A knight, a magician.

"I'm going alone. I'll only be gone six months."

"Alone? What did you say?" I lose sight of myself.

"It's only six months, Honey. What are you going to do, quit your job? And when we get back, what will you do?"

I'd rather he'd have slapped me. He can't leave me here. He can't go without me. "I want to come with you. I don't care about work. I'll figure something out."

"Six hours ago you had an interview for a new job. Wasn't that you?"

"I didn't stay for the interview. I don't want that job. I don't want any job. I just want to go with you."

"You can't. I want to go alone. I just want to go and finish the book and come home. Six months. I'll be back in six months."

I feel something brewing inside of me. A wildness thrashing about deep inside. "John, I don't understand." My voice startles me. It's so calm. It's untouched by the wildness. The wildness spreads, multiplying itself in an instant. The wildness has taken over my organs. It has become my heart, my brain, my blood. Wildness streams down my back instead of my hair. Wildness covers my body instead of skin.

"Let's see, six months. That means you'll be gone for Christmas."

John nods slowly. He reaches for my hand but jerks back suddenly. He sees the wildness. I can tell he sees it. I see the fascination in his eyes.

"You'll be gone for Christmas." I repeat it steadily. I walk out of the kitchen. I don't know where the wildness is taking me. We stop, me and this untamed force, by the hall closet. I reach in and start taking out boxes of Christmas decorations. I put aside everything that is not an ornament. I scoop up five boxes of ornaments. With the wildness helping to balance them, I carry them into the kitchen. John is sitting at the table, his green eyes soaked.

I take out the ornaments and one by one I smash them on the tile floor. Splinters of glass fly like shiny moths about the room. I keep at my work. When I'm finished, when all the ornaments are broken, there's something beautiful about the shattered colored glass glistening in the kitchen light. I walk out of the kitchen and take the wildness into our room to lie down.

"John has been gone a month." Molly lights a cigarette and flicks nonexistent ash off her satin blouse. "And you're still alive." She hands me a memo. It's about an industry charity dinner honoring Len as Humanitarian of the

Year. "We have to fill up five tables." I think about the month. And I think how the world did not stop turning itself around and around.

"I'll fill the tables, don't worry." Molly grabs the memo out of my hand. Molly hates to strong-arm people to go to these kinds of industry dinners. But she's smiling. Molly is in love again. Joe is back. This love makes her patient with me. Love can be great that way. It can make you feel patient, generous, even wise. Molly treats me like a young widow. A young widow needs sympathy, but there is life up ahead for a young widow. She teases me and invites me on dates with her and Joe. Sometimes I go with them to a movie. I sit in the dark with the wildness and we watch the movie. I think how I don't feel like the widow, but rather like the one who died. Like the one who wakes up one morning and finds there is no longer any floor upon which to walk. I sit and wonder who I might have become if I hadn't fallen in love with John. Wondering who I might have become takes up a lot of my time. It is nearly a full-time job. My real job, though, is wondering if John will come back.

Emma buzzes. "Len is waiting for you in the conference room." From time to time Emma tells me how hard it must be on John to be away from home. Emma doesn't think anything is hard on me. Emma doesn't think things are hard on women in general. And if they are, they should act, like I'm acting, as if everything is easy. Emma clips out articles about Mexico and puts them on my desk. Maybe she thinks articles about the peso's devaluation or some new disco in the Zona Rosa will make me miss him less. I don't read the articles.

I walk into the meeting. "Sorry I'm late, Len. I couldn't get off the phone."

Len says, "No problem, Babe. Let's get started. You know Reggie Nouri, don't you?"

"Sure." I shake hands. He tries to kiss me, but he's not fast enough. Reggie Nouri has just come from shooting his movie. He's still in full makeup and costume. This is great. Everyone is acting like it's perfectly normal for the producer to come to an ad presentation dressed like a 1920s gangster.

CREATIVE DIFFERENCES

Reggie puts his feet up on the conference table — the sign that he's ready. On his feet are spats. I laugh. Len tries to strangle my laugh with a look. I start the presentation. Reggie interrupts. I let him. You don't expect a tough guy to have manners.

He says, "I don't want an ad illustrated by that guy who did the ad for my last movie." I have eight boards against the wall, all drawn by this illustrator. I say nothing, figuring he won't recognize the artist's work. I start again. He interrupts again. He reaches into the top part of his sock and pulls out a crumpled piece of newspaper. Carefully he unwraps it and smooths it with his hands and passes it to me. Unfortunately, his hands have makeup on them and he has smudged the ink and it's unreadable. I imagine it is some item from an obscure gossip column, probably from his hometown paper, saying something unflattering about him. He says he will get me another copy. I say thanks, like he'll be sending along a page of the Gutenberg Bible. I begin the presentation.

I think about how I mailed the article in *Metropolitan* to John two weeks ago. Only the article. No letter. No note. When the article came out and people read it, and it was Xeroxed and synopsized in the daily summaries, and some people even sent me copies, like I might have missed it, most said it was flattering. It wasn't. But people are impressed with you when you are written about in a prestigious magazine. You enjoy, for a few seconds, a special kind of notoriety that people in the movie business appreciate. You join a club. A club whose members have suffered through seeing their names in print and reading what other people think of them. A club whose members are then thought to be a little bigger than life. Not as big as the movies, but bigger, say, than the square footage of their offices.

Reggie is walking his spats up and down the side of the room examining the ads. He doesn't mention the illustrator. Damned if he doesn't stop in front of the best ad. Tough guy radar I guess you could call it. Len's secretary comes in and says Mr. Nouri is wanted on the set. He flashes us a smile of good-bye. With all the money he's made, why can't he afford better teeth?

Len is winding up the meeting. He asks everyone to a luncheon meeting tomorrow. "Everyone except you, Jerry."

I look over at Jerry, wondering if he has asked to be excused or something. Usually my staff asks me about missing meetings, but now and then I see them talking to Len about conflicts on their schedules. I understand it, though. You have to be sure your boss's boss knows who you are.

"Jerry, I saw you having lunch with Marshall yesterday." I don't like the sound of Len's voice. It sounds like it could blast through about eight feet of solid rock. "You don't work here anymore, Jerry."

Everyone at the table freezes, furiously scanning their memories for things they might have done recently that they didn't know were disloyal sins.

Jerry looks at me. But I am back in Las Vegas, years ago, and Len is saying he is going to fire Etta. Poor, weird, bald Etta. I stopped him then. I stopped him without even thinking very much about it. I've already thought too much about this. He's firing someone who works directly for me without even asking me. I can't allow this. I decide to say nothing. I decide not to try and save what is already lost. I decide to go along with the code. It's a real humanitarian code. Getting up to leave, I feel Len's eyes on me. I look past him. I leave the room and walk the wildness back into my office.

EXECUTIVE VICE-PRESIDENT

19

"*M*orning."

"Morning." I show the guard in the lobby my I.D. card. He knows me and I know him. For maybe ten years. But I always show my card. Other senior executives refuse. They act like it's demeaning. Considering what we do for a living, I think they're a little confused about the definition of demeaning. Besides, when you work late hours in a big office building and you're by yourself and it's 10:30 at night, you like to think there are no crazies waiting in the stairwells or behind the Xerox machines. That's what you like to think.

"I hear we're being taken over." The red label on his blazer is inches from my face.

I pull back. "Taken over?" Now that's a stupid thing to do. Repeat something. I love it when the lobby guys know more about my company than I do.

"Yeah. CC and L." I must look even stupider now because he spells it out: "Commercial Credit and Lending Corporation."

I laugh at him and at the idea of a takeover and go on to the elevator. I tell myself to keep calm. Act in a way befitting the big corner office they've given me. I feel an icicle forming inside my body. If I breathe too deeply, I might freeze.

I ride up in the elevator with a do-not-disturb look hanging on my face. At each floor, a part of me descends. I get to the thirty-fifth floor, my floor, and feel that most of me lies at the bottom of the elevator shaft. Crumpled. Taken over. Can't be. Wouldn't Jake have told me? Maybe Jake doesn't know.

The small reception area outside my office is crowded with people drinking coffee, smoking, gossiping. It might be a cocktail party. It's my staff waiting for me. "Morning."

"Morning." Emma looks up slowly. The distance from her desk to my face might be a thousand miles. She knows, too.

"I'll just be a minute and then you can all come in." I go inside my office and shut the door. My office looks the same. I feel a little sorry for it. It doesn't know its world is about to be turned upside down. I hang my fur coat on a quilted hanger inside the small closet and lock it. When John bought me this coat last year I told him I couldn't possibly wear it to the office. It might get stolen. He smiled. "Whatever you want." I love his easiness. It's an easiness I look for in myself and never find.

I buzz Emma and ask for some herbal tea. I wish I could call John and have his secretary put me right through. The new one. She doesn't have that proprietary way about her that his other secretary had. She doesn't care who John speaks to. Just connect him up, type his letters, Xerox, file and go home. I wonder who she works for now. I decide to try Molly.

"Molly?" She tells me to hold on a second. I got home late last night. I made myself some cinnamon toast and cinnamon rose tea. Work has been keeping me so busy I hardly ever eat a proper dinner at the same time on week nights anymore. I've stopped saying I'm sorry to myself. I'm still sorry, but how many times can you apologize for the same thing. I figure I should either stop doing it or stop apologizing. Lately work has been following me home. It lives with me like a boarder.

"Molly? A takeover. CC and L." Molly is quiet for so long I think we might have been disconnected. She's probably wondering why I'm talking like a Western Union operator. She's probably wondering why I haven't called her in weeks.

"CC and L? It will be all right." The way she says CC&L, I know it won't be all right. She keeps talking. Trying to soothe me. I stop listening. I want her to say this is terrible. I want her to be outraged for me. Suddenly I am so tired I could cry. I want to sleep. A dark, starless sleep. Last night I lay awake running through my life like so much footage through a projector. I just about had it all straight when it got light and I fell asleep. Now I'll have to start all over again tonight. I look outside. The park is white. It hasn't had enough time to get dirty. I can only see the tops of people's heads. It's so cold, everyone walks with his head down, against the wind.

"I'm still here. We could do that. One o'clock. That would be great. I'll have Emma make us a reservation."

She tells me she has something to tell me. "Don't worry." She hangs up. It's not that I worry, exactly.

The door opens and my staff walks in. "Morning."

No one has a folder. They just want to talk. They're worried. It's not yet ten and I wish the day were over. I wonder if I should call Jake. It's almost seven in Los Angeles. He won't be awake. I buzz Emma anyway and tell her to call and leave word with his butler, Sam.

They all know. The lobby guys must have been pretty busy this morning. I never get over how quickly word travels around an office building. It's like a giant just dunked the whole building in a tub of gossip.

I sip my mint tea and pretend it's got caffeine. Someone is leaking the information about the takeover. I wonder why. I wonder why it's being done this way. Why is it companies act like they can't be bothered with the people who work for them? I look back out the window, hide a yawn. My eyes water. Some mornings life just gets too close.

I tell the staff I only know what they know. They don't believe me. They figure as part of senior management, I know everything but have been sworn to secrecy. They do their figuring out loud. I can tell that the idea that I might not know what's going on disturbs them as much as the idea of a takeover. If they want to believe I know more, let them. I should know more.

Emma buzzes. She tells me Len is on the phone. I ask her to make a lunch reservation for me. I pick up on Len.

"Morning, Babe." He doesn't even try to hide the excitement in his voice. He asks if I'm alone. I'm tempted to say yes to find out what he knows. Some people are easy to pump for information. Len is one of them. He can't bear to keep things to himself. What good is knowing insider stuff if you can't tell other people what you know?

"How about lunch?" he asks.

"Fine." He gives me the name of the restaurant a long way from the office. I hang up knowing he doesn't want us to be seen together. The intrigue starts. I'm interested. I ask Emma to call Molly back and tell her I can't make lunch. Something's come up. The staff quiets. They sit in such a way I know they think they're entitled to be told what I found out from Len. They're not.

I ask a few questions about work. Their answers are startled and short. They can't believe I can talk about work at a time like this. I'm a little surprised myself. But I wonder who they think is going to open two movies in the next five weeks while we all sit around and wonder what being taken over is going to do to our lives.

I ask what they've heard about CC&L. The head of CC&L, whose name no one can remember, hates to have his picture taken. Someone says he's sixty-five. Someone else says he's forty-five. He's an accountant. He's a lawyer. Harvard, B.A. Wharton, M.B.A. Harvard, LL.B. He's educated, that much is clear. He started the business with a five-thousand-dollar loan from his wife's father. Someone says he has a friend whose cousin works for CC&L in San Francisco and says they're horrible. This is just the kind of unfounded, dangerous gossip we all eat up.

I watch as each one of my staff meets his or her own fears. The five vice-presidents and the one senior vice-president who report to me have all worked together for a long time. A long time by movie standards, that is. We know each other in ways our lovers, wives, husbands, don't know us. Working in an office with people for years means you watch them come face to face with life's curves. Sometimes their work gets screwed up and you have to get involved in their personal lives. Try and sort things out for the company's sake. Sometimes you get involved because you like them. Because you'd help a drowning person. Sometimes it's the only way of holding on to yourself. When work slaps you around a little too hard, the people you work with are there to remind you to keep going. They remind you not to let your life be eroded away by worry.

"You know we'll all probably lose our jobs." My creative director manages a smile.

Lose our jobs. Out of work. Unemployed. Not a fun thought. As much as you hate work sometimes, as much as you fantasize about escaping from it, you never fantasize about being fired. You're always quitting.

The thought of losing my job flies about the room like a bird that's just escaped from its cage. The thought of losing my job distracts me. It makes me angry. It reminds me of how little control we have over our lives. It's easy to forget you work at the pleasure of some distant force. It's easy to forget the movie business is a business.

The silence in the room catches me up. I smile at them. A motherly kind of smile that surprises me. The room starts to hum again. They know I will try to take care of them.

"Remember when we thought we were being taken over by a network?" I say.

A few heads bob, remembering. Telling stories. We love to do it. We do it well. We talk about the old times and we give them and ourselves a grace we did not have at the time. There is a particular brand of story we like to tell when we are worried. It is the how-dumb-we-once-were story. Someone starts. I buzz Emma to ask if Jake was there.

"His butler said Mr. Tyler is out of town," she says. Calling Jake Mr. Tyler throws me. For an instant I think she's talking about his father.

"Mr. Tyler is out of town." I repeat it. "Is there a number? Will Sam be speaking to him later?"

"I've already left word at the number." Emma frosts up.

"Where is he, Emma?"

She doesn't know. I hang up the phone. Everyone seems relaxed. They ask me to tell a story. A part of me wants everyone to get out of my office so I can get some work done. But I can't do that to them. Not yet.

"I had just been made a publicist." I laugh at the expression "made a publicist." It sounds like a fairy godmother in stacks of crinoline comes down and touches you with a wand and poof! you're a publicist. My staff is waiting for me to go on.

"I didn't know anything." I tell them my story. I was doing the rounds. Taking all the editors to lunch. One day I had lunch with a senior editor at a big woman's magazine. We went to the Tea Room. She was known there. We sat in one of the tiny booths in front where she could see everyone come in. A lot of people leaned over to kiss her. Sometimes she'd introduce me, but mostly she'd wait until they walked away and then tell me a little detail about some private scandal that had wrecked their lives. Or made their lives.

This editor was probably twenty-five years older than I. She was very stylish, divorced with a grown son. She tried to make me feel comfortable. I wasn't uncomfortable. I felt like I used to when a friend's mother came to prep school and took us out to dinner at the most expensive restaurant in Boston.

We talked movies. She asked me about these two actors that were making a movie for us in England. I told her a couple of stories. Nothing really bad. Just libelous stuff. About a week later I read these same stories in a gossip column. Reading them gave me the creeps. I couldn't understand how my words got into this column. I was hoping no one would read the summaries that day. I was hoping no one would notice. It turned out that everyone noticed, including the two actors in England. This column was syndicated. It appeared in a New York paper one day. Then in a Los Angeles paper the next. In a London tabloid three days later. Then in Chicago. There seemed no end to seeing my stories in print.

My boss asked the whole staff into his office. I told him that I had told an editor and she must have told the columnist. My boss looked at me like I was impossibly thick. The other publicists wouldn't look at me at all. I figured my brief career as a publicist was over. I imagined myself sitting back out in the hall in front of a typewriter for the rest of my life. But my boss started to laugh. You'd have to call it a laugh because of the way his face looked. But it didn't sound like a laugh. He told me the editor I had had lunch with *was* the gossip columnist. She just used a different name for the column. And everyone knew it. Everyone, that is, but me.

The staff wanders out of my office. I suspect to wander downstairs into someone else's office. They will keep talking about the impending takeover all day. Every day. Until someone tells them what the hell's going on.

I buzz Emma and start making calls. Between calls I stare out the window. I wish Molly were still here. She'd be philosophic. She'd poke fun at me for ever thinking I was in control of my life at the office. But Molly is the director of communications for a museum now. She goes home at 5:30. She is married. She is pregnant. I think of her as having moved to another planet.

It's 12:40. I'm not hungry. Now I wish I hadn't told Len I would meet him for lunch. I think I'm going to throw up. I miss John. I miss him like you miss food or oxygen or sleep. Emma buzzes. It's Gene Reismann. I pick up on the producer of a movie that was released two weeks ago. It isn't making any money.

"We can't spend any more money midweek. I'm sorry, Gene."

"That's not what Len told me on Saturday."

I take a deep breath. The icicle has sprouted branches and is now growing throughout my four limbs. Gene Reismann is looking for someone to blame for his flop. I think he just found someone.

"I'm sure Len wanted to see the weekend figures before committing to any more money. Now we've had an opportunity to study the figures."

"Shit. You can't do this to me. People like this movie. My barber told me he was going to see it next weekend."

People don't like this movie. That's what I want to say. But I don't. I can hear in his voice that he has just now realized someone else is in control of his movie's fate. I'd like to tell him we have something in common. We both just found out we're not in control. We're driving cars without brakes. It doesn't matter the cars are Jaguars. But I just tell him again why the company can't spend any more money advertising his movie. I love that about his barber.

"I'm calling Jake," he says. "I'll call you back." He hangs up before I can give him the number where Jake's butler says he is.

I pick up on Manfred Wilkes, the unit publicist for a comedy we have in production. It's shooting in New York for two weeks. He tells me he's set up the meeting I asked for with the director and the star. It's for 11:30 tomorrow night. I say okay and hang up.

I brush my hair and put on some red lipstick. I unlock my closet, fight a desire to hide in it and take out my coat. I drop the index cards that need retyping on Emma's desk. I ignore the overly brisk way she scoops them up. I go out into the hallway, press for the elevator and stare up at all the shiny, gold statues of Oscar in the glass case.

20

"No, thanks. I'm fine."

A young girl stands half in and half out of the trailer. She is wearing a sheepskin jacket, fur-topped boots and a ski mask. The ski mask is folded up so I can see her face. She's probably pretty enough when she gets sleep.

"You sure?" She nods at me a little disappointed that my demands aren't going to keep her inside a little longer. Down goes the mask. "'Bye."

It's eighteen degrees outside. It feels about thirty-five in here. I didn't think it was such a good idea to wear my fur coat to a movie location. I was wrong.

It's almost one o'clock in the morning. The star and the director were supposed to be here at 11:30. I'm going to kill Manfred Wilkes. In the ninety minutes I've been waiting, I have read an out-of-date *Time* twice, memorized the production's bulletin board, fantasized about all the mean things I'm going to say when the director and his actor finally do show up. I've had two cups of bath-warm tea and one package of Fig Newtons. The Fig Newtons were delicious. Now I am counting the squares on the linoleum floor. How could I ever think of giving up show biz?

I could go outside and see what's happening. The young girl said they were having trouble with the scene they're shooting. It's being shot outside. She said it shouldn't be much longer. They've shot it five times. Must be real comfortable shooting outside in the winter. I think I'll stay here. I fish an envelope out of my pocket. It's a letter from John. I've read it maybe twenty times. In it, he says he has to stay longer—a couple more months. He hasn't finished the book. Since I thought there were only about four poets in all of Mexico, I can't understand what's taking him so long.

John wouldn't be keen on my doing this tonight. Keen really isn't the right word. He would say I was crazy to go to a late-night shoot. He would say I should send someone who works for me. Then I would say something mean. He would look at me for a second as if he finally understood how men are driven to hit women. The funny thing is John's right. In a way. But the movie business just doesn't work that way. The right way.

I study the letter. I am looking for where he's written in code that he's really not coming back at all.

The door opens and tomorrow's newspapers are slung inside. The trailer door closes. Sounds like a meat locker clicking shut. I rush over to the papers like I've been without human contact for months. I settle into the one comfortable chair and open the paper. I read the paper the way I've been reading it for fifteen years. Front page, entertainment page. Check our ads. Check the competition's ads. Read the columns.

I turn to the gossip. I stop. Can't be right. I reread the lead item. The item says that certain key executives at my company are thrilled with the rumor that CC&L may be acquiring the studio. Same executives hope this will mean the end of Jake Tyler. I fight nausea. My body feels as if it has been dipped in a near-frozen river. I read it again. Something's not right. I go back over yesterday's lunch with Len.

What Mr. Expedient wanted to talk to me about was joining forces with him to help CC&L get rid of Jake. For the longest time I sat there thinking he was joking. I don't know why I didn't remember this was the same guy who would have pushed Marshall off the boat if he hadn't jumped first.

CREATIVE DIFFERENCES

I sat there watching him drink Japanese beer, poke at his sushi and talk about doing in our boss. I sipped some green tea and pushed a flat porcelain spoon around a black plastic soup bowl. We were sitting next to a rock garden. I kept looking at it. It was like the whole world in miniature. And the world seemed so simple. I listened to the water dripping down over the tiny, flat rocks.

I didn't say much. I did say something about it practically being Jake's studio. Something about Jake's loving movies. Len's look told me he couldn't understand how I had gotten to where I had in the corporation thinking that way. And at that moment, I agreed with him. I thought I understood corporations. I thought I understood office politics, thought I even played a fair game. Suddenly I felt way out of my league. Until then I didn't know I had been playing softball. Len had brought a hardball to lunch and all I wanted to do was find some way of staying on the bench. I didn't want to play in this game.

Len said Jake's leaving would be good for both of us. I got the feeling it would be good for him. The way he talked, I was pretty sure CC&L hadn't decided about me yet. Len kept talking. He does that. He could talk you to death. A lot of times I say yes just to shut him up and save my life.

Thinking back I wonder why I didn't say, Fuck you, Len. I wonder why I let him think I might throw in with him. I wonder why my affection for Jake didn't give me courage. I read the item again. Something's still not right. This column closes at two o'clock. At two o'clock yesterday Len and I hadn't even ordered dessert yet. This item was planted before lunch. Len gambled I would go along with him. Not much of a gamble on his part. I've gone along with him before. All of a sudden work seems about tests of courage and loyalty and survival and all I want to do is sell movies.

Certain key executives. There aren't that many of us. How many has Len gotten to? I wonder what he said to them. I try to imagine how you get to a point in life where you can go around planning out loud how to destroy someone's career. People keep treating you like you've suggested nothing unusual. That's how I treated him. I wonder if when you look in the mirror you look different. I close the paper. I don't know anymore.

The way I've been feeling about work lately is probably the same way you feel when you fall out of love with your husband but are too lazy to get a divorce. I look at the company like it's my husband. Everyone—Jake, Len, the finance guys, the filmmakers, my staff—is one demanding husband. Sometimes my husband is happy with me and lets me alone. And then I start to think I could love him again. But then something goes wrong and he yells at me even when it's not my fault. He makes me feel terrible. I don't tell anyone this. It's degrading to admit your marriage is bad. But the thought of splitting up after all these years overwhelms me. It's more than being overwhelmed. It would mean I had failed. I tell myself to work a little harder and to try not to care so much about what my husband thinks of me.

The trailer door opens. Two men come inside. They stamp their feet like the cold is sticking to the bottoms of their shoes. I fold up the paper and put it in my shoulder bag.

"Morning, gentlemen." My voice is even and friendly. Warm. They smile, ready to give me anything I want. What I want is to go home. Go home, pack a few things and run away with John for a few thousand years. What I get is a promise of twenty minutes of footage for the trailer, a special photography session once they're back in Los Angeles and a grudging consensus that it's best to sell their film as an all-out comedy rather than as a relationship movie. Not a bad night's work. Too bad this isn't really my work anymore. All this is just a sideline.

We bundle up and walk outside. The director wants to gossip about the gossip.

"Think CC and L will fire you?"

The only malice I hear in his question is against CC&L. Even so, the word "fire" summons up an old, icy fear. It's like the yardstick you've been measuring yourself by was just snapped in two. He stands waiting for me to answer in such a way I know he's glad a studio executive is finding out what it feels like to be insecure. I smile my answer, shrug my shoulders and get into a warm, idling limo. They walk back out toward the drafty set. A long pier on the Hudson.

CREATIVE DIFFERENCES

"Morning." Len opens the door to the hotel suite. It's 8:00 A.M. He helps me off with my coat. I place six ad boards face to the wall and toss two fire-engine red folders onto the low oval glass table. I fix myself a cup of milky coffee from the large room service table. I pass over the toast, the muffins, the Danish, the pain au chocolat. There's enough food here for ten meetings.

"What kind of meeting is this going to be?" I hate having to ask Len this. But I want to know. It's been two weeks since the first rumors of the takeover surfaced. While I wait for Len to answer, I look around the room. It's a grand room. It's big enough for three couches. Lots of brocade, petit point pillows and tiered drapes. Very posh. It doesn't look quite like someone's home, but it's a little friendlier than the average hotel suite.

"Just a meeting. Meet and greet. I've told him all about you."

"Thanks." I want to kill him. I can imagine what he's told Mr. CC&L about me. I wonder if he's told him I can be counted on during the coup. The fact is Len hasn't mentioned getting rid of Jake since our lunch two weeks ago. He acts as if he's never talked to me about doing Jake in. I've seen him with Jake, and there's no way anyone could tell he wants to push Jake off a twenty-story building.

"Did you read the paper this morning?" I try to sound casual. I think I sound casual.

"No." The same way Len wonders how I've moved ahead in the corporation, I wonder how he has. I wonder if he takes lessons at night to act so stupid. I tell him there's an item in one of the columns saying everyone in senior management will be replaced six months after the takeover.

"Oh, that." Len slumps into a plump club chair. He lights a cigarette, checks to see if the tip is lit and smiles at me. I look past him toward the wall of windows at the far end of the room. The windows go from the floor to the ceiling. The heavy, blood-red curtains have been drawn back. They are held open by thick red ropes with pink tassels. Winter sunlight pours in. It isn't this bright down on the sidewalk, but up here, twenty-five stories closer to the sun, it's brilliant. Len in direct sunlight is not a pretty sight. His skin is dry. His nerves have jerked tiny lines into his cheeks and across his forehead. I wonder how I look in sunlight.

I see how Len has gotten to where he is. He has no loyalty. He thinks loyalty is for saps. He's probably right. There really isn't any place for loyalty in a business like ours. In any business, probably. It gets in the way. It gets in the way of change. Businesses like their employees to be loyal to the concept of authority, not to any one person in authority. He's read the paper. He's waiting for me to ask if it's true. I'm not going to. Instead, I ask if he wants to make the presentation to Mr. CC&L.

"No, Babe. This is your show." He gets up and walks slowly around to where I've stacked the ads. He stands flipping through them. There is something so disgustingly smug about the way he stands here. He thinks being here, in this expensive hotel suite with Mr. CC&L just on the other side of the door in his bedroom means he's made it. Mr. CC&L has asked him to his home to do business. The way I see it, Mr. CC&L was probably just too lazy to get dressed and limo across town in eighteen-degree weather to have an early morning meeting with the managers of his newest acquisition. We've been invited to his home about as much as the maids who clean it are invited.

"Hello. Sorry to keep you waiting. I'm Leland Alexander. Everyone calls me Sandor. I hope you will, too."

I give my hand to Leland Alexander. He looks into my eyes. I look back, unflinchingly. In that quick look I know he wants to win me over. And I'm afraid he just might be able to.

He turns to shake hands with Len. Len claps him on the shoulder and I'm sure I see Leland Alexander flinch. I don't think it's proper to touch the shoulder of a man who heads a *Fortune* 500 company.

Leland Alexander sits down on the billiard green couch. A young man appears out of nowhere and places on the table in front of Alexander a cup of coffee, a gold cigarette case, a thin onyx lighter and a small leather notepad. Then he leaves. I think Mr. CC&L is going to fit right into the movie business. Anybody who has someone else carry his cigarettes will love the little extras our filmmakers request from time to time.

"How's morale?" This throws me. I don't expect men like Leland Alexander to have this word in their vocabulary.

"It's not good."

Len pushes his cigarette lighter against a white marble ashtray. It makes a clattering sound. If this coffee table weren't made of glass, I'm sure Len would have kicked me just now.

"Well, you'll have to tell me what I can do about it."

"Buy some other studio."

Leland Alexander laughs. Laughing at my jokes always goes a long way with me. Even when I'm not making a joke.

"She doesn't mean that, Sandor." This meeting isn't going the way Len planned it at all. I don't think he told Mr. CC&L about my mouth.

"Please don't tell Mr. Alexander what I mean, Len."

"Please call me Sandor. I insist." I love when people pretend to ask you to do something for them when it's really a command.

"Sandor wants the truth, Len. Don't you?" I study Leland Alexander. He's taking so long to answer you'd think I just asked him the $64,000 question. Leland Alexander is not what I expected. He's not much older than I am. He's attractive. His eyes keep darting over my head like there's someone standing behind me.

"Of course, I want the truth."

Well, that's a relief. The man knows how to lie, at least. I can tell this isn't exactly how Leland Alexander wants the meeting to go either. He doesn't want me asking the questions.

He begins a corporate monologue. I like his voice. I lose the sense of what he's saying. I'm busy figuring out what it will take to keep my job. I struggle against a yawn.

He tells me he knows nothing about movies. And nothing about how to sell them. I believe his first admission. I don't believe his second. For a second.

Len is listening to him and by the look on his face I'm afraid Len might turn into a puppy if Sandor keeps this up much longer. He's very good, this Mr. Leland Alexander.

Mr. CC&L leans on one elbow and rests his head on an upturned index finger. He seems weary all of a sudden. His eyes skate across my face as if looking for a resting place. For some reason I hope he finds one. Just for a moment. I feel the anger inside start to thaw. I am filled with something all too familiar. I can hear myself saying I can deal with this. I can get along with this man. That's the thing about business. You get yourself all worked up thinking that some new thing—some new boss, some new rule, some new something—is really the last straw. You tell yourself you're not going to take it. And then you find you can take it.

People in offices find ways of accommodating almost anything. It doesn't make us good people. And it doesn't make us bad either. It's just what we've been taught to do. Get along. Imagine what would happen to businesses if people lit out every time something came up that bothered them. It's more than hanging around to get a paycheck. You get to where you take some comfort, some pride out of being a part of the overall scheme. You're part of something. You matter to that something. And you tell yourself you matter when that something forgets. You get to where you can't allow all the time you've put in to be washed away. You get to where you'll fight to keep your job.

"I haven't been to a movie in ten years." His confidence is a little suffocating.

I stand up and lean over the back of the chair to retrieve the boards. I feel his eyes on my calves. With my back to him I say, "I wouldn't let that get out."

"What? What did you say?" He's restless. His composure's steady, but his fingers vibrate slightly lighting what must be his fourth cigarette. He's a little bored with Len and me.

"I said your secret's safe with me, Sandor." I start the presentation and for now he's too much of a gentleman to interrupt to put me in my place. Fact is, I won't tell anyone. It would just open up the "how can you work for a man who doesn't know anything about the movie business" can of worms.

I show him six ads. He looks at them as if I'm holding them a hundred feet away. Surely he's seen ads before. I point to the ad Jake and I like. I point to the ad the filmmakers prefer. I act as if Len doesn't exist.

Leland Alexander looks up. His brown eyes seem to hunt for me. He can't place me. I think about the rumor that he has a mistress in San Francisco and a wife miles away in Chicago. And for some reason I think he always keeps his eyes open when he makes love.

"Whatever you and Jake think is right, is right." Doesn't sound to me like he wants Jake out. "The filmmakers should respect your expertise." Leland Alexander stands up. The meeting is over. He's at the door to his bedroom. Unseen hands open it. He turns back. "I wonder if you can do something for me?"

"Yes, Sandor."

"Would you please find out who planted the item in this morning's paper and let me know?" He might as well be asking me to get the Japanese to arm. I shrug my shoulders. It's my way of dismissing the assignment. He's still standing at the door waiting for my answer. Maybe I've lost the touch of shoulder shrugging. I toy with the idea of asking him if the item is true.

"Sandor, it's very hard to find out that sort of thing."

"We've never found it hard at CC and L. I'm sure you can find out. And I want a retraction." His voice could cut wood.

I decide right now to call Danny Castle. Not to find out who planted this item. I don't care. No. I'm going to ask Danny to have something planted about me. Since items seem so important to Alexander, a good one about me can't hurt.

"I'll do my best."

"I know you will." He smiles, but his eyes are having none of it. "There's one more thing. I don't care for the copy line on the ad you want to go with. Please have it changed."

I look at the ad and read over the line. Is this the same man who seconds ago told me he didn't know anything about selling movies? "What don't you like about it?"

Leland Alexander's body jerks like someone put the brakes on too fast. He's not used to people asking him to explain himself.

"Don't worry, Sandor. We'll fix the line," Len speaks up. He's on his feet, ready to do anything, promise anything, be anything. He's making a big mistake.

Sandor is gone. I have to admit the room seems shrunken without him.

21

*T*his weekend our adventure movie opened to record business. The producer sent everyone champagne. I just saw Len in the lobby. He's on his way to see Leland Alexander. Probably to explain what record business means. Jake should be here soon. He's spending this week in New York. I'm taking Friday off.

I'm going to Bermuda for a long weekend. I haven't been to the beach in a long time. It's like spring outside. This morning the item Danny Castle planted about me ran. It says CC&L is busy renegotiating my contract and hoping to make a new four-year deal with me. Thanks, Danny.

I buzz Emma. "Get me Fred on the phone, please."

"Before I get your tea?" I see not everyone is as happy as I am this morning.

"After will be fine. Can I have the call sheet from yesterday?" Emma comes in and places it in the in-box. She hands me a memo. I don't recognize the stationery. Now I see the dark navy letters. CC&L. It's about some meeting. Emma stands in front of me. She doesn't say anything. Emma almost never talks to me about her personal life. She'd rather talk to other secretaries. She believes in a caste system. You just don't get chummy with your boss. It is one of the reasons I like Emma. I get the feeling she's about to break her own rule.

"Would you have some time today?"

"Of course. What is it?"

"How about after lunch before your three o'clock meeting?"

"What three o'clock meeting?" I pick up the index card Emma leaves every night on the far right side of my desk under the glass paperweight John gave me two years ago when I moved into this office. There is no three o'clock on it.

"Mr. Alexander's office called early this morning."

"How early?"

"About eight o'clock."

"What were you doing here that early?"

Emma shrugs like it's none of my business and goes on. "His secretary said Mr. Alexander would like you to meet with Larry Riddel at three o'clock today. You were free, so I said okay." Emma's got me there. In the two months since CC&L officially acquired the studio, I have met with six people that Mr. Alexander's office asked me to see. I have, at Len's urging, hired one of them. I tell Emma to get me some tea and then call Fred.

"By the way, Emma, who is Larry Riddel?"

She looks at me like I should know. I love that. I love when my secretary looks at me like I'm stupid. "He works for CC and L." She waits. I nod. She's going to string this out. "He's Mr. Alexander's right hand." I nod again. All of a sudden a sense of dread dives through my body. "He's head of research." I watch her walk out of my office. I fight an undertow inside my body right under my heart. I am being pulled under.

Emma buzzes. "Fred's line is busy." I tell her to try the head of finance for me. He comes on the line.

"Any idea when you're going to approve the budget for our next release? I've been waiting for almost three weeks."

"Soon. I hope soon." I let him struggle for a few seconds. Finance guys don't usually hope for things. They approve, disapprove, review, analyze. Not hope. I'm wasting my time. I let him off the hook and hang up. No one can make a decision around here anymore. My division is still busy, but for all the others it's as if the company has gone out of business. No new movies have started, no budgets have been approved. The whole company is waiting for Mr. CC&L to make all the decisions. If you ask me, the only decision he needs to make is whether or not he's firing Jake and the rest of us.

Emma buzzes. "Fred is on eight." I pick up the phone.

"Any luck in tracking down that item I asked you about last week?"

"Yes, I have." We both ignore this morning's item about me.

"Were you planning to tell me about it?" Fred apologizes. He doesn't get my joke. He says he's sorry in a couple of ways. I have time to think that the last few weeks I have spent a great deal of time tracking down items for Mr. Alexander. Every time one of the columns writes something negative about CC&L, he circles it in pencil on the summaries and sends it to me. Across the top he writes the same thing. Who is planting this? The latest item took a swipe at Alexander himself. He called me. He was upset. I felt a little sorry for him. The item said a certain widowed society lady wasn't going to wait much longer for her lover to get over his newfound interest in the movies and return to the City by the Bay. I asked him if it could be anyone at CC&L. Anything this personal, I prompted him. He assured me all his guys, he called them lieutenants, were loyal. Stand-up guys. The way he said it, I believed him. I believe Alexander commands loyalty the way they do in the military. Under threat of death.

"Hold on a second, Fred. Yes, Emma." She tells me the producer and director, my 9:00, are on their way up from the lobby. She says they gave the lobby guard a hard time when they were asked their names. I tell her to offer them some coffee. Too bad we can't put a little Valium in it. I punch up Fred again. "So?"

"The item was planted by someone who knew what he was talking about. Someone at CC and L. It was planted by a guy who works for Leland Alexander." I think it would hurt Alexander less if I just pumped a couple of bullets into him.

Emma buzzes. "The producer and the director don't want coffee. They want you." She also says the director's agent is with them. Bringing your agent to the kind of meeting we are going to have is a little like bringing your lawyer to traffic court.

"Fred, thanks." I ask him not to say anything to anyone else about this. He says he won't. "Fred, could you do one more thing for me? It's important."

"I'll try."

"Find out the man's name." Fred starts to tell me how hard this is, how careful he had to be to find out what he had. Fred wants to relive his detective work. He wants me to tell him how great he is. But I cut him off. "Do what you can." I sound as if it's not so very important after all.

I hang up. The director, his agent and the producer spill into my office like a tidal wave. I scribble something on the CC&L memo and tell Emma to have it hand delivered to Mr. Alexander's office.

While we wait for my creative director, Randy, the director starts to talk about his movie. He pauses to look at his agent, who nods, and he keeps talking. I'm not listening.

"So, what we mean is." I perk up. The producer points to a framed poster hanging on my wall. "We don't want an ad like this. That's terrible."

I laugh. Six eyes stare at me. He's not joking. The ad he just pointed to was the ad for one of his own pictures. The movie grossed $140 million. I never knew he hated the ad. Randy comes in before I can say anything.

Randy sets up nine boards. He talks about each one of them. Randy is probably the most talented art director that's ever worked for me. But he rubs people the wrong way. In the movie business only the filmmakers are supposed to be opinionated.

"This is the ad." Randy sits down. He lights a thin, black cigarette. His Armani jacket is perfectly wrinkled. I bask in his arrogance.

"These ads are awful. Terrible. I'm so disappointed." The director turns his back on the ads and stares out the window. Now all three of them are talking. They act like Randy and I aren't even in the room. I feel sorry for Randy. I went to the design studio with him last night and stayed until ten o'clock. He stayed longer. He's tired. And now his feelings are hurt. He begins to hate these men. And a part of him is fighting the idea that they might be right. Maybe these ads are terrible.

This happens in business. Someone says your work isn't any good with such conviction that for a second that seems to span an eternity, you believe him. Maybe you're not very good after all. Maybe you're a fraud. Then, little by little, violence by violence, you realize that saying something is bad doesn't make it so. The trick is not to pay too much attention to what anybody says. Randy hasn't learned this trick yet.

"Gentlemen." I point to an ad that Randy dismissed in his presentation. "Here is a good ad." Randy never knows which of his ads is the best. You wouldn't expect a mother to pick out her best child. The ad is more than good. "It's more attitude than advertising."

"Mr. Alexander's secretary is on the phone."

I look up from the ad board. Emma is standing at the opened door. "Mr. Alexander's secretary is on the phone."

"I hear you, Emma. Can you take a message?" The filmmakers stop talking. For a moment we are all the same. All of us in this room. We are all at the mercy of Leland Alexander.

"She wants to speak with you."

I have no intention of talking to Sandor's secretary. Especially in front of these men. Emma has no intention of leaving. The call button keeps blinking. My old secretary, Lisa, would have tried to handle it herself. Emma knows when she's wasting her time. I'm going to give in. I know it and she knows it. I'm just not the kind of executive who yells at her secretary when things don't go my way.

"Hello."

"This is Jane Foreman, Mr. Alexander's executive assistant."

"Yes, Jane. What can I do for you?" Emma visibly shrinks at my emphatic sweetness. She wants to walk out of my office in protest. But she isn't going to. The filmmakers are chatting with Randy. He thinks they're making up to him. They're not.

"I received your note just now saying you're not available on the twenty-third for a meeting with Mr. Alexander."

"That's right."

"Before I tell Mr. Alexander, I just wanted to check and make sure." She says his name with such respect, it's almost touching. "Mr. Alexander will want to know why you won't be attending the meeting."

"I can't attend the meeting because the twenty-third is a Saturday and I don't work on Saturday." This is not, strictly speaking, true. I have worked a million Saturdays.

"All right. That's what I'll tell him." Jane thanks me and hangs up. My smile at Emma says she can go back to her desk now. Her smile says I have a lot of nerve tampering with her job security. What's a Saturday if it keeps peace in the house?

I go back to the ad. They love it. They only love it because they think I have, in some way they don't completely understand, just stood up to Mr. CC&L.

Emma buzzes. "Mr. Alexander on 09."

Great. "Gentlemen, if you'll excuse me. Our boss is calling me."

The filmmakers laugh at my joke. They gather up their stuff. Randy is slow to get up. I think for a moment he's going to stay. They all wander out of my office. Slowly, like the tide going out.

"Hello, Sandor." My sweetness quota for the day is being taxed.

"I've changed the meeting. For you. It's this Friday."

"Oh."

"Aren't you going to thank me?" I think he's flirting with me.

"Friday's no good." I'm a little surprised at my own directness. This is a little like driving a sports car fast. Very fast. I go on. "I'm going away for the weekend." I lie and say with my husband.

"I see." He's not flirting anymore. "What time were you leaving?" I tell him about the one o'clock flight to Bermuda.

"I see. Come to the meeting. You'll be finished by one o'clock. I'll have my plane take you and your husband to Bermuda." The way he says husband catches me up. He thought I was single. I look at my hand quickly to see if my wedding ring fell off sometime and I didn't notice it. It's there.

"Thank you, Sandor. That's very nice of you. By the way, I found out who planted that item."

"Who?"

"I don't know his name, but he works for—"

He interrupts me. "When you get his name, call me." The phone goes dead.

I look at my watch. I'm supposed to be in the screening room with Jake to see Quinn Lilley's movie. The studio finished it for him. Releasing Quinn Lilley's movie is one of Leland Alexander's priorities. He's tired of paying the interest on the money. He's only been paying it for two months. Jake's been paying it for two years.

I brush my hair. It looks great. My blouse is white silk, like something a dame in a 1940 movie would wear when she tells her husband she's cheating on him. All I did was accept a private plane. I wonder how much the free ride is going to cost.

I walk down the hall toward the executive screening room. I notice two secretaries reading the *Wall Street Journal*. Following the upward rise of CC&L's stock, no doubt. We all look in the oddest places for some sign of what's going to happen to us.

Jake's New York secretary is waiting for me at the door. "He just started it." She hands me a box of popcorn. You always get popcorn at Jake's screenings.

"Thanks." I stand in the back of the room waiting for my eyes to adjust to the dark. I see Jake sitting next to Len. There are two other men sitting in the front row. I don't know them. Probably CC&L guys. I sit down next to Jake. He sees me. He leans over and kisses me. "Hi ya."

I watch the movie, but I'm thinking about Quinn. I think I could have loved Quinn. It wouldn't have been the way I love John. I was not exactly the same person with Quinn. Would he still be alive if I had let myself love him? If I had stayed in that crazy house longer?

Jake smacks his forehead with an open palm. In the dark, it sounds like a firecracker.

"What's the matter?"

"That. Up there." He gestures at the screen. I swivel back to face the screen. I don't say anything. It's best not to let Jake get started. I'm never as direct with Jake as I want to be. With Molly gone, Jake is my best friend at work. Except not quite. I sneak a look at him. He misses Quinn, too. His best friend is gone.

The screening ends. The two men walk over. Gray suits, shirts so white they give bleach new meaning. For a second I think they're twins. They shake hands with Len and Jake. They look at me like I'm someone's wife. They leave.

"Good movie," says Len. "Should do some business this summer. I think we should open in about eight hundred theaters." Len's voice is all business. On some level he believes what he's saying.

Jake turns his popcorn box upside down into his palm. All that's left are unpopped kernels. He chews them. "Are you out of your fucking mind, Len? Eight hundred screens? Are you nuts?"

Len studies his cigarette tip. He seems a little bored with Jake and me. I can tell he doesn't want to answer.

"The company has to try and recoup the money. Sandor wants a broad release." It took him just thirty-five seconds to use Sandor's name.

I put my hand across Jake's arm. But I don't need to. He's not going to kill Len. Jake stands up. He turns to me. "Want to get a drink?"

I follow him out of the screening room. It's 11:30 in the morning.

Jake orders a double Scotch. I order a Perrier with lime. We are sitting at the top of the skyscraper next door to our office building. We are in a bar sixty stories high. I feel as if we're in an airplane. It's cloudy outside. Spring sure gave up easy.

He tells me Leland Alexander is a dangerous man. I was hoping he would tell me something I didn't know, maybe talk about what he's going to do. About what I should do. But instead he's talking about Leland Alexander. He keeps pushing at the square gray cocktail napkin, running his thumbnail back and forth across the bar's embossed logo. The way he talks about Alexander, I feel ashamed for thinking I might be able to get along with him.

"I've been walking on the beach a lot. Thinking. I'm almost fifty. I don't know what the point is anymore." It occurs to me that if the whole company were in Los Angeles where Jake always said we belonged, CC&L wouldn't have been able to find us. Jake keeps talking about the beach. I signal the waiter for another round. I love the shirt Jake is wearing. He doesn't look fifty. I picture Jake's beach house. It must be tough getting up every morning to blue sky.

"Let him make Len head of the company," he says.

I feel like my bar stool just slid a few inches. Is that what Alexander is planning to do? I decide to change the subject, reel Jake back in.

"We should talk about Friday's meeting. The presentation to Sandor's board of directors. Don't you want us to be good?"

With an effort, he lets go of the damp napkin and looks up at me. "You must have me confused with someone who gives a shit."

I feel my face getting warm. I feel like I was just slapped. I squeeze my Perrier glass for a few seconds and lay my now-cold hand on my face. Why do I care about Friday's presentation? Do I think some stupid presentation is going to save our jobs? Save my job? Save Jake. I look at Jake. He doesn't know what I'm thinking. Funny how you can get to be this old and still find parts of yourself you didn't know existed. Bad parts. Scared parts.

"I've talked to a couple of other studios. I've been thinking about making my own movies." Jake's voice makes me jump.

"What?" I find his eyes. They are racing ahead, but I make him look at me. Now I get it. He's got everything figured out, figured out for himself. I guess I thought my loyalty to the company would hold us all together. Like glue. Hold Jake and me together, at least.

"Remember the last time we went drinking together?" he says. I let him have his eyes back.

"I remember, Jake."

We had just come from the police station. I had been asked some questions. It turned out I was the last person to see Quinn alive. I have never been the last person to see anyone alive. The police kept asking me why he did it. It seemed a pretty stupid question to me. I went back to L. A. for the memorial service. I told John I was doing it for Jake. John said I was doing it for myself, which was okay. He just didn't think I should drag Jake around as my excuse. John likes Jake. The funny thing is, I was doing it for Jake. I didn't bury Quinn until much later. There was something easy about being melancholy. Quinn wouldn't have liked it. But I didn't want to give it up.

We are downstairs now standing on the street. It's snowing. But it's warm the way it can be sometimes when it snows. The city feels like it's inside a warm glove.

"What happened to you and John?" He asks me this like he might be asking me to explain the theory of relativity, in layman's terms, of course, and hurry up 'cause it's so damned cold standing here.

"He's finishing his book."

"I didn't think anything could bust up you two. You should have found time to have a kid. Should have made time."

I'm amused that Jake thinks it was just a matter of finding time. It kind of lets me off the hook. I might take this explanation as my own. When someone asks me if I have children, I'll just say I couldn't find time.

"He sent me a book he thought might make a movie. Always liked John."

"He's not dead, Jake. Will it make a good movie?" I don't think of us as busted up. I think of us as sort of a piece of string. A long piece of string that is laid across the country, up and down hills, threaded through towns, resting against the pavement, slanting down toward Mexico. Loose and no longer tangled, just straight and long. So long I can't see the end, his end.

Jake is talking, but now I can't keep my mind on what he's saying. The street is beautiful. I watch a woman in a mink walk by. There are snowflakes clinging to her coat. The snow is making everything quiet. The snow is calming everyone down. It's almost two o'clock. Jake wipes a snowflake out of his eye. A snowflake lands on my upper lip. I lick it off. I swear I can almost feel its five little points scrape the inside of my mouth.

"Goddamn New York weather. I could never live here again." Jake jerks up the collar of his camel's hair coat. He holds a nearly finished cigarette between his fingers. He looks as if he's debating whether or not to throw it into the street. He does.

"Jake?"

"Yes?"

I bend down and scoop some snow into a ball. I reach up and smash it into his neck. "See ya."

22

*L*en is waiting for me in the lobby of the CC&L Building. His gray suit and oyster-colored shirt look real nice. He doesn't look like he's in the movie business. But I guess that's the point. I'm wearing a forest green challis dress. Len tells me right away that I look nice.

"Need any help, Babe? I unpacked your boards and got them ready for you upstairs."

I'm so surprised I slip a little on the greasy-looking marble floor. Len catches me by the elbow and rows us both toward the elevator. Over the years, Len's limp has gotten less and less noticeable. But today his walk is uneven.

"Thanks, Len. What time do we go on?"

Len looks at his watch. It's a gold Rolex. I don't remember seeing it before. "In twenty minutes. They're doing the forest products now."

"Now there's a tough act to follow."

Len looks at me, not getting my joke. He's nervous. I'm not. I was a few days ago but not anymore. I figure they're going to get rid of me, so why be nervous.

I ask Len if Jake is coming. We step onto the elevator. It's paneled and dark brown.

"I don't know."

"He'll be here. He'll come in late. But he'll come."

Len lets me chatter on for a few more seconds. Then he shuts me up. "Jake was fired last night. They bought out his contract. He's gone."

We ride up. Inside I'm screaming. Fired? Fired last night? I guess they fired him and then broke all his fingers. Otherwise he would have called me. He wouldn't have let Len be the one to tell me.

"Here, Fred asked me to give you this." I take an envelope from Len's hand. He pulls his hand back and cracks his knuckles. Pretty disgusting. He should consider saving that for the presentation.

We walk into the boardroom. Ten men are sitting at a horseshoe-shaped mahogany table. The table looks big enough to double as a helicopter pad. I am the only woman. These guys look as if they're on loan from the Politburo.

A young man greets us. I order hot tea with honey. I could have said sugar, but why be easy? I've heard Alexander has a personal chef at his office. He must have honey.

I sit down in one of the four dark brown armchairs. I can't keep my hands off the leather. This chair probably cost more than Quinn Lilley's film will eventually gross. Gee, that's funny. I just admitted to myself that Quinn's movie isn't any good. Yesterday there was an item in the paper about how expensive and how bad Quinn's movie is. The item went on to say CC&L expected their executives to be able to pick better movies in the future and expected them to market them better. I should have realized then that Jake wouldn't be here today. That he was history. Another item. Someone at CC&L prefers to send messages to their employees via the gossip columns. Not my way of doing business, but it's effective. Effective the way a bomb is effective. Of course a pistol would have done the job just as well. But someone on the planet might have missed it. I felt sorry for Jake when I read it. I doubt he will even see it. He's probably on a plane back to Los Angeles. Back to the sun.

There was something about the item that made me think the old days are gone. Sitting in my office last night finishing up some notes for this presentation, I thought this is what it must feel like to row out to the middle of a huge dark lake and let your small boat float undisturbed as you look down, down, down into the black deepness that has no bottom. You go through life trying to connect with people. You try to forge single moments of connection, of recognition. Of course, sometimes you don't have to try. Like when you fall in love. Then the moments come easily. Only you get a little greedy. Simple moments are not enough. You want an eternity.

Molly called me just as I was leaving. I had already turned off the light on my desk. The light from the hall drifted into my office like hot summer moonlight. Molly's voice is like a beacon. I follow it and moor my small boat near shore. She says she misses me and misses the way we talked everything to death. For a second I want to go back in time, inch my way out of now.

She asks about John. Tenderly, I tell her I don't think he's coming back. If I could see through the phone I know I would see Molly leaning gracefully against a wall, her head up, her throat exposed, as though waiting for a knife.

She says she read the item in the paper about Quinn's movie. "The part about your hating the movie. That must have hurt you." I've never told Molly anything about Quinn. All I say is yeah.

"How you doing with the CC and L guys?"

"Not real well," I say, staring down at the item circled in red lying on my desk.

"Well, I know you can handle them." I slip off the phone pretty quickly after this.

I pick up the agenda that's on the white marble cube in front of me. The agenda has been printed on a heavy stock in dark blue CC&L ink. It's the classiest agenda I've ever seen. I used to do agendas for meetings with Jake. He used to tear them up. I stopped doing them. I see I am to speak first, then Len. No Jake.

Len chatters in my ear. He's acting like my best friend. You might call his constant noise a pep talk. I ignore him and he doesn't know it. I smile at Sandor and nod my head. I love my manners. The bridge of his nose wrinkles a little. I wonder if this is some sort of secret sign. Some apology for having made me come here to talk about my work to men who are embarrassed by the movie business. To men who are not embarrassed by the AIDS joke they just told one another.

Sandor is talking. I've got to pay attention. I shuffle my index cards. Len lights his fourth cigarette.

"Before we begin, I've asked Larry Riddel to give us his thoughts about the business." I sag back into the soft leather chair and let my head ride against its high back.

Larry Riddel points to the young man who just served my tea on a heavy silver platter. The young man pushes two buttons on a control panel and one half of the far wall disappears. In its place we see several tables, graphs and an organizational chart. Riddel selects a wooden pointer from the corner. He hefts it like a pool cue. He begins to talk about numbers and percentages and projections. He points to his chart like he's pointing to the Magna Carta.

A few weeks ago Larry Riddel came to see me. He was wearing a three-piece blue suit with a gold fob spread delicately across his toned middle. His breathing was shallow, as if there were invisible gas in my office that might be poisonous. I was ready to hate him. The odd thing was, I liked his voice. It had a nice, soft tone to it. He talked and I watched him. It was kind of like watching a movie. He made almost no eye contact with me. He talked about his plans for the movie business. I made a few jokes. I could tell by how his eyes jumped that he got the jokes. But he didn't laugh. Riddel reminded me of a career military man who, into his middle age, wonders if he should have become a priest instead.

I haven't met very many men like Riddel. I guess that makes me lucky. Except I was unprepared. I've met a lot of difficult men. Demanding, crazy, talented, neurotic men. But no one like Riddel. No one bloodless. He talked about selling a movie as if he were planning the invasion of Normandy all over again. He called filmmakers employees. He referred to my staff as triage. When he sensed I wasn't buying, he grabbed a legal pad and drew a picture on it with a black marker. Pictures of hills being attacked. Flanking. Outflanking. Guerrilla warfare. He sure as hell wasn't talking about the movie business. But I wasn't worried. I was sure Jake wasn't going to let some research guy—to use one of Riddel's phrases—get a foothold in our area. I even thought Len would pound down a couple of stakes in the Keep Out sign. I was wrong.

If I were one of these board of directors guys, it would seem to me that Riddel has all the answers. He's here to help. Here to protect the financing. Minimize the downside risk. Here to take the guesswork out of making movies.

A soft click and more charts. It's a chart of my department. Except there are only half the number of jobs on this chart. I look at Len. He stares at the chart. He knows. He knows they are planning to cut my department by half.

For some reason I start to think about the time John and I were in the Sistine Chapel in Rome. We got there early so we could crane our eyes to the ceiling without being crushed by tourists. Among the forty or fifty early birds was a young mother and her son. Her son looked to be about ten. After looking up at one of the Western world's greatest triumphs, he turned to his mother and said: Is this it? Sitting here listening to Mr. Research talk about previously new methods—previously new, isn't that old?—I'm wondering if this is it? If this is what I'm meant to be doing with my life?

I can't think of one thing I've done in the last sixteen years that has really meant anything. I figure that each day I must have done something. But now, thinking back on all those days rolled into one another, I can't name one thing I did that really mattered. Loving John mattered. The days spent with John mattered. I can hear John telling me to stop putting my life on hold until I get to some place up ahead. I don't think I put my life on hold. I was just looking for something; a sign, a pattern. Something that would make work make sense and then I could forget about it. Forget about it the way you forget about gravity. Maybe that's what really bothers me. The randomness of it all. The random way people rise in corporations. Smart or dumb, good at their jobs or just good at keeping their jobs. The random way people's careers are cut off. The random way you fall in love. And out of love. It shouldn't be this random.

I remember the note Len gave me on the elevator. I read it. I'm not surprised. Fred says the man who has been planting all the items about our studio, about Alexander, about me, is Larry Riddel. Alexander's stand-up guy.

Alexander introduces me. I stand up and toss the index cards with my speech on them back onto my seat. "Morning, Gentlemen. I don't agree with one thing Mr. Riddel has said about the future of the movie business. I'm going to tell you why, and I hope at the end of my presentation some of you will agree with me." I turn and give Larry Riddel one of the best smiles. He looks like someone just shot in the belly. Len looks as if he'd like to strangle me. I can almost hear him saying, I unpacked her goddamn boards for her. Len hates to feel like a sap.

The man farthest from me is going through his papers looking for something. I keep talking. He finds what he's looking for and settles down. I keep talking. I'm pretty good at this. Sometimes it's easy to talk about what you like to do, what you've spent your life doing. I tell them about movies and their place in the world of commerce, in the world of commercial art. You'd think I was an evangelist trying to convert them to my religion.

The man with the piece of paper passes it to the man next to him. They whisper. Then the second man begins to read it. I don't get it. No one was reading when Larry Riddel was talking. I focus on Leland Alexander. He's listening. He's enjoying my performance. He appreciates business theater. The paper reaches the fifth man. I walk closer to the arc of the horseshoe. I stand in front of the man who is reading the paper now. I can read upside down. What they've been passing around and whispering about while I've been standing up here talking is personnel's biography of me. My résumé. The sixth man passes it on to the seventh. This paper is more real to them than I am. This piece of paper with my job titles, with my salary history, with how much money I administrate, with how many people report to me, is, as far as these men are concerned, me. A more real me than the one standing in front of them.

I walk over and pick up my shoulder bag and walk out of the room. I walk down the hall, hoping I am headed toward the elevators. There they are. I press for an elevator. Leland Alexander is beside me.

"You can't do this to me."

"Sandor, for someone who doesn't go to the movies, that sure sounds like movie dialogue to me." I shift my leather bag onto my other shoulder. I am inches closer to him now. "Your buddy Riddel planted the items you've been acting so concerned about."

Sandor doesn't take his eyes off of me.

"Did you hear me? Riddel—your stand-up guy—planted the items. All of them. Items to hurt you, to hurt your family. Items meant to destroy CC and L. Your company. Items, Sandor, to try and destroy my company. My career. He's a dangerous guy."

Sandor lights a cigarette. He holds his thin onyx lighter like he wishes it were a set of brass knuckles. "Let's talk about this later."

"You don't get it, do you? Riddel doesn't care about CC and L. And he sure as hell doesn't care about the movie business. Promising all those guys in there he can get rid of the risk. Get rid of the risk? Risk is what it's all about. All Riddel wants is power. Power to have it his way. Power to control people. Power to humiliate people if they move out of line." Sandor looks behind him wondering, I suppose, if anyone is overhearing us. Possibly looking for an escape. "Riddel's a bad guy, but you're worse." I feel like a slalom skier. "You think you need a guy like Riddel. Bad cop to your good cop. Only you're not a good cop, Sandor."

"You don't know what you're talking about." A stillness comes over me and I hate it but I'm actually waiting for him to convince me that I'm wrong, that I don't know what I'm talking about.

"I don't give a shit what the press writes. I can control Riddel. Riddel has a role in this company. Guys like Riddel and Len have their place in business whether you like it or not. Whether you want to admit it or not." Sandor's voice is hard, each word a piece of steel. He lays down his argument like laborers might hammer down a railroad track. Symmetrical, rigid, unmovable. "Riddel got carried away. It happens. But the fact of the matter is, he did what I asked him to do. What needed to be done. I fired Jake Tyler, the head of the company, and the stock didn't go down one penny."

"I see, Riddel did a good job. And as soon as I taught Riddel everything I know, you were going to get rid of me. And give my job to Riddel. A kind of bonus for a job well done. I just beat you to it."

"You little fool." Sandor grabs my arm. He holds it the way an exasperated lover might. The shock of familiarity runs through my body. "I was planning to promote you. Not get rid of you. I have plans for you. We're a lot alike. More than you know. We can make good movies. You'll see. You're not going to leave."

Leland Alexander is looking at me like I'm on fire. He thinks I'm going to change my mind. I don't want to think about what job he was planning to give me. I feel like an addict face-to-face with my ultimate drug dealer.

The elevator doors open.

I sit very still. I begin to thaw. I listen to the icicles inside my body split and melt. I am ready to move on. A part of me feels crazy. Crazy the way a prisoner might who has just been found innocent after spending years in jail. A part of me feels back home. That part of me I lent to work, to the company. The part I thought they owned. But I was wrong. I belong to myself. I belong to John.

The stewardess offers me another Perrier. I am her only passenger. Leland Alexander called me last night and asked me to reconsider leaving. I told him I had to visit someone and that I was leaving in the morning. He offered me his plane. I took it. He thinks I will reconsider. He thinks a couple of rides in a Gulfstream will make me reconsider.

Make me reconsider if I want to work for him and find out that he's right; we are a lot alike. Find out I can put up with that one thing I was sure I couldn't put up with. Find out I can handle it. Sandor's wrong. I'm not going to reconsider. The way I see it I'd be considering a bigger job and a smaller life. God, there wasn't anything Sandor didn't offer me last night. It was pretty easy to say no, though. It's easier somehow when the person doesn't believe you. Sandor didn't believe me. He talked to me like we had had a lover's quarrel over something hurtful but something ultimately pretty silly. The sound of his voice was unhurried. You know the kind that says if I have to call you every day, twenty times a day, I will, because you're going to buy what I'm selling. Sandor is a great salesman. I know, I'm a great salesman, too.

"Phone call for you."

I freeze up and like a car out of control I skid about inside my head. The phone is maybe five inches from me, but it might as well be five miles.

"Are you going to take it?" The stewardess is leaning in toward me, encouraging me the way a mother might encourage her child who has just decided after standing in line for twenty minutes that the Ferris wheel is too high.

I grab the phone. "Sandor, just leave me alone."

"It's Jake."

"Jake?" Jake? I can't figure this out. Am I disappointed it isn't Sandor begging me some more? Yeah, maybe a little. God, this is nuts. "Jake, how did you find me?"

"Heard you were free."

"Free?" I repeat the word as if I have never heard it before.

"Thought you might want to work for me. I got a studio to give me a lot of money and I need someone to help me. They've promised to leave me alone." He's laughing over the bit about the studio's promise. "Come on, what do you say? We'll be our own assholes."

"Hard to turn down an invitation to be an asshole, Jake. Maybe. I'm not sure."

"Not sure. Who is? Think you'd be better off with Leland Alexander?"

"No. It's just that—maybe I could. Jake? Are you still there?" The phone is dead. I lost him. Work for Jake? I could work for Jake again. I wonder what John would think. John would think I'm crazy.

I think about why John left. He didn't leave because I lost the baby. He didn't leave because of another woman. John didn't leave me because I wasn't home enough. Or because I complained about work too much. John left me because he had trouble finding me. There is a part of me I used to hide from John, a part I used to take to work and, like a balloon, inflate each day and then deflate each night. Somehow this part grew so big that it hid the part of me John fell in love with. I grew out of proportion.

CREATIVE DIFFERENCES

I think I've found the part of me he loved, or used to love. It's hard to be a person and a businessperson. A lot of people can do both—work flat out and live flat out. I guess I'm not one of them after all. Work isn't set up to keep track of your life. It's set up to keep track of its life. Maybe my mother was right all along. I hear her words, and this time they sound gentler somehow. Now what I hear is a mother's love ground down into a gentle warning. She might have told me to put on my boots or take my vitamins or not to swim right after lunch. She could have told me any of these things. But she chose to tell me to watch out for the business world.

The stewardess puts a cassette into the video player and places a box of popcorn, hot and buttery from the microwave, on the seat next to me. The screen comes alive. It's a movie I first saw eighteen years ago during a Christmas vacation from college. It's John's favorite movie. You see, I'll try anything to recapture what I've lost. Molly wouldn't tug at it. She'd let it be. She sure as hell wouldn't quit her job and go two thousand miles to see someone who made it pretty clear he doesn't want to see her. I'll try anything—old movies, decoder rings, Jake's numerologist if I knew her number—anything that might magically get things back to where they were. I think about John.

I pull at the string. Carefully, I start to wind it into a ball. As I fly across the country, I scoop it up, taking care not to break it.

I'm tired. And now I'm scared. Maybe I should have called John. Told him I was on my way. Maybe he won't like being surprised. He said he was going to stay in Mexico for a while longer. I think about John's leaving. I think about how I missed the moment when he realized he could leave me. The actual moment. When did it come? Did he wake up one morning knowing he was going to leave me? Was I in his arms that morning? Was he kissing me, knowing he was going to leave? How come I didn't feel it? Or see it?

I think about the months without him. Each day I woke up certain that today would be the day I would finally stop missing him. Today would be the day when the hourglass was full up and I could turn it over and let him drain out of me. Never got to that day. I think of the months without him. Without making love. I can feel his hand on the back of my neck. I'm falling asleep. I should have called. Maybe he will have forgotten about us, forgotten how we loved. Forgotten we were congruent. His short letters say he's forgotten. His few calls say he's forgotten. I haven't forgotten. I remember. I should have called him to remind him about our love. Too late now.

I am dreaming of making love with John. Our bed is big, acres of white cotton. His great green eyes steady me and then they lay themselves down before me like a magic carpet and I am aloft. My body swells to his. And when he is finally inside of me, I feel like you do when, after swimming under water, you break to the surface and suck in air and revel in the sunlight you've inexplicably missed so much.

I am dreaming of you, John. I am dreaming of love. Of children. Of light. We are kissing. Yes, yes, this is it.

The stewardess wakes me. We will be on the ground in a couple of minutes. She sets a Perrier down on the tray next to me. I look out the window and watch the ground getting closer and closer. The plane lands. I feel the ground under me. It feels solid.

I get out my brush and makeup. I look into the mirror. I see a gray hair. I always thought when I saw the first gray hair I would be upset. I'm not. I like it. I brush my hair and then pull the gray strand free of the others. It looks great.

I haven't cut my hair in almost a year. It's pretty long. I look in the mirror again, trying to decide if I should get my hair cut. I'll ask John.